TRUSTING
Miss
Trentham

EMILY
LARKIN

Trusting Miss Trentham / Emily Larkin. ~ 1st edition

ISBN 978-0-9951358-1-9

Cover Design: Jane Smith (JD Smith Design)
Larkin Font Design: Georgina Kerby (Georgie Graphic Design)
Series Logo Design: Kim Killion (Killion Group)
Author Photo: Tim Cuff (Nelson Creative)
Silhouette Effect: Melissa Evans (SunRoom Web Design)
Regency Audiobook Listener:
Emily Gee in combination with Midjourney

A Baleful Godmother

Novel

It is a truth universally acknowledged,
that Faerie godmothers do not exist.

CHAPTER 1

October 31st, 1808
London

$\mathcal{M}$iss Letitia Trentham, England's wealthiest unmarried heiress, received her eighteenth proposal of the year at the Hammonds' ball. The Little Season was drawing to its close and the company was thin, but more than a hundred people crowded the ballroom. Four of them were currently angling after her fortune.

When Laurence Darlington suggested that they sit out their next dance, Letty experienced a sinking feeling. When Darlington suggested that they repair to the conservatory, the sinking feeling became stronger. The conservatory adjoined the ballroom—was in fact in full view of the ballroom, had a table of refreshments and an attendant footman, and could hardly be called secluded—but it was secluded enough for a proposal.

Experience had taught Letty that it was better to get proposals over with as swiftly as possible, so she let Darlington lead her down the short flight of marble stairs.

The musicians struck the first notes of a *contredanse*. "Champagne?" offered the footman.

Yes, a big glass, Letty thought. "No, thank you," she said.

Laurence Darlington led her to the farthest end of the conservatory, where there was a stiff array of ferns and a row of gilded chairs precisely aligned. Only a glimpse of the ballroom could be seen. Music floated down the steps. The smell of the ball—sweet perfumes, spicy pomades, and pungent sweat—smothered any scent of greenery.

Letty sat and smoothed the sea-green silk of her ball gown over her knees and braced herself for what was to come. For the past two weeks, Laurence Darlington had been doing a good impression of a man falling in love. It was one of the better impressions she'd seen this year, although not as good as Sir Charles Stanton's. *That* had been masterful.

Laurence Darlington sat alongside her and gazed ardently into her eyes. A very handsome man, Darlington. The most handsome of this year's crop of fortune hunters. And up to his ears in debt.

"Miss Trentham," Darlington said, emotion throbbing in his voice. "What I am about to say can surely come as no surprise to you."

No. It was no surprise.

Letty heard the proposal with weary resignation. It was a pretty speech. Darlington wasn't fool enough to call her beautiful; instead, he praised her character and her intelligence. Even so, his words resonated with falsehood. When he finished, he said passionately, "There is no one I would rather marry. No one! You are everything I could ever wish for in a wife." The first half of that statement rang with a clear, bell-like tone. It was actually the truth. The second half gave a discordant *clang* in Letty's ears.

"I lay my heart at your feet."

Darlington was a good actor. He did almost look like a man who'd laid his heart at his lover's feet. His handsome face bore an expression of hopeful longing and his eyes burned with passion.

Passion for her fortune.

"You love me, Mr. Darlington?"

"Yes," Darlington said fervently.

"And my fortune . . . ?"

"Means nothing to me!"

Darlington's delivery was perfect—the earnest expression, the vehement tone. Letty might have believed him, if not for the dissonant *clang* in her ears, like a cracked church bell being struck. She took a moment to be thankful that she had a Faerie godmother, that she'd been given a wish on her twenty-first birthday and that she'd wished as she had, that she *could* hear Darlington's lies.

"Tell me, Mr. Darlington, if we married, would you be faithful?"

Darlington blinked. He hadn't expected that question. None of her suitors ever did. But she always asked it. "Of course!"

Clang.

Letty nodded, as if she believed him. She looked down at her hands and smoothed a wrinkle in one of her gloves. "Is it true that you're a gambler, Mr. Darlington?"

Darlington appeared not to have expected this question either. There was a short pause, and then he said lightly, "I roll the dice occasionally."

Letty glanced at him. More than occasionally, and more than just dice. Cards. Horses. Dogfights. Cockfights. Prizefights. Anything and everything, if what she'd heard was correct.

"And is it true that you're almost bankrupt?"

It was a shockingly rude question to ask, one she wouldn't have asked in her first season, or even her third, but years of fortune hunters had taught her that bluntness was best.

Darlington stiffened. The mask of passionate lover slipped slightly. His smile was fixed, almost a grimace.

They stared at each other for a long moment, while the strains of the *contredanse* drifted down from the ballroom,

3

and then Darlington relaxed and laughed. "My dear Miss Trentham, I can assure you that—"

"I sympathize with your financial troubles, Mr. Darlington," Letty said brusquely. "But I will not marry you."

Darlington lost his smile. He closed his mouth. The glitter in his eyes wasn't passion. Color rose in his cheeks. Not embarrassment, but anger.

His jaw tightened. He stood stiffly and turned from her without speaking, strode across the marble floor, climbed the shallow steps to the ballroom.

Letty watched him disappear among the dancers. Fury surged through her, fierce and bitter. How dare he? How dare any man pretend a love he didn't feel and vow a fidelity he had no intention of keeping?

On the heels of fury was an urge to cry. Tears stung her eyes. Letty blinked them back. She would *not* cry over a man like Laurence Darlington. She wouldn't cry over *any* false suitor—a promise she'd made to herself in her first season.

But that promise was becoming harder to keep. The proposals had always hurt, but this year they hurt more than ever. This year, each proposal made her feel older and plainer and lonelier. Lonelier than she'd ever felt in her life. A hopeless, aching loneliness. And while part of that loneliness was because her cousin Julia had died last year, an equal part of it was because she was twenty-seven and still unmarried.

Would no man ever love her for herself?

After all these years on the Marriage Mart and nearly two hundred proposals, it seemed unlikely.

I wish I wasn't an heiress. For a brief moment, Letty indulged in a dream of going somewhere far, far away where no one knew who she was, and winning true love, like a princess dressed as a pauper in a Faerie tale.

She snorted under her breath. Princesses in Faerie tales were always beautiful, and she was most definitely *not* beautiful.

Perhaps that's what she should have wished for on her twenty-first birthday? Beauty, not hearing lies. But then she would have been a beautiful heiress, besieged by suitors and unable to hear their falsehoods—and *that* road must surely have led to misery.

"Miss Trentham?"

Letty glanced up. A man stood before her. He was tall, taller than Darlington, and broad in the shoulder. He was dressed for dancing in a tailcoat and knee breeches and silk stockings, but despite those clothes he looked as if he had no place at the Hammonds' ball. No languid tulip of the *ton*, this man. He was whipcord lean, his skin tanned brown, his expression unsmiling. He looked almost dangerous.

Letty felt a slight flare of nervousness. She looked for the footman. Yes, he still manned the refreshment table.

"Miss Trentham?" the man asked again. The tan gave a misleading impression of health. He wasn't just lean, he was gaunt. His tailcoat, for all its fine cut, hung on his frame.

A soldier back from India, invalided out? His dark brown hair was clipped short and his bearing was military.

"Yes."

"My name is Reid. I wondered if I might have a few words with you?" She saw exhaustion on his face, and tension.

Letty hesitated, wishing for the nominal chaperonage of Mrs. Sitwell, currently ensconced in the card room. "I'm engaged for the next dance, but until then you may certainly speak, Mr. Reid."

"Thank you." He gave a curt nod.

Letty folded her hands in her lap and gazed up at him, trying to look politely expectant, not nervous.

Mr. Reid gave her a long, frowning stare and then said abruptly, "You have a reputation for being able to distinguish truth from lies."

Letty tried not to stiffen. "Some people believe I can." She said it with a smile of amusement, as if she thought it a joke.

Mr. Reid didn't return the smile. "Can you?"

It wasn't the first time Letty had been asked this question. She'd learned to turn it aside with a jest, with a lie. But something about Mr. Reid made that impossible. His eyes were intent on her face. They were an extremely pale shade of gray, almost silver. She had an odd sense that his gaze was razor-sharp, penetrating skin and bone. Her awareness of him became even stronger—his tension, his exhaustion. There was something very wrong with this man.

"Sometimes," Letty said, and heard a *clang* in her ears at the lie. "Sit down, Mr. Reid. Tell me what it is you wish to know the truth of."

Reid hesitated, and then pulled one of the gilded chairs out of line and sat at an angle to her. He moved like a soldier—precise, controlled movements with no graceful flourishes.

Once seated, he was silent for several seconds, then spoke tersely: "There are two men here in London—I served with them in Portugal—one of them passed information to the French."

Letty blinked, hearing the truth in his words.

"I've spoken with them, and they both say they didn't, but *someone* did, and they were the only ones who knew other than the general and myself. The general didn't tell anyone. *I* didn't tell anyone. One of these two men lied, and I can't tell which one. Would you be able to?"

Letty released her breath slowly and sat back in her chair. "Perhaps." *Clang.* "If one of these men is a traitor, what will you do?"

"I don't know."

Clang.

"That, Mr. Reid, is a lie."

Hope flared in his silver eyes, flared on his gaunt face. He leaned forward. "You *can* tell."

"What will you do to him?" Letty repeated.

"Probably kill him." This time, Reid spoke the truth.

Tiny hairs pricked up on the back of Letty's neck. She glanced at the footman, stationed at the refreshment table, and back at Reid. Common sense urged her to push to her feet and walk from him as quickly as she could—run, if she had to. This man was *dangerous,* possibly even deranged.

Wary caution kept her where she was. "I need to know more before I decide whether I can help you."

Reid sat back in his chair, even tenser than he'd been before. "What do you want to know?"

"Everything."

He stared at her for a long moment, grim-faced, and then began to speak. "I was on General Wellesley's staff, an exploring officer. Reconnaissance. We'd been in Portugal less than a month. We engaged the French at Roliça, and then four days later at Vimeiro."

Letty nodded. She'd heard of the battles. Victories for England, both of them. "August of this year?"

"Yes." Reid's hands were clenched together, his knuckles sharp ridges beneath the gloves. "I had three local scouts. I went out daily with them. Not all together, you understand. I'd go with one man; the others would scout alone. We met each evening. On the day before Vimeiro, just on dusk, we were captured. The scouts were summarily executed."

Killed in front of him, was what he meant. Letty swallowed. "Why weren't you executed?"

"I was in uniform; they weren't."

She nodded.

"The French were waiting for us. It was an ambush. And *I* had chosen our meeting place. Other than the general, only two men knew of it. They both claim not to have told a soul—and yet one of them *must* have."

"Who are these men?"

"Wellesley's aides-de-camp."

Letty frowned. "Surely such men would be trustworthy?"

"Someone told the French," Reid said flatly. "It wasn't me, it wasn't the general, it wasn't my scouts."

Letty gazed at him uneasily. Did she want to go further with this? Reid's tension was disturbing. He seemed balanced on a knife-edge. What if he killed a man based on her say-so?

She opened her mouth to tell him that her rumored ability

to distinguish truth from lies was merely a trick, that she'd only guessed he was lying earlier—and then closed it again.

What if she *didn't* help Reid, and he killed the wrong man?

Letty chewed on this thought for a moment, and then said, "Tell me about the two men, Mr. Reid."

"They were new. I didn't know them well. Didn't like them much. Playing at soldiering." His upper lip curled. "Wellesley didn't like them either. They'd been foisted on him."

Letty raised her brows. "You didn't know these men well, and yet you told them where you and your scouts would be?"

"Wellesley had asked me to keep him informed of my movements. He was in a meeting when I left, so I told his aides."

"And both these men are currently in London?"

Reid nodded.

"Isn't that unusual?"

"One sold out, the other was cashiered." His lip curled again.

"Cashiered? You mean dismissed? Whatever for?"

"Dereliction of duty. He spent the Battle of Vimeiro in his billet, too drunk to stand up."

Letty nodded, and looked down at her hands. She plucked at the tip of one finger, pulling the glove. Did she want to become involved in this?

"The man who sold out is Reginald Grantham."

Letty's head jerked up. "Grantham?"

"A suitor of yours, I'm given to understand."

She nodded, mute.

"When you next see Grantham, could you ask him for me?" Reid's voice was neutral, almost diffident. "Please?"

His voice might be neutral, but nothing else was—the sharp-knuckled hands, the intensity of his gaze, the way he sat—stiff, leaning forward slightly. This meant a great deal to him.

"Please?" Reid said again, and emotion leaked into his voice: a faint edge of desperation.

For some reason, that edge of desperation made her rib-cage tighten. Letty looked down at her own hands. "Were the scouts close friends of yours, Mr. Reid?"

Reid didn't speak for several seconds. "No. I barely knew them."

Letty glanced up. He was no longer leaning tensely forward. The intensity was gone from his face. He looked tired and ill and defeated, as if he expected her to refuse.

"What sort of men were they?"

"Good men. Brave men." His mouth tightened. "Peasants."

Did he think that that admission would make her less likely to help him? Yes, he did; he was pushing to his feet.

"Sit down, Mr. Reid."

Reid cast her a sharp glance, hesitated, and then sat again.

Letty looked back down at her hands, rather than his hopeful eyes. "How did you hear of my . . . knack?"

"A friend. He told me Grantham was at your feet, and that you'd be certain to kick him away because you always knew when your suitors were untruthful. He said you had an uncanny talent for distinguishing truth from lies."

"Which friend?"

"Colonel Winton."

Letty saw the colonel in her mind's eye—stocky, graying, eagle-eyed—and nodded. "Tell me about yourself."

There was a pause. She glanced up to see Reid's brow wrinkle. "Me?"

"Who are you, Mr. Reid?"

Another pause, and then Reid said, "My father was Sir Hector Reid of Yorkshire. I'm the youngest of five sons. I joined the Thirty-third Foot as an ensign. Flanders first, then India." His delivery was flat and unemotional. "After the Battle of Mallavelly, Wellesley took me for one of his aides. I was on his staff for five years, then Gore's. Wellesley requested me back for Copenhagen. After Copenhagen, we were to sail to South America, but we were sent to Portugal instead."

"What's your rank?"

Another pause. "I was a major."

"You've been invalided out?"

"I resigned my commission."

"Because of what happened in Portugal?"

"Yes."

Letty studied his face. A career soldier didn't resign his commission because of the deaths of three peasants he barely knew. "Something else happened, didn't it?"

Reid's face tightened. "Yes."

"What?"

Reid's face became even tighter. He didn't speak.

"Major Reid, if you're not truthful with me—"

"It's not fit for your ears," he said flatly.

Letty closed her mouth, hearing the bell-like chime of truth in his words. Something terrible had happened in Portugal. Something terrible enough to make this man resign his commission.

She studied Major Reid's face—the skin stretched taut over his bones, the tension, the exhaustion. She'd been right to think there was something seriously wrong with him. He was brittle, ready to break.

Up in the ballroom, the musicians stopped playing. The *contredanse* was over. It was time for her to leave the conservatory and find her next partner.

Letty stayed seated. "Who is the second man?"

"George Dunlop."

"I don't know him."

"He's in Marshalsea."

Letty jerked slightly. "Prison?"

"He's a debtor."

"Major Reid, I can't . . ." Letty shook her head silently. She couldn't enter a prison.

Reid leaned forward on his chair. The tension and the fierce hope were gone. He looked drained. More exhausted than anyone she'd ever seen. "Miss Trentham, I'll be dead before the end of the year and I need to make this right before I die. Please, will you help me?"

Letty stared at him, hearing the truth in his words. Muscles constricted in her throat, but she wasn't entirely certain why. Because Reid was dying? Because he was begging? Both? "Of course I'll help," she heard herself say.

Reid closed his eyes briefly. "Thank you." He exhaled a low breath and straightened in the chair, but his exhaustion didn't ease. Everything about him was weary—his long limbs, his gaunt face, his silver eyes. Even his hands were weary, no longer clenched.

"But you must promise not to kill the traitor."

Reid's eyebrows came sharply together. The weariness evaporated. He was suddenly taut, tense, dangerous.

"I will *not* be responsible for deciding whether a man lives or dies," Letty said firmly. "A military court is the place for that."

Reid stared at her for a long moment, his eyes boring into her—and then he gave a stiff nod. "Very well."

"You must *promise* me you won't kill him. On your word of honor."

"You have my word of honor I won't kill him." The words came from his mouth reluctantly, but they were the truth.

Letty almost wished he had refused. Did she *really* want to be involved in this? "I ride in Hyde Park most afternoons. Meet me there tomorrow. I'll ask Grantham to join me."

"Will he come?"

"I'm the heiress he's angling to marry," she said tartly. "Of course he'll come."

Reid's eyebrows lifted slightly at her tone, but he made no comment.

"You may ask Grantham your questions; I'll tell you whether he's lying or not."

"You *will* be able to tell?"

Letty nodded.

"How?"

11

"I hear it."

"This knack of yours, is it . . ." His brow creased as he searched for a word. "Infallible?"

"I hear every single lie, Major Reid."

He frowned. "How?"

Letty shrugged lightly. "A quirk of my birth. You may test me tomorrow, if you disbelieve me." She stood. "Now, you must excuse me; I'm engaged for this dance."

Reid stood, too.

"Three o'clock at the Grosvenor Gate."

"Thank you."

Letty could think of no suitable reply. *You're welcome*, and *It's my pleasure*, were both lies. She settled for a nod.

She climbed the shallow steps and emerged into the ballroom with a sense of having woken from a disturbing dream. *This* was normalcy—the rustle of expensive fabric and glitter of jewels, the scents of dozens of different perfumes, the babble of voices, the gaiety. The fortune hunters.

Letty glanced back, almost expecting Major Reid to have disappeared. But no, he stood in the conservatory, tall and gaunt, watching her. With a black cloak and scythe, he'd be the Grim Reaper.

And she had agreed to help him. *Not smart, Letitia. Not smart at all.*

Letty shivered, and set out across the dance floor in search of Lord Stapleton.

CHAPTER 2

November 1st, 1808
London

$\mathcal{I}$carus Reid arrived at the Grosvenor Gate ten minutes
before the hour, riding a hired hack. Miss Trentham arrived
three minutes later. *Her* mount was definitely not hired, a
dapple-gray mare with an excellent gait.

Behind her, on horseback, was a hulking man in livery.
Groom, or guard? *Both,* Icarus decided.

He watched Miss Trentham approach, and reviewed what
Colonel Winton had told him about her. Intelligent. Reserved.
Not a lady to indulge in flirtations. Enormously wealthy, but
not extravagant. Not tight-fisted, either; her dead mother had
established a lying-in hospital for poor women, and foundling
homes and a charity school, and Miss Trentham spent a small
fortune supporting these enterprises.

Miss Trentham halted. "Good afternoon, Major Reid."

Icarus bowed in the saddle. "Miss Trentham."

Miss Trentham's riding habit was severely plain. She had
no knots of ribbon, no braiding, no frogging. No curling
ostrich feathers in her hat, no ringlets in her hair. She didn't

look like an heiress. Nor did she look like a woman who gave thousands of pounds to the destitute.

"Do you care to ride with me?" Miss Trentham's tone was faintly aloof.

"It would be my pleasure," Icarus said, for the groom's benefit.

"Shall we canter, then?" Miss Trentham's voice might be aloof, but her gaze was wary, telling him that she wasn't comfortable.

A gentleman would have begged her pardon and taken his leave, but Icarus was no longer a gentleman. Honor, integrity, pride, decency, courage—everything that had made him who he was had been stripped from him in Portugal. What remained was this person he was now, a sack of skin filled with blood and bones and single-minded purpose. He would beg if he had to. Hold this woman to her unwilling promise if he had to.

They cantered for several minutes, then slowed to a walk. "Grantham promised to meet me at three thirty," Miss Trentham said. "Until then, you may test my knack, if you wish."

Icarus glanced over his shoulder. The groom was a discreet distance behind, out of earshot. "I do wish." He turned his gaze to her.

Miss Trentham was no beauty—she was too tall, too thin, her nose too long, her mouth too wide, her hair an undistinguished shade between brown and blonde—but she had poise, and a disconcertingly direct gaze. "Tell me twenty things, Major Reid," she said, "and I'll tell you whether they're lies or not."

"Mister," Icarus said.

A wrinkle creased her brow. "I beg your pardon?"

"I prefer to be called Mister." Major Reid had died at Vimeiro.

Miss Trentham examined him for a moment, her eyebrows slightly raised, and then gave a short nod. "Twenty things, Mr. Reid."

Icarus frowned, and tried to think of something besides Grantham and Dunlop. It was a struggle. "Uh . . . my father wanted me to join the army."

"False."

"He wanted me to join the navy."

"True."

"One of my uncles was an admiral of the fleet."

"True."

"One of my brothers is a commodore."

"False."

"He's an admiral."

"True."

"He was wounded at Trafalgar."

"False."

"One of my brothers died at Trafalgar."

"True."

I have died many times, Icarus almost said. He closed his mouth tightly, and racked his brain, and said, "I had a dog when I was a boy."

"True."

"His name was Cerberus."

"False."

"His name was Ulysses."

"True."

"He had three black paws."

"True."

"He died when I was sixteen."

"True."

"I buried him in the Home Wood."

"True."

That wasn't twenty things, but it was enough. Icarus stared at Miss Trentham through narrowed eyes. "How do you do it?"

She returned his stare coolly. "I told you last night: I hear lies."

"But *how*?"

Miss Trentham gave an elegant shrug, and a wry half-smile. "I inherited it from my mother."

She glanced ahead, then back at him. "I have a lot of suitors, Mr. Reid. It's something of a nuisance. So much of a nuisance that my stepbrother keeps a man on retainer to make inquiries about them."

Icarus blinked. "He does?"

"Strangely, all my suitors prove to have financial problems." Miss Trentham's smile wasn't wry this time, it was more of a grimace. "Grantham was investigated last month. He's a younger son. Spends beyond his means, gambles too much, drinks too much. He sticks at nothing—the law, politics, soldiering. He left the army under something of a cloud—apparently Wellesley dislikes laziness in his officers."

Icarus grunted. "Sounds like Grantham." And Wellesley, for that matter.

"There was no hint of treason."

"It happened," Icarus said. "Grantham or Dunlop, one of them passed information to the French."

Miss Trentham surveyed him coolly, and then glanced ahead again. "Here's Grantham."

The Honorable Reginald Grantham had the type of good looks that Letty most disliked: blond, florid, and with a tendency to stoutness. His manner annoyed her, too—the *I'm a viscount's son* self-importance, as if he'd be doing *her* a favor if he married her.

Letty gritted her teeth and smiled at Grantham politely. "Mr. Grantham. How nice of you to join us. I believe you know Mr. Reid?"

Grantham gave a stiff nod. "Major."

"Grantham."

"Shall we ride together?" Her suggestion made Grantham bristle slightly, like a dog guarding a bone. Did he see Reid as a rival? Letty almost snorted. There was nothing of the lover about Mr. Reid. He saw her as an instrument, not a woman.

They trotted along the bridle path, Reid to her left, Grantham to her right, the groom two horse-lengths behind. After several minutes, Letty slowed to a walk. Grantham maneuvered himself between her and Reid, as if trying to cut Reid out. The way he sat on his showy chestnut made Letty think of a cockerel strutting in a hen yard, chest puffed, tail feathers on display.

"Nice mare you've got there, Miss Trentham," Grantham said. "My father, the viscount, has a similar one in his stables."

Letty almost rolled her eyes. *My father, the viscount,* was one of Grantham's favorite utterances. She'd heard it times past counting, the last fortnight. "Does he?" she said, and then, before Grantham could elaborate on this subject: "Mr. Reid has been telling me about Portugal."

"Portugal? Nasty, squalid little place. Nothing you'd be interested in."

"Actually, I find myself quite interested in Portugal," Letty said, an edge creeping into her voice. What did this patronizing idiot know of her interests? "Mr. Reid has posed some questions, and I find myself curious to hear the answers."

"Questions?"

"About what happened the day before the Battle of Vimeiro."

Color flushed Grantham's face. "Lord, Reid, you're not still going on about that? You're dicked in the nob, is what you are! I told no one!"

Clang.

Letty's eyebrows rose slightly. She glanced past Grantham. Reid's silver eyes were fixed on her with hawk-like intensity. He looked tense, taut, unbreathing.

Letty looked back at Grantham. "But you *did* tell someone, Mr. Grantham."

"What?" Grantham seemed to swell with indignation. "I did not!"

Letty smiled at him without warmth. "Mr. Grantham, I have a knack for knowing truth from lies, and this knack tells me that you *did* tell someone."

"I didn't!"

Letty reined her horse to a halt. "You did."

Grantham halted, too, blocked by Reid's mount. "What's this about?" he blustered. "My father's a viscount!"

"We can continue this conversation here," Reid said, in an iron-hard voice. "Or at a court-martial. Which do you prefer?"

Grantham's gaze darted right and left. There was a faint sheen of perspiration on his cheeks. "I told Wellesley!"

Clang. Letty caught Reid's eye and shook her head.

"Dunlop told Wellesley," Reid said. "Who did you tell?" His hand was on Grantham's reins, holding the horse in check. The animal's head was up, its ears back.

Grantham glared at Reid. Reid stared implacably back. The threat in his silver eyes made Letty's scalp prickle. She found herself holding her breath. This silent staring match was a duel. She had no doubt who'd win.

Grantham looked away. "I told Cuthbertson."

Letty met Reid's gaze and nodded.

"Anyone else?"

"No!" Grantham snarled, his color high.

Letty nodded again.

Reid released Grantham's reins.

Grantham dug his heels into his mount's flanks, shoving Reid aside. "You have the manners of a yokel!"

Letty watched him ride off. The Honorable Reginald Grantham didn't look ashamed of himself; he looked puffed up with righteous indignation.

What an unpleasant man.

She looked at Reid, expecting to see contempt on his face. He was frowning.

"Cuthbertson?" she asked.

"Colonel Cuthbertson."

"A colonel? It wouldn't be him then, would it?"

Reid said nothing. He continued frowning.

Letty nudged her mare into a trot, then a canter. Reid kept pace with her. After half a mile, she slowed to a walk again. Reid fell in beside her.

"You want me to visit Marshalsea Prison." It was a statement, not a question.

"Yes."

Letty halted. "Mr. Reid, surely you must realize that I *can't*."

Reid halted, too. He looked at her without speaking.

Letty listened to the clatter of a phaeton driving past on the carriageway—and the sound of her lie reverberating in her ears. Of course she could visit Marshalsea. Anyone could.

"Think of the scandal!" she protested. "The gossipmongers will have a field day!"

"Only if they know of it."

Go secretly? Letty stared hard at him—the gaunt, tanned face, the silver eyes. "Are you after my fortune?" she demanded.

Reid blinked. "Me? No."

"If I accompany you to Marshalsea, will you give me your word that you won't compromise me, or damage my reputation in any way?"

Reid's eyebrows drew together over his nose. "Miss Trentham, I have absolutely no interest in your fortune." There was hauteur in his voice—and a clear, bell-like tone of truthfulness. "I don't want a wife. *Any* wife. If you accompany me to Marshalsea, I won't compromise you, or damage your reputation—or allow anyone else to do so."

Letty eyed him narrowly, and then nudged the mare into a canter. Thoughts jostled in her head like dancers at a ball. Should she go secretly to Marshalsea Prison with Mr. Reid? *Could* she?

After five minutes of mulling, Letty knew that she could; the question was, did she dare? She slowed to a trot, trying to sort through her emotions. Reluctance. Fear. A prickle of excitement. A faint itch of curiosity.

You're so cautious, her cousin Julia had said once, trying to persuade her to go to a not-quite-respectable masked ball at Ranelagh, and when Letty had replied, *My fortune is ten times yours; I have to be ten times more cautious than you,* Julia had laughed and said, *Nonsense!* And while it hadn't been nonsense, perhaps she was overcautious, because Julia had gone to the ball and not been caught by a fortune hunter.

Letty let the mare drop to a walk, and glanced at Reid. His expression was unreadable.

Dared she go with him?

Julia would have dared, without hesitation.

Letty halted.

Reid halted, too, and met her gaze straightly. He said nothing. No arguments, no persuasions, no entreaties. He didn't look tense or taut or exhausted; he looked almost calm.

They stared at one another for a long, silent moment.

"Meet me outside Hatchard's tomorrow at two o'clock," Letty said.

Reid nodded. No flicker of surprise crossed his face.

Somehow, he'd known she would agree.

CHAPTER 3

November 2nd, 1808
London

Letty met her friend Miss Torpington at Hatchard's bookshop at one thirty, and sent her own maid home. They browsed the books for twenty minutes, and then Miss Torpington departed. Letty assured her that her maid was in the shop. The lie clanged unpleasantly in her ears, but Miss Torpington didn't hear it.

Letty watched her friend disappear from sight and felt ashamed of herself. She almost hurried after Miss Torpington and told her the truth—that her maid *had* left and she would be glad of an escort back to Hill Street—and then she thought of Mr. Reid and his three executed scouts and blew out a breath. For their sakes, for Reid's sake, she would do this.

She waited two minutes, drew a heavy veil out of her muff and arranged it over her hat, and boldly emerged onto Piccadilly. Mr. Reid stood outside, like a guardsman at parade rest. His gaze flicked to her—and stayed. Veil or not, he had recognized her.

She hoped no one else would.

Letty crossed to him. "Mr. Reid."

"Miss Trentham." He gave a curt nod.

"This afternoon I'm Miss Smith."

Reid gave another curt nod. He glanced behind her. "Your maid?"

"My maid thinks I'm with a friend, and the friend thinks I'm with my maid."

Reid transferred his gaze to her veiled face and nodded a third time. He held out his arm. "Shall we?"

Letty had placed her hand on a man's arm hundreds of times before. Thousands of times. But this time it felt reckless and dangerous. She had the sense that she was about to walk along the edge of a cliff—and that falling was a distinct possibility.

Marshalsea Prison lay in Southwark, on the far side of the Thames. The hackney carriage Mr. Reid hailed was the most dilapidated vehicle Letty had ever ridden in. The seats were stained, the floor filthy, and there was a strong odor, a mingling of sweat, urine, onions, and some other scent that her nose couldn't identify.

Reid didn't appear to notice the stains or the smell. He sat silently, his attention directed inwards. He didn't attempt to engage her in conversation.

Letty cast him a sidelong glance, seeing the firm mouth, the resolute jaw, the jutting cheekbones. He was a very different man from Grantham. No weak, blustering nobleman's son, but a career soldier, sharp-eyed and intelligent and tough.

And obsessed. Obsessed with whatever had happened in Portugal.

Letty turned her attention to the view out the window. They were passing through a London she'd never seen before, much shabbier than Mayfair, shabbier even than Holborn, where her mother's lying-in hospital and other charities were located. The streets teemed with hawkers selling from barrows and baskets. People thronged everywhere. Letty stared at them, fascinated. These were London's coal-haulers and dustmen and bricklayers, its rat catchers and rag-and-bone men, fishwives and washerwomen. Perhaps even its prostitutes and pickpockets.

The streets became shabbier, the hawkers fewer. An extremely unpleasant smell forced its way into the hackney. The vehicle rattled across London Bridge. Letty's nervousness increased until it felt as if she had a nest of mice tucked beneath her breastbone.

She glanced at Reid again. He was still sunk in his thoughts, a tight frown on his brow.

The hackney entered Southwark. Beneath the nervousness, Letty became aware of a peculiar sensation, a sensation she'd never felt before: an oddly exhilarating tingle in her blood.

It took several minutes before she found a word for it. That exhilarating sensation was *freedom*. The hackney might be filthy, her destination might be a prison, but for the first time in her life, she was actually *free*. Free of servants, free of chaperonage, free of being an heiress.

The hackney drew to a halt.

Letty gazed out the window. She saw two large buildings, one old, with crumbling whitewash and small windows, the other built of brick, with high windows and columns at one end. "Which one is Marshalsea?"

"They both are."

Reid handed her down from the hackney and paid the jarvey, requesting the man to wait for them. Letty's heart began to beat slightly faster. She glanced cautiously around.

The street wasn't busy, but neither was it empty. Men and women loitered. Urchins played in the gutter. A scrawny dog slunk past with its tail between its legs.

Reid gave her his arm. He seemed not in the slightest intimidated by their surroundings. His face was bony and weary, but his posture was erect and his gaze alert. She watched him briefly examine the street, his silver eyes flicking from face to face, doorway to doorway.

Together, they crossed the dirty roadway. Letty wanted to clutch Reid's arm tightly; she made herself rest her gloved hand lightly on his sleeve. She was conscious of people watching them, assessing the cost of her cloak, her shoes, her muff, her veiled hat.

A voice in her head noted that she *should* feel afraid, but she wasn't. Nervous, yes. Apprehensive and uneasy. Curious. But not afraid. Not with Reid at her side.

Reid was dangerous. More dangerous than any man on this street.

They entered the prison. Icarus felt Miss Trentham shiver as she crossed the threshold. She gazed around the narrow cobblestone courtyard.

"Anyone may enter Marshalsea," Icarus told her in an undertone. "But not everyone may leave."

Miss Trentham nodded, and shivered again.

Icarus led her across the courtyard. The man he'd been before Vimeiro would never have brought a well-bred young lady to a place such as this. The man he was now felt nothing more than a faint twinge of shame, easily ignored.

On the far side of the yard, they passed through an iron-bound door, and then a second. Icarus greased each turnkey in the fist.

They climbed a flight of narrow stairs and walked along a dark corridor lined with doors, most of which stood open.

Dunlop was in the third room along, a cramped space with two beds and four inhabitants.

Icarus halted in the doorway. Miss Trentham's hand didn't tighten on his arm, but he sensed her tension.

He tried to see the room as she did: the crooked blinds, the battered table and lopsided stools, the two beds with their tangle of dirty sheets. A washstand with a cracked pitcher and bowl stood in one corner. The smells of chamber pot and unwashed male, tallow candles, tobacco smoke, sour ale and pickles filled his nostrils. God knew he'd seen worse in his life, smelled worse, but Miss Trentham wouldn't have.

Icarus experienced another faint twinge of shame. He had sunk very low to bring her here.

Of the four inhabitants of the room, one lay snoring, two sat at the table with tankards of ale at their elbows and greasy cards laid out between them, and the fourth hunched on a stool by the window, stitching a threadbare waistcoat.

Icarus stepped half a pace into the room.

The man at the window glanced up, then returned his attention to his stitching.

Dunlop didn't look up. He was focused on the cards. His face was unshaven, his shirt open at the throat.

"Dunlop," Icarus said.

Dunlop tilted his head back and blinked blearily. "Tha' you, Reid?"

"Yes."

Dunlop grunted, and looked back at his cards.

Icarus was aware of Miss Trentham standing stiff and silent beside him. Was her tension due to revulsion, or fear?

Get this over with, he told himself. *Fast.*

He reached into his pocket, brought out a handful of guineas, and clinked them loudly in his palm.

Dunlop looked up. So did his fellow card player. So did the man darning at the window.

Icarus clinked the coins again and held his hand open, letting them all see the golden guineas. "A word with you, Dunlop."

Dunlop glowered at him for several seconds, then threw down his cards.

"Gentlemen, if you wouldn't mind giving us some privacy?"

25

For a guinea apiece, neither man minded. One took his tankard, the other his sewing, and they both left the room.

Icarus closed the door and turned to Dunlop, still glowering at the table. "Vimeiro," he said, conscious of Miss Trentham standing at his elbow.

Dunlop lowered his head pugnaciously. "What about Vimeiro?"

"My rendezvous with the scouts. Who did you tell about it?"

Dunlop's eyes flickered. He was thinking; Icarus could almost see the cogs turning slowly in his head.

"Who, Dunlop?"

"Wellesley."

"Who *other* than Wellesley?"

Dunlop's gaze tracked across the room. More cogs turned slowly. "Matlock was with Wellesley. He heard."

"Who else?"

"No one."

Miss Trentham stirred slightly. She shook her head.

"*Who?*" Icarus said.

Dunlop pushed up from his stool, staggered, and caught his balance. "Get out."

"Not until you tell me who else you told."

"Fuck you," Dunlop said, pushing his chin forward belligerently. "And fuck your money."

Icarus placed the guineas back in his pocket. He took a step towards Dunlop. "Who else did you tell?"

"Go to hell! Think I'm afraid of you? Wellesley's golden boy? He thought the sun shone out your—"

Icarus caught Dunlop by the throat and took two swift strides across the narrow room, lifting him, slamming him back into the wall.

The man on the bed stopped snoring.

Dunlop's heels scrabbled frantically, half a dozen inches off the floor. His fingers clawed at Icarus's gloved hand.

Icarus counted to ten in his head, while Dunlop choked

and gurgled, and then let him slide down the wall. He eased his grip on the man's throat. "Apologize to the lady for your language, Dunlop."

Dunlop inhaled a wheezing, desperate breath. His face was puce. "Bastard!"

Icarus tightened his grip again, held Dunlop off the floor again. He counted five seconds, while the man on the bed resumed snoring.

This time, when he eased his grip, Dunlop apologized.

Icarus bared his teeth in a smile. "Now, let's consider my question again. Who—other than Wellesley and Matlock—did you tell?"

Dunlop hissed a swearword.

The man was a slow learner. Icarus tightened his fingers and forced Dunlop's chin up. "Who?"

"Green," Dunlop said truculently.

Icarus put up his eyebrows. "Green?"

"My manservant."

Icarus remembered the man—young, wiry, quiet. "Where is Green now?"

"How the devil should I know? Turned him off in Basingstoke last month. M' pockets were to let; couldn't afford him."

Icarus glanced at Miss Trentham, standing by the door, veiled and aloof and utterly out of place. His conscience gave an even stronger twinge. She shouldn't be witnessing this.

Miss Trentham gave a short nod.

He turned his attention back to Dunlop. "Anyone else?"

"A sergeant. He was looking for you. I told him where to find you." Dunlop croaked a laugh.

"Which sergeant?"

"How should I remember a damned sergeant's name?"

Icarus tightened his grip again. "Which sergeant?"

"The one who lost his arm at Vimeiro," Dunlop said in a sullen, breathless voice.

The aftermath of Vimeiro was a blank. He'd been out of his

mind with fever, with torment. If a sergeant had lost an arm, he didn't know who he was. "Leishman? Day? Houghton?"

"Houghton."

Icarus grimaced inwardly. Poor Houghton. "Who else did you tell?"

"No one."

He glanced at Miss Trentham. She shook her head; it was a lie.

Excitement flared in Icarus's chest, hot and fierce. Dunlop *was* his traitor. "Who else?" he asked, flexing his fingers around Dunlop's throat when what he really wanted to do was rip the man's head off.

"Cuthbertson," Dunlop wheezed. "He already knew."

"Not one of the villagers?"

"No."

Icarus glanced at Miss Trentham. She nodded. *That* wasn't a lie.

"One of the French?"

"No!"

Miss Trentham nodded again.

The excitement died in Icarus's chest, leaving him hollow again. Dunlop wasn't his traitor.

"Anyone else?"

"No, curse it!"

Another cool nod from Miss Trentham.

Icarus released Dunlop and stepped back. "I entrusted you with a message for General Wellesley's ears only, and you told not only Wellesley, but Matlock, *and* your man Green, *and* Houghton, *and* Cuthbertson?"

"Cuthbertson already knew," Dunlop said sullenly, massaging his throat.

Every muscle in Icarus's body vibrated with fury, with disgust. "A flogging would be too good for you."

Dunlop spat at him. The spittle landed on the floor alongside Icarus's left boot. Icarus glanced at it contemptuously, turned his back, and crossed to Miss Trentham, cool and aloof in her cloak and veiled hat.

He fished the guineas from his pocket again, slowly and insultingly selected one, and dropped it on the floor. He held out his arm to Miss Trentham, opened the door, and escorted her from the room.

When they were several steps down the corridor, Dunlop shouted after him, "Go to hell, Reid!"

Too late, Icarus told him silently. *I'm already there.*

CHAPTER 4

The hackney trotted back towards the Thames. Letty stared out the window but it wasn't Southwark she saw; it was Mr. Reid pinning Dunlop to the wall.

Such casual violence, performed as effortlessly as breathing.

She glanced at Reid. He was sunk deep in thought, his brow furrowed.

Her gaze dropped to Reid's hands, clenched in his lap. They looked like gentleman's hands, clad in leather gloves, but they weren't; they were fighter's hands, large and strong and brutal.

She knew she should be repelled by him—but she wasn't.

Reid was tougher than any man she'd ever met. He was more a *man* than any man she'd met. He was dangerous. And because of those things—perversely, and against her better judgment—she was attracted to him.

He's not attracted to me, Letty thought wryly. She was nothing more than a tool to Mr. Reid.

The hackney crossed London Bridge. A foul smell pushed its way into the carriage again. "What's that smell?" Letty asked.

"Smell?" Reid blinked, and looked up. "The tanneries."

They fell into silence again, traversing streets and

neighborhoods Letty didn't recognize. Finally, the hackney turned into the Strand. A few minutes more, and they'd be back at Hatchard's. She smoothed her gloves on her hands, tweaked each fingertip, and silently acknowledged a truth to herself: she didn't want to go home.

"I apologize," Reid said abruptly. "I should never have taken you to Marshalsea. It was unconscionable."

Letty glanced at him. His expression was grim. Was he in the throes of a fit of conscience?

"It was interesting," she said, and heard the bell-tone of truth in her words. It *had* been interesting—the sordid room, the coarse language, the violence. More interesting than any afternoon in her life. "Matlock. Would that be Lieutenant Thomas Matlock? The Earl of Riddleston's brother?"

Reid put up his brows. "You know him?"

"Extremely well. He's a close friend of my cousin, Lucas Kemp."

"I don't think it was Matlock."

"He's in England at the moment. Did you know? He's on leave."

From Reid's expression, he hadn't known.

"My cousins hold a house party in Wiltshire every year, before the hunting season starts. I'll be there. And so will Tom Matlock."

"I don't think it's Matlock," Reid said again.

All too soon, the jarvey deposited them opposite Hatchard's. Letty stared across at the bookshop. Barely an hour had passed since she'd last seen those wide bow-fronted windows, and yet she'd been to another world and back.

"How do you intend to . . ." Reid's brow knitted. "To reenter your life? Will your maid meet you here?"

Letty shook her head. "I'll pretend my friend sent a footman to escort me home—she lives only one street over from me."

"An invisible footman?"

"A footman I dismissed on my doorstep."

Reid looked dubious. "Will it serve?"

"It will," Letty said. "If only because no one expects subterfuge from me. I'm extremely cautious, Mr. Reid—and my servants know it. I never go *anywhere* unattended. I have no wish to be trapped into marriage!"

Reid didn't state the obvious: that she hadn't been at all cautious today. "You live on Hill Street, I understand?"

"Yes."

"I shall escort you."

They walked along Piccadilly, and turned into Berkeley Street. Their strides matched. Reid walked silently. It was a novel experience to be in the company of a man who wasn't trying to impress her with his wit or his charm or his antecedents.

Letty glanced at his profile. Reid would be a handsome man if he wasn't so gaunt. Even gaunt, he was striking. *What will you do now?* she wanted to ask. But she knew. Find Green. Find Houghton. Find Cuthbertson.

And then die.

Her throat tightened painfully. A chilly breeze found its way through her veil, making her eyes sting.

Berkeley Square opened out in front of them, lofty houses with windows reflecting a darkening sky. Hill Street was on the far side. They walked around the winter-bare fenced garden in the middle of the square. The house she'd hired was just visible: tall and brick, with a gabled roof and crown cornices, as lofty as its neighbors.

The house was no prison, as Marshalsea was—and yet it *was* a prison. Her prison. Walls hung with silk, Aubusson carpets, gilt-edged dinner sets. The housemaids and the liveried footmen, the housekeeper and the butler, her chaperone Mrs. Sitwell, were all her warders.

Letty's steps slowed. She didn't want to go back.

What she wanted was to go to Basingstoke with Mr. Reid and discover whether Green was his traitor. But that would entail lies. Many lies.

She frowned down at the pavement. Three Portuguese scouts. Good men, Reid had said. Brave men. Men who'd been betrayed to their deaths.

In her mind's eye she saw a set of scales. The justice the scouts deserved weighed down one pan heavily. In the other pan were today's lies. One to her maid. One to Miss Torpington. And one lie yet to be told, to her butler when he opened the door and saw no footman at her heels. Compared to the three deaths, the lies weighed almost nothing. They were . . . acceptable? No, not acceptable, but at least excusable. Small untruths uttered in the pursuit of one great truth. But if she went to Basingstoke she would have to tell more lies. At what point would the balance tip? When would the weight of lies become more than the weight of those deaths? When would the lies become *in*excusable?

Perhaps it would be better to tell none at all? To let Reid struggle on alone.

But he was *dying*.

Letty worried at her lower lip with her teeth, and thought about the scales—and then she looked at Reid, and the decision made itself. She *would* help him.

A carriage passed with a rattle of wheels on cobblestones. Mr. Reid stepped onto the roadway. Letty stayed where she was.

Reid halted, and glanced at her. "Miss Trentham?"

"Let us go to Basingstoke and look for Mr. Green." Letty heard the words with faint shock. Had she truly said that?

She saw her own shock reflected on Reid's face. He came back to her side. "Miss Trentham, it's one thing to absent yourself from your household for an afternoon; it is quite another to go to Basingstoke. It's all of fifty miles!"

"Don't you wish for my help?"

Reid was silent for a long moment. "Yes," he said finally. "But not if it means your ruin."

Letty gave a humorless laugh. "If only my suitors had your decency, Mr. Reid. Most of them would jump at ruining me if it meant I had to marry them!"

Reid's face stiffened. "Decency? You know I have no decency. Not after Marshalsea. No *decent* man would have exposed you to such brutish behavior!"

"It was extremely interesting," Letty said.

Reid's eyebrows lifted.

"If you're concerned about Dunlop's language, it was shocking, but I assure you I didn't understand everything he said. There was one word I've never heard before."

Reid clearly understood which word she was referring to. His lips tightened. "An unpardonable piece of crudity."

"And I must be lacking in sensibility, because I thought he quite *deserved* to be throttled."

Reid gazed at her. His expression was bemused.

"Have I shocked you, Mr. Reid?"

Reid considered this question, and didn't answer it directly. "I'm relieved the experience didn't overset you."

"I'm not a chit from the schoolroom to be thrown into the vapors by such a scene," Letty told him. "I'm a grown woman. And I wish to go to Basingstoke with you. I believe it can be done without anyone being the wiser."

"I don't see how—"

"I'm engaged to stay with a friend in Andover for four nights, on my way to Wiltshire. I shall write to her, putting off my visit. Helen will think I'm still in London, and everyone else will think I'm in Andover."

Reid frowned. "Your carriage—"

"I shall travel post this time, because . . . because I've decided my traveling chaise needs to be reupholstered!"

"And your maid?"

"I'll give Pugh leave to visit her sister in Chertsey for a few days. I can set her down on the way, and she can travel on to Whiteoaks by stagecoach. And as for my chaperone, Mrs. Sitwell, she never goes to Wiltshire. She detests the countryside."

Reid's frown deepened. "Your maid will hardly leave you unattended in a post-chaise."

"I shan't be unattended. *You* will meet me in Chertsey. You'll be sent by Helen, to escort me as an outrider."

"Would your maid leave you in the care of just an outrider?" His tone suggested he didn't think so.

Letty didn't think so, either. She chewed on her lip, and then said, "You'll have to hire a girl to pretend to be one of Helen's maids. She won't need to say a word, just wait at the posting inn in Chertsey with you. If Pugh sees you *and* a maid, she'll be satisfied."

"A pretend maid?" Reid said, in the same tone he'd said *An invisible footman?*

"Yes. A few minutes' work for a couple of shillings—I'm sure you could find someone willing to do it."

"What about Basingstoke? You'd need a maid there."

"We'll say my maid has fallen ill. A chambermaid can help me with my buttons."

Reid frowned at her.

"We choose a quiet inn in Basingstoke, where neither of us is known, and put up for a few days."

Reid's frown deepened. "As man and wife?"

"We look too dissimilar to be brother and sister, don't you think? We'd have separate chambers, of course!" Letty flushed, glad of the thick veil, and hurried on: "It shouldn't take more than a day or two to discover Green's whereabouts, if he's still in Basingstoke. And if he's not . . . Well, we'll deal with that if it happens! And then I'll take another post-chaise to Wiltshire. You may come if you wish, and speak to Tom Matlock."

Reid turned his head away and looked across the square, his eyes narrow.

Letty watched him, and listened to the echo of everything she had said: Andover and Chertsey, outriders and maids. So many lies to be told. She was aware of a sick feeling in the pit of her stomach. Did she truly want to do this?

"I don't like it," Reid said finally. "But it could work." Both statements were the truth. He regarded her for a long moment, as if trying to see through the veil. "Are you certain you wish to lend yourself to such a deception?"

No, she wasn't certain.

Letty hesitated, on the brink of balking—and then she thought of the scales again, thought about betrayal and death and justice and truth and lies. She gave a decisive nod. "Yes." She *was* certain. She would do it for the dead scouts. She'd do it for Reid, who was dying. And she'd do it—shamefully—for herself, because she wanted to spend more time in his company, because she wanted not to be an heiress for a few days—and that was selfish and wrong, but at least she would be honest to herself and not pretend it wasn't true.

"The risk to your reputation—"

"If it doesn't bother me, it shouldn't bother you."

Reid gave her an extremely saturnine look. Too late, Letty realized she'd offered him a deep insult. A gentleman *would* be bothered by the risk to a lady's reputation.

Reid's lips compressed. Letty found herself holding her breath.

"Very well," Reid said, finally. "We'll attempt it. When?"

"I'm due to leave for Andover in six days." Letty's mind skipped over the hurdles and fastened on the goal at the end: Basingstoke. "Meet me in the park tomorrow. We'll ride again, and discuss the details."

This time, when Reid crossed the roadway, Letty matched her stride to his. He halted when they reached Hill Street. "I'll come no further. Will you be safe?"

"Perfectly. Good-bye. Three o'clock in the park. Don't forget!"

When she'd gone two steps, Reid said, "Thank you."

Letty stopped and looked back. She gave him a nod. "You're welcome."

After a moment, he nodded back.

Letty turned away and walked down Hill Street. Emotions churned in her stomach: trepidation, a twinge of doubt, excitement. She climbed the steps to her front door and glanced back at Reid, tall and lean and motionless at the end of Hill Street. She couldn't make out his face from this distance, but she saw it in her mind's eye: weary and gaunt, with sun-bronzed skin and silver eyes—and a frown, because Reid was always frowning.

She would like to see him smile.

Letty pulled off her veil and shoved it inside her muff. *Do not become attached to this man, Letitia,* she told herself sternly. *Remember: he's dying.*

Her eyes stung. This time, she knew she couldn't blame it on the cold breeze.

CHAPTER 5

*I*carus traveled post to Basingstoke on the sixth, arriving at dusk. On the seventh, he walked around the market town, inquiring after Mr. Green at the inns and looking for a hostelry for himself and Miss Trentham. By noon, he'd found a suitable establishment—on a quiet backstreet, modest but clean—and booked rooms for himself, his wife, and his wife's maid for four nights, plus a private parlor. He didn't find Green. That afternoon, he posted back to Frimley, halfway between Basingstoke and Chertsey, where he canceled Miss Trentham's booking from Frimley to Andover the following day, and arranged instead for a carriage to convey himself and his wife to Basingstoke.

On the morning of the eighth, he hastened to Chertsey. Midday found him in the yard of the King's Head, dressed as a servant. Not a liveried footman, but a sober and respectable steward. Alongside him, equally sober and respectable, was a young washerwoman, clad in her Sunday best. Hired that morning, the washerwoman had professed herself quite happy to assist in a clandestine tryst. *Course I won't tell a soul,* she'd said, accepting a silver crown. *If you want to put your leg over someone else's wife, who am I to mind?*

Just after noon, a post-chaise swept into the yard, drawn

38

by sweating horses. The ostlers ran forward, the postilions dismounted; all was bustle and noise.

"This it?" the washerwoman asked.

"Yes."

Two ladies descended from the carriage: Miss Trentham, cool and aloof in dove gray, and a short middle-aged woman with blunt features and a brisk, no-nonsense manner.

Icarus stepped forward, and bowed. "Miss Trentham?" he said, in a servant's polite, uninflected voice.

Miss Trentham ate her luncheon at the King's Head. By the time she'd finished this repast, the maid had been borne off by her sister and the washerwoman had departed. Icarus handed Miss Trentham into the post-chaise, and swung up on the horse he'd hired.

Chertsey to Frimley was a little over twelve miles. Not far, by a soldier's reckoning, but more than far enough for a man who'd spent six weeks confined to bed with the fever. When Icarus dismounted at the posting inn in Frimley, his legs were shaking.

Miss Trentham and her outrider arrived in Frimley; Mr. and Mrs. Reid departed from it. Icarus sank gratefully onto the soft squab seat across from Miss Trentham. Damn it, he was as weak as an old man.

No, he was as weak as a *dead* man—because that's what he was: dead. An animated corpse with one task to perform before he could crawl back into his grave.

Frimley to Basingstoke was almost eighteen miles. They accomplished the journey in silence. Not a chatterer, Miss Trentham. Icarus stared out the window and watched the sky darken, while his thoughts ground through their inevitable circuit: Vimeiro, the ambush, the executions, and finally, the creek.

It always came back to the creek. Everything came back to the creek.

When the carriage slowed to enter Basingstoke, Icarus roused himself from his memories. "We're putting up at the Plough." His voice was harsh. He cleared his throat and strove for a milder tone. "It's plain, but clean. I hope you'll be comfortable there."

"I have no doubt I will." Miss Trentham didn't sound tired; she sounded alert and cheerful. "What should we call one another, Mr. Reid? If we need to speak in front of the servants."

"I shall go by my own name; you may choose whatever name you prefer."

Miss Trentham was silent for a moment. "The truth, I think. You may call me Letty."

"My name is Icarus."

"Icarus?" The coach was now too dark for him to see her expression, but he thought she sounded faintly surprised. "An unusual name."

Icarus shrugged. "A family name."

The post-chaise deposited them at the Plough. The innkeeper bustled out, short and stout and bobbing his head. "Mr. Reid, Mrs. Reid, welcome, welcome. A cold night. I've lit the fire in your parlor. Come in, come in."

They stepped inside. Icarus watched England's wealthiest heiress examine her surroundings—the simple furnishings, the humble drugget carpet. No disdain came to her face. Rather, her expression was wide-eyed and curious.

"My wife's maid took ill this morning," Icarus said. "We hope she'll be well enough to join us tomorrow."

The innkeeper arranged his face into a sympathetic smile. "Not to worry, Mr. Reid. My daughter will be pleased to wait on your wife. A good girl, she is. I'm sure you'll find no fault with her."

Miss Trentham murmured her gratitude.

The innkeeper led them upstairs. Their bedchambers were side by side, low-ceilinged and old-fashioned, with tiny-paned windows.

"Charming," Miss Trentham said, with apparent sincerity.

They ate dinner in the parlor he'd hired, just the two of them. The repast was substantial, but simple: fried sweetbreads and a raised mutton pie, with curd pudding to follow. The curtains were drawn, a fire burned in the grate, candles glowed in the sconces, and it was as intimate as if they truly were husband and wife.

Icarus laid his knife and fork neatly on his plate and glanced at Miss Trentham. An unmarried lady. An heiress.

Miss Trentham didn't look like either of those things. She looked like someone's wife, cool and mature and well into her twenties. Her husband was clearly a man of only moderate means; her clothing had none of the embellishments a wealthy woman would sport.

"Is that all you're going to eat?" Miss Trentham said.

"I have no appetite." It was another of the many things he'd lost at Vimeiro.

"Nonsense! You've not eaten enough to keep a sparrow alive. No wonder you're so thin. Eat!"

Icarus looked down at his almost-full plate. "I'm not hungry."

"Eat!"

Icarus was too weary to argue. He sighed, and picked up his knife and fork again, and ate another sweetbread.

"And some pie," Miss Trentham said, in a tone that brooked no argument.

Icarus ate some pie, too.

Miss Trentham didn't cease harassing him until his plate

was half empty. "You must have some curd pudding, too," she said firmly.

"I'll be ill if I eat any more," Icarus said.

Miss Trentham cast him a sharp glance, but didn't argue; she must have heard the truth in his words.

Icarus went to bed with his stomach uncomfortably full. Perhaps it was the food, or perhaps the exhaustion of riding twelve miles on horseback, but he dropped almost instantly to sleep.

He fell asleep in Basingstoke, but woke in Vimeiro, face down in a creek. Someone knelt on his back. Hard fingers gripped his hair, knuckles digging into his scalp. He fought, bucking and twisting until it seemed that his heart would burst with effort, but he couldn't break the rope that bound his arms behind him, couldn't dislodge the man on his back, couldn't tear his hair free.

"C'est vrai?" a voice snarled in his ear. "Dis-moi! Tell me!"

The knuckles pressed harder into his scalp—and shoved his head underwater.

Icarus bucked and fought. Water filled his eyes, his nose, his mouth, his lungs. He was choking, drowning—

He woke abruptly, lurching upright, fighting with the bedclothes, lungs heaving, a scream in his throat.

The room was dark, and for a panic-stricken moment he thought he truly *was* back in Vimeiro—and then reason caught up with him. His arms and legs were unbound. He was in a nightshirt, not a uniform. He was in bed. He was dry.

Icarus dragged air into his lungs. With heroic effort, he managed not to vomit up his dinner.

After a moment, he lay back down. His body shook uncontrollably, deep wracking shudders, and his throat felt as raw as if he'd been screaming. He wiped his face with trembling hands, smearing away sweat and tears.

Slowly, his breathing steadied. Slowly, his heart stopped its frantic, futile pounding.

At last, the shaking died to mere tremors. Clumsily, Icarus reached for the tinderbox and lit a candle.

The tiny, golden flame showed him the bedchamber: beamed ceiling, four-poster bed, drugget rug.

There were no bodies. No harsh-faced French soldiers crowding round.

And no creek.

Icarus fumbled for his watch on the bedside table. Two o'clock. The longest sleep he'd had since Vimeiro.

CHAPTER 6

November 9th, 1808
Basingstoke, Hampshire

Letty woke at dawn. She rang for hot water. The land-lord's daughter, Sally, a cheerful, round-faced girl, laced her into her stays.

"Do you know if Mr. Reid—if my husband is awake?"

"He were up before anyone this mornin'. In the parlor, he is, readin'."

Letty stood still while the girl fastened the buttons at the back of her gown. "Did you hear any odd noises in the night?"

"Noises? What sort of noises, ma'am?"

Letty frowned at herself in the mirror, trying to find words to describe the noise that had woken her. A cry? A scream? "I thought I heard someone shout."

"Shout? It'd've been someone on the street, ma'am. Jug-bitten." The girl fastened the topmost button. "And your hair? How would you like it dressed?"

"A knot, thank you."

Sally undid the plait, brushed out Letty's hair, twisted it into a knot, and anchored it with hairpins. "There you are, ma'am."

"Thank you." A glance in the mirror, a twitch of her cuffs, and she was ready to face Mr. Reid.

Letty went down one flight of creaking stairs and entered the parlor. Reid was in an armchair by the fire, legs crossed, reading. He closed his book, stood, and bowed. "Good morning."

"Good morning." She examined his face. Reid looked no more or less exhausted than he had yesterday. "How are you? Sally said you were up before anyone this morning."

"I'm an early riser."

The Plough laid on a simple breakfast: eggs, sausages, and a pot of tea. Letty ate with relish; Reid picked at his food, and pushed his plate away after eating one egg and half a sausage.

"Don't be ridiculous," Letty said, putting the plate back in front of him.

"I've eaten my fill."

"You may *think* you've eaten your fill, but you haven't," she said firmly.

"I assure you, I have."

"I assure you, you *haven't.*"

They matched stares. Beneath his weariness, Reid looked annoyed. "I'm not your child or your employee, Miss Trentham. You can't compel me to eat more than I wish to."

"But as your *wife,* I really must insist on it!"

Reid didn't smile at this sally. He pushed his plate away again.

Letty placed it back in front of him. "Mr. Reid," she said bluntly. "I don't have to help you. I'm doing you a favor—a rather large favor—a favor that could see me ruined! In return, all I ask is one very *small* favor from you: that you eat more."

Reid's expression became saturnine. "Blackmail, Miss Trentham?"

Letty pursed her lips and considered this accusation. "A bargain. I help you find your traitor; you humor me by eating more."

Reid blew out his breath. He picked up his knife and fork again. "How much would you like me to eat?" he inquired, with sour politeness.

Letty wanted him to eat everything that was on his plate, but she compromised with: "At least one more egg, and a whole sausage."

Reid ate precisely what she'd told him to eat. His plate was still half-full when he'd finished. Letty watched him lay down his knife and fork. His hands were large, with strong, lean fingers. Fighter's hands. Hands that could hold a man pinned to the wall.

Her gaze lifted to his face. The sun had been only an hour in the sky, and already Reid looked exhausted, lines of weariness etched into his skin. "What time did you get up, Mr. Reid?"

He glanced at her, and away. "I'm an early riser."

That wasn't an answer, it was an evasion. Letty frowned at him. "Did you hear someone crying out in the night?"

"No."

The landlord's daughter bustled cheerfully into the parlor. "Would you like anything more, ma'am, sir?"

"No, thank you, Sally." Letty placed her napkin on the table and pushed back her chair. "My husband and I are going for a walk."

Basingstoke was a market town, and Wednesday was market day. The street that the Plough lay on was quiet enough, but the main square was chaos and commotion. Half the folk of Hampshire had apparently come to sell their produce, and the other half to buy it.

Letty peered through her veil. The square was crammed with stalls and barrows and carts and livestock of every description, and people, hundreds of people, all of whom seemed to be calling out to one another.

"Good Lord," she said.

Reid halted, and looked slightly daunted.

Letty stared around the market square. The impression of bedlam didn't ease.

"Someone here must have seen Mr. Green!" she said firmly. "It's simply a matter of finding them."

Reid's eyebrows twitched up, but he didn't say what they were both thinking: *As easy as unearthing a needle in a hayrick.*

They eased their way into the market, pressed close on all sides by housewives, tradesmen, and farmers in leather waistcoats and hobnailed brogues. Letty could scarcely hear herself think.

"Excuse me, we're looking for a friend of ours. A young man named Green. He was released from service here last month. His employer was a Mr. Dunlop. Have you perhaps seen him, or heard of him?"

Reid asked the question until he was hoarse, but none of the busy vendors or their customers knew of Mr. Green.

At noon, they returned to the Plough. Luncheon consisted of last night's raised pie and curd pudding, reheated. They ate silently. Letty kept an eye on Reid's plate. When he made to put down his knife and fork, she said, "You haven't finished your pie."

Reid shot her a narrow glance, but didn't argue. After he'd chewed his way through the rest of the pie, he laid down his cutlery. "Satisfied?"

"Yes. Now do let me serve you some of this delicious pudding!"

A muscle in his jaw twitched, but he said nothing.

Reid ate three mouthfuls of curd pudding, and then put down his spoon. "I can't eat any more." Letty heard the truth in his words.

He eyed her for a moment, and placed his bowl to one side, waited another moment, then folded his napkin. Letty wasn't sure whether to be offended or amused. Was she such a dragon?

If Reid had looked weary at breakfast, he looked exhausted now.

"Would you like a nap?"

Reid stiffened in his chair. An expression of affront crossed his face. "No, thank you."

Letty sighed inwardly. Dare she bully him into a rest? "Then let's return to our task."

They worked their way outward from the square, asking questions of the butcher and the baker, the apothecary, the tailor and the cobbler, the wainwright and the cooper, even venturing into a fragrant brewery. Letty found the experience interesting. These were the sorts of places—brewery, bakery, cooperage—that the children who grew up in her mother's foundling homes were apprenticed in.

No one they spoke to had heard of Green. The overcast sky became darker, the clouds denser and lower. A damp, chilly breeze plucked at Letty's cloak and stirred her veil. She watched Reid closely. By late afternoon, he was gray beneath his tan.

"I have to rest," Letty announced. "All this walking! I need a cup of tea. That inn looks the very place."

Reid didn't protest.

The inn in question was a humble establishment, with faded paintwork and a lopsided sign, but the coffee room was empty, and a fire burned in the grate, and the serving woman's apron was *almost* clean.

Letty pushed back her veil and examined Mr. Reid. He looked as if he needed more than a cup of tea. "A pot of tea, please, and an ale for my husband."

The ale *did* revive Mr. Reid. He looked much less gray by the time he'd drained the tankard.

"We haven't asked here," Letty said. "Perhaps this is where Dunlop and Green stayed."

"I asked at all the inns on Monday."

"We should ask again," Letty said firmly. "Someone may have lied."

"Why would they?"

Why, indeed? Letty sighed. "Dunlop turned Green off in Basingstoke, which means he *stayed* in Basingstoke; he'd hardly throw the man out of his carriage as he passed through town."

Reid rubbed his face. "Maybe he did."

"In which case, someone would have noticed!"

The briefest and faintest of smiles crossed Reid's face—and instantly vanished. "I should have asked Dunlop where he stayed. At least, we'd have a starting point."

"Do you think he'd have remembered?" Letty said dryly. "He couldn't even remember that sergeant's name—and the man lost an arm!"

Reid shrugged.

Neither of them made a move to leave. It was warm in the coffee room, and cold outside. The door to the corridor stood open a crack. The serving woman's voice floated in. "We don't want no one like you workin' here."

"Oh, but please—"

"If you want a roof over yer head, go to the workhouse."

"Green could be in the workhouse," Reid said, with a frown. "Or an almshouse."

"Yes." Letty's attention was only partly on Reid; most of her attention was on the conversation taking place out of sight.

"But it wasn't my fault!" The speaker was a young woman. Desperation and truth rang in her voice.

"I don't care whose fault it were. Yer not wanted here. Out!"

"Excuse me," Letty told Mr. Reid, pushing up from her chair and hurrying from the room.

Only one person stood in the corridor: the serving woman, her mouth pinched tight, her hands fisted on her hips. The door to the street was just swinging shut.

Letty hastened outside. A woman stood on the flagway, wrapped in a cloak, a carpetbag at her feet, her head bent in despair.

"I beg your pardon," Letty said. "I couldn't help overhearing . . ."

The woman looked up. She was very young, dark-haired and slender, with a pale, tearstained face that might, in other circumstances, have been pretty.

"What is your trouble?" Letty asked gently. "Can I help?"

The girl's face twisted. Tears started in her eyes. "No one can help."

"I think I probably *can* help you . . . but not unless you tell me what's wrong."

They stood in silence for a long moment, while a cold wind whistled down the street. Then, the girl looked away. "I'm pregnant," she said bitterly.

Letty nodded, unsurprised. "What did you mean when you said it wasn't your fault?"

The girl looked back at her. "I meant that his son raped me, is what I meant!" she said fiercely. "But Sir Malcolm wouldn't believe it—turned me off!—and my aunt won't believe it either! No one will believe me!"

"I believe you," Letty said.

The girl's fierceness drained away. The despair returned. "What use is that?"

Mr. Reid emerged from the inn. Letty waved him back with a flick of her hand. The girl didn't notice.

"How old are you?"

"Seventeen, ma'am."

"What about your parents?"

"Dead last year," the girl said, wearily. "That's why I went into service."

"Housemaid?"

"Up at the manor."

"Well, it so happens that I'm in need of a maid myself for a few days. That will give us time to come up with a solution to your problem."

"There is no solution!"

"There most definitely *is*. For a start, you need somewhere to live until the baby's born."

The girl stared at her. "Where?"

"*Not* the workhouse!" Letty smiled at her. "Come now, be my maid until Friday—I'm in desperate need of one, I assure you."

Incredulous hope was dawning on the girl's face. "You mean that, ma'am?"

"Of course, I mean it! Now tell me, what's your name?"

"Eliza Marshall, ma'am."

Letty beckoned to Reid. "My name is Mrs. Reid, and this is my husband."

Eliza bobbed Reid a shy curtsy.

"Eliza has agreed to be my maid while we're here," Letty informed him.

Reid received this news impassively. He acknowledged Eliza's curtsy with a polite nod.

"We're staying at the Plough," Letty said. "On Beadle Street. You know where it is?"

Eliza nodded.

A sudden thought struck her. "Er . . . do you know the family who runs it?"

To her relief, Eliza shook her head.

"Good! Tell them you're Mrs. Reid's maid. There's a room hired for you. Make sure the fire's kindled, and ask for your dinner if you're hungry."

Eliza picked up the carpetbag and hugged it to her chest. "Thank you, ma'am."

"I shall see you in an hour or two, Eliza."

"Yes, ma'am. Thank you, ma'am!" Eliza bobbed another curtsy, and scurried off.

Letty watched her out of sight, and turned to Reid. He was looking at her, his expression inscrutable. "Pregnant?"

"Raped by her master's son and turned out. And her aunt won't help her."

Reid glanced at the inn. "That's the aunt?"

"I assume so."

Reid made a sound, part grunt, part snort, wholly contemptuous. He glanced in the direction Eliza had gone. "And when we leave here?"

"I shall send her to Holborn. There's a lying-in hospital there, a very good place—a charity I support—and Eliza may stay there until the baby's born. The child can go to a foundling home—a *good* one—and then all that will remain is to find Eliza another position." Letty forcibly stopped this train of thought. "But *that* can all be dealt with later," she said briskly. "For now, let's visit the workhouse and see if Mr. Green ended up there."

*C*HAPTER 7

G reen hadn't found his way to the workhouse, or to any of the almshouses. Dusk was darkening the sky. The wind carried the occasional drop of rain. "We'll try all the inns tomorrow," Letty said. "I know there's no *logical* reason why anyone would lie, but there's no harm in checking, is there?"

Reid glanced at her, and clearly decided that the question was rhetorical.

A gust of wind almost lifted Letty's hat from her head. In its wake, the rain began to come down in earnest.

Miss Trentham, England's greatest heiress, never ran; Mrs. Reid did, clutching her hat with one hand and holding her skirts up with the other. She arrived at the Plough puffing and laughing and feeling like a girl again, and clattered breathlessly up the stairs to her room, where Eliza waited to help her out of the damp clothes.

The Plough had begun to feel almost like home, comfortable and familiar, with its warm, low-beamed bedchambers and snug parlor. Dinner was giblet pie and rice pudding. Letty, who'd never eaten giblet pie before, found it surprisingly tasty. Mr. Reid—with an expression of silent long-suffering—ate almost half a plateful, but refused the rice pudding.

Upstairs in her bedchamber, Letty allowed Eliza to

unbutton and unlace her, and then sent the girl to bed.

"But your hair, ma'am. Don't you wish me to brush it out?"

"I'll do it myself tonight. Go to bed. You look exhausted. And don't worry! You will *not* be turned out into the street."

Grateful tears filled the girl's eyes. "How can I ever thank you enough, ma'am? You're an angel!"

"I can assure you I'm no angel. But I'm an orphan, myself; I know what it's like. Now, off to bed, my dear!"

Eliza bobbed a tearful curtsy. "Thank you, ma'am. Good night, ma'am."

Letty brushed out her hair, plaited it, and changed into her nightgown. An angel? No one in the *ton* would call her an angel. Cold, yes. Proud and standoffish. In the words of one of her rejected suitors, an unfeeling bitch.

But not an angel.

Letty climbed into the high bed. She didn't immediately blow out her candle, but lay watching the candlelight flicker over the walls, enjoying the coziness of the bedchamber and the sound of rain pattering against the window panes. *I wish I could stay here forever.* It was wonderful being plain Mrs. Reid. Wonderful not to be hemmed about by servants, wonderful not to have people toad-eating her whichever way she turned.

Dimly, a clock struck the hour. Letty counted the strokes. Ten. She snuffed her candle and burrowed into her bedclothes.

The sound of rain lulled Letty to sleep; the sound of someone calling out woke her. She blinked her eyes open and lay almost unbreathing, tense, straining to hear. Utter silence. Utter darkness. And yet she had the sensation that someone was in her bedchamber, that they'd made a noise . . .

Minutes crawled past. Letty found the courage to roll over and locate the tinderbox and light her candle. Light sprang up. The shadows drew back into the corners. No housebreaker cowered by the little washstand or behind the chair.

Letty got up and checked under the bed. Nothing. She padded shiveringly across to the door. It was still latched on the inside.

She blew out a breath, annoyed with herself. A dream, that's what it had been. Or perhaps she'd heard a drunkard on the street. How had Sally phrased it? Jug-bitten.

Letty turned back to the bed—and the sound came again. A choked-off scream that made the hairs on the back of her neck stand on end. It was close. So close it seemed almost inside her room.

She stood for a moment, her scalp prickling, her heart pounding with terror—and then common sense reasserted itself. That was no one jug-bitten; that was pure distress. Whoever had made that sound needed *help*.

Letty hurriedly put on her slippers, threw a shawl around her shoulders, picked up her chamberstick, and let herself out into the corridor. She turned towards Eliza's room, but even as the floorboards creaked beneath her feet, the noise came again.

Not Eliza's room; Mr. Reid's.

Letty crossed to his door and knocked quietly. "Mr. Reid?"

No one answered her.

Letty cautiously tried the door. It was unlatched.

Dare she enter Reid's room?

While she hesitated, shivering, the sound came again, a gasping cry that made her heart clutch in her chest. Was he being murdered?

No, what was *far* more likely was that he was raping Eliza. The girl was pretty, and her pregnancy scarcely showed, and she was young and vulnerable and easy prey to an unscrupulous man.

Letty wrathfully flung open the door.

Reid wasn't raping anyone. He lay in bed, alone and

asleep—but he wasn't sleeping restfully. Even as she watched, he thrashed against the bedclothes.

He was in the throes of a nightmare. And clearly one that put every nightmare she'd ever had to the pale.

Letty crossed swiftly to the bed. "Mr. Reid, wake up."

Reid thrashed again. He seemed to be having difficulty breathing. Sweat stood out on his face. Tendons strained in his throat.

"Mr. Reid! Wake up!"

Reid's face was so twisted by distress that it was almost unrecognizable.

Letty grasped his shoulder and shook him. "Icarus! Wake up!"

His eyelids sprang open. He stared at her without recognition, his silver eyes wide and wild, and sat suddenly upright and struck her.

His arm tangled in the bedclothes, blunting his blow. Even so, the punch knocked her flying. Letty hit the floor. The chamberstick spun from her hand, plunging the room into darkness.

She lay where she'd fallen, almost too afraid to breathe. The animal savagery on Reid's face—the blind wildness in his eyes—the swiftness of the blow . . . He could kill her without realizing it.

She lay silently, fearfully, listening to Reid's harsh, disrupted breaths, feeling the imprint of his knuckles on her cheek, tasting blood in her mouth. He sounded as if he was sobbing, choking, unable to get enough air into his lungs. Was he still caught in his nightmare?

A minute passed. It appeared that Reid wasn't going to climb from the bed and beat her to death. Was he awake? Did he even realize she was in his room?

"Mr. Reid?" Letty said cautiously. "Are you awake?"

His breath caught, as if she'd startled him. There was a moment of silence, and then: "Miss Trentham?"

Letty carefully sat up and fingered her cheek. "Yes."

She heard fumbling, and then the tinderbox sparked and a candle flared alight.

CHAPTER 8

*I*carus stared at Miss Trentham. What was she doing in his bedchamber? Why was she on the floor?

"Are you all right?" she asked.

No, he wasn't. His body still thought he was drowning. His lungs were laboring, every muscle in his body shuddered violently, and he wanted to vomit. "Why are you on my floor?"

"You had a nightmare. I tried to wake you, and you hit me." Miss Trentham groped for two objects: a chamberstick and a candle.

"I hit you?"

Miss Trentham touched her cheek. It was pink. "Yes."

He'd *struck* her? Cold horror filled his belly. "Are you all right?"

"I believe I'll live," Miss Trentham said, with a wry smile. There was a tiny smear of blood at the corner of her mouth.

"You're bleeding," Icarus said, even more horrified.

Miss Trentham touched a fingertip to her lips, found the blood, and wiped it off. "It's nothing."

"I'm sorry," Icarus said, appalled. "I didn't mean to."

"Of course, you didn't." Miss Trentham climbed to her feet, crossed the room, and closed the door.

Icarus blinked. He hadn't even noticed the door standing open.

Miss Trentham came back to the bed and surveyed him. "You're not all right, are you?"

"It was just a nightmare," Icarus said, avoiding the question. "Everyone has nightmares."

"You had one last night, too, didn't you?"

The shudders were dying to shivering. "You should go," Icarus said, hauling the bedclothes up around his shoulders. His voice was hoarse. Had he been screaming again? Was that why she was here? "I apologize for waking you."

"You do that a lot, you know. Don't think I haven't noticed." Miss Trentham lit her candle from his, and sat on the end of his bed.

"What?" Icarus discovered that his face was damp. Tears, or sweat? He wiped his cheeks hastily.

"You don't answer the question I've asked. Is it because you don't want to tell the truth?"

Of course it was. "You should go," Icarus said again. "It's not proper for you to be in my bedchamber."

Miss Trentham gave him a look that told him she'd noticed the evasion. "Do you have nightmares often, Mr. Reid?"

"Everyone has nightmares once in a while. Please go, Miss Trentham. Before someone finds you here." He couched the request as an order, but Miss Trentham didn't scramble off his bed and obey.

"What would it matter if someone did? Everyone here believes me to be your wife."

Icarus gazed at her, shivering. At least his breathing was under control now.

Miss Trentham gazed back at him. Dressed in a nightgown and shawl and with her hair in a disheveled plait, she didn't look at all aloof. "I think we should discuss your nightmares."

Icarus didn't agree. "Please leave my bedchamber."

"Certainly. Once we've discussed your nightmares."

"My nightmares are no concern of yours," Icarus said stiffly.

"You've woken me two nights running, and you've struck me to the floor. I'd say your nightmares *are* my concern." Miss Trentham tilted her head to one side. "Are the nightmares about India?"

"No."

"Portugal?"

Icarus thinned his lips. "Please leave."

"Did the French torture you?"

The muscles in his face tightened. Icarus tried to inhale, and discovered that his lungs had frozen.

Miss Trentham's expression changed. Was that pity in her eyes? "They did, didn't they?"

Icarus struggled to find his voice. "An officer in uniform is a prisoner of war, not a spy. He would not be tortured."

"Yes, or no, Mr. Reid."

"Please leave my room."

Miss Trentham stayed where she was, on the end of his bed. "Yes, or no?"

Icarus flung back his bedclothes and stalked across to the door, wrenching it open. "Leave!"

Miss Trentham sighed. She climbed off his bed and walked to where he stood. He could clearly see where he'd struck her. "Talking about things often helps, you know."

"I've not told anyone what happened in Portugal," Icarus snapped. "And I'm hardly likely to start with you!"

"Perhaps you should," Miss Trentham said seriously. "It might help you sleep better."

Nothing would help him sleep better.

"Good night," she said, and then she surprised him by standing on tiptoe and lightly kissing his cheek.

By the time Icarus found his voice, Miss Trentham had gone. He closed the door and touched his cheek. What had moved her to kiss him?

Pity?

There was no sleeping after a nightmare; Icarus had learned that early. He read for four hours, then stripped out of his nightshirt, sponged himself down with cold water, and dressed for the day. Another hour's reading, and the inn stirred awake. Icarus rang for hot water, shaved, and went down to the parlor to wait for Miss Trentham. She appeared an hour after dawn.

Icarus stood. "Good morning."

"Good morning." She advanced into the room. "I hope you got some more sleep?"

Icarus ignored this question. "Your cheek? How is it?" The left side of her face looked slightly swollen, and the left half of her mouth.

Miss Trentham wasn't diverted. "I hope you got some more sleep?"

"It's stopped raining," Icarus said.

"Did you sleep again?"

Icarus pulled out a chair for her at the table. "After you."

Miss Trentham folded her arms. "Did you sleep again?"

Icarus pressed his lips together and didn't answer.

"Do you *ever* sleep again?"

"Sit," Icarus said, losing his patience.

"I appear to have married a tyrant," Miss Trentham said dryly, and sat.

The landlord's daughter served them breakfast. At Miss Trentham's request, Icarus forced himself to eat two eggs and two sausages. If he was a tyrant, Miss Trentham was a damned despot.

"Have you tried laudanum?" Miss Trentham asked, when he'd finished eating.

Icarus didn't pretend to misunderstand her. "I have," he said curtly. "And I dislike it." Dislike was an understatement. The orderlies had forced it on him when he'd been in the throes of fever, violent in his delirium. It had made the nightmares a hundred times worse. He'd been unable to break free of them, unable to wake up, unable to breathe.

"I think you should talk to someone about what happened in Portugal. If not me, then someone you trust. A chaplain, perhaps."

"Can we please not discuss this?"

Miss Trentham leaned forward. "It could help you!"

"I don't need help," Icarus said flatly. "I told you, I'll be dead by the end of the year."

Her eyes narrowed. "What is it you're dying of, Mr. Reid?"

Icarus pushed back his chair and stood. "Shall we make a start?"

Basingstoke was a small town, but it was fifty miles from London—a convenient day's ride—and boasted a disproportionate number of inns for its size. Icarus knew, because he'd visited them all on Monday. Visiting them all again on Thursday was a waste of time—but it was better than discussing his nightmares or the state of his health.

They started with the Plough, and then crossed the King's Arms, Toby House, and Hogshead off the list. Next was the Red Lion.

"Dunlop? Green? Never heard of 'em," the landlord said impatiently. He was an overfed man, his waistcoat straining to accommodate his ample girth. "I told you that before."

Icarus turned to go; Miss Trentham stayed where she was, her gaze on the landlord's face. "But you *have* heard of them."

Icarus swung back to the landlord.

The man flushed. "You calling me a liar?"

"Yes," Miss Trentham said matter-of-factly. "I am."

"Now, look here—" The landlord broke off as Icarus stepped towards him.

"Do you know where Green is?" Icarus asked bluntly.

"No, I don't! And you can't browbeat a man in his own—"

"What's your name?" Miss Trentham asked.

"Busbee. And I must ask you to leave—"

"Mr. Busbee knows where Green is," Miss Trentham said.

"Does he? How interesting." Icarus flexed his hands and took another step towards the landlord.

"He's in the stables!" Busbee cried.

Icarus halted. "The stables?"

"He's one of my ostlers."

*C*HAPTER 9

*G*reen was indeed in the stables behind the Red Lion, shoveling manure. Icarus blinked, scarcely able to recognize him. "Mr. Green?"

Green straightened wearily. "Sir?" He was a slight young man, unshaven and grimy, wearing a filthy shirt and even filthier breeches. The fragrance of horse dung wafted from him.

"My name is Reid. You may remember me from Portugal."

Green looked at him more closely. "Major Reid."

"You're a hard man to find. We've been looking for you for several days."

"Looking for me?" Green said blankly. "Why?"

"Cast your mind back to the day before the engagement at Vimeiro," Icarus said, watching the man's face intently. Was this his traitor? Somehow, he didn't think so. "Do you remember Dunlop mentioning me at all?"

"He mentioned you most days, sir. Jealous of you, he was. Called you the general's golden boy."

"On *that* particular day, Dunlop told you of my rendezvous with my scouts. Do you remember that?"

Green thought for a moment, his eyes unfocused, and then nodded. "Yes, sir."

"Did you tell anyone what he told you? Where we'd be? And when?"

Green's brow wrinkled. "Of course not!" The note of indignation in his voice was perfect.

Icarus glanced at Miss Trentham.

She nodded. Green was telling the truth.

Icarus sighed. "Thank you."

Green shrugged, and turned back to the pile of manure.

"Ah . . . if you don't mind my asking . . . why are you here, Mr. Green?"

Green stabbed his shovel into the manure. "Mr. Dunlop done a runner, is why I'm here," he said bitterly. "Left me to pay *his* shot and *my* shot—which I couldn't do, seeing as how he owed me three months' pay. It's either this, or debtors' prison."

Icarus's eyebrows rose. "Who told you that?"

"Mr. Busbee."

Icarus glanced at Miss Trentham. She nodded. Green was telling the truth again.

"How much did Dunlop owe you?"

"Ten quid."

Icarus pulled out his pocketbook, extracted a ten-pound note, and held it out.

Green's mouth dropped open. "Sir?"

"Go on, take it."

"But—"

"Take it."

Hesitantly, Green did. "Thank you, sir." Moisture sheened his eyes. He blinked several times.

"How much is there still to pay?"

"Less than a quid. Busbee's keeping tabs. But I can pay *that* now—"

"You're not responsible for that obligation. Dunlop was. And since he neglected to discharge it, *I* will." Icarus used his major's voice: authoritative, brooking no argument.

Green hesitated, clutching the note in his dirty fingers, and then said, "Thank you, sir," again.

Icarus tucked the pocketbook back in his coat. "It may interest you to know that Dunlop is currently a resident of Marshalsea Prison."

Green blinked. "Marshalsea? Mr. Dunlop?"

"He's not enjoying the experience."

Green grinned. It transformed his face, making him look like a schoolboy at a fair. "Hard to see as how *anyone* could enjoy that!"

"Indeed." Icarus studied the young man. Green had been competent at his job, as far as he could recall. "I have no man-servant at present," he said abruptly. "I can offer you a month's employment, and a good reference at the end of that."

Green's eyes widened. "Me, sir?"

"If you would like."

"Yes, sir!"

"I'm staying at the Plough, on Beadle Street. Present yourself there once you've cleaned yourself up. I'll pay your shot here."

"Yes, sir! Thank you, sir!" Green hurried off, leaving the shovel jammed in the manure heap.

Icarus turned to find Miss Trentham watching him, her veil pulled back and her eyebrows slightly raised. "Very chivalrous, Mr. Reid."

To his annoyance, Icarus felt himself flush.

"Busbee sounds like rather a villain," she said, twitching down her veil again. "Surely the debt was Dunlop's, not Green's?"

"He sounds very much like a villain." Icarus set his jaw and strode back into the Red Lion. It would give him great pleasure to rip Busbee's head off and shove it up his posterior.

By the time he ran Busbee to ground—in his storeroom—Icarus had rethought his tactics. "I understand that Dunlop departed without paying his shot," he said, in a reasonable tone.

Busbee eyed him warily. "That he did! More'n eight quid, he owed me. A week's board for him and his man, plus three bottles of my best wine each night."

"Ah . . . I think you might be mistaken," Miss Trentham said gently. "Are you certain it was so much?"

Busbee swelled. "Positive!"

Miss Trentham shook her head.

"I'm sure Mr. Busbee keeps accounts," Icarus said, with a tight, unfelt smile. "Shall we examine them?"

Busbee thought of several reasons why he couldn't possibly allow them to view his books. Icarus grew impatient. "Then perhaps we should take this matter to the magistrate?"

Busbee led them to his office and sullenly produced his ledger. Icarus bent over the desk and ran his finger down the columns. "Four nights' accommodation. Three dinners and . . . seven bottles of wine. This is your handwriting, I take it?" He tapped the sum that had been scrawled at the bottom.

"Yes," Busbee said, even more sullenly.

"Not eight pounds," Icarus said, straightening. "Not even close."

"I misremembered!"

Icarus studied the man's face. "Did you tell Mr. Green that he'd go to debtors' prison if he couldn't pay what his master owed you?"

Busbee flushed. "Of course not!"

"I think you're misremembering again," Miss Trentham said.

Busbee cast her a resentful glance. "I'm not an almshouse. Seven bottles of my best wine! Someone had to pay for it!"

"I sympathize with your problem," Icarus said. "But not with your method of achieving redress. Mr. Green was even more Dunlop's victim than you were."

"Why should *I* be out of pocket?" Busbee muttered. "It's not fair, is what it is."

"Mr. Green has worked for you for . . . how long? A month? Without wages. Is *that* fair?"

Busbee folded his lips together and didn't answer.

"How much do you pay your ostlers?"

"A shilling a day."

"Ah . . . Mr. Busbee?" Miss Trentham said.

Busbee gave her a surly glance. "One and six a day."

Icarus looked at the dates in the ledger. He did some mental arithmetic. One and a half shillings a day, multiplied by thirty . . . "So he's earned two and a half pounds in your service. I think you'd better pay him, don't you?"

"Why should *I* be out of pocket?"

Icarus reached inside his coat and pulled out his pocket-book. "Who says you will be?"

Busbee considered the matter for several seconds, then unlocked a drawer in his scarred desk and counted out two pounds and ten shillings. Scowling, he shoved the money at Icarus. "That's all I owe him. Now what about what Dunlop owes *me*?"

Miss Trentham cocked her head. "Are you certain that's all you owe Green, Mr. Busbee?"

Icarus glanced at her sharply. So did Mr. Busbee.

"I don't owe Green nothing more!" Busbee protested loudly. His voice was fractionally high-pitched, fractionally off-tone. Even Icarus heard that he was lying.

"That does it," he said, losing his patience with the man. "The magistrate. Now." He strode round the desk and reached for Busbee.

Busbee scrambled backwards and fell over his own chair. "All right! All right! I'll give it to you!"

Icarus halted.

Busbee crawled to his feet and fumbled with the drawer again. He counted out more money. He was sweating profusely, giving off a rank animal odor. Icarus's nose recognized the smell for what it was: fear.

"What's this?"

"Green gave me some of his things as . . . as payment." Busbee glanced at Miss Trentham, and slid his hand into his waistcoat pocket and brought out a watch. He placed it on the pile.

"You took Green's watch and pawned his belongings?"

Busbee glanced at him, and had the intelligence not to speak.

Icarus could barely speak, either. Outrage tightened his throat and thickened his tongue. "Is that everything you owe Mr. Green?"

Busbee nodded.

"*Say* it," Icarus said, between his teeth.

"It's everything."

"Mr. Busbee is telling the truth for once," Miss Trentham said.

Icarus counted out the money. Three pounds ten. Plus the watch. "I can understand not wanting to be out of pocket, but this is far more than that! You *profited* from it!"

"Perhaps the magistrate would be best?" Miss Trentham said coolly. "He does seem an out-and-out rogue."

"No!" Busbee cried. "Please! I promise I'll never do it again!"

Icarus glanced at Miss Trentham, aloof behind her veil, and then fastened his gaze back on Busbee. "I need a better guarantee than that, Mr. Busbee. Your word. Your *word* that you will never be dishonest in your dealings with anyone, *ever* again." He showed his teeth in a smile. "And you'd better mean it."

Busbee wet his lips. Sweat stood out on his doughy cheeks, on his domed forehead. He darted a glance at Miss Trentham. "My word," he said. "I'll never be dishonest in my dealings with anyone ever again."

"Does he mean it?"

Miss Trentham nodded.

Icarus put Green's money in his pocket, along with the

watch, and opened his pocketbook. Carefully, he counted out the exact sum that Dunlop owed and, equally carefully, placed it on the ledger. What he really wanted to do was bury the money in the manure heap and make Busbee dig for it.

CHAPTER 10

*R*eid walked fast, practically striding, his arm taut beneath Letty's hand. She stretched her legs to keep up and glanced at his face. A magnificent man when he was angry, with those blazing silver eyes, that knotted brow, those flared nostrils. She could imagine him facing Achilles on the battle-field at Troy—and winning.

Reid's pace slowed. He exhaled, and almost visibly shed his anger. His arm relaxed. He glanced at her. "Luncheon?"

"Luncheon."

Now, he no longer looked magnificent; he looked gaunt and weary. Letty had a flash of memory: Reid as she'd seen him last night, in the throes of his nightmare, crying out in anguish.

She soberly matched her steps to his, along Beadle Street to the Plough. Reid bespoke a room for Green and then they ate a silent lunch. "Will you come to Wiltshire?" Letty said, when they'd finished. "Talk to Tom Matlock?"

Reid shrugged. "May as well."

"And then what?"

Reid ran a hand through his hair, and sighed. "I made some enquiries before I left London. Houghton's from Bristol. He'll have gone back there."

"Bristol's not far from Wiltshire . . ."

Their eyes met.

"To try a trick like this once is rash," Reid said. "To try it twice?" He grimaced. "Foolhardy."

He was correct, but even so . . .

"I want to go to Bristol," Letty said.

"Do you know anyone there? Could you perhaps visit—"

Letty shook her head. "I don't know anyone in Bristol."

Reid frowned, and raked a hand through his hair again. "Do you think you can get away with it a second time?

"I don't know that I've got away with it *once*," Letty said.

The frown vanished. Reid huffed a breath, almost a laugh. "That's true."

Letty's heart gave a thump. That fleeting smile, the barely-glimpsed amusement in his eyes . . .

"Colonel Cuthbertson sold out after Vimeiro," Reid said. "Which is odd."

"But surely a *colonel* wouldn't be a traitor?"

"Why did he sell out?" Reid countered. "I understand why Grantham sold out, but Cuthbertson? He was a career officer. More than twenty years' service." He frowned, and looked down at his napkin, folded it in half, folded it again. "He was wasteful with his money—always outrunning the constable—but I can't imagine him *selling* information . . ." His frown deepened. He shook his head. "Inconceivable!" And then he hesitated, and said, "And yet I can more readily believe it's him than Matlock or Houghton."

The landlord entered the parlor. "Begging your pardon, Mr. Reid, but your man's arrived. I've settled 'im in his room, and he's wishful to see you."

"Excellent." Reid stood. "Come on in, Green."

Mr. Green stepped shyly into the room. Clean-shaven, he was even younger than Letty had thought. Twenty? Twenty-one? No scent of the stables accompanied him into the parlor. He looked as if he'd scrubbed himself to within an inch of his life.

"Your wages," Reid said, placing the money on the table. "Plus what Busbee owed you for your belongings. Plus your watch."

Letty almost laughed at Green's expression. He couldn't have looked more incredulous if Reid had conjured the items out of thin air.

"Are those the only clothes you have? Did Busbee sell the rest?"

Green swallowed, and found his voice. "Most of them, sir."

"I suggest you spend the rest of the afternoon replenishing your wardrobe. I shan't need you until evening."

"Yes, sir. Thank you, sir!"

Letty waited until the boy had gone. "You've acquired a worshipper."

"Me?" Reid's face stiffened, as if she'd slapped him. "I'm the last person anyone should worship."

Letty eyed him thoughtfully—and returned to the subject they'd been discussing. "Where does Cuthbertson live? Do you know?"

"Near Exeter."

Exeter? Letty was dismayed. "Exeter is . . . rather far."

"Yes." Reid leaned his shoulders against the wall.

They looked at each other for a long moment. Letty thought about the deception required to travel to Exeter in Reid's company—and then she thought about the three scouts and the justice they were owed. "It could be done," she said, finally. "West to Bristol, south to Exeter, back to London. A week. Maybe ten days."

"Eliza?"

Letty considered this question. "She'll come with us. I shall take her to the lying-in hospital myself, when I reach London."

Reid's mouth compressed.

"What?" Letty said. "Have you something against the girl?"

Reid lifted his brows. "Eliza? Of course not."

"Then, what?" Why did he not look pleased? "Have you changed your mind? Do you not want to pursue this?"

Reid looked away from her.

"What?"

Silence grew in the room, then Reid looked back at her. "I want to pursue it." His voice resonated with truthfulness. "But I dislike the risk to your reputation. I dislike being indebted to you."

"I suggest you reconcile yourself to it," Letty said briskly. "Because I want to see this to its end."

Later that afternoon, while Reid was at the posting inn arranging conveyance to Wiltshire on Saturday, Letty slipped out to visit the apothecary. A bell tinkled above her head as she stepped inside the cool quietness of the shop. Mingled scents filled her nose: lavender and *sal volatile* and a dozen others she didn't recognize.

The shop was a small one, with row upon row of shelves crammed with bottles and flasks and jars and vials. A thin, balding man stood behind the counter, mixing a liquid. To one side of the counter, in an upright chair, sat an elderly woman tucked all around with shawls, busily knitting. She had the sunken mouth and cheeks of the toothless, and large arthritic knuckles. Letty spared her a glance, and stepped up to the counter.

"Won't be a moment, ma'am," the apothecary said.

Letty waited while the man poured his liquid into a tiny flask and inserted a stopper. *Click click click,* went the knitting needles.

The apothecary brushed his hands tidily together and smiled at her. "How may I help you, ma'am?"

"My husband suffers from insomnia," Letty said. "He

refuses to take laudanum. Have you something else that would help him sleep?"

"Sleep," the old woman cackled.

The apothecary pursed his lips thoughtfully. "Has he tried valerian?"

"I don't know."

"Valerian," the old woman cackled. *Click click click.*

"The taste is . . ." The apothecary's nose wrinkled. "I'll let you smell it."

He crossed to one of the tall shelves, took down a flask filled with dark brown liquid, and removed the stopper. A smell wafted out, pungent and musty.

"Not very pleasant, is it?" The apothecary reinserted the stopper.

It was very *un*pleasant, in Letty's opinion. And overpowering; the valerian had quite smothered the other scents in the shop. "How does it compare to laudanum?"

"Laudanum," the old woman cackled, her knitting needles going *click click click.*

"Oh, much milder, and not at all addictive. It's not an opiate. It won't put him out, but it will help him drop off. The effect isn't instantaneous; it might take an hour or more."

Letty thought about it for a moment. "I'll take some," she decided.

The apothecary carefully poured some valerian into a vial and sealed it with a cork.

"How much does one take?"

"One teaspoon."

Letty took her purse from her reticule and paid. *Click click click,* went the knitting needles.

"I hope it helps your husband to sleep," the apothecary said politely, handing her the vial.

"Sleep?" cackled the old woman. "There's two things as make men sleep. Liquor and sex. Liquor and sex."

The apothecary blushed a puce color. "Please excuse my mother, ma'am. She's a little touched. Doesn't know what she's saying."

"It's perfectly all right," Letty assured him, choking back a laugh.

Click click click, went the knitting needles. "Three husbands I had, and they was all the same. The feather bed jig allus sent 'em straight to sleep."

Letty bit the tip of her tongue. The apothecary's blush intensified. Even his balding pate reddened. He hastened out from behind his counter, ushered Letty to the door, and opened it for her. *Tinkle,* went the bell, and *click click click,* went the knitting needles. "Nothing like a good tumble to put a man to sleep," the old woman said.

The apothecary practically pushed Letty out the door. The bell tinkled again as it shut. "Mother!" she heard him say in a faint, anguished voice.

CHAPTER 11

*D*inner was chitterlings, and a suet pudding. "Chitter-lings?" Letty said, trying to determine what exactly was on her plate. Some kind of sausage? "What a curious name. Do you know what it is?"

"Pig intestines," Reid told her.

"Oh." Letty cut herself a small piece and chewed dubious-ly. But the chitterling, stuffed with savory breadcrumbs and fried with bacon, was surprisingly tasty. "It's good. You must have some."

Reid glanced at her sardonically. Did he take her comment as a request?

Letty kept an eye on his plate while she ate. He did eat quite a few chitterlings, and he even suffered to eat several mouthfuls of suet pudding. Not nearly enough food for a man of his size, but significantly more than he'd eaten their first night here.

"Do you prefer brandy or port, Mr. Reid?"

His eyebrows rose. "Now?"

"In general."

He shrugged. "Brandy. Why?"

"Just curious."

Later that evening she had a discussion with the landlord, which resulted in the man bringing her a bottle of his best brandy, a glass, and a teaspoon. Letty placed the tray on a chair by the door, out of the way. "I shall take you to London next month," she told Eliza, while the girl brushed out her hair and plaited it neatly. "To a very good lying-in hospital in Holborn. It's a little early, I know, but I think it's the best place for you."

The girl's eyes met hers in the mirror.

"It's a charity hospital, but I promise you it's very clean and respectable. You'll be quite safe there."

After a moment, Eliza bit her lip and nodded. "Thank you, ma'am."

Her hair plaited, Letty turned to face the girl. "I imagine you'd prefer not to keep the child, but . . . I may be wrong?"

Eliza shuddered, and shook her head. "I don't want it, ma'am."

The poor wee thing, unwanted before it was even born. "Then it shall be placed in a foundling home. I know some very good ones. You may be certain the child will be well cared for. And when it's old enough, it can go into service. How does that sound?"

Eliza's eyes filled with grateful tears. "It sounds perfect, ma'am."

Letty looked the girl up and down. "You need a new gown. That one's looking tight. I'll buy you one tomorrow."

"I can let out the seams again—"

"A new gown," Letty said, firmly. "Now, off to bed with you. I shan't need you any more tonight."

Eliza smiled through her tears and bobbed a curtsy. "Thank you, ma'am. Goodnight, ma'am."

78

At a quarter past one, Letty woke to the now-familiar sound of Mr. Reid's nightmares. She lit her candle, threw a shawl around her shoulders, shoved her feet into slippers, and grabbed the tray.

Tonight, she wasn't hesitant; she entered Reid's room without knocking, put the tray down, and hurried to his bedside.

This wasn't sleep; this was torment. Reid thrashed, his tendons standing out, muscles straining, sweat beading his skin. His breathing was loud, harsh, irregular.

"Icarus! Wake up!"

Reid was locked in his dream. His face twisted. His breathing became harsher. He bucked wildly. A cry of pure distress tore from his throat.

"Icarus!" Letty grabbed his shoulder and shook him hard. "Wake up!"

Reid's eyelids snapped open. His arm lashed out at her.

Letty ducked back swiftly. "Icarus! It's me."

Reid lunged up from the bed, murderous savagery on his face.

"Icarus! *Stop!*"

He halted, half out of the bed, one bare foot on the floor. He blinked—and she saw him come back into himself. Awareness, understanding, and recognition flooded his face.

Letty watched warily as Reid fumbled for the bed and sat. Her heart hammered loud and fast at the base of her throat. Lord, he'd been as mad as a berserker.

But Reid no longer looked dangerous. His skin-tone was gray and he was perceptibly shaking. He rubbed his face hard, as if trying to scrub the nightmare away.

"Back into bed!" Letty said briskly.

She plumped the pillows, hauled the sheets and quilt into order again, and put Reid to bed as if he was a child, propping him up to half-sit. He obeyed without protest, shivering hard. He looked slightly dazed, as if his body was in Basingstoke, but his thoughts were somewhere far, far away. His breathing had a faint hitch to it.

Letty poured a generous glass of brandy and handed it to him. "Drink this."

Reid obeyed, gulping a mouthful. He inhaled sharply, and coughed. "Jesus!" It took him several seconds to catch his breath. The dazed look was gone and there was faint color in his cheeks. "What the devil?"

"It's brandy," Letty said.

"I realized *that*."

"I thought it might help." She perched beside him on the bed, curling her feet under her. "Go on, drink it all."

Reid hesitated, and took a sip.

Letty sat quietly, watching him. How could a man go from terrifyingly dangerous to heartrendingly vulnerable in the space of a few minutes? It was more than the tremor in his hands and the hitch in his breathing. It was his hair, disheveled and damp with sweat. It was the hollow at the base of his throat, glimpsed through the open collar of his nightshirt. It was the bare wrists, exposed where his cuffs had ridden up.

For some reason, that shadowy hollow, those exposed wrists, made Reid seem so defenseless that Letty's throat tightened painfully. She swallowed twice, and cleared her throat. "Is the brandy any good?"

"Tolerable." The silver gaze settled on her face. "Thank you."

Letty almost blushed. "You're welcome."

Sitting beside Reid on the bed, she could smell him, smell fresh male sweat. Inexplicably, it made her want to lean closer and inhale deeply, made her want to fill her lungs with his scent.

Letty looked away. The small vial of valerian caught her eye. One hurdle at a time.

She glanced back at Reid. His eyelashes were astonishingly long, and spiky with moisture. Had he cried in his dream?

He took another sip of brandy, rubbed his face roughly, sighed.

Letty wasn't sure if it was the sigh, or the damp eyelashes, or the bleak weariness on Reid's face, but she experienced an almost overwhelming urge to lean over and hug him.

She buried her hands in her lap and looked away again.

When Reid finished the brandy, Letty took the glass. "Would you like more? There's a whole bottle."

"I should be in my cups if I had any more."

"Why not? If it would help you sleep."

"I never sleep again."

Letty's eyebrows rose. This was unprecedented openness from Mr. Reid. "What else have you tried? Other than laudanum?"

He looked away. "You should go to bed."

"What else have you tried?"

Reid glanced at her. His jaw tightened. A flicker of annoyance crossed his face. "It doesn't matter. I told you, I'll be—"

"Dead by the end of the year. Yes, I know." Letty crossed to the tray. "I bought some valerian. Have you tried that?"

Reid didn't reply. She looked over her shoulder to find him eyeing her narrowly.

"The apothecary said valerian's not at all like laudanum. It's not an opiate. It won't put you to sleep, but it will *encourage* you to sleep."

Reid's eyebrows flicked slightly in disbelief. He said nothing.

Letty picked up the vial and the teaspoon and brought them to the bed. "I should warn you, it does smell rather bad."

Reid eyed her even more narrowly, and then sighed, not a sigh of annoyance, but of resignation. "How bad?"

Letty uncorked the little vial and held it out.

Reid sniffed. His head jerked back. "Jesus!"

"Please?" Letty said. "Just once?"

They matched gazes for several seconds. Finally, Reid

looked away. "All right, I'll try it. Once." There was an undertone in his voice that took her a moment to recognize: wryness. He was humoring her.

Letty measured out the valerian.

Reid swallowed it, and grimaced.

"Would you like a little more brandy to wash it down? Just a mouthful?" Letty splashed a small amount into the glass and held it out to him.

Reid swallowed the brandy, too.

"Do you normally read now?" A glance around his bedchamber showed her six books stacked in a pile. "Which one are you reading?"

"The second volume of *The Odyssey*."

Letty fetched the book, but she didn't hand it to Reid; instead, she sat cross-legged on the end of his bed, and opened the volume. "From the beginning?"

"I am perfectly capable of reading myself," Reid told her. The wryness was gone from his voice; in its place was a faint edge of irritation.

"I enjoy *The Odyssey*." Letty opened the book—it was Alexander Pope's translation—smoothed her hand over the first page, and began to read.

At the end of the third page, she risked a glance at Reid. The irritation had faded from his face. He looked almost relaxed.

By the end of the seventh page, his eyes were heavy-lidded and drowsy. Letty lowered her voice and spoke more slowly.

By the tenth page, Reid was asleep.

Letty closed the book quietly and crept off the bed.

She stood for a long moment, looking down at him. This was a Reid she'd not seen before. All the tension, the grimness, the bleakness were gone from his face. He didn't look dangerous; he looked peaceful.

His hands lay limply. Beautiful hands. The sort of hands a Greek sculptor would prize, large and strong and lean-fingered.

They seemed very brown against the white of the sheet.

She wanted to reach out and take one of them, wanted to lay her palm against his, slide her fingers between his. She wanted to lean down and kiss him, kiss those cheekbones, kiss that mouth.

Liquor and sex, the old woman had said. The feather bed jig.

I wish I truly was Mrs. Reid.

Letty picked up her chamberstick and tiptoed from the room.

CHAPTER 12

November 11th, 1808
Basingstoke, Hampshire

$\mathcal{I}$carus woke to the sound of someone moving quietly in his bedchamber. He blinked his eyes open. For several disorienting seconds, he didn't know where he was. India? Portugal? England?

"Good morning, sir."

Icarus stared at the young man blankly—and then recognition came. Green. With the recognition came comprehension, and memory. Basingstoke. The Plough.

"Good morning," Icarus said, and pushed back the bedclothes, feeling dazed and off-balance. Where had Miss Trentham vanished to? Why were the shutters open? Was it actually *daylight* outside?

He looked around the bedchamber with incredulous disbelief. He'd fallen asleep again? "What time is it?"

"Ten o'clock."

"Ten?" Icarus felt even more off-balance, even more incredulous.

"Mrs. Reid said to let you sleep, sir."

Icarus stared around the bedchamber again. There was the brandy, there the vial of dark liquid, there *The Odyssey*.

"I have hot water, sir. Do you prefer to shave yourself, or would you like me to do it?"

"Uh . . . I'll shave myself." Icarus rubbed his face, ran his hands through his hair, shook off the incredulity.

"Very good, sir."

Half an hour later, washed, shaved, and dressed, Icarus went down to the parlor. Miss Trentham was there, reading. She looked up at his entrance and studied his face. What she saw made her smile. "Good morning."

"Good morning." Icarus eyed her. How in God's name had she managed to send him to sleep again?

The landlord's daughter bustled in, carrying two plates. Not sausages this morning, but fried ham. The scent made Icarus's mouth water.

Miss Trentham was some kind of witch, he decided, as they sat at the table.

"Three eggs today, don't you think?" Miss Trentham said, unfolding her napkin. "And two slices of ham."

A bossy, *despotic* witch.

After breakfast, they went their separate ways, Miss Trentham to buy Eliza a new gown, Icarus to arrange for an outrider to accompany the post-chaise into Wiltshire tomorrow. They met again for a late luncheon, when Miss Trentham forced him to eat rather more than he wished to.

"What I should *really* like to do this afternoon," Miss Trentham said, putting her napkin neatly beside her plate, "is go riding. Do you think that's possible?"

"Very possible." He examined her face. There was no sign of the blow he'd struck her two nights ago. He felt relief that the injury had been minor—and horror that he'd hit her in the first place.

The Plough had no suitable hacks, but the commercial stables had a neat bay mare that Miss Trentham liked the look of, and several geldings that were up to his weight.

"What do you ride, sir?" the groom asked, sizing him up. "Twelve stone?"

Icarus swallowed the *fifteen* he'd been about to utter. "Thereabouts." Twelve stone? Had he really lost that much weight?

They followed the man's directions, rode south to the downs, and put the horses to a canter. Icarus hadn't known where he was when he woke this morning, but there was no mistaking where he was now—the gently undulating hills, the neat hedgerows, the plump sheep. It was utterly unlike India. Utterly unlike Portugal.

When they dropped to a walk, Miss Trentham came up alongside him. "May I ask you a question, Mr. Reid?"

Icarus eyed her warily. Was this about his nightmares? Because he was damned if he was going to discuss them with her.

"As a soldier, you've killed men, haven't you?"

Icarus felt himself blink, felt himself stiffen. "In battle, yes."

"Did it bother you?"

"I didn't enjoy it, if that's what you're asking." He'd vomited after his first battle. Vomited after his second one, too.

Miss Trentham's brow creased slightly "And yet you enjoyed soldiering?"

"There's a lot more to soldiering than killing people," Icarus told her. Some of his affront leaked into his voice. What did she think he was? A murderer?

"Have you ever tortured anyone, Mr. Reid?"

Icarus rocked back in his saddle. "I beg your pardon?"

"Have you—"

"Of course I haven't!" The gelding caught his outrage

and tossed its head and skittered two steps sideways. Icarus brought the animal under control, and glowered at Miss Trentham.

"Does it happen?"

He opened his mouth to tell her hotly that British soldiers weren't barbarous savages—and then closed it again. Sometimes, they were.

Miss Trentham watched him steadily.

"I can't tell you that it never happens in the British Army," Icarus said, uncomfortably. "One hears rumors from time to time. But I *can* tell you that I've never witnessed anything that could be classed as such."

Miss Trentham nodded. She was going to ask another question—he could see it on her face—and he knew where that question was leading: Vimeiro.

"Let's ride," he said curtly, putting his heels to the gelding's sides. The animal plunged forward.

Icarus held to a canter for almost a mile. His hot outrage dwindled to mere anger, and then to annoyance and a reluctant acknowledgment that Miss Trentham's questions had been valid. Any English man or woman had a right to ask them. As a soldier, he'd been answerable to his superior officers. To the king. And to the people of England.

He slowed to a trot, and managed a polite smile. "Ready to turn back?"

Miss Trentham met his gaze squarely. "I apologize if I offended you, Mr. Reid. It was not my intention."

Icarus drew his horse to a halt. "You did offend me," he told her. "But you're not a soldier. You don't understand soldiering. We're not blackguards and murderers."

"I didn't think you were."

Icarus looked away from her, and then back again. "There are soldiers who're little better than criminals," he admitted. "But I assure you I wasn't one of them."

"I didn't think you were," Miss Trentham said again.

The last of his annoyance evaporated. Icarus gave a nod.

They trotted leisurely back to Basingstoke and returned the horses. Icarus felt weary, but not exhausted. His legs were barely shaking.

"Spare a penny for an old soldier?" he heard someone say distantly, as he walked across the square with Miss Trentham.

Icarus glanced around. A beggar sat on a bench outside the Hogshead. He had a graying beard, a crutch, and only one leg.

The townsman the beggar had petitioned—stout and self-important, with a beaver hat and a topcoat with three capes—walked past without acknowledging the man.

Icarus halted.

"Spare a penny for an old soldier?" the beggar said again, to a housewife bustling past, who also ignored him.

Icarus dug in his pocket. "Won't be a minute," he told Miss Trentham.

*C*HAPTER 13

*L*etty followed Reid across the cobblestones. The beggar looked up as they approached. He was a thin man, with leathery skin and a shaggy salt-and-pepper beard. "Spare a penny for an old soldier?"

Reid gave him a handful of coins.

"Lor' bless me!" the man said, almost falling off the bench. "Thank 'ee, sir."

"What regiment were you in?"

The man squinted up at him. "Twelfth Foot, sir."

"Twelfth Foot? You're a long way from home. East Anglia, isn't it?"

"Come down 'ere to be with me sister."

"She lives in Hampshire?"

"Used to. Dead a few years back."

"Were you at Mallavelly?"

"That I were."

Reid looked at Letty, a question in his eyes. She nodded; the beggar was telling the truth.

Reid glanced at the beggar, and at the bench, and then back at her. She read that question, too, and answered it by stepping closer to the bench and sitting down.

Reid sat next to the beggar. "I was at Mallavelly."

Letty half-listened while the two men talked, exchanging military reminiscences. *You don't understand soldiering,* Reid had told her. *We're not blackguards and murderers.*

And then he'd admitted that some soldiers were.

Letty plucked the fingertips of her gloves thoughtfully. What had happened to Reid in Portugal?

She knew what she *suspected* had happened to him.

Letty glanced at Reid, seeing the way his clothes hung on his gaunt frame, seeing the hollows of his cheeks. He and the old beggar were now talking about Seringapatam, during which battle the soldier had injured his foot. "Nothin' more'n a scratch. But the gangrin came in. Fair stinkin' it were."

Reid grimaced. "I know the smell."

"Had to take off half me leg. Took three men to hold me down," the old soldier said proudly.

After a few minutes, Reid turned the conversation back to England. The beggar talked of his sister's death. "Fever, she 'ad."

"Fever? I had the fever in Portugal. Almost cocked my toes up."

The beggar nodded sagely. "You don't look none too spry, sir, if you don't mind me sayin'."

Reid shrugged agreement and asked further questions. The beggar described his slow slide into destitution.

"What about the workhouse?" Reid suggested in a neutral tone.

"Workhouse?" The old soldier spat expressively. "Don't never want to end up there. I'd rather die in a ditch!"

Reid turned the conversation again, told a story about a man he knew who'd unexpectedly come into five hundred pounds—and run through it all in less than a year. Letty listened intently; Reid was lying.

"What a looby," the beggar said with disgust.

Reid shrugged. "Who wouldn't do the same?"

"*I* wouldn't," the old soldier said indignantly. "I'd go 'ome to Sudbury and buy meself a cottage and live there quiet-like. Five hunner quid! I could live the rest of me life on that—*and* 'ave some to spare!"

Reid glanced at her, his eyebrows lifted in query. Letty nodded; everything the beggar had said was the truth.

"Well, soldier, you're going to have the opportunity to do just that." Reid pulled out his pocketbook, extracted five banknotes, and held them out to the man.

The beggar's mouth fell open. He was missing several teeth.

Reid closed the man's fingers around the bills, and stood. "Good-bye. It's been a pleasure meeting you."

Letty stood, too, and watched the old soldier's face. His mouth worked, but no words came out. He groped for his crutch, and tried to stand.

"No, don't get up," Reid said, reaching down to grip the beggar's hand. "Put that money away, man. Else someone will take it."

The old soldier fumbled the bills into an inside pocket of his threadbare coat. "Sir," he said, tears standing out in his eyes. "Sir . . ." He swallowed audibly. "Sir, how can I ever thank you?"

Reid smiled down at him. "By buying that cottage." He touched a finger to his brow, almost a salute, and turned away.

Letty matched her stride to his. On the far side of the square, she glanced back. The old soldier was still sitting on the bench, scrawny and grimy and dumbfounded. She looked at Reid. "Do you do that often?"

"I've done it a few times." Reid walked several paces, and halted abruptly. "That man risked his life for England—gave his *leg*, for Christ's sake!—and now he's reduced to begging?" He was fierce, impassioned, glaring at her from beneath lowered brows.

Letty met that silver glare steadily.

The animation drained from Reid's face, leaving him

haggard once more. He turned away and began walking again. "I beg your pardon. It's a sore point with me."

Letty said nothing. She matched her stride to his again.

Reid glanced at her. "I made my money soldiering—prize money. It seems only right that I share it with those who were less fortunate than I was."

Letty nodded. Her mother had expressed almost that exact same sentiment on a number of occasions: *Our wealth doesn't make us better than other people; it makes us luckier. It behooves us to share that luck with those who've not had our good fortune.*

She examined Reid's bony face. "And when you die? What happens to your money then?"

The blunt question didn't appear to shock Reid. "Veterans' charities," he said. "All of it."

Dinner that evening was muggety pie, and apple fritters.

"Muggety pie?" Letty said, eyeing her plate.

"Made with muggets," Reid said.

"Yes, but what *are* muggets?"

"Your guess is as good as mine."

Muggets were offal, Letty discovered, but exactly what part of an animal's entrails—or indeed, which animal they came from—she had no idea. The pie was well-seasoned with herbs and surprisingly tasty, and the apple fritters were delicious, golden and crisp, dusted with sugar and served with thick cream. Letty had no difficulty persuading Reid to eat his dessert.

"You had the fever in Portugal?" Letty said, while she debated whether to have a third fritter.

Reid nodded.

"You almost died?"

Reid shrugged. "So I was told. I wasn't aware of it at the time."

Letty decided to have a third fritter. She doused it with cream. "How long were you ill?"

"Long enough."

Another of his evasions. "How long, Mr. Reid?"

"I was six weeks in my bed."

Her gaze jerked to his face. "Six *weeks*?"

Reid nodded again.

Letty stared at him. Six *weeks* in bed with the fever. No wonder his clothes hung on him. "How long have you been out of your sickbed?"

"Nigh on a month."

"You should have stayed there!" Letty told him. "You shouldn't be traipsing about the country. You should be *resting*."

"I don't have the time," Reid said flatly.

Letty pushed her dessert away and leaned forward on her elbows. "What exactly are you dying of, Mr. Reid?"

Reid's face stiffened.

Letty met his affronted stare. Yes, it was an unpardonably rude question, but she wasn't going to apologize for it, or retract it.

"That is none of your business, Miss Trentham," Reid said, after a moment.

Letty examined his face—the skin stretched tautly over jutting bones, the stony expression, the flat, silver stare. "You're not dying of the fever, are you?"

Reid made no reply.

"And you're not dying of an injury, as far as I can tell."

Still, Reid made no reply.

"And you're not dying of your nightmares, are you?"

"Good night, Miss Trentham." Reid pushed back his chair, thrust his napkin on the table, and walked from the room.

The door shut quietly behind him.

Letty sighed. Stupidly, she felt like crying. She looked at the chair Reid had sat in, and the balled-up napkin, and the half-eaten fritter stranded on his plate. Couldn't he see that she was trying to *help* him?

That night, Mr. Reid slept until one o'clock before becoming ensnared in his nightmare. Letty half-expected his door to be latched, shutting her out, but it opened to her touch. She hurried to the bed. "Reid! Wake up!"

He wasn't thrashing and flailing so wildly tonight; he was twisting beneath the bedclothes, choking and gasping, weeping in his sleep.

"Icarus!" Letty grasped his shoulder and shook him hard.

Reid woke with a jolt.

He didn't strike out, didn't lunge up in berserker fury; he gave a hoarse, wheezing, desperate gasp, as if he'd been holding his breath for a long time, and then turned his head into the pillow with a groan. His body trembled violently. His breathing was short and sobbing.

He was crying.

Letty bit her lip, and turned away to grant him privacy. Her heart ached sharply in her chest. The brandy was where she'd left it last night. She walked across to it slowly, uncorked it slowly, poured a large glass slowly, giving Reid time to compose himself. When she turned back, he was wiping his face roughly with his hands.

She spent another minute fiddling with the brandy bottle, pushing the cork back in, and then crossed to the bed. "Here."

Reid sat up, moving as if his bones ached, and took the glass. Their fingers brushed.

Letty busied herself rearranging his pillows. "Lie back."

Reid obeyed. He looked like a man who'd been to Hades and back, haggard and utterly drained. Tremors ran through his hands, making the brandy tremble in the glass. His breathing was hoarse, catching in his throat with each inhalation.

Letty sat on the bed and watched him sip the brandy. Reid had parted from her in anger that evening, but either he'd forgotten or he no longer cared. He didn't ask her to leave, didn't speak to her at all, just slowly sipped. Gradually the tremors stopped. His breathing quieted. The faint hitch was no longer audible.

When he'd finished the glass, Letty measured out a teaspoon of valerian.

Reid swallowed it without protest. He didn't even grimace at the taste. He was utterly passive. It was as if the nightmare had drained him of himself—his essence, his spirit, whatever it was that made him Icarus Reid—and left a half-alive husk in its place.

Perhaps the nightmares *were* what was killing him?

Letty fetched *The Odyssey* and sat on the end of his bed to read. Reid didn't object. She wasn't sure he even noticed. He lay limply, his gaze unfocused. If she hadn't seen his chest rise and fall, hadn't seen the slow blink of his eyes, she'd have thought him dead.

Letty read in a low voice, glancing at him often. His eyelids lowered by increments.

It took half an hour for Reid to fall asleep. Letty continued reading for another ten minutes, and then stopped. She closed the book and sat quietly, watching him. Icarus Reid. A complicated man—driven and dangerous, tough, obstinate, evasive—and yet also disarmingly kind.

And damaged. Deeply and terribly damaged.

Letty sighed, and climbed down from the bed, and put the book back where she'd found it.

She tiptoed over to look down at Reid. He was soundly asleep, his breathing slow and even. The candlelight cast shadows over his face, making his cheeks seem even more hollow than they were.

A painful emotion stirred in her breast. *It's pity,* Letty told herself. But she knew it wasn't. She grieved for Icarus Reid, but she didn't pity him. Reid was not a man to be pitied.

Letty reached down and stroked his hair. "I wish you would tell me," she whispered, and then she bent and pressed her lips—lightly, daringly—to his.

Reid didn't stir.

Letty sighed, and picked up her chamberstick and left the room.

CHAPTER 14

November 12th, 1808
Whiteoaks, Wiltshire

On Saturday, Letty went back to being an heiress. The journey from Basingstoke to Whiteoaks in Wiltshire was thirty-odd miles. In the post-chaise, Letty considered spinning a tale for Eliza and Green that explained why she was going to stay with her cousins and Reid wasn't. A mysterious family feud, perhaps? And then she saw a set of balance scales in her mind's eye, weighed down by three deaths on one side and by her lies on the other. No, she'd tell no more falsehoods than were absolutely necessary.

"My husband prefers to stay in Marlborough when I visit Whiteoaks," she said, and left them to make their own guesses as to why that might be. "Eliza, you'll stay in Marlborough, too. I shan't need you at Whiteoaks, but next week we'll go to Bristol, and then perhaps down to Exeter."

"Yes, ma'am."

Letty glanced at Reid. Last night's nightmare still clung to him. He'd been quiet all day. Broodingly quiet. Bleakly quiet.

He'd have another nightmare tonight. And tomorrow night. And the night after that.

And she wouldn't be there to help him.

Reid and Green and their luggage—along with Eliza's carpetbag—were deposited at the Castle and Ball in Marlborough's wide High Street. "Remember to leave the brandy and valerian beside his bed," Letty told Green, for what must be the fifth time that day. "With a glass and a teaspoon."

"Yes, ma'am."

Eliza came as far as Whiteoaks for propriety's sake, peeping wide-eyed out the window as the post-chaise drew up in front of the great portico. A butler and two footmen emerged and trod down the marble steps.

"Good-bye, Eliza. I'll see you in a week."

The carriage door swung open. Letty descended demurely, the luggage was unloaded, and then the post-chaise—postilions, outrider, and maid—swept back to Marlborough.

Letty watched it clatter from sight, and then turned to gaze at the vast marble façade of Whiteoaks, with its Corinthian columns and rows of windows and the bas-relief crowning the portico.

Much as she loved her Kemp cousins, she didn't want to be here. She wanted to be at the Castle and Ball with Reid, making sure he drank his brandy and swallowed his valerian and went back to sleep again.

"Ma'am?" the butler said.

Letty sighed, and marched up the long flight of marble steps. Her heart quailed in her chest as she stepped into the entrance hall. Had her deception been discovered?

"Letitia!" Her eldest cousin's wife arrived with a flurry of scarves and perfume. "They sent you in a post-chaise! How shabby!"

No, not discovered.

Letty embraced Almeria, and assured her that it wasn't shabby at all; on the contrary, she had enjoyed it enormously; and yes, Helen had sent an outrider; and yes, Helen had sent a maid—and those words were even more lies to go on the scales—but although part of her regretted each and every lie she'd uttered this past week, part of her *couldn't* regret them. Not if it meant redress for the dead scouts. Not if it meant that Reid found his traitor.

More cousins appeared. Letty looked around eagerly for Julia—and then memory slapped her in the face: Julia was dead. She'd been dead these past seventeen months.

Pugh clucked over the state of her hair. "Pulled back so tightly! Not flattering, not flattering at all!" Letty paid no attention. Propped up on the mantelpiece in the Lilac Bedchamber were two letters, one thick, one thin. The handwriting on both was extremely familiar. She knew what each letter held before she even picked them up: the thick one contained the monthly summaries on her mother's lying-in hospital and foundling homes and charity school; the thin one, the investigator's report on her most recent suitors.

The seal on the second letter had been broken. Letty repressed a spurt of annoyance. Her stepbrother paid for the investigator; of course he had a right to read those reports before she did.

She settled on the chaise longue to read, while Pugh unpacked her trunk, muttering direly over every crease she discovered. Conscientiously, Letty examined the monthly summaries first: numbers of women admitted to the hospital, numbers of births, numbers of babies accepted into each of the homes, numbers of children apprenticed and where to. The superintendent of the charity school had appended a note: *One boy showing extraordinary talent in mathematics. I suggest extra tuition.* Below that, her man of business had scrawled: *Arranged.*

The summaries read, Letty unfolded the investigator's report. Her gaze skipped down the page—Frederick Ashburton—Roger Pinkney—and Icarus Reid.

She forced herself to read the paragraphs on Ashburton and Pinkney first. They merely confirmed what she had suspected; both men were deeply in debt, Pinkney almost bankrupt.

She'd requested as much information as possible on Reid, and the investigator had obliged.

Icarus Reid. Fifth and youngest son of Sir Hector Reid of Wetherby, Yorkshire. Born 1778.

1778? That meant Reid was only thirty. He looked much older. Letty frowned, and read further. *Grandson of Admiral Titus Reid. Nephew of Admiral Virgil Reid. Brother of Admiral Socrates Reid. Joined the 33rd Foot as an ensign in 1795. Distinguished himself in the action at Mallavelly, 1799. Mentioned in the dispatches. Promoted to lieutenant and attached to Lieutenant Colonel Wellesley's staff as aide-de-camp.*

Seven years of campaigning in India had followed, during which time Reid had been promoted to captain, and then major, and earned significant wealth. *Estimated prize money, £25,000.* Letty's eyebrows rose. A genteel fortune.

Wellesley had taken leave of absence in 1805. When he resumed his military career in 1807, Reid rejoined his staff. *According to my sources,* the investigator wrote, *Wellesley specifically requested Major Reid.*

Reid had returned from India in time to participate in the Battle of Copenhagen. Then, in July of this year, he'd sailed with Wellesley to Portugal. *Following the Battle of Vimeiro (August 21st), Reid was on the invalids' list for several weeks. He resigned his commission and returned to England in mid-October.*

As far as I can ascertain, Reid has no debts. Further, it appears that his fortune is untouched! Letty didn't begrudge the man his exclamation mark. In over one hundred reports, this was the first time he'd investigated a suitor who wasn't a fortune hunter.

At the bottom, the investigator had made notes on Reid's character. *My sources all spoke highly of Major Reid. He's said to be an even-tempered, intelligent man, and a courageous and resourceful soldier. I found no indications of profligacy. By repute, he is neither a gambler, nor a drunkard, nor a philanderer.* The investigator didn't write—*In my opinion Reid would make an excellent husband*—but it was clearly implied.

Letty sighed, and refolded the sheet of paper. There were two surprises in the report—Reid's age, and his fortune—but nothing to tell her what had happened to him at Vimeiro. "I need some fresh air, Pugh. I'll be back in an hour."

It was a year since Letty had last been at Whiteoaks. Then, Julia's death had been fresh: the riding accident, the broken neck. Now the mourning blacks were put away, but it still seemed to Letty that a melancholy air hung over the estate. Perhaps it was due to the season—the bare trees, the chill in the air, the drifts of dead leaves—but she thought it was more to do with Julia.

In London, Julia's absence had been a dull ache, something she'd learned to ignore. At Whiteoaks, memory of Julia was everywhere. Here was the shrubbery where they'd played hide and seek, here the stream where they'd paddled barefoot with the boys, searching for frogs, and here the long avenue of oaks where they'd raced their ponies. Memory upon memory. Julia stuck up a tree, Julia falling in the river, Julia with mischief on her face and mud on her dress and torn flounces hanging around her ankles.

Letty wandered slowly along the avenue, stirring the dead, damp leaves with her boots. She'd walked here with Julia when they'd last been at Whiteoaks together. Walked, talked, laughed. Boisterous, harum-scarum Julia, who even in adulthood hadn't outgrown her tomboyish ways. Julia, who'd made everything seem fun, who'd joked while they fended off fortune hunters together, who had made the Marriage Mart bearable.

A strange feeling grew while she walked, a sense that Julia was nearby. Letty could almost see her, like a shimmering afterimage on her retina. *If I turn my head fast enough, I might glimpse her.*

Ahead, two riders entered the avenue. Even at a hundred yards' distance, Letty recognized them. Julia's twin, Lucas. And Tom Matlock.

Someone whooped distantly—Tom, she guessed—and the horses were urged into a canter.

The sensation that Julia was nearby intensified—so sharp, so strong, that Letty could have sworn Julia stood alongside her—and then abruptly vanished.

The riders swept past with a thunder of hooves—it *was* Tom whooping—and pulled up in a showy scattering of gravel and dead leaves. Tom leaped down and caught her in a rib-cracking hug, lifting her off her feet. "Tish, m' love. God, but it's good to see you."

Letty hugged him back. He smelled of horse and leather and clean linen.

Tom set her on her feet, and then Lucas hugged her, too, and they were all laughing and it felt so *good* to be together again.

"When did you arrive?" Lucas asked. He looked nothing like Julia—his hair, his eyes, the arrangement of his bones, were all different—and yet he was *so* much like her. She saw Julia in his grin, Julia in the way his eyes crinkled at the corners, Julia in the tilt of his head.

"An hour ago. How are you both?"

"In fine form," Lucas said. "What's the count now?"

"Eighteen so far this year."

Tom exchanged a wry glance with Lucas, dug in his pocket, and flipped a half-crown at his friend.

"You'll find a couple of 'em here this week, Tish," Lucas said, pocketing the coin. "Bernard nagged m' brother into inviting them. Stapleton's already arrived, and Henry Wright's coming on Monday. Wright's a decent fellow—he was at Eton with us—but I don't think much of Stapleton."

"A new wager." Tom fished another half-crown from his pocket and waggled it at Lucas. "Stapleton *and* Wright to propose by the end of this week."

"I *am* here," Letty said indignantly.

"I know, love." Tom grinned at her. "Walk back with us?"

Letty tucked her hand into the crook of his arm and looked at him—the merry face, the laughing green eyes. No, Tom was no traitor. But he might know what had happened to Reid at Vimeiro. "I met an acquaintance of yours in London last week. Icarus Reid. He was a major before he sold out."

"Reid?" Tom's eyebrows lifted.

"He said he'd be passing through Wiltshire. I told him you were here, suggested he look you up."

"I hope he does," Tom said cheerfully. "Good man, Reid."

Twenty-eight people sat to dinner that evening. Letty found herself with her stepbrother on one side and Lord Stapleton on the other.

"Letitia," her stepbrother, Bernard, said with cool politeness. "How pleasant to see you." Letty heard *that* lie.

Bernard made no mention of the latest report during dinner, but he took her aside once they'd repaired to the drawing room. "This Major Reid is an interesting development. No title, of course, but a respectable fortune. I hope he may offer for you." *That* was the truth.

"I don't think he's looking for a wife."

Bernard frowned, creases furrowing on either side of his nose and pinching between his eyebrows, giving him a bird of prey look. "Then why did you add him to the list?"

Because she'd wanted to find out more about him. "Because I'm not certain," she said.

Bernard grunted sourly, and looked across the room to

where Lord Stapleton stood. Stapleton was a man of moderate height, moderate build, moderate good looks—and an expensive gambling habit.

"I view Stapleton favorably. His debts are manageable. You'd do well to encourage him."

"I'd rather have Sir Henry," Letty said. "At least *his* debts are none of his doing."

"Then I suggest you accept his offer," Bernard said coldly. "He asked my permission to pay his addresses."

"You gave it, of course."

"Of course."

"And Stapleton?"

"Him, too."

Letty repressed a tart comment. Bernard had been wanting to be rid of her since the day his father had married her mother. Of *course* he'd given his permission.

Letty sat down to a game of Speculation with the younger members of the house party—a Kemp tradition. The game rapidly degenerated into noisy merriment. Time blurred. Tonight could be any one of a hundred similar nights over the years: Tom telling jokes, Lucas laughing quietly, people slapping down counters, slapping down cards. For a moment Letty's eyes told her that Julia sat across from her, giggling— and then she blinked and saw it was Almeria's eldest daughter, Selina.

Letty looked hastily away. She fumbled for her handkerchief and blew her nose.

"I win!" Lucas said—and Letty looked at him, golden-haired and laughing, and made a discovery. Lucas was only laughing with his mouth, not his eyes.

After that observation, Letty found herself unable to

recapture her pleasure in the game. She played her cards, offered up her trumps for sale, added counters to the pot, even won a round, but all the while she was more aware of Lucas than anything else. Lucas, who no longer wore black for his dead twin. Lucas, who was pretending to be happy.

Towards the end of the game, Letty became conscious that she wasn't the only person watching Lucas. Tom had seen it, too—and was worried by it. "Come riding with me tomorrow morning," she said to Tom when the game was over and they were putting away the counters and the cards. "Before church. I need to talk with you."

Tom grinned. "An assignation, Tish?"

"Eight o'clock."

Tom laid his hand to his breast. "I'll be there, dear heart."

CHAPTER 15

November 13th, 1808
Whiteoaks, Wiltshire

Tom Matlock was good to his word. He strolled into the stableyard at eight the next morning, very smart in a military-cut riding coat and gleaming boots. "This may be the most exciting morning of my life," he confided, once they were trotting along the oak avenue. "Trysting with an heiress! Is it to be a special license, Tish, or do you want the banns to be read?"

"Tom, do be serious."

"But," Tom said, ignoring this request. "I feel it's only fair to tell you that my heart belongs to another." His tone was bantering, but there was a ring of pure truth to his words.

"I want to talk about Lucas," Letty said.

Tom dropped his lightheartedness. "What about him?"

"How is he? Truly."

Tom looked away from her, down the long line of leafless oak trees.

Letty waited.

"Let's canter," Tom said, abruptly.

Tom chose a route that took them along the River Kennet and up onto the Marlborough Downs, to a wooded height that commanded a sweeping view. Here, he halted. Whiteoaks lay spread before them: the parkland, the folly peeping from the trees, the smooth, green expanse of lawns, the palatial house. Mist lay in the hollows and along the river.

"Have you seen much of Lucas this past year?" Tom asked.

Letty shook her head. "He's been dealing with his god-father's estate. He only came back to town last month. He seemed . . . I thought he seemed happier. He wasn't wearing blacks."

"When did you see him last?"

"The beginning of October. I asked him to dine with me on his birthday, but he'd already accepted an invitation elsewhere."

"Had he?" Tom looked down at Whiteoaks. "He didn't go. I arrived in London the evening of his birthday, went round to his rooms, found him sitting in the dark with the fire gone out, so drunk he couldn't even stand up." His lips compressed. "He'd been crying."

Letty stared at him. It was several seconds before she found her voice. "But he seemed almost his old self!"

"He's not," Tom said flatly. "He puts on a good act, but he has days where I don't think he'd even get out of bed—let alone shave or dress—if not for that man of his."

Letty's horror grew. How had she missed seeing this?

"You know how wounded animals hide themselves away? That's what he did after Julia died—and I understand he needed to be alone afterwards—you don't have to tell me how close they were—but he needs to crawl out of his cave and learn how to be happy without her."

"I thought he had," Letty said, troubled. When she'd asked how he was, Lucas had said "Better," and it had been the truth.

But better didn't necessarily mean happy.

"No." Tom shook his head. "I asked for an extended leave of absence. Wellesley gave me until the end of the year."

"For Lucas?"

"Of course, for Lucas!"

"Can I help?"

"I don't know. I don't even know that *I* can help." Tom gazed down at Whiteoaks, and his lips thinned further. "I don't know that coming here was a good idea. This place is full of Julia." He shook his head. "Come on, let's ride."

They galloped on the downs, and came back through the park, dropping to a slow trot when they reached the avenue. Letty's mood was somber. Tom had been correct; Julia was everywhere.

Everywhere, and nowhere.

But if Lucas had lost his twin, he still had his best friend, and if anyone could help Lucas, it was Tom. Tom, with his grin and his banter and his dog-eared sketchbooks. Tom, who was mercifully still alive despite six years as a soldier.

"How are you enjoying soldiering?"

Tom gave a shrug. "Oh, I like it well enough."

Letty considered this ambivalent answer. "You'd rather sell out and be an artist?"

Tom laughed ruefully. "You know me too well."

"*Could* you sell out?"

"Only if I marry an heiress." He gave her a cheerful leer. "What do you say, Tish? Want to marry a youngest son with not a penny to his name?"

"Your heart belongs to someone else," Letty reminded him.

Tom's grin faded. He looked almost sad. "So it does."

They rode in silence. Letty's thoughts grew even more somber. Lucas wasn't the only person at Whiteoaks pretending to be happy. And then she straightened in her saddle. "Tom, if you had twenty thousand pounds, would you sell out?"

"Yes, but I don't." He turned the subject: "There's to be a ball this week. Did Almeria tell you?"

"Tom . . . I can *give* you twenty thousand pounds."

"What?" Tom looked startled. "Don't be ridiculous."

"I'm not being ridiculous. Let me give you twenty thousand! Then you can sell out!"

"Thank you, but no," Tom said firmly.

"Why not?"

Tom reached over and took her gloved hand and kissed her knuckles. "Tish, I love you dearly, but I *won't* take your money." Truth rang in his voice.

"But—"

"No," Tom said. "Don't feel sorry for me, Tish. Soldiering suits me well enough. I'm better off than a lot of younger sons." He thought for a moment, and added: "And heirs, for that matter. I'm a thousand times better off than m' brother, saddled with Father's debts. Or Henry Wright. Poor devils."

"Yes, but if I give you—"

"Lord, Tish, you're like a terrier at a rabbit hole! I *don't* want your money."

Letty sighed.

They reached the end of the avenue. Whiteoaks came into sight. Tom glanced at his watch, and tucked it back in his waistcoat pocket.

"Tom . . . will you tell me about the Battle of Vimeiro?"

"Vimeiro?" Tom lifted his eyebrows. "What do you want to know?"

"Everything."

Tom looked at her as if she'd sprouted a second head, and then shrugged. "The battle was straightforward. We outnumbered the French. Not many casualties."

"Did you fight?"

"Me? I carried orders, mostly."

"Carried orders?"

"The general can't be in more than one place," Tom explained. "So his aides-de-camp relay his orders. Vimeiro was pretty busy—we were down a couple of officers—one drunk, the other missing—I went back and forth a score of times. Quite wore out my horse!"

They dismounted in the stableyard. Grooms hurried forward to take their mounts. Letty looped the long skirt of her riding dress over her arm.

Another horse clattered into the yard behind them. A liveried servant leaned low over the horse's withers and passed something to one of the grooms.

"Lieutenant Matlock, sir?" the groom called out. "A message for you."

Tom's eyebrows flicked up. "For me?"

The groom hurried over, holding out a letter. Tom broke the seal and read swiftly. He crossed to the mounted servant. "Tell him yes. Two o'clock."

The man touched his forelock, turned his horse, and trotted from the stableyard.

"Yes, what?" Letty asked.

"Major Reid's in Marlborough. He's coming to visit this afternoon." Tom shoved the letter in his pocket. "Hurry up, Tish. We'll be late for church!"

*C*HAPTER 16

*I*carus reached Whiteoaks a little after two. The big gray he'd hired was a handsome Roman-nosed beast, but it had a hard mouth and recalcitrant nature and had already tried to unseat him twice.

Whiteoaks was built in the style of Palladio, with white marble and tall columns and perfect symmetry. Icarus didn't particularly care for it. He preferred rambling, red brick manors with ivy growing up their walls and odd turrets and strange staircases and no symmetry at all—buildings that looked as if they'd *grown,* not shining, hard-edged, white monoliths.

"Major Reid!" someone called cheerfully, as he trotted into the stableyard.

Icarus swung down from the saddle. "Matlock. How do you do?"

Matlock strode over, grinning.

They shook hands. Matlock's grip was strong. "Lord, Major, you look like death warmed over!"

Matlock was closer to the mark than he realized. What would he say if Icarus told him the truth? That he *was* dead. That he'd been dead since Vimeiro.

"Fever take you again, sir?"

Icarus shrugged. "You know how it is."

Matlock took this as a *Yes*. Miss Trentham wouldn't have. "Let me introduce you to m' host, Major, and then we'll have a chat about old times."

Icarus met half a dozen Kemps in a green and gold salon, bowed and shook hands and exchanged commonplaces for ten minutes, and then Matlock slid them out of the room and he found himself outside again, strolling in the shrubbery.

"I haven't seen you since Portugal, Major! Seems so long ago, now."

"A lifetime," Icarus said. He cast a frowning glance around. Where the devil was Miss Trentham? She'd promised—

"I don't need to introduce you to Miss Trentham, do I?" Matlock said, as they rounded a hedge and came upon a lily pond and fountain.

The tension in Icarus's shoulders eased. "No."

Miss Trentham sat on a stone bench carved with acanthus leaves. She wasn't alone. A tall man with guinea-gold hair was leaning over her, one booted foot on the seat, a smile on his fatuous, good-looking face. One of her damned fortune-hunting suitors. Icarus's jaw clamped tight, and he quickened his step—and took in Miss Trentham's posture. There was nothing remotely stiff or uncomfortable about her bearing. In fact, she was laughing at something the man had said.

Illogically, Icarus's irritation increased.

Matlock made the introductions. The Adonis was Miss Trentham's cousin, Lucas Kemp. Icarus bowed punctiliously.

"Pleased to make your acquaintance, Major." The Adonis's handclasp was strong, his smile friendly. "Tom's told me about you. Sang your praises, rather."

The compliment caught him like a kick in the stomach. Icarus felt his face stiffen. "Don't believe a word of it," he said, trying to make his reply sound like a joke.

"Nonsense!" Matlock said. "You weren't Wellesley's favorite for nothing!"

Icarus tried to smile, but his mouth felt as if it was carved from stone. He glanced at Miss Trentham. She was watching him.

"Is it true you used to go behind enemy lines in British uniform?" the Adonis asked.

"Yes," Icarus said flatly, almost curtly—and caught himself. This was the direction he *wanted* the conversation to go in. He tried to relax, to smile more naturally. "Yes, I did."

They strolled in the shrubbery. Miss Trentham hadn't been exaggerating when she'd claimed to know Matlock well; there was no formality between them at all. They talked to one another as if they were brother and sister. Icarus had seen Miss Trentham aloof and cool in a sea-green ball gown. He'd seen her aloof and poised in riding dress, aloof and mysterious in a cloak and veiled hat, aloof and sober in traveling dress. Today, she wasn't aloof at all. She was approachable, friendly, relaxed—another woman altogether. The shape of her face altered when she smiled—not a small, polite society smile, but a genuine smile that did something to her cheeks, so that her mouth didn't seem too wide, or her nose too long.

Tish, the two men called her, and she did look like a Tish, not a standoffish Miss Trentham.

Icarus told two of his more amusing reconnaissance tales, trying not to be irritated by the way the Adonis walked arm in arm with Miss Trentham—and then said, "By the by, Matlock, I ran into Dunlop in town last week."

"Dunlop?" Matlock's lip curled contemptuously.

"He mentioned . . . I don't know if you recall, but he said you were present when he told Wellesley where I'd be meeting my scouts. I wondered whether perhaps you'd told anyone."

"Me? No."

Icarus almost didn't bother to look at Miss Trentham—he *knew* it wasn't Tom Matlock—but he did look, and Miss Trentham nodded.

"How long are you on leave?" Icarus said, turning the conversation.

"Until the end of the year," Matlock said. "Wellesley's got that dashed court-martial—cross as a bear!—said he doesn't want me under his feet."

Icarus lifted his eyebrows. "Two months? You'll fill up a few sketchbooks. Has Matlock shown you his Portuguese sketches, Miss Trentham? They're first rate."

"I've seen 'em," the Adonis said.

"*I* haven't," Miss Trentham said. "Did you bring them with you, Tom?"

Matlock grinned. "You'll be sorry you asked."

They strolled for the better part of an hour. The Adonis wasn't fatuous at all. He seemed a pleasant man—quiet-voiced and sensible—apart from his annoying habit of walking arm in arm with Miss Trentham, or with his arm around her shoulders, or once—which made Icarus grit his teeth—holding her hand.

His irritation annoyed him. Was he a dog guarding a bone? He didn't even particularly *like* Miss Trentham. She was bossy and despotic and interfering and nosy, and the way she had of ignoring his wishes was infuriating—but he'd actually missed her at the table, watching his plate and insisting that he eat more dinner, insisting he eat another egg for breakfast, and last night when he'd finally clawed his way back to consciousness, he'd wanted nothing more than to find Miss Trentham in his bedchamber, holding out a glass of brandy, measuring out a teaspoon of vile brown liquid, and then sitting cross-legged on his bed and reading Homer until her voice lulled him to sleep.

He *missed* her, damn it, and that was profoundly annoying. Missed her not because he liked her, but because of the way she treated him.

An unwelcome moment of insight came as they wandered through a knee-high boxwood maze: *Miss Trentham treats me as if she's my nursemaid.*

Icarus halted. Miss Trentham treated him as if she was his nursemaid—and he liked it?

"Are you all right, Mr. Reid?"

And there she was, doing it again, watching him with those damned *nursemaidish* eyes.

"I'm fine," Icarus said, curtly. He was thirty, not five. A soldier, for Christ's sake! He didn't need a nursemaid, and he most certainly didn't *want* one.

Miss Trentham ignored this comment. "Shall we turn back? I confess, a pot of tea and something to eat would be nice."

You don't need refreshments, Icarus thought sourly. *But you think I do.*

"It's the macaroons you want," Matlock said, with a sly grin. "Don't think I didn't notice how many you ate yesterday, Tish. Six!"

"They're extremely tasty," Miss Trentham said, unembarrassed. "I'm sure Mr. Reid will eat six, too."

Icarus saw the glint in her eyes and realized that this wasn't a comment; it was a command.

Icarus ate six macaroons in the green and gold salon. Quite a number of other people ate macaroons, too, and honeycomb cake and seed cake and a dark, rich plum cake. The salon was cheerfully noisy. He counted eighteen people and five different conversations and one lapdog yapping to be picked up.

Miss Trentham didn't revert to her society manners, but she became a little more formal. So did the Adonis and Matlock. Like children in the presence of their parents, Icarus thought, refusing a seventh macaroon.

He glanced around as the door opened to admit two new arrivals. The Adonis grimaced. "Keep your head down, Tish."

Icarus studied the newcomers. Both were male, and both were headed their way. "Who are they?"

"The prim one is Tish's stepbrother," Matlock said, in an undervoice. "And the peacock is Lord Stapleton."

Matlock made the introductions. The stepbrother's

eyebrows rose faintly. "Major Reid? I do believe I've heard of you."

Prim wasn't the correct word, Icarus decided after three minutes' conversation with Bernard Trentham. Supercilious fitted better. Two minutes after that, he realized that Trentham believed him to be an aspirant to his stepsister's hand. Indignation almost rendered him speechless. To be thought a fortune hunter!

"Are you in the neighborhood long?" Trentham asked, in a cool, disinterested voice. "You must visit again. I'm sure Letitia would be delighted to go riding with you."

Icarus blinked, his indignation punctured.

"My cousin, Robert Kemp, is holding a ball this week. You must come if you're still here." A thin, condescending smile, a faint bow, and Bernard Trentham took his leave.

Icarus stared after the man, bemused. Had he just been *approved* of?

He shook himself, and looked around for Miss Trentham. Whatever her faults, she wasn't arrogant.

Miss Trentham was talking with Lord Stapleton. There was no trace of the woman who'd walked arm in arm with her cousin in the garden; her manner was quite altered, polite and aloof, and her face had changed, too—nose too long, mouth too wide.

"Stapleton will be number nineteen this year," someone murmured in his ear.

Icarus glanced round. Matlock stood at his shoulder. "Nineteen?"

"To offer for Tish's hand. A low count, this year. It's usually well over thirty, but I guess Julia's death accounts for it."

"Julia?"

"Lucas's twin sister. Tish wore blacks a full year. Her best friend, Julia was. Bernard was none too pleased."

Icarus had the feeling that he'd lost track of the conversation. "Not pleased about what?"

"The blacks. It put the suitors off. Ah, good. Lucas is going to the rescue."

"Why would Miss Trentham's stepbrother be displeased?" Icarus asked, still baffled.

"Wants to be rid of Tish, doesn't he?" Matlock said, as the Adonis removed Miss Trentham from Stapleton with a smiling apology and a claim of prior commitment.

Icarus wrinkled his brow. He'd lost a thread somewhere.

"Tish and I are going for a ride," the Adonis announced. "Care to join us, Tom? Major Reid?"

"Ah . . ." Matlock glanced at him.

"I must be going," Icarus said.

"Then we'll ride as far as the road with you," the Adonis said.

Icarus made his bows to his host and strolled round to the stableyard again. The mounts were saddled and brought out, Miss Trentham joined them in riding dress, slightly out of breath—"Lord, Tish, you kept us waiting an *age*," Matlock said, grinning—and two minutes later they were trotting four abreast down a long avenue of oaks.

"How long will you be in Marlborough?" Matlock asked Icarus.

"A few more days. Maybe a week."

"Then you must visit again. We'll go for a ride. There's some good country round here."

Icarus glanced at Miss Trentham. Her eyes were on him. She gave a slight nod, telling him to say yes.

"Thank you," he said noncommittally.

"And don't think I didn't hear dear Bernard invite you to the ball," Matlock said.

"*Bernard* invited him?" the Adonis said.

Matlock's grin widened. "Nice of him, wasn't it? Seeing as how it's not his house *or* his ball!"

The Adonis snorted. So did Icarus's mount, and then it tried to unseat him.

"That's a nasty trick," Matlock said, when Icarus had the beast under control again.

"Hmm," Icarus said. His opinion of the gray wasn't fit for Miss Trentham's ears.

They parted ways at the gatehouse. "Come again," Matlock said cheerfully. "Tomorrow afternoon? We can ride up on the downs."

Icarus glanced at Miss Trentham. She was watching him, an imperative expression on her face, as if she was trying to pass on an urgent message. He could almost hear her voice in his ears: *We need to talk about Bristol.* Or perhaps she was trying to say, *Make sure you eat your dinner.*

"Very well," he heard himself say. "Tomorrow afternoon."

CHAPTER 17

"So that's the famous major," Lucas said, trotting slowly on Letty's left. "Not what I expected."

"Not what I expected either," Tom said, on her right. "He's altered almost past recognition." He cast a frowning glance back at the distant figure on horseback. "I don't like that gray. Hope it doesn't throw him."

Letty didn't like the gray either. She twisted in her saddle and watched Reid for a moment. "An unusual man. He seems fairly . . . taciturn."

"Wouldn't say that," Tom said.

Letty waited for an enlargement of this comment, but none was forthcoming. She glanced back at Reid again. He'd disappeared from sight. "So how *would* you describe his character?"

"Reid? Oh, he's a great gun. A regular Trojan!"

"Yes, but what's he *like*?" she said, exasperated.

Interest sparked in Tom's eyes. "Fancy him, do you, Tish?"

Letty felt her cheeks grow pink. "Of course not. I'm curious, is all."

Tom looked as if he didn't believe her, but he let it slide. "You couldn't find a better soldier. Reid didn't purchase his promotions; he *earned* them. The men all respected him. He was Wellesley's favorite." He shrugged, as if this said every-thing, and urged his horse into a leisurely canter. "The downs or the river? Your choice."

Letty tried a different tack that evening; she asked to see Tom's sketchbooks of Portugal. "If you want to," Tom said, and fetched them down from his room.

Being Sunday, there was no card-playing after dinner. The younger members of the party were loudly debating the merits of cross-questions over jackstraws, their more sober elders were settling themselves on various sofas, settees, corner chairs, and bergères, Almeria's two daughters were at the pianoforte arguing over the sheet music, and the pug was yapping. "The library," Tom said, with a jerk of his head.

They retired to the library. Lucas came, too. The three of them settled by the fire, pulling the winged armchairs close together.

Tom had four dog-eared sketchbooks from Portugal: one large, and three small enough to fit in his coat pocket.

Letty took the large one first. She turned the pages, mar-veling at Tom's skill, quite forgetting that she was trying to learn more about Reid. How on earth did he do it? A few pencil strokes, a dab of watercolor, and he created scenes that were so vivid, so textured, that she could almost *smell* Portugal. She glanced up at Tom. "These are incredible."

Tom shrugged. "Pretty rough. Didn't have a lot of time."

Letty went through the entire sketchbook slowly, and then flicked back through it: scrubby hillsides, villages of stone houses with pantiled roofs. "Is this Vimeiro?"

"Roliça. Vimeiro's later." He showed her.

Letty stared at the page. A cobbled square. A church with a small peak-roofed belltower. Two tethered donkeys. A flower pot on a step. The sky was tinted with a wash of palest blue, the church roof was terracotta, the donkeys dun and black, and the flowers a cheerful poppy red.

Vimeiro looked quiet, sleepy, rustic—and yet terrible things had happened there.

Letty closed the sketchbook soberly and picked up the first of the small ones. It was filled with drawings dashed out in pencil: donkeys and mules, mongrel dogs, goats and goatherds, peasant women wearing headscarves, a priest in his cassock. And soldiers. Soldiers eating, talking, laughing, playing cards, sleeping stretched out on the ground.

A middle-aged man with a jutting nose featured in several of the sketches. "Who's this?"

"General Wellesley."

Letty turned more pages. Here was Grantham, looking sweaty and peevish, and here Dunlop, with an irritable set to his mouth, and here, with his head thrown back laughing, was Reid.

"My goodness," Letty said, her voice incredulous. "That's Mr. Reid!"

Lucas craned closer. "So it is. Lord, I'd scarcely recognize him."

"I nearly didn't this afternoon," Tom said. "Got a deuce of a shock. Looks ten years older. Thin as a damned skeleton."

Letty stared at the sketch. So this was what Reid looked like when he was happy. That laugh on his face, the carefree way he sat, slouching, his arm slung over the back of the chair next to him . . .

Her heart clenched painfully in her chest. She hastily turned the page. Here was the man with the large nose again. Reid's general. Wellesley. And here a donkey carrying panniers. And here a peasant with a face creased into a thousand wrinkles. And here was Reid again.

Reid featured twice in that sketchbook—once laughing; once with Wellesley, both men frowning over a map—and once in the next book, dozing on a bench.

Letty stared at that sketch. Reid was half-asleep, his eyes heavy-lidded, his head tilted back against the wall behind him. He looked weary, but not in the way he was weary now. This wasn't the strained exhaustion of a man worn almost to the bone. This was the physical tiredness of a strong, healthy man.

She closed the book. "May I see the last one?"

Tom handed it to her. It was the tattiest of the three little sketchbooks. "Not much in it. Spilled tea over it."

Tom had indeed spilled tea over it. The pages were warped and stained and only a quarter of them were used, but one sketch was of Reid. It was one of Tom's two-minute portraits. Reid stared directly out from the page, his face captured in a few slashing pencil strokes. Letty stared back at him. This was Reid as he'd been three months ago. A man in his prime. Alert, focused, vigorous.

"You're right; he does look ten years younger." Reid was smiling ever so faintly, humoring the artist, a slight quirk to his lips, a minuscule lift to his eyebrows. "And not nearly as grim as he does now."

"Grim?" Tom said indignantly. "Reid's not grim!"

Letty closed the sketchbook. "How would you describe him, then?" she said, handing it back.

"Good sense of humor. Gets along with everyone. I've never seen him lose his temper."

That wasn't the Reid she knew.

Letty had a flash of memory: Reid half-throttling Dunlop.

She picked up the first small sketchbook again and flicked through it. Tom had captured his subjects with quick pencil strokes, hasty shadings, rough smudges of his thumb—and yet they were so alive, she almost expected them to move. "Your landscapes are beautiful, but the people . . ." She touched a portrait of a grimy-faced foot soldier. The man's lips were slightly parted. He seemed on the verge of drawing breath, of speaking. "How on earth do you do it, Tom?"

"Good, isn't he?" Lucas said, as proudly as if the sketch were his own.

Tom was better than good; he was superb.

Letty turned the pages until she came to Reid laughing. Again, her heart clenched painfully in her chest. What terrible thing had happened to alter him so greatly?

She gave the sketchbook back to Tom. "Tom . . . when I first met him, Reid told me a little about Vimeiro. He said he and his scouts were captured, and the scouts were killed."

Tom blinked. "Reid told you that?"

Letty nodded. "Do you know anything about it? Do you know what happened?"

"Know?" Tom grimaced. "I was the one who found him."

"Found him?"

Tom stacked the sketchbooks one on top of the other, not looking at her. His mouth was compressed, his eyebrows drawn down.

"Was it very bad?" Letty said hesitantly.

"Bad? Not really. Not like battle." Tom put the sketchbooks to one side, got up, stirred the fire with the poker, added another log.

Letty glanced at Lucas. Lucas shrugged.

Tom prodded the log, adjusting its position.

Letty waited silently. So did Lucas.

Tom turned away from the fireplace and settled back in his armchair. His lips were still pressed together and his eyebrows still drawn down. Letty exchanged another glance with Lucas.

"What did Reid tell you?" Tom asked, finally.

"That he was caught close to dusk, when he met up with his scouts, and that the scouts were summarily executed as spies, but he wasn't, because he was in uniform."

Tom grunted. "The liaison officer was killed, too, and he *was* in uniform."

"Liaison officer?"

"Portuguese lieutenant. Pereira. Acted as translator. Reid can't speak Portuguese, y' know."

Letty raised her eyebrows. Reid hadn't spoken of a liaison officer. "They executed him, too?"

"No." Tom shifted in his armchair, shifted again, blew out a breath. "The battle was over by midday. Reid still hadn't returned, been missing all night, so Wellesley sent me to look for him. Took half a dozen men with me."

Silence fell. The crackle of the log burning was loud.

"And you found him?" Lucas prompted.

"Found them all, in a gully. Reid's rendezvous point. The scouts had been shot. The liaison officer . . ." Tom kicked the heel of one boot against the armchair. "Don't know what killed him, but I can guess."

Silence fell again.

"What?" Lucas asked.

Tom kicked his heel against the armchair, *thock, thock, thock.* "They drowned him."

Letty put up her eyebrows. "Drowned him?"

"There was a creek."

Half a minute of silence elapsed. "And . . . ?" Lucas said.

Tom sighed, a deep exhalation of air. "Reid and Pereira were on the ground, bound hand and foot. Pereira was dead, Reid was alive. Both soaked to the bone. It hadn't rained. They'd been in the creek for sure."

Letty digested this information. "What did Reid say?"

"Nothing, far as I know." *Thock, thock, thock.* "He was out cold when I found him, not breathing that well. Portugal in August, it's hot, but he was shivering like it was the middle of winter. He came down with a fever and inflammation of the lungs, was out of his mind for weeks, nearly died three or four times."

Letty looked down at her lap and plucked at a fold of silk. "Had he been injured at all?"

"No."

Letty twisted the silk between her fingers, and then smoothed it and looked up. "Do you think . . . the French were torturing him?"

Tom jerked back in his chair. "What? No. Of course not!"

"What, then?"

Tom grimaced, and looked at the fire. "I think they were having some sport and it went too far." His boot began to swing again: *thock, thock.*

"Nasty," Lucas said quietly.

Tom shrugged. "Battle's far nastier. Wait till you've seen a man get disemboweled. Or a horse—" He stopped kicking the chair and sat upright. "I beg your pardon, Tish. Not a topic for your ears."

Letty surveyed him soberly. "You don't draw those things."

"Who would want to?"

The library door opened. "There you are, Letitia! I've been looking everywhere for you."

Tom, his back to the door, pulled a face.

"Oh, Lord," Lucas muttered under his breath.

Bernard entered the library and closed the door with an irritated *snick.* "What are you doing in here?"

"Looking through some of Tom's sketches," Lucas said mildly.

Bernard sniffed. "I should have thought daylight was better for that. Lucas, Thomas, if I may please have a private word with my stepsister?"

Lucas hesitated, and climbed to his feet. Tom gathered up his sketchbooks.

Bernard stood primly beside the fireplace while they left the room, his lips pursed, his hands clasped behind his back.

Letty used the few seconds to compose her face into a courteous expression.

"Really, Letitia, I'm disappointed," Bernard said, once the door had shut behind Tom. "Lord Stapleton came all this way to further his acquaintance with you, and you persist in spending your time with your cousin and Matlock! One would think you're avoiding the earl."

Letty fixed her gaze politely on Bernard's face and said nothing.

"And now I find you *hobnobbing* in here with them. Alone. At night!"

Hobnobbing? Letty almost snorted. "I've always spent a great deal of my time with Lucas and Tom," she said calmly. "You've never objected before."

Bernard gave another of his sniffs. "That was when Julia was alive. It's different now. It would give Stapleton a very odd notion of your character if he'd seen you in here with them."

"Why should it?" Letty said, holding on to her temper. "Lucas is my cousin, and Tom's practically family. I've known him since I was a child."

"You're not a schoolgirl now!"

"I haven't been a schoolgirl for a long time. I'm twenty-seven, Bernard. Old enough to be in the library alone with my two oldest friends." Letty stood. "Is that all?"

"I wish you to spend more time with Lord Stapleton," Bernard said stiffly.

"I've no intention of marrying Stapleton."

"He's barely in debt—"

"Stapleton inherited a fortune, and gambled it away in less than two years. I shall not give him *my* fortune to gamble away, too!"

"He's barely in debt," Bernard repeated. "And he's an earl."

"What has his title to do with anything?" Letty said, cool amusement in her voice.

Bernard's cheeks seemed to quiver. His nostrils pinched. He stood a little straighter. Letty recognized the signs; her stepbrother was about to lose his temper.

"Is Lord Stapleton in the drawing room now?"

"Of course he's there now," Bernard snapped.

"Then I shall speak with him." Letty gave Bernard a civil smile, and left the library.

*C*HAPTER 18

November 14th, 1808
Whiteoaks, Wiltshire

*L*etty was unable to speak privately with Reid on Monday. She rode out with him, and Lucas and Tom, and Almeria's eldest daughter, Selina, and Lord Stapleton. Back at Whiteoaks, eating macaroons and sipping tea, Stapleton attentive at her side, she stewed with frustration.

"It's young Oscar's birthday soon," Lucas said, reaching for a piece of plum cake. "What the devil shall I give him?"

Tom shrugged. "He's your nephew. How should I know?"

"He's mad about the knights of the Round Table," Lucas said, chewing meditatively. "Imagines himself as Sir Gawain."

"He's already got every book about the knights there is," Oscar's sister Selina said.

"I know *that*," Lucas said. "I was thinking . . . Could you paint Sir Gawain, Tom?"

"Of course."

"If I model for Gawain, can you make me look like Oscar?"

"Of course," Tom said again.

Letty saw her opportunity. "What an excellent idea! And

I know the perfect setting: the folly! We should all ride over there tomorrow afternoon." She turned to Stapleton. "It's a ruined castle, you know. Wonderfully gothic. There's even a secret passage." A secret passage, and all sorts of nooks and crannies where she'd be able to get Reid aside for a few minutes' conversation about Bristol. "And you must come, too, Mr. Reid."

Reid cut her a glance. He'd heard the note in her voice. He nodded.

"That's settled, then," Letty said. "*Do* have another macaroon, Mr. Reid."

Sir Henry Wright arrived later that afternoon. Lord Stapleton, correctly perceiving him as a rival, became even more attentive. He paid Letty compliments all through dinner, solicitously arranged her chair at just the right distance from the fireplace in the drawing room afterwards, and when she retired for the night, bowed over her hand, kissed it, and requested in a low voice the pleasure of her company for a walk in the gardens after breakfast.

Thus, Letty received her nineteenth proposal of the year in the bare-leaved garden at Whiteoaks. Gray clouds scudded overhead and a chilly wind whipped at her cloak. Stapleton had taken pains with his appearance. He strolled alongside her, wearing mirror-bright Hessians, pantaloons in a delicate shade of yellow, a long-tailed coat of blue superfine, and a slender-brimmed beaver hat. His neckcloth was tied in a style that must have taken a good half hour to achieve.

"My dear Miss Trentham," Stapleton said, in an earnest tone. A gust of wind made the tails of his coat flap and lifted his hat from his head. Stapleton caught it before it could fly away. His hair was brushed into a fashionable Caesar, glistening with pomade. "My dear Miss Trentham," he said again.

Letty schooled her face into an expression of polite interest, and listened to Lord Stapleton's proposal. He had rehearsed it; the sentences came fluidly off his tongue. At least he wasn't pretending to be in love with her. His tails flapped while he professed an affectionate regard for her, emphasized his earldom, and expressed the earnest hope that she'd do him the honor of becoming his wife.

"You feel affection for me?" Letty said, when he'd finished.

"Yes," Stapleton said, gripping his hat while the wind tugged at it. "And the deepest respect." Both statements rang false in Letty's ears.

"Tell me, Lord Stapleton. If we were to marry, would you be faithful to me?"

"Ah . . ." Stapleton's eyelids flickered, and then he smiled. "But of course."

Clang.

"And do you intend to moderate your gambling? I understand you've lost more than forty thousand pounds in the last two years."

Stapleton's eyelids flickered again. His smile disappeared.

Letty met his gaze coolly. Would he tell her it was none of her business?

The silence between them grew. Letty wondered which would win out: Stapleton's pride, or his need for money.

"Perhaps we shouldn't suit, after all," Stapleton said stiffly.

"No," Letty said. "I think not."

Stapleton made her a wooden bow, wished her good day, and walked off, trying to look dignified. The wind hustled him along, crowding his coat-tails between his legs.

The Whiteoaks' folly perched on a wooded height, a small and ruined castle that looked as if it had been there for centuries—roofless, with half-collapsed walls and crumbling staircases and a derelict tower—but the disintegration was purely artistic; the folly was less than eighty years old.

They made quite a large party: Lucas and Tom, Reid, Sir Henry Wright, Selina and her younger sister Emma, and the grooms who were to look after the horses and set up the picnic. Letty stayed close to Reid as they climbed the fifty-two steps up to the castle and entered the grassy courtyard. Sir Henry gazed around, and laughed. "Fabulous!" He was a stocky young man, with a square, good-humored face and no pretensions to dandyism.

"Isn't it just?" Letty said. "There's a dungeon *and* a secret passage."

They traipsed down to the dungeon first. Daylight slanted in through an iron grille, illuminating a dank and dismal little cell. Attached to one wall were rusting lengths of iron chain.

Sir Henry laughed again when he saw the chains. "This is almost too good to be true!"

"Wait till you see the secret passage," Tom said.

"Where is it?" Sir Henry demanded.

Tom grinned. "You find it."

Sir Henry accepted this challenge.

Letty took hold of Reid's wrist and tugged him towards the stairs. Together they climbed back up to the courtyard. She led him across to a ruined gothic arch with a fine view of the downs, and sat on a tumbled block of stone. "Bristol," she said.

Reid leaned against the arch.

"Let's leave on Saturday. I'll say I'm going to stay with Helen again. For ten days. That will give us time to go down to Exeter, if we have to."

Reid gazed out over the downs, his eyes narrowed against the weak glare of the sun. "And your maid? Your *real* maid?"

"I'll give her leave to visit her sister again."

Letty turned her head at the sound of laughter and voices. Sir Henry, having assured himself that the secret passage didn't start in the dungeon, emerged into the sunlight again, trailing an audience.

"Won't she think it's unusual?"

"Perhaps a little, but I'm sure she'll be glad of an extra holiday."

"Hmm," Reid said, watching Sir Henry enthusiastically inspect the ruined walls.

Letty studied his face. "Don't you wish to pursue this?"

Reid transferred his gaze to her. "I do."

Tom's description flashed into her mind, vivid and terrible. Her imagination built a picture: a scrubby gully, a creek, four dead men, and Reid lying unconscious, bound hand and foot, barely alive. "Then we leave on Saturday," she said.

Reid looked at her a moment, and nodded. "I'll arrange for a post-chaise."

Letty looked down at her hands. She tugged at one gloved fingertip. "How's Eliza?"

"Fine."

"And you? How are you?" She looked up at his face again.

"Fine."

"Are you using the valerian?"

"Yes."

"Is it working?"

"You're not my nursemaid, Miss Trentham."

Letty recognized one of his evasions. "Have you been falling asleep again? Yes or no?"

Reid's jaw tightened. He didn't answer.

"Have you been eating enough?"

A muscle twitched in his jaw; he was gritting his teeth. "You're not my nursemaid," he said again.

They matched gazes. "It's *got* to be in this wall," Letty heard Sir Henry say. "The others aren't thick enough."

Letty looked away, out over the treetops. "My cousin Robert is holding a ball tomorrow night."

"I know. I've been invited."

"You're also invited to dine with us beforehand."

Reid was silent.

Letty glanced at him.

Reid's silver eyes were narrow, his expression annoyed. "Your doing?"

She shook her head. "Lord Stapleton is leaving early. Almeria doesn't like uneven numbers at the table. Not when it's a formal event."

Reid couldn't hear the truth in her voice. He looked as if he didn't believe her.

A crow of triumph told her that Sir Henry had found the entrance to the secret passage. Letty didn't bother to look around. "I hope you'll accept the invitation," she told Reid.

That was the truth, too. But of course he couldn't hear it.

Letty looked down at her gloves. She smoothed them from fingertip to wrist.

Breathless voices came from above them, and laughter. She glanced up. Five cheerful faces peered down at them from the ruined tower. Letty smiled and waved, and returned her gaze to Reid. His eyes were still narrow, his expression still annoyed. He looked nothing like the man Tom had sketched laughing in Portugal, nothing like the man Tom had described. "Tom says he's never once seen you lose your temper."

The muscles in Reid's face tightened fractionally, as if her words had been a slap. He looked abruptly away.

Letty bit the tip of her tongue. She hadn't meant to upset him. She looked down at her hands again, tugged slightly at each gloved fingertip, smoothed the kidskin over her wrists, and glanced at Reid. His profile was grim. "I beg your pardon. I shouldn't have said that."

"My temper isn't what it used to be," Reid said stiffly, not looking at her. "The apology is mine to make. I regret if my manner has offended you."

"It hasn't," Letty told him. "You have no idea what a relief it is to talk with a man who's not trying to charm me."

Reid turned his head and looked at her.

"I wish you would let me help you."

"You are helping me."

"I don't mean help you find your traitor; I mean help *you*."

Reid looked away again. "I'm beyond help, Miss Trentham."

Letty's eyes filled with sudden, stinging tears. At this moment, the two grooms arrived with the picnic. Letty blinked, and surreptitiously blotted her eyes, and watched the men open the wicker basket and begin laying out plates and linen napkins.

She looked up at the ruined tower. It was empty again, but the five explorers didn't spill out into the courtyard; Sir Henry was following the passage all the way to the bottom.

Reid glanced at the picnic preparations. An expression of resignation crossed his face. "How many macaroons do you wish me to eat?"

Letty tried to smile. "I'm a great trial to you, aren't I, Mr. Reid?"

He transferred his gaze to her, a frowning appraisal that lasted several seconds. "Yes," he said. "But you're an even greater help. You've helped me more than I deserve. If I succeed, it will be because of you. I'm more grateful than I can express."

This brought another rush of tears to Letty's eyes. She looked away, and blinked fiercely. "Five macaroons," she said, when she had control of her voice. "And a piece of plum cake."

*C*HAPTER 19

November 16th, 1808
Whiteoaks, Wiltshire

*I*carus accepted the invitation to dine at Whiteoaks before the ball, and when Matlock urged him to come riding beforehand, he found himself agreeing to that, too. Matlock seemed almost as determined to look after him as Miss Trentham was. Was he such a pathetic-looking creature, that everyone must need watch over him?

Icarus decided not to answer that question.

He rode over to Whiteoaks beneath a bright, pale sky. The big gray only tried to unseat him once.

He hacked around the park with Matlock and the Adonis, Miss Trentham, and a burly young baronet. They trotted through a bare bluebell dell, cantered under the great oaks, jumped a stream, and indulged in a brief gallop along a lane hedged with hawthorn. Icarus was conscious of both Matlock and Miss Trentham sending him occasional glances. *Checking to make sure I'm not overtaxing myself,* he thought sourly. And sure enough, at the end of the lane, Matlock suggested they turn back.

They looped around to the stream again and jumped it—whatever the gray's faults, he had a powerful jump—and cantered leisurely beneath the oaks. Halfway along, the gray stopped dead. Icarus almost went over its head.

"Take care!" the Adonis said sharply, reaching out to grab the bridle.

The gray put his ears back, and looked as if he wanted to bite the man's hand off.

"That's a damned brute of a horse."

"He shan't throw me," Icarus said, settling himself firmly into the saddle.

The Adonis released the bridle. "That's how my sister died," he said abruptly. "Came off a horse. Broke her neck." For a moment his expression was unguarded and Icarus saw something raw and dark and painful in his eyes, and then the Adonis shook his golden head and smiled and said lightly, "But I imagine you've ridden worse beasts in your time, Major."

Icarus nodded, at a loss for words.

Ahead, the others halted and looked back. "Everything all right?" Matlock called.

The Adonis waved them on, and nudged his horse into a trot.

Icarus followed, his gaze resting thoughtfully on the man's back. There was more to the Adonis than appeared at first glance. Beneath that handsome, golden exterior, the man was hurting.

And then he mentally picked himself up by the scruff of his neck and gave himself a sharp shake. *The man has a name. Use it.*

He sipped tea and ate macaroons—a familiar ritual, now—and rode back to Marlborough. A wash, a change of clothes, and it was time to depart for Whiteoaks again. This time, he went by carriage.

Icarus had anticipated the evening with grim resignation—and even more so when he entered the dining room and discovered he was seated alongside his nursemaid, Miss Trentham—but the dinner and ball proved enjoyable. Bernard Trentham *was* irritating, with that way he had of looking down his nose and the condescension of his manner, but Matlock and Lucas Kemp were good company, and Miss Trentham didn't press too much food on him, and the punch served in the ballroom was astonishingly good. Icarus leaned against the wall and sipped, trying to distinguish the different flavors. The base was an alcoholic cordial of some kind. Blackberry, he decided after another sip, with oranges, a tart hint of lemon, perhaps a dash of rum, and that tingle on his tongue was definitely champagne.

"Tasty, ain't it?" said Matlock, propping up the wall alongside him.

"Extremely." Icarus sipped again, and let his gaze drift over the crowded ballroom. The musicians were playing a lively Scottish reel and at least two dozen couples were dancing. Miss Trentham was on the dance floor. Icarus studied her face, trying to determine whether her partner was a suitor or not. Not, he decided; her manner wasn't off-puttingly aloof.

"Who's that dancing with Miss Trentham?"

Matlock scanned the ballroom and found her. "Arnold Kemp."

"Another cousin?"

"Of Tish's? Yes. As much as any of them are cousins of hers. Tish ain't actually related to the Kemps."

"Oh? I assumed . . ."

Matlock glanced at him. "You assumed Tish's fortune and the Kemp fortune were connected? No." He put his glass down on the ledge behind him, reached into his breast pocket, and drew out a small, slender book and a stub of a pencil.

"You bring a sketchbook to a ball?" Icarus said, putting up his eyebrows.

Matlock shrugged. "Never know when I'll see something worth drawing." He flicked to a blank page, drew a stick figure at the top of the page, and labeled it *OMT*. "Old Man Trentham had three children." He drew three lines descending, with stick figures at the end of each. "An heir, a spare, and a daughter." He labeled the first two new stick figures *Heir* and *Spare,* and drew a bonnet on the third. "The spare never married, so we can forget about him." Matlock put a cross through the spare's stick figure. "The daughter married William Kemp, the eldest son of a nabob. When the nabob turned up his toes, she and her husband inherited this place and became rich as Turks. Had eight children. Robert's the oldest, Lucas and Julia were the youngest. Got it?"

Icarus nodded.

"Now the heir, he married a duke's daughter. Old Man Trentham left him a modest fortune and a drafty old manor house. The heir had two children, Bernard and Caroline, and then his wife died."

Icarus nodded.

"The heir didn't mind being less wealthy than his sister, but Bernard and Caroline *did* mind. However, they had one thing their cousins didn't have: their grandfather was a duke. You've met Bernard; Caroline's even worse. Takes her pedigree *very* seriously. Exceptionally high in the instep."

Icarus nodded again.

"Several years after his wife died, the heir met a widow with an enormous fortune and a young daughter. Fell in love. Married her, took her daughter as his own." Matlock closed the sketchbook and tucked it back into his pocket. "Bernard and Caroline were *not* pleased. Especially when the heir let his new wife will her fortune solely to her daughter. Bernard hasn't seen a penny of it. That's one of the reasons he dislikes Tish so much."

"The heir didn't want the fortune?"

Matlock shrugged. "It was a love match. He wasn't interested in her money. He even helped her set up several charities.

A lying-in hospital, some foundling homes, a school. *Don't get Bernard started on those.*"

"Huh," Icarus said, and found Miss Trentham on the dance floor. Was that what she was searching for? A man like her stepfather, who cared nothing for her fortune?

"Bernard and Caroline were pretty beastly to Tish—Caroline was an absolute cat—Tish's birth is respectable, her father was a gentleman, but from the way Caroline carries on he may as well have been a shopkeeper—and to make matters worse, the will was extremely odd. Tish wasn't allowed to make her début until she was twenty-one. Her mother died when she was, oh, sixteen I think, and her stepfather cocked up his toes a couple of years later, so it fell to Bernard and his wife to bring her out. Bernard was *not* pleased."

"Huh," Icarus said again.

"Robert and Almeria helped, of course. The Kemps have always treated Tish well."

"She seems very close to Lucas."

"Lord, yes! Lu and Ju and Tish practically lived in each other's pockets when they were growing up. And me," he added reflectively. "The four of us were inseparable. Did everything together."

The Scottish reel came to its end. There was a surge of movement from the dance floor. Icarus lost sight of Miss Trentham. He sipped his punch, savoring the flavors on his tongue. When the next dance was called—a *contredanse*—his gaze wandered down the lines of dancers until he found her again. He knew instantly that her partner was a suitor. Her manner was more aloof, her face plainer. "Who's Miss Trentham dancing with now?"

Matlock shrugged. "Don't know him. Another hopeful." He glanced at Icarus, a gleam in his eyes. "Why, sir? You interested?"

"No," Icarus said, in a quelling tone. "I have no need for a wife. Or a fortune."

The gleam in Matlock's eyes faded. "Shame. Tish could

do with a good husband, and she's not the sort men fall in love with. She's not pretty, and she's got all that money—and no one sees past those two things." His gaze returned to the dance floor, where the dancers were now bowing to one another. "Got a style of her own, Tish has."

"Tom, darling." Almeria Kemp bustled up in a waft of French perfume. "Miss Ulverton needs a partner. Would you mind?"

Matlock met Icarus's eyes ruefully, and allowed himself to be towed off.

Icarus stayed where he was, leaning against the wall, sipping his punch. He watched the dancers. Matlock was correct: Miss Trentham had a style of her own. Austere wasn't the correct word for it, although it came close. Her gown was unembellished by frills or flounces or knots of ribbon. Her hair was dressed in an upswept coronet of braids, with not one single curl. She wore no jewelry other than a solitary strand of pearls at her throat and matching pearl eardrops—no brooches or bracelets, no diadem or jeweled combs. The girl next to her in the set was pretty, extremely pretty, but alongside Miss Trentham she looked overdressed, too many glittering trinkets, too many ruffles on her gown, too much lace, and far too many curls clustering around her face.

Icarus emptied his glass. Elegant. That was the word he'd been searching for. Miss Trentham looked austerely, coolly, and understatedly elegant. And, given her height and her angular, boyish figure, surprisingly graceful as well. A good dancer.

A footman with a tray halted in front of him. "Champagne, sir? Punch?"

Icarus chose more punch, and ran his gaze over the dancers again. Matlock was dancing with a pretty little blonde, and Lucas Kemp was partnered with a striking brunette. *Overdressed,* Icarus thought, taking in the profusion of lace decorating the blonde's ball gown. *Overdressed,* glancing at the diamond tiara in the brunette's hair.

His gaze drifted back to Letitia Trentham.

She wasn't pretty or beautiful, but he'd been harsh to think her plain. Icarus turned words over in his head, rejected *homely* and *ordinary,* and decided on *interesting.* Miss Trentham had an interesting face. The face of an intelligent, strong-minded woman.

"Major Reid." Almeria Kemp reappeared in a wave of perfume.

Icarus straightened away from the wall. "Mrs. Kemp."

"Would you like to dance? I can introduce you to a charming young lady."

"Ah . . . I might look into the card room." He smiled and made his escape, glass in hand. But the card room was populated mainly by dowagers and elderly men, and he was no more in the mood for whist or loo than he was in the mood for dancing. Icarus drifted out to the ballroom again.

The next dance was called. Miss Trentham was partnered by her cousin, Lucas Kemp. In his company, there was nothing remotely aloof or standoffish about her. She smiled in a way that made her look quite eye-catching.

After that dance came supper. Miss Trentham and Matlock bore Icarus off to the supper room. "You must try the lobster patties!" Miss Trentham said.

Icarus ate a lobster patty.

"And one of these cherry tartlets."

Icarus ate that, too. Slowly. He was beginning to feel uncomfortably full.

"I saved a cotillion for you," Miss Trentham told him. "If you would like to dance? But don't feel that you have to. Tom will partner me otherwise."

Did she want to talk with him privately, or was it the disinterested offer it sounded like? Icarus studied her expression. It was extremely neutral. She didn't seem to be trying to convey any message at all.

He chewed his last mouthful of cherry tartlet while he considered Miss Trentham's suggestion. It did seem foolish to attend a ball and not dance at least once. "I should like that," he said, and wondered how it had sounded to her ears. Truth, or lie? He wasn't certain himself.

Miss Trentham nodded. "Another tartlet?"

"I can't."

That was definitely the truth, and Miss Trentham heard it. She didn't press him to eat any more.

The cotillion came two dances later. To his surprise, Icarus found himself enjoying it. He and Miss Trentham were well-matched as dancers. Miss Trentham seemed to enjoy it, too. She wasn't wearing her standoffish face, or even her polite face. She looked like she had when she'd danced with Lucas Kemp: friendly and approachable. This surprised Icarus so much that he almost missed his cue. Did she consider him her friend?

He recovered his concentration and danced the main figure with Miss Trentham. When they'd circled back to their places, standing side by side, he glanced obliquely at her. Not standoffish at all, or even aloof. And then Icarus realized why. It wasn't that she thought of him as a friend; it was because she knew he didn't want to marry her.

Miss Trentham caught his glance before he could look away. Her eyes were almost the same muted sea-green as her ball gown. "Come riding tomorrow, Mr. Reid. Two o'clock. We may be able to discuss Bristol."

Icarus nodded.

"And even if we can't talk privately, there'll be macaroons afterwards."

Despite himself, Icarus smiled.

Miss Trentham smiled back. When she smiled like that, with her whole face, a glint of humor in her eyes, she was actually very attractive.

Icarus almost missed his cue again.

*C*HAPTER 20

November 17th, 1808
Whiteoaks, Wiltshire

*T*he following afternoon, Letty rode out with Lucas, Tom, Sir Henry, Reid, Selina, Emma, and her cousin, Arnold. There was no galloping; Tom had an easel strapped to his saddle. They cantered leisurely, taking a path through the woods that led to the folly. Here, Lucas and Tom dismounted.

"Let's go up on the downs," Selina said. "I should like a good gallop!"

They jumped the stream, trotted through the bluebell dell, and came upon the path leading to the downs. Here, Letty declared that she felt a trifle peaked and would prefer to go back. "You go on. I'll be perfectly happy by myself! Enjoy the downs."

"I'll accompany you," Reid offered. "I'm feeling rather tired myself."

No one argued with him. He did look tired. Tired and heavy-eyed.

They waited until the others had gone, then turned their mounts towards the stream. "Bristol," Letty said.

"Bristol." The big Roman-nosed gray tried to unseat him. Reid brought the horse sternly under control. "A post-chaise will pick you up at ten. I've hired an outrider, and Eliza will be in the chaise. I've written ahead to book rooms in Bristol. Four nights at the Swan. I'm told it's a quiet place, away from the main thoroughfares."

Letty nodded. "And after that, Exeter."

"If necessary. I hope it's not."

"You think it's Houghton?"

Reid shook his head.

Letty frowned. "Then why did you say you hope we don't have to go to Exeter?"

"Because the longer we're absent, the greater the risk you'll be discovered missing."

"I'm not worried about that."

"Well, you should be!"

Letty nudged her horse into a canter. Reid was correct; she *should* be worried—the scandal would be ferocious, her reputation in smithereens—and in a small way, she *was* worried—but her concern for her reputation was eclipsed by her concern for Reid. If he was going to Bristol, so was she. If he went to Exeter, so would she. Her reputation was important, but not as important as making sure Reid ate enough and that he slept again after his nightmares. She and Reid were embarked on different quests now. His was to find a traitor; hers was to restore him to the man he'd been before Vimeiro.

The stream came into sight. Letty picked up her pace. Alongside her, the big gray stretched his legs. Letty glanced at Reid. *I'm beyond help,* he'd said at the folly. Well, she was going to prove him wrong.

She shifted her weight as her horse took the jump. Out of the corner of her eye, she saw the gray stop dead on the bank.

Reid plunged over its head.

A huge *splash* sounded.

Letty landed badly, hauled on her reins, and scrambled

from the saddle before her horse had halted. "Reid!" She tripped over her long skirts, caught her balance, and plowed into the water. "Reid!"

Reid hadn't broken his neck. He was flailing to his feet in thigh-deep water, coughing, spluttering, gasping for breath. Letty ran to him, stumbling on rocks, her wet skirts twisting around her ankles. "Are you all right?" She grasped his arm.

Reid wrenched free and struck out, a wild blow that caught her on the shoulder.

Letty sat down hard in the icy water.

Reid swung towards her, the blind, berserker look on his face, teeth bared, fists raised.

"Icarus!" Letty cried sharply, pushing to her knees. "*Stop.*"

Reid stopped. Water streamed down his face, streamed from his hair, streamed from his coat.

Letty stared into his silver eyes, almost afraid to breathe. Her heart beat hard and fast in her chest.

Reid blinked. The wild, blind look faded. He lowered his fists.

Letty scrambled to her feet. "Are you hurt?"

Reid didn't appear to hear her. He turned away and blundered to the bank, moving with frantic haste, lurching and stumbling. Once on dry ground, he bent over and vomited.

Letty followed him from the water, slowly, soberly. Tom's description of Vimeiro echoed in her head. The creek. The dead, drowned Portuguese officer. And Reid, bound hand and foot, barely alive. *I think they were having some sport and it went too far.*

Reid stopped retching. He was shaking convulsively, hands braced on his knees. His breathing was hoarse and irregular. Letty halted a prudent distance away. Would he recognize her? Strike out at her? "Icarus?" she said quietly.

Reid turned his head and looked at her blankly, then recognition came into his eyes. He straightened, and turned from her and walked back to the stream, moving as stiffly and haltingly as an old man. He stripped off his gloves and scooped up a handful of water, rinsed his mouth and spat, rinsed again, spat again.

From the opposite bank, the Roman-nosed gray watched, its ears set belligerently.

Reid turned back to her, wiping his mouth with the back of one hand. His face was gray beneath the tan.

Letty reached out and gently took his elbow. "Come over here. Sit down for a moment. Catch your breath."

Reid let her draw him away from the stream to a patch of grass. He was shivering. His breath wheezed in his throat.

"Sit."

Silently, he obeyed, bowing his head into his hands.

Letty knelt in front of him. "Are you hurt at all?"

He shook his head.

Letty peeled off her wet gloves—hesitated—and then damned propriety to perdition. She put her arms around Reid's shoulders and gathered him close, cupping the back of his head with one hand.

Reid didn't tense. He was as passive as he'd been that final night in Basingstoke, shivering hard, a faint hitch to every breath. She wasn't real to him right now; Vimeiro was.

Letty rested her cheek on his wet hair and felt a fierce mixture of tenderness and grief and protectiveness, and an overwhelming need to make everything right for him.

But she didn't know how to do that. How did one fix something like this?

Gradually Reid's breathing steadied, gradually his shudders eased. He didn't draw away from her. His forehead rested against her shoulder. He smelled of river weed and wet wool.

Letty stroked his damp hair. *Icarus Reid,* she whispered silently. *What am I going to do about you?*

He hadn't been physically wounded at Vimeiro, hadn't had his flesh hacked by sabers or his bones shattered by musket balls, but he *had* sustained an injury, even if no one could see it—and pretending it hadn't happened, trying to bury it, wasn't helping him at all. "Icarus, I know what happened at Vimeiro—Tom told me—and you need to *talk* to someone about it. A military chaplain, or another soldier, or someone in your family."

Reid stiffened. He lifted his head from her shoulder and pulled away from her.

"They almost drowned you, didn't they?"

His face tightened. He averted his head and made to stand.

Letty grabbed his sleeve, digging her fingers into the wet superfine, hauling him back to his knees. "Icarus, you have to *talk* to someone about it!"

He turned his head to look at her. His eyes were hard and bright, his face so taut it seemed hewn of wood. "They didn't almost drown me," he said flatly. "They drowned me until I died. Over and over and over."

Letty stared at him. He was telling the truth. Horror stopped her breath. She released her grip on his sleeve. "Why?"

"To make me tell them what they wanted to know."

Letty swallowed. "Icarus . . ." She touched the back of his hand.

Reid's eyes became even brighter. "I told them," he said, and then—shockingly—he began to cry.

146

CHAPTER 21

$\mathcal{L}$etty reacted instinctively, putting her arms around Reid, gathering him close again, holding him tightly. His words echoed inside her head, sharp-edged and terrible. She pressed her face into his damp hair, and rocked him. "Hush," she whispered mechanically. "It's all right. Hush." But she knew it wasn't all right.

Reid inhaled a huge, shuddering breath, and stopped crying. He tried to pull away from her.

Letty didn't release him; she tightened her embrace. "Whatever you told them didn't matter, Icarus," she said fiercely in his ear. "Wellesley *won* that battle! The French pulled out of Portugal. Whatever you told them—*it didn't matter.*"

She felt him tense, felt him repudiate the words.

Maybe it *had* mattered. Had men died because of what he'd told the French? Letty hesitated, uncertain what to do, what to say. She needed to know the facts. "What did you tell them, Icarus?"

Reid pulled away again. This time she let him. "Icarus . . . what did you tell them?"

He scrubbed his face with his hands. His cheeks weren't flushed from crying. He looked bloodless beneath his tan.

Letty reached out and touched his arm. "What did you tell them?"

Reid shook her hand off and looked away, to where her horse stood cropping grass.

"What, Icarus?"

He looked back at her. His lips compressed. "They wanted to know if it was true we had no troops on the northeast ridge."

"Was it true?"

"Yes."

"And you told them that?"

His lips thinned even further. He nodded.

"How did that affect the battle?"

Reid looked at the horse again. "They tried to take the ridge, but Wellesley saw the advance. He countered it."

"So it didn't matter?"

Reid didn't answer.

Letty tried to read his profile. Bleak, bitter. "It did matter?"

Reid shook his head, still not looking at her. "No."

He spoke the truth, but he was also lying, even if there was no *clang* in her ears. It might not have mattered to the outcome of the battle, but it *had* mattered to Reid. It had mattered terribly. The expression on his face, the tone of his voice . . .

Reid was somewhere far beyond guilt or shame. He hated himself.

Letty felt helpless. What should she say? What should she do? Reid had been brutalized by the French until he'd betrayed his own side. Did he think himself a coward and a traitor?

Of course he did.

"Icarus . . ." She rose on her knees and caught his chin, brought his head round to look at her, held those silver, de-spairing eyes in a fierce stare. "You are *not* a coward. You are *not* a traitor."

She saw denial on his face, in his eyes. He tried to jerk his chin free.

"You're *not*," Letty said vehemently, and then—prompted by instinct—she leaned forward and pressed her lips to his.

She felt Reid stiffen in surprise.

Letty kissed him again, softly, gently, trying to tell him that even if he reviled himself, she didn't.

For a fleeting second Reid's lips clung to hers, cool and salty with tears, and then he pulled away, twisting his chin free. He stared at her. His expression was wholly shocked.

"You're not a coward or a traitor," Letty told him firmly.

The shock vanished. Reid's face tightened. He averted his head and climbed to his feet.

The big gray was still on the far side of the stream. Reid looked across at the animal, and then down at the water. A muscle tightened convulsively in his jaw.

Letty realized that he couldn't bring himself to step into the creek.

"You're not riding him," she said brusquely. "Look at him! He wants nothing more than to throw you again. One of the grooms can fetch him."

Reid glanced at her.

"The folly's two minutes away. Lucas and Tom are there. You can take one of their horses."

Reid took Lucas's mount because Tom stopped painting and rode back with them. "Took a toss, did you?" Tom said cheerfully. "Lord, but you're wet, the pair of you! You'll borrow my clothes, of course, Major. We're almost of a height."

Letty caught Tom's elbow in the stableyard. "He needs something hot to drink," she hissed in his ear. "And some brandy."

When she next saw Reid, he was in the green and gold salon, eating macaroons and wearing a coat that was half an inch too long in the sleeve. He looked as gaunt and weary as ever, but his hair was dry and the gray tone gone from his skin. Letty sat alongside him on the sofa, and cast Tom a grateful glance.

Reid didn't stay long. He ate one more macaroon and took his leave, promising to return Tom's clothes tomorrow.

"How are you getting to Marlborough?" Letty asked. "Not that gray!"

"Lucas's curricle," Tom said. "One of the grooms will bring it back."

He went out to see Reid off, and returned two minutes later.

"How do you think he is?" Letty asked.

"He's perfectly well. Stop fussing, Tish. It'd take more than a toss to upset a man like Reid!"

Letty stayed awake for a long time that night, thinking about what had happened at the stream, remembering the despair she'd seen in Reid's eyes. She thought back to her first meeting with him. *I need to make things right,* he'd said.

She had assumed he was on a personal crusade for revenge, but it seemed to her now that she'd been wrong. Reid's quest was more than vengeance; he sought expiation as well.

But was expiation possible? Reid couldn't *undo* what had happened. He couldn't take back what he'd told the French.

Letty pondered that question for several hours, and came to an unsettling conclusion. Expiation *was* possible.

The penalty for cowardice was discharge—and Reid had resigned his commission.

The penalty for treason was death—and Reid had told her he'd be dead by the end of the year.

He'd refused to tell her what he was dying of, but she thought she knew.

Icarus Reid intended to kill himself.

CHAPTER 22

November 18th, 1808
Whiteoaks, Wiltshire

In the morning, her nighttime fears seemed faintly foolish. Letty's certainty became doubt. By the time she'd eaten her breakfast, she'd convinced herself that her imagination had been overactive. Reid was no more going to kill himself than he was going to grow wings and fly to the moon. His bleakness yesterday, the despair she'd glimpsed in his eyes, were entirely natural—given what had happened to him at Vimeiro—but he had too much strength of character to commit suicide. Reid was a soldier. If he was backed into a corner, he'd fight his way out; he wouldn't turn his face to the wall and die.

Accordingly, when Sir Henry Wright asked to speak with her privately, Letty was able to give him her full attention.

Sir Henry didn't make the mistake of trying to propose in the windswept, leafless garden. Nor did he make the mistake of trying to present his offer as anything other than what it was: a marriage of convenience.

"You know my circumstances, I think," he said bluntly,

151

when they were seated across from one another in the cool privacy of the library.

"Yes," Letty said. Wright's father had left him saddled with massive debts.

"I can't offer you anything—except a baronetcy." He made a throwaway gesture with one hand, as if to indicate how worthless that title was. "The manor's well enough, but nothing compared to Whiteoaks."

"What are your feelings for me?"

"I think we could be friends," Sir Henry said, and meant it.

Letty nodded. She thought they could be friends, too. "If we were to marry, would you be faithful to me?"

Sir Henry flushed faintly. He glanced away from her, and then back. He met her gaze squarely. "No. But I'd never give you cause for embarrassment."

Letty nodded again. She looked at his forthright face and steady brown eyes. She liked this man. "If I was looking for a marriage of convenience, I'd accept your offer. But I'm not. I'm very sorry, Sir Henry."

He shook his head. "It's what I expected. A one-sided bargain, after all. I can see what's in it for me—but not what's in it for you." He smiled ruefully. "To tell the truth, I'm almost relieved. Marrying for money is not . . ." An expression of distaste crossed his face. "Not something I ever envisaged myself doing."

"What will you do now?"

Sir Henry looked down at his hands. "What I *want* to do . . ."

"What?"

He looked up and met her eyes again. "What I want to do is sell everything, right down to the last teaspoon. Get rid of the whole mess."

Letty listened to the bell-like tone of his words. He meant it. "Would that cover the debts?"

"Just."

"And your family?"

Sir Henry shrugged. "My sisters are both married. They'd be sorry to see the manor go, but they have their own homes."

"And you? What would you do?"

Sir Henry smiled faintly. "Take the king's shilling."

"The king's shilling? You can't *enlist,* Sir Henry!"

He looked almost amused. "Any man can enlist."

Letty stared at him. "Do you *want* to be a soldier?"

"Begged m' father for a commission when I came down from Oxford, but he wouldn't hear of it. Nothing he can do about it now." Sir Henry grinned, as if he found this amusing.

"Yes, but an *enlisted* man!"

The grin faded. Sir Henry shrugged again. He didn't tell her that commissions cost money; she knew that.

"A cavalry regiment?"

Sir Henry shook his head. "The Ninety-fifth Rifles."

Letty lifted her eyebrows. "You *have* thought about this."

"A lot." Sir Henry pushed to his feet. He held out his hand. "Thank you for your time, Miss Trentham."

Letty stood and clasped his hand—and didn't release it. "I don't wish to marry you, Sir Henry, but I *do* wish to buy you a commission. I hope you'll accept it."

Sir Henry opened his mouth, and then closed it. He blinked, swallowed, spoke: "Miss Trentham, you can't—"

"Yes. I can."

Sir Henry looked at her for a long moment. "Why?" he said, finally.

"Because I like you. You tell the truth. You are *exactly* the sort of man who makes a good officer. I shall write to my man of business today and set it in motion."

"Miss Trentham . . ."

Letty kissed his cheek, part farewell, part blessing. "Enjoy your soldiering, Sir Henry."

"Thank you," he said, looking almost dazed. "I . . . Thank you!"

Letty composed a letter to her man of business, not merely about Sir Henry's commission, but also about securing a place for Eliza at the lying-in hospital next month. *I know it's too early,* she wrote, *but she has no relatives and I wish for her to be somewhere safe and comfortable.* That done, she ate a light luncheon, changed into her second-best riding habit—her favorite was still damp from yesterday's drenching—and sat in the blue parlor awaiting Reid's arrival. The window seat had a good view of the carriage sweep. At five after two, she saw him trot past on a chestnut horse.

Letty caught up her gloves and riding crop and hurried out to the stableyard. Reid was just dismounting.

"Mr. Reid! Good afternoon."

He gave her a nod. "Miss Trentham."

"Would you like to go for a ride? I'm just heading out myself."

Reid seemed to hesitate. "Alone?"

"Sadly, yes," Letty said, trying to decipher his expression. Did he not want to go riding with her? "Lucas and Tom are already over at the folly, Almeria's taken the girls to Marlborough to look at fabric, and Sir Henry left not an hour ago. I should be glad of your company."

Again, that infinitesimal hesitation. "Of course I'll accompany you," Reid said politely.

Letty turned to one of the grooms. "The bay mare, please. The one with the white socks."

The groom hurried off.

A saddlebag was strapped behind the chestnut's saddle. Reid unfastened it and handed it to a groom. "Please have this taken up to Lieutenant Matlock's room."

"Yes, sir."

The bay mare was brought from the stables and led to the mounting block. Letty climbed into the saddle.

Reid swung up on the chestnut again. The horse was a good hand shorter at the withers than the gray had been.

"Is that horse up to your weight?" Letty asked.

"Barely. I'll take care not to use him too hard."

They trotted from the stableyard. Letty was aware of an awkwardness between them, a constraint in Reid's manner. She didn't need to wonder why. It was because of what had happened at the stream yesterday. Because of what he'd told her.

She studied Reid's profile. It seemed to her that he held himself more tautly than usual. Whether his tension was due to shame that she knew his secret or fear that she'd reveal it, she couldn't guess.

"I shan't tell anyone," Letty said. "You have my word."

Reid glanced at her. He gave a short nod, but didn't speak.

They rode silently, at a trot. Reid's horse had a placid, knock-kneed gait. The sky was overcast, the wind damp, the woods dank and gloomy. Dead leaves squelched beneath the horses' hooves. The trees stood like great, gray skeletons. The bleakness of the day pervaded Letty's mood. Her thoughts swung back to her nighttime fears. "Mr. Reid," she said abruptly. "You don't intend to kill yourself, do you?"

Reid's head swung round. She saw his astonishment—and then he blinked, and his face became expressionless. He didn't answer her. He looked away again.

Letty's stomach contracted. "You do, don't you?"

"Shall we canter?"

Letty leaned over and caught his arm. "Mr. Reid, tell me! Are you planning to kill yourself?"

Reid shook her hand off. "That is absolutely none of your business, Miss Trentham."

The evasion was an answer in itself. Letty stared at him, aghast. "But *why*?"

Reid didn't reply. He nudged the chestnut into a canter.

Letty followed. She felt almost stupid with shock. Horror grew in her chest; horror, and fear, and a terrible sense of urgency. Thoughts swarmed in her head, as frantic and disordered as bees chased from their hive. Reid was going to kill himself?

It was several minutes before Letty was able to think coherently. *Don't panic,* she told herself sternly. *Find words he'll listen to.*

Reid chose the path up to the downs. They cantered slowly, not pushing the horses. Letty fastened her gaze on Reid's back and cudgeled her brain, turning over arguments, examining them, discarding them. By the time Reid dropped to a trot, she thought she'd found the words she needed. She came abreast of him. "There's a good viewpoint ahead. You can see Whiteoaks."

Reid made no reply, but he let her take the lead.

At the viewpoint, Letty halted. Reid came up alongside her. They gazed down on Whiteoaks—the black river, the dark woods, the ruined castle on its rocky prominence. "We should ride back past the folly. You'll want to take your leave of Tom."

Reid nodded.

Letty fixed her gaze on his face. "They did the same to that Portuguese officer, didn't they? Drowned him over and over."

Reid glanced at her—his eyes meeting hers briefly—and then away. After a moment, he nodded.

"What was his name?"

For several seconds, she thought Reid wouldn't answer, and then he said, "Pereira."

"Was he a good soldier?"

"Yes."

Letty took a breath, and prayed that Reid would listen to her. "If Pereira had told the French what they wanted to know—and if he'd survived—would you have wished to see him hanged as a traitor? Or would you have thought that he'd already suffered past human endurance? That he'd already *died* several times, and that perhaps what he deserved most was forgiveness?"

156

Reid's face tightened. He turned his head even further from her. All she could see was the hard right angle of his jaw.

Letty bit the tip of her tongue against further arguments. Let him think it over. She nudged her horse into a trot.

CHAPTER 23

Letty held the bay at a slow pace. She wanted Reid to concentrate on what she'd said, not on his horse. At the folly, she dismounted. Lucas and Tom's horses were standing hip-shot and half-asleep.

She glanced at Reid. He was looking particularly grim. What was he thinking behind that shuttered expression?

"You never saw the secret passage, did you? It starts down here." Letty crossed to one of the crumbling stone buttresses. "See? This is actually a door." She leaned her weight against a block of stone. It pivoted, exposing a steep, narrow staircase. She looked back at Reid. "Come on. We don't need a lamp."

For a moment it seemed that Reid would refuse, and then his mouth tightened and he crossed to the doorway, ducked his head, and entered. His glance as he passed was like a slap. Dislike glittered in his eyes.

Letty found herself frozen, unable to follow him, almost unable to breathe. *He hates me.*

She pressed her hands to her cheeks and inhaled a shaky breath.

Above, Reid's boots scuffed on the stone steps.

Letty lowered her hands and blinked fiercely. She was *not* going to cry. She swung the door shut and set off up the staircase. It was almost as steep as a ladder. Daylight shone in from artistically placed gaps and—as they climbed higher—arrow slits.

These steps were steeper than those outside. It was exactly thirty-nine steps to the courtyard, and another twenty-one to the tower. Reid climbed all the way to the top, and halted. "How does this open?" There was no curiosity in his voice, no interest; just curtness.

"Press that stone there."

The door swung open with a faint, gritty whisper.

Letty followed Reid out into the roofless tower. The crumbling walls soared high, pierced by arrow slits and little arched windows. Pigeons had nested on some of the sills. The floor was speckled with bird lime.

Reid crossed to the farthest windows and stared out towards the downs. Letty looked at the set of his shoulders, the set of his head, and turned away from him. She walked to one of the arrow slits above the courtyard and pressed her hands to her cheeks again. Foolish tears welled in her eyes. She blinked, and blinked again.

Lucas and Tom were visible below, Tom at his easel, Lucas in the gothic archway, feet apart, legs braced, shoulders back, an old rapier in his hand. He looked ready to spring into battle.

Letty blinked again, and sniffed. She was *not* going to cry.

Tom laid down his paintbrush. He walked over and took Lucas's chin in his hand, tilted his head slightly—and kissed him.

Letty's breath choked in her throat. Tom was *kissing* Lucas?

She looked away, blinked several times—and looked back.

Lucas had dropped the sword. He was returning Tom's kiss with fervor.

Letty had to remember to breathe, to swallow. Her heart was beating fast with shock, with disbelief.

She turned away from the arrow slit, her mind almost blank with panic. She knew only one thing: Reid mustn't see Tom and Lucas kissing.

She crossed to where Reid stood, staring out at the downs, and tried to find her voice. "That's where we just were. See?" She pointed. "And over there, that single oak, they call that the gallows tree—not that anyone's ever been hanged there, but it *looks* like a gallows—and up on that hill are two standing stones. There are lots of standing stones in Wiltshire! There's a huge ring near Avebury, dozens of stones. And Stonehenge, of course. You've heard of Stonehenge?" She was babbling, the words spilling from her mouth. How long would Lucas and Tom kiss for? "Can you see the two standing stones on the hill? If you look hard, you might be able to make them out."

She left Reid at the window and hurried across to the arrow slit again. To her relief, Tom and Lucas were no longer kissing. Instead, Tom knelt in front of Lucas as if he was praying.

What were they doing?

Realization dawned. Tom was kissing Lucas down *there*.

Letty stared, transfixed with horror.

Lucas tipped his head back. His eyes were closed, his lips half-parted, an expression of pure bliss on his face.

Letty swallowed the lump in her throat and looked back at Reid. He was turning away from the window. She hurried across to him, feeling breathless with panic. "Let's go back down to the horses."

Reid put up his eyebrows. "But—"

"Tom's busy painting. We don't want to disturb him."

"But—"

"We don't want to disturb him!"

Reid's eyebrows arrowed together in sharp suspicion. He stepped past her.

Letty grabbed his wrist. "No."

Reid flexed his wrist and broke her hold. He crossed to the arrow slit in three swift strides and looked down—and froze.

Letty hastened after him. "Reid," she said in a desperate whisper, tugging at his arm. "Please."

Reid didn't try to break her hold again. He turned and practically bundled her back to the secret doorway. "Down," he said, his hand between her shoulder blades.

They descended the staircase in hasty silence. Letty's thoughts tumbled over themselves. Lucas and Tom? Tom and Lucas? At the bottom, she opened the door and stumbled out into daylight. The horses stood where they'd left them. Letty stared at them. Shock rang in her ears. Lucas and Tom?

Reid caught her by the shoulder. "You did *not* see that," he said fiercely.

Letty stared at him, unable to speak. Tom and Lucas?

"Do you hear me?" Reid shook her. "You did *not* see that. You are *not* going to tell anyone about it."

Letty swallowed. "Of course I won't tell anyone!"

Reid released her and turned away. He strode to her horse and cupped his hands. "Mount."

Letty obeyed, putting her boot in his hands, letting him fling her up into the saddle. Reid swung up onto his chestnut. He looked extraordinarily grim, grimmer than she'd yet seen him.

They rode from the folly at a quiet trot. When they'd gone a hundred yards, Reid picked up the pace, keeping them at a canter all the way to the avenue of oaks. There, he slowed again. Letty came up alongside him. "Mr. Reid . . ." Her voice dried in her throat. She had no words to express her confusion, her dismay.

Reid halted. "If you have any regard for Matlock and your cousin, you'll forget what you just saw."

Letty gazed at him. Shock still rang in her skull. "Are Lucas and Tom . . . ?" She swallowed. "Are they . . . ?" She couldn't bring herself to articulate the words.

"Matlock and your cousin are lovers," Reid said bluntly. "And if you tell anyone, you'll ruin them both."

"Of course I'm not going to tell anyone! I tried to stop *you* from finding out."

"So you did." Reid's expression relaxed fractionally. He gave a short nod.

Lucas and Tom were lovers? It seemed to Letty that the world had shifted on its axis, that everything had tilted sideways, that she was in danger of losing her balance.

"Their relationship is their private business and the best thing you can do—for them and for yourself!—is to forget what you saw." Reid's eyes held hers. "It didn't happen."

Letty swallowed, and found her voice. "It didn't happen."

Reid gave a curt nod, and nudged his horse into a trot.

Letty followed, feeling subdued and off-balance.

She didn't see Tom until evening. He entered the salon where the household gathered for dinner and made his way across to her. "Tish, m' love," he said cheerfully. "Did you have a good afternoon?"

"Yes," Letty lied. "I went riding with Mr. Reid. He asked me to pass on his regards; he's leaving Marlborough tomorrow."

"Leaving? I'm sorry to have missed him. A good man, Reid."

"Yes." Letty studied his face—an attractive, merry face. Tom Matlock. Earl's son, artist, soldier. Sodomite? She should feel revulsion, but she didn't. She *couldn't*. She loved Tom as much as she loved Lucas. Tom was family.

No, it wasn't revulsion she felt; it was worry. Reid had been correct: one word, and Tom and Lucas would be ruined. They could end up in gaol, or worse, hanged.

The gong rang for dinner. Soberly, Letty made her way into the dining room. Soberly, she sat. She found Lucas at the long table—almost opposite her—and Tom, three places down from her. She unfolded her napkin and laid it on her lap and watched Lucas look round and locate Tom. The two men exchanged a glance.

It was the tiniest glance, no more than a second or two, and yet it was as private and intimate as if they'd reached across the table and touched each other's fingertips.

Letty stared down at her lap. Her throat felt tight. She

swallowed, and smoothed a wrinkle in her napkin. She'd known Lucas and Tom since she was a child. How had she failed to see that they loved each other?

It wasn't until morning that Letty had a chance to speak with Lucas alone. She captured him in the breakfast parlor. "Come to the library; I need to talk with you."

"Sounds ominous," Lucas said. "Should I be worried?"

Letty closed the door and stood with her back to it, examining Lucas's face. "How are you?" she asked bluntly.

"Never been better!" Lucas gave her a cheerful grin, and strolled across to one of the tall windows.

Letty followed him. "Truthfully, Lucas. How are you?"

"Never better," he said firmly. "Do you think it will rain? I hope not. That painting's still not quite finished."

"Lucas, the *truth*."

Lucas glanced at her, his grin still fixed on his face. "I told you—"

"I can hear when you're lying."

Lucas's grin congealed into a grimace. He looked away, out the window. After a moment, he said, "So you can still do that trick?"

"Yes."

Lucas exhaled. The sound was almost a sigh.

Letty took his hand, interlacing their fingers. "Truthfully . . . how are you?"

Lucas was silent for a long time. "I've been better," he said finally. "But don't worry about me, Tish. It takes time, is all."

"Is there anything I can do to help?"

He gave her a sidelong glance and a wry, affectionate smile. "No. But thank you."

Letty bit her lip, and then said, "I'm glad Tom's back."

"So am I." Lucas looked out the window again.

"Does it help?"

"It helps a lot." Lucas gazed out at the bleak winter landscape. Letty saw his lips compress. "I think he's my savior," he said, almost sadly, and then he shrugged off his pensive mood and grinned and said, "Or perhaps my ruin." It was a joke—his flippant tone invited her to laugh—but her ears told her it *wasn't* a joke, that he spoke the utter and absolute truth.

Letty found herself unable to return Lucas's grin. She remembered the kisses she'd witnessed, remembered the intimate glance she'd observed at the dinner table. Theirs was a perilous relationship. One misstep and they *would* be each other's ruin.

Lucas lost his grin. "Tish, don't worry about me," he said firmly. "I'll be all right."

You need to be more careful, she wanted to tell him. *Someone might find out.*

Letty bit the tip of her tongue, holding the words back. She nodded, as if she believed him, and released Lucas's hand.

Lucas took this as a signal the conversation was over. He turned away from the window. "When are you leaving?"

"At ten."

"I'm going to Cornwall next month." He crossed the library and held the door open for her. "Tom hasn't seen Pendarve yet."

Letty halted in the doorway.

Lucas raised his eyebrows. "Tish?"

"I love you," Letty told him. "And if there's ever anything I can do for you—*anything*—I hope you will tell me."

"Of course I will," Lucas said. "Honestly, Tish, don't worry about me."

Letty hugged him, burying her face in his shoulder for a brief moment, then stepped back. "Be careful!" she said fiercely.

Lucas blinked. "I'm always careful." He looked at her, and his brow creased quizzically. "Tish? What's this about?"

I know about you and Tom, she almost blurted.

"Nothing. Good-bye!" She smiled brightly and left Lucas standing in the doorway, a puzzled expression on his face.

CHAPTER 24

November 19th, 1808
Bristol

$\mathcal{T}$hey reached Bristol shortly after dusk. The Swan was a larger establishment than the Plough, and considerably smarter. The bedchambers were well-appointed, the private parlor tasteful rather than cozy, and the meal laid on the table included not only soup, a roasted chicken, and a vegetable pudding, but a dish of tongue with red currant sauce, and a syllabub.

Letty sat and surveyed the food spread before them, and then lifted her gaze to Reid's face. He was examining the meal, his expression impassive. After a moment, he looked up.

In Basingstoke, and during those first days at Whiteoaks, she'd thought she and Reid had almost become friends. The incident at the stream and its aftermath yesterday had altered that. A huge gulf seemed to have grown between them. Reid's eyes held a warning, as did the set of his jaw. He would not tolerate further discussion of Vimeiro, the creek, the drownings, or his intention to die.

Letty looked down at her plate. He needn't worry. She wasn't going to repeat herself.

They ate silently. She hoped he was mulling over what she'd said on the downs, hoped the words had burrowed into his brain, hoped they were making him *think*.

"How do we locate Houghton?" she said, when they'd finished eating.

"He'll be receiving an out-pension from Chelsea Hospital. That's a parish matter."

"How many parishes are there in Bristol?"

"At least a dozen, I should think."

The landlord, when applied to, was able to sketch a rough map of Bristol and mark thirteen parishes. "There are more, but I can't bring 'em to mind just now," he said apologetically.

Letty studied the sketch. "Which ones might I visit without my husband, and which are in neighborhoods that are . . . insalubrious?"

The landlord scratched his bald pate, and then leaned over the sheet of paper again. "You'd be quite safe to visit these, ma'am," he said, jotting down the names of four parishes in the bottommost corner, and then, after a moment's thought, a fifth.

"We'll be faster if we split up," Letty said, when the landlord had gone. "I shall inquire after Sergeant Houghton at these parishes; they're perfectly respectable." She tapped the five jotted names with a fingertip.

Reid frowned. "Bristol is a city neither of us is familiar with. It seems unwise for you to venture out alone."

"I won't be alone. Eliza will accompany me."

Reid examined the sketch. He looked extremely weary. Had he slept last night at all? "It's not safe."

"If you can explore behind enemy lines, then I can surely visit a few churches in an English city," Letty said tartly.

He glanced at her.

"I'll visit these five, and no more. I won't take any risks. I shall be a pattern card of prudence and caution."

"If you're certain . . ."

"I am." Letty tore off the corner and folded the list in half.

A flicker of relief crossed Reid's face. Relief that their search would be prosecuted more swiftly? Or relief that he wouldn't have her company tomorrow?

The latter, probably.

Letty looked down at the table, blinked several times, looked up and smiled. "That's settled, then," she said briskly. "If you'll excuse me, I think I'll turn in. Good night, Mr. Reid."

Again, she saw relief on his face.

Letty climbed the stairs, clutching the folded list, blinking back tears. Damn Reid. How could he make her cry so easily? She opened the door to her bedchamber. Eliza was there, laying out her nightgown. Candles burned in the sconces and on the bedside table, and a fire burned merrily in the grate.

Letty summoned a smile. "How cheerful this looks."

Eliza helped her out of her gown, unlaced her stays, fetched warm water for her to wash her face and a hot brick for the bed. "I like how your hair is done," she said shyly, when Letty sat on the stool to have her hair brushed out. "It's so pretty like this, with the braided bun. It looks . . . it looks *regal*."

Letty found herself laughing. "Regal?" She glanced at herself in the mirror, and sobered. Not regal, and definitely not pretty. An ordinary face. A spinster's face, or perhaps the face of a governess. Plain and sensible and matter-of-fact. Not a face a man would fall in love with.

The urge to cry came again. Letty blinked several times. "Ringlets don't suit me," she said brusquely.

"I wish I could dress your hair like this," Eliza said, unpinning the bun.

"Practice, if you wish."

For the next half hour, Eliza did just that. Her fingers tugged and twisted, she created a braided bun, and then a Psyche knot with braids wound around it. Finally, she brushed out Letty's hair and replaited it into one single braid. "Is there anything else, ma'am?"

"No, thank you."

Reid's bedchamber wasn't next to hers, but across the corridor, a circumstance that worried Letty. Would she hear him if he cried out in the night?

It worried her so much that she found herself unable to sleep. She lay in the dark, the bedclothes pulled up to her chin, her ears straining for the slightest sound. She heard the distant clatter of carriage wheels on cobblestones, heard faint, faraway voices, heard the creak of floorboards in the corridor, heard embers shift in the fireplace.

An hour passed, and a second hour, and she was still awake, still worrying, still straining to hear. Finally, Letty climbed out of bed, unlatched her door, and propped it open with her stool.

It seemed that she'd only just crawled back into bed when the sound she'd been waiting for came: a faint, barely-heard cry of distress.

Letty sat bolt upright. Reid was drowning again.

She threw back the bedclothes and groped for her tinder-box. Candle. Slippers. Shawl.

At Reid's door, she hesitated—would he *want* her help tonight?—and then the choked-off scream came again. Letty shoved open his door. Whether Reid wanted her help or not, he was getting it.

She strode to the bed, grabbed Reid's shoulder, and shook it hard. "Icarus! Wake up!"

Reid jolted awake.

Letty stepped back as he lunged up from the pillow, his eyes wild, the berserker fury on his face. "Icarus! *Stop*."

Reid's head jerked back. He blinked, his expression confused—and then understanding flooded his face. He groaned and bowed his head, pressing the heels of his hands to his eyes.

Letty wanted to slip an arm around his shoulders and hug

him; instead she busied herself with the brandy. The bottle stood on Reid's dressing table, along with a glass and a teaspoon and the vial of valerian. She blessed Green silently, and poured a generous glass.

Reid was still sitting hunched over, head bowed, hands to his eyes. His breathing was ragged. Letty laid her hand on the nape of his neck for a moment, offering silent comfort. "Here," she said. "Brandy."

Reid lowered his hands. He didn't look at her. He took the glass wordlessly.

Letty closed both their doors while he sipped the brandy, and then looked through the books by his bed. It appeared that he'd finished *The Odyssey* and started on Herodotus's *Histories*—which told her how little he'd slept the past week.

She kept an eye on Reid. When he'd finished the brandy, she poured a teaspoon of valerian. Again, Reid accepted it wordlessly. She tried to read his expression. Exhaustion, she decided. Physical and emotional exhaustion.

"Lie down," she said. "I'll read for a bit."

"You don't have to."

"I know you dislike me," Letty said brusquely. "And that you wish me to Jericho, but I'm reading to you—whether you want me to or not!"

Reid's gaze shifted fractionally, his eyes met hers for a brief moment, and then he looked away again. He lay back on his pillows.

Letty sat cross-legged on the very end of his bed. She opened the book to the page Reid had marked and started reading aloud. She concentrated on the text, not on Reid, concentrated on keeping her voice low and calm and not letting any trace of emotion color her tone. She didn't glance up when she turned that page, or the next one. It wasn't until she reached the history of Periander of Corinth that she paused and lifted her gaze from the book. Reid was watching her, his eyes heavy-lidded, drowsy.

Letty looked back down at the page. Names caught her eye: *Procles, Lycophron.*

"I don't dislike you," Reid said.

Letty glanced up. "I beg your pardon?"

"I don't dislike you. You make me angry, but I don't dislike you."

Letty's throat closed. She looked back down at the book, and blinked several times.

"I know you're trying to help, but I wish you wouldn't." Reid spoke slowly—half-drunk, half-drugged, close to sleep. "I'm dead already, don't y' see? Been dead for months."

The words were terrible in themselves, but what was far more terrible was the clear bell-tone of truth in them. Reid truly believed he was dead.

Letty's gaze jerked to his face. His eyes were fully closed.

"You're not dead!" she said sharply, closing the book with a snap. "Do you hear me, Icarus Reid? You're *not* dead." She scrambled down from the foot of his bed and went to lean over him like the nursemaid he'd accused her of being. "You're only dead if you *think* you are. It's in your head! Do you hear me?" She took his shoulder and shook it hard.

Reid's eyelids lifted. His silver eyes were drowsy and dilated. He focused slowly on her. A tiny frown creased his brow. "Don' cry."

Letty discovered that she was, tears spilling fast and hot from her eyes. "Damn you, Icarus Reid. You are *not* dead!" And she leaned down and kissed him, trying to force the words into him. "You're not! You're *not*!"

Reid's hand rose and gripped her arm as if to push her away—and then his fingers relaxed, and his mouth relaxed, too, and he kissed her back.

Letty had never kissed a man properly before. She didn't know *how* to kiss a man properly, but somehow that was irrelevant. She pressed her mouth urgently to Reid's, tears running down her face. He was *not* dead. He was *not*.

"Don' cry," Reid murmured again. His arm slid around her, pulling her close.

The frantic grief subsided. In its place was shyness. Shyness, and a growing sense of wonder. Icarus Reid was *kissing* her.

His lips parted. He tasted her lips with the tip of his tongue.

The tears stopped flowing so swiftly. Letty sniffed, and caught her breath on a sharp hitch.

"Don' cry," Reid murmured again and gathered her even closer, so that she lay nestled against him. He touched her lips with his tongue again.

Letty kissed him back as best she could, mimicking him. Reid tasted of brandy and the salt of her tears. She parted her lips to his questing tongue, and shivered with pleasure.

Reid's mouth was slow and sleepy and warm. And perfect. More perfect than she had ever imagined any mouth could be. Lips, tongue, teeth. All perfect.

They kissed for long minutes, unhurriedly, leisurely. Letty felt Reid's breath feather over her cheek, felt the heat of his arm around her, felt the warm solidity of his body beneath the bedclothes.

The kiss became even slower, even more leisurely. Letty finally drew back. "Go to sleep," she whispered.

Reid was almost already there, his eyes closed, his arm slack around her. He muttered something in his throat.

"Sleep," Letty whispered again.

She doubted he heard her. He was utterly relaxed, no tension in his body, no tension on his face.

Letty lay quietly, drinking in the sensations: the warmth of his arm around her, the soft sound of his breathing, the brandy-and-tears taste in her mouth, the smell of clean linen and sandalwood soap and fresh male sweat. She touched his jaw with a light fingertip, felt the heat of his skin and prickle of his stubble. Icarus Reid.

His breathing was deep and low and regular. He was asleep.

Letty carefully extricated herself from his half-embrace. She climbed off his bed, pulled the covers up around his throat, bent and pressed her lips to his cheek, and tiptoed from the room.

*C*HAPTER 25

November 20th, 1808
Bristol

*I*carus drifted awake. He blinked his eyes drowsily open, saw a bedchamber and faint light creeping through chintz curtains, and closed his eyelids again, sinking back into warm, lingering contentment, sliding back towards sleep. The sound of his door quietly opening caught his attention.

Icarus reluctantly opened his eyes again.

Green peered around the door. The young man's face lit up. He advanced into the room, a steaming ewer in his hands. "You're awake, sir!"

Regretfully, Icarus abandoned thought of sleeping again. He levered himself up to sitting, and yawned. He felt deliciously relaxed, deliciously rested. He rubbed his face, raked his hands through his hair, yawned again. "What time is it?"

"Half past eleven, sir," Green said, putting down the ewer and drawing open the curtains.

"Half past eleven?"

Green grinned, an expression almost of pride on his face. "You slept the clock round, sir."

"Half past *eleven*?" Icarus repeated foolishly, his brain still half-asleep.

"Mrs. Reid said not to wake you. And she said to tell you that she's gone visiting some churches, and she'll be back for luncheon at one, and she's ordered breakfast for you, and it's eggs and sirloin, and you're to eat *all* of it." Green said this all in a rush, with an expression on his face that made Icarus think of a puppy wagging its tail, eager to please.

Eggs and sirloin? All of it? Icarus tried to feel annoyed by this high-handedness, but all he felt was hungry. Green was still looking at him with that eager-puppy expression. Clearly a response was required. "Very good," Icarus said.

Green grinned again, and busied himself at the washstand, laying out Icarus's razor and a towel, pouring hot water into the bowl. "Would you like some tea, sir? I can fetch a pot right up."

What he most needed was to pee. "Yes, thank you," Icarus said.

He pissed in the chamber pot while Green was gone, and placed it back under the bed. The brandy bottle caught his eye. Memory surged back. Miss Trentham sitting cross-legged on the end of his bed, the taste of brandy on his tongue, the sound of her voice, cool and melodic, easing him towards sleep.

The surge of memory rolled over him like a tidal wave: he'd told her he was already dead, and she'd cried, and he'd kissed her.

Icarus halted, barefoot on the rug.

He'd made Miss Trentham cry? He'd kissed her?

He shook his head sharply and advanced to the washstand. That wasn't memory; it was a dream. Of *course* he hadn't kissed her. But even as he washed his hands, he knew he was lying to himself. Miss Trentham had definitely cried last night, and he had definitely kissed her. Kissed her for a long time. Kissed her until he'd fallen asleep.

Icarus found himself reluctant to face Miss Trentham over luncheon. He washed and shaved quickly, went down to the private parlor and ate three eggs and a piece of sirloin, and took the stairs two at a time back to his room, where he shrugged into his greatcoat and tucked the landlord's map into a pocket. He pulled on his gloves and set his hat on his head. "Mrs. Reid will be back shortly," Green said, observing these signs of imminent departure.

"Tell her I'm sorry to have missed her, but I have some business I must attend to." Miss Trentham would have heard the lie in his words, but Green didn't. "I'll see her this evening at dinner."

He hastened down the stairs and out into the street, telling himself that he was *not* fleeing—but he knew this for self-deception. He *was* fleeing. He didn't feel remotely up to facing Miss Trentham. How on earth was he going to look her in the eye? He'd *kissed* her, for Christ's sake! And not just a peck on the cheek. A thoroughly intimate kiss, his tongue in her mouth.

Icarus winced. How had he forgotten himself so far as to do that? It was beyond improper!

He hurried off, his gaze fixed on the grimy cobblestones. If Miss Trentham was coming along the street, he didn't want to see her.

He hailed a hackney and chose a parish at random. By the time he discovered the churchwarden's name, located the man, and ascertained that Sergeant Houghton wasn't one of the parish's pensioners, it was nearly two o'clock. He visited three

175

more parish churches, with similar lack of results. At dusk, he gave up and walked wearily back to the Swan. Coalsmoke was acrid in his mouth. A light drizzle fell. He turned up his collar and hunched his shoulders. A hackney clattered past, but Icarus ignored it. He was in no hurry to return to the Swan, and in no hurry *at all* to dine with Miss Trentham. Lord, how was he going to meet her eyes? What on earth was he going to say to her?

An apology was clearly required.

Icarus spent the next twenty minutes trying to come up with one. The trouble was, they were all so damned stilted and awkward and—if he wasn't careful—obliquely insulting to Miss Trentham. And on top of that, whatever he said had to be *truthful*.

He settled on a beginning—*I apologize for my lapse of good manners last night*—and an end—*I give you my word of honor it won't happen again*—but the middle eluded him.

His steps slowed when he neared the Swan. The cobblestones were slick with moisture and slightly slippery. At the corner, Icarus halted and gazed across at the inn. He was nervous, and that realization annoyed him. He was thirty years old, for Christ's sake. It was *absurd* to be put out of countenance by a kiss.

He crossed the street briskly. He'd made a mountain out of a molehill. It was quite simple: go in, meet her eyes, apologize. His apology didn't need to be grandiloquent. It didn't need a flowery middle. A beginning and an end were fine. *I apologize for my lapse of good manners last night. I give you my word of honor it won't happen again.* Short and simple. And then they could go back to how things had been.

Even so, he was extremely relieved not to meet Miss Trentham on the staircase, and equally relieved to find the door to her bedchamber closed. Icarus gave Green his hat and greatcoat to dry, washed his hands and face, tied a fresh neckcloth, and went reluctantly down to the private parlor. He took a deep breath, and opened the door.

Letty lifted her gaze from her book. *Don't blush,* she told herself sternly. She closed the book and put it aside, trying to look calm, but she wasn't calm at all. Her heart was beating far too fast and her lungs seemed to be half the size they normally were.

Icarus Reid had *kissed* her last night.

Reid shut the door. She thought his cheeks colored faintly beneath his tan, and realized that he was just as embarrassed as she was.

That realization gave Letty a little courage. She found a smile. "Good evening, Mr. Reid."

"I apologize for my lapse of good manners last night," Reid said, and his cheeks definitely *did* color. "I give you my word it won't happen again."

Letty's smile faded. Reid regretted kissing her. Of *course* he regretted kissing her. She was no beauty. How could she have thought that he wouldn't regret it?

A tight, nauseous feeling grew in her belly. *Make a joke of this,* she told herself. *Don't let him see you're upset.*

"What a shame." Her voice was light and amused. "I had quite hoped it would." The truth, spoken as if it was a jest, as if his kiss hadn't been the most important thing to ever happen to her.

"Of course not!" Reid said. "It would be grossly improper and . . . and *wrong.* Your reputation—"

"My reputation?" What that was this was about? "Mr. Reid, if we're discovered traveling in each other's company, my reputation will be worth no more than a ha'penny. Less, probably!"

Reid grimaced, and didn't dispute this truth.

Letty tried to read his face. Did he want to kiss her again, or not?

She hadn't the courage to ask him directly so instead she

said, in as careless a tone as she could manage, "And if we're not discovered, then it doesn't matter what we do, does it?"

CHAPTER 26

"$\mathcal{I}$t's not honorable," Icarus said lamely, and even as the words left his mouth, he heard how hypocritical they were. Taking Miss Trentham to Marshalsea hadn't been honorable. Taking her to Basingstoke hadn't been honorable. And bringing her to Bristol certainly wasn't either. In fact, nothing he'd done had been honorable.

He looked down at the floor. He'd had honor once.

Miss Trentham rose from her chair and came to stand in front of him, not too close, just out of arm's reach. "The only reason not to do it again would be if one or the other of us doesn't wish to."

Icarus reluctantly met her eyes. He'd thought they were sea-green, but he'd been wrong; they were blue, almost the same shade as her gown.

"For my part, I would be happy to do it again. But if you don't wish to, I perfectly understand." Miss Trentham's tone was almost offhand, and there was a faint, ironic smile on her face, as if she was inviting him to laugh *with* her and *at* her at the same time.

Icarus stared at her, unable to think of a response, and while he was staring at her he became aware of just how much effort it was taking her to stand there looking cool and unflustered and amused, because she wasn't cool and unflustered and amused, it was a mask, and underneath it she was far more nervous than he was.

And with that insight came a second one: Miss Trentham would make a droll joke when he turned her down, be poised and confident and unconcerned, but that would be a mask, too, and beneath it she'd be hurting, because she was cursed with a fortune and a face that wasn't pretty and no man had ever wanted to kiss her for herself before.

It suddenly became even more important to find the right words. But what? What could he possibly say?

An honorable man would gently tell her that he couldn't kiss her again because it was wrong, and it would be the truth.

A kind man would tell her something different.

Icarus swallowed, and found his voice. "I wouldn't mind either."

Two waiters laid a substantial repast on the table—Icarus counted seven different dishes—and departed. "Did you have any luck finding Houghton?" Miss Trentham asked, unfolding her napkin.

"No. You?"

She shook her head.

They ate in near-silence. Icarus was aware of a self-conscious awkwardness between them. She'd admitted she wanted to kiss him. He'd admitted he wanted to kiss her. Where did they go from there? He served himself at random. It wasn't until he'd finished, that he realized how much he'd eaten. He looked at his empty plate with astonishment.

"Would you like some ratafia pudding?" Miss Trentham asked.

Icarus glanced at the pudding, opened his mouth to say *No,* and realized it was a lie. "A very little."

The ratafia pudding was extremely tasty. Icarus ate more than a little. Finally, he forced himself to put down his spoon and push his bowl away.

Without the business of eating and the faint clatter of cutlery, his awareness of Miss Trentham increased. Annoyingly, so did his self-consciousness. He was *thirty*, for crying out loud. Well past the age of self-consciousness.

Icarus reached into his pocket, took out the sketched map, unfolded it, and laid it on the table. "I went to these four," he said, matter-of-fact and businesslike. "And you visited all five on that list?"

Miss Trentham nodded.

"Which leaves us with four more. Plus any the landlord forgot."

"Then we should find Houghton tomorrow."

"With luck." Icarus studied the map for a moment, then glanced at her. "Do you wish to accompany me tomorrow, or wait until we know which parish he's in?"

"What would you prefer?"

Icarus hesitated, and wished that Miss Trentham's ear for falsehoods wasn't quite so infallible. "I would be glad of your company," he admitted.

Miss Trentham looked down at the table. Perhaps it was the candlelight, but he thought that faint color rose in her cheeks. "Will it be safe?"

"With me? Yes. And if for some reason I think it's not, I'll bring you back here immediately. You have my word on that."

Miss Trentham bit her lip, and glanced at him. "Then I shall accompany you."

"Good." Icarus refolded the map and placed it back in his pocket. That business sorted, the rest of the evening loomed before him. What did Miss Trentham expect of him?

Nothing, it appeared. She was pushing back her chair and bidding him good night.

Icarus stood politely. "Good night." He watched Miss Trentham leave the parlor with a strong sense of relief— and a faint pang of opportunity lost.

CHAPTER 27

$\mathcal{H}$is arms were bound tightly behind him. Someone knelt on his back. His face touched the surface of the creek. With each wheezing, desperate breath, he sucked a little water into his mouth. Iron-hard fingers gripped his hair, digging into his scalp. "C'est vrai?" a voice asked in his ear. "Dis-moi! Tell me!"

Icarus squeezed his eyes shut, and wheezed for air. His throat was raw from vomiting. His lungs ached.

"Dis-moi!" the voice said again, and the fingers clenched even tighter in his hair, pressing his head lower. Each inhalation was now half water, half air. His panic grew until he could barely breathe. Hot tears squeezed from beneath his eyelids.

His captor ruthlessly thrust his head under water. Icarus bucked and thrashed and tried to dislodge the man on his back, tried to tear his head free, tried not to breathe—but eventually came the moment when he *had* to breathe, sooner this time than the last time, and the water rushed into his mouth, down his throat, into his lungs—

"Icarus!"

Icarus lunged up into wakefulness, flailing out with arms that were suddenly free. He was half out of the bed, his heart beating a thousand times a second, when he recognized the figure standing before him. Miss Trentham in her nightgown. Full awareness flooded him with the suddenness of a blow to the head: he wasn't at Vimeiro. For a moment, he stood stunned, and then half-collapsed back on the bed. Every muscle in his body trembled violently. His lungs were laboring, not quite believing they could get enough air. The urge to vomit was strong.

He scrubbed his face with shaking hands while Miss Trentham busied herself with the brandy. The bottle clinked faintly against the rim of the glass. Icarus closed his eyes and tried to calm his breathing—there *was* enough air, even if it didn't feel like it.

"Here," Miss Trentham said.

Icarus opened his eyes. She was holding a very full glass of brandy.

He sipped while she rearranged his pillows. Small, cautious sips, partly because he could barely hold the glass steady, partly because his breathing was still jerky.

"Sit back," Miss Trentham said.

Obediently, Icarus did.

Miss Trentham smiled crookedly at him, and smoothed his hair back from his brow, and turned away.

The brandy was warm in his mouth, warm in his throat, warm in his belly, and he wanted to keep sipping until the glass was empty—but memory of what had happened last night between himself and Miss Trentham was vivid.

Icarus lowered the glass and tried to think, before he drank too much.

His first thought was that he should send her from his room, now. His second was that he wanted to kiss her again. His third was that *she* wanted to kiss *him*.

Icarus stared down at the brandy, trying to decide what to do.

It would be selfish of him to kiss her. Selfish and dishonorable. But everything he'd done in the past three weeks had been selfish and dishonorable. He was using Miss Trentham, allowing her to risk her reputation in pursuit of his traitor, and he was giving her nothing in return, absolutely nothing, because he had nothing to give her, not a husband's protection, not his heart, nothing. Except perhaps this. A kiss.

Did it make it right that he didn't only want to kiss her for himself? That he wanted to kiss her because she *deserved* to be kissed? Because it was the one thing he could give her?

Of course it didn't.

Icarus looked at his reflection in the brandy and felt ashamed of himself, and then he looked at Miss Trentham and the shame was superseded by an emotion almost like longing. He wanted her to stay with him. Wanted her to sit on his bed and read to him. Kiss him. Come to Exeter with him. Be with him during the last few weeks he had on this earth.

He took another sip of brandy, felt it slide down his throat, warm and potent and relaxing, and it was tempting to keep sipping until the very last drop was gone—but he resolutely handed the glass back to Miss Trentham.

"Don't you want it?"

Yes, he did; and no, he didn't. Icarus selected his answer with care. "I don't wish to drink too much tonight."

Miss Trentham nodded. She'd heard the truth in his words. She poured him a teaspoonful of valerian.

Icarus swallowed it.

She rearranged his pillows, fetched Herodotus, and perched herself on the end of his bed.

Icarus relaxed back against the pillows.

Miss Trentham opened the book and found her place. "At length, when the time came for parting, Procles . . ."

It was her voice he liked. Low and musical. She made Herodotus sound like poetry. Icarus listened without paying any attention to the words. His eyelids grew heavy. After some time, he became aware that Miss Trentham had stopped reading. He blinked his eyes open. She was still sitting on the end of his bed, but her gaze was on him, not the book.

"You're almost asleep, aren't you?" Miss Trentham put

Herodotus aside, and climbed down from the bed and came quietly to stand alongside him. She reached out and smoothed his hair, and then bent and kissed him lightly, pressing her mouth to his.

Icarus remembered her lips from last night. Warm and soft and wonderfully responsive. He made a low murmur of pleasure in his throat and reached for her, drawing her closer.

They kissed. And kissed some more. And then some more. And somehow she ended up lying on the bed with him, and his arms were around her, and his tongue was in her mouth, and he was kissing her. Deep, slow, sleepy kisses. Comforting kisses. Kisses that made him feel warm and safe and happy in a way he hadn't felt for a very long time.

Icarus didn't remember falling asleep, but it must have happened, because he woke in a vaguely familiar room with the sense of having slept for a long time. Daylight leaked through the chintz curtains. His bladder told him it was late morning.

He stretched and yawned and rubbed his face, and climbed out of bed and attended to his bladder. Then he opened the curtains and leaned his hands on the windowsill and gazed out at Bristol, gray and hazy with coalsmoke. He felt rested, and hungry, and oddly content.

He ate a late breakfast of eggs and sirloin, and set out with Miss Trentham to visit the final four parishes. There was no self-consciousness between them today, just a feeling of comfortable familiarity and something that was almost friendship.

The search went more quickly than yesterday, but none of the churchwardens knew of Houghton. They were, however, able to supply him with the names of the three Bristol parishes the landlord had forgotten. It was almost dusk by the time the hackney coach drew up outside the third and final church.

The churchwarden was in the vestry, preparing for evening prayer. "Sergeant Houghton? No, can't say as I've ever heard of him, sir."

"He's a Chelsea Hospital out-pensioner," Icarus explained, for the seventh time that day. "Lost an arm in Portugal three months ago."

"Only a few pensions from Chelsea come through here, and none of them are your sergeant. Have you tried the other parishes?" The churchwarden was a colorless man, with mild, earnest blue eyes.

"All of them. You're the last." Icarus raked a hand through his hair in frustration. "He's from Bristol."

"Which parishes have you tried?" the warden asked helpfully. "Perhaps you missed one."

Icarus handed him the sketched map and explained where they'd been. The churchwarden pursed his lips. "There are a few outlying parishes you could try, sir. And then there's Bedminster and Horfield and Westbury, which aren't Bristol of course, but most people think of them as such." He cocked his head. "Shall I write the names down for you?"

"Please."

They followed the churchwarden into his small, cluttered office. Icarus examined the furnishings while the man found a quill and sheet of paper. The carpet was worn almost through and the curtains had faded to an indeterminate gray. Not a wealthy parish, this.

The churchwarden blotted his list, folded it, and held it out. "Failing these, I suggest you write to Chelsea Hospital, sir, to find out where they're sending the sergeant's out-pension."

"I'll do that," Icarus said, tucking the list into his waistcoat pocket. "Thank you. We're much obliged to you." He pulled out his pocketbook and extracted a five-pound note.

"Oh," the man said, his cheeks flushing faintly at the sight of such largess. "Thank you! That will go to good use, sir. Very good use!"

Outside, Icarus stood for a moment. Frustration fermented in his chest. He'd *been* in London; why the devil hadn't he thought to visit Chelsea Hospital and furnish himself with Houghton's direction?

He expelled a sharp breath, and looked round for a hackney. Dusk was falling rapidly. The evening worshippers would soon be arriving.

"Spare a penny for a wounded soldier?"

Icarus glanced to his right. There, leaning on a crutch, was a grimy young man. "Soldier?"

"Twenty-eighth Foot." The man shuffled forward, hobbling awkwardly. "Hamstrung at Alexandria."

"Hamstrung?" Icarus grimaced. He'd seen men hamstrung in battle, and horses. He felt for his pocketbook—and was arrested by a light touch on his arm. Miss Trentham.

He glanced at her, and saw her shake her head.

Icarus slid the pocketbook back into place. "Not hamstrung?"

"And not a soldier."

Icarus turned back to the beggar. His pity metamorphosed into disgust. He wanted to pick the man up by his collar and shake him like a terrier shaking a rat. "The fellows of the Twenty-eighth would give you a good thrashing if they knew your game. Since they're not here, seems I should do it for them." He took a step towards the beggar.

The man turned and ran, pelting down the darkening street, legs pumping frantically, crutch tucked under one arm.

Icarus halted. *Definitely* not hamstrung.

His disgust died as abruptly as a candle being snuffed. Not hamstrung, and not an ex-soldier, but undoubtedly poor, undoubtedly hungry, and undoubtedly in need of a few pennies. He sighed, and turned back to Miss Trentham.

She was watching him, her expression neutral, neither condemning nor approving.

Shame heated Icarus's face. "I beg your pardon." To offer violence to a beggar—in *front* of her. "I wouldn't have hit him."

"I know." Her smile was small and wry and sympathetic, and made him feel even worse.

He hailed a hackney, handed Miss Trentham into it, and sat on the lumpy squab seat beside her, sunk in unwelcome thought. He was turning into someone he didn't recognize. Someone he didn't like.

Behind them, he heard church bells begin to ring, calling parishioners to evening prayer.

"I'm sorry," he said.

"It's all right, Icarus." Miss Trentham slipped her hand into his.

Icarus held on to it and allowed himself to feel slightly comforted, even though he knew he didn't deserve it.

CHAPTER 28

"We'll give Bristol one more day," Icarus said, when they'd finished dining. "If we don't find Houghton tomorrow, we'll head down to Exeter." Which he didn't want to do. Exeter was so damned far from London.

"You said you don't think it was Houghton."

"No," Icarus admitted, fiddling with his napkin. "Houghton was a good soldier. I liked him." He folded the napkin in half, and then in half again. "I didn't like Cuthbertson."

"Why not?"

"Why not?" Icarus shoved the napkin aside. Cuthbertson had been like a bitch in heat, always swaggering past on the way to a sexual liaison or just back from one—and ready to boast of it. *On my way to take a flourish,* he'd say with a wink. Or, *Just had myself a buttered bun.* "He, ah . . . was rather too much given to gallantry for my taste."

"Gallantry?" Her eyebrows rose. "You mean he was a philanderer?"

Icarus nodded.

Miss Trentham's eyebrows rose even higher. "You mean . . . with other soldiers?"

"Lord, no!" Icarus said. "There are camp followers and, um, local . . . uh, women."

Miss Trentham's eyes narrowed. Her head tilted to one side. "You mean prostitutes?"

Icarus found his napkin again. "Yes." He folded it into quarters, unfolded it, pushed it aside. How had they got onto this subject? "Houghton was an excellent sergeant. Tough, but fair. The men respected him."

Miss Trentham accepted this change of topic. "Is he quite old?"

Icarus shrugged. "My age, or thereabouts."

"Oh." She looked faintly surprised. Had she been expecting a grizzled sergeant with salt-and-pepper whiskers?

"It's a great shame he lost his arm. To my mind, he would have made a good officer."

"Can an enlisted man become an officer?"

"An officer can be raised from the ranks." Icarus brought out the churchwarden's list and unfolded it. "I'd like to find him." He pondered the list for several minutes, and looked up to find Miss Trentham watching him. She was wearing a gown in a soft shade of slate gray. Her eyes were gray, too. Icarus frowned. Hadn't they been blue yesterday?

Miss Trentham smiled at him. "We'll find Houghton." And then she pushed back her chair and bade him good night.

The next time he saw Miss Trentham, she was in her nightgown, standing in the middle of his bedchamber. Icarus stared at her blankly, wheezing for breath. What? Where? And then the fog of nightmare lifted from his brain.

He heard himself groan, and closed his eyes and lay back on the pillows, trying to catch his breath. After a moment, he realized his face was wet with tears. He wiped them clumsily away.

"Here."

Icarus sat up slowly and accepted the brandy. She'd given him less tonight; the glass was only half full.

Miss Trentham plumped his pillows. "Sit back."

He did, and sipped. Blessed brandy.

Miss Trentham sat beside him on the bed, not saying anything, a quiet and comforting presence. When he'd drunk half the brandy, he handed the glass back to her. She took it without a word, and gave him a teaspoon of valerian. "Must be close to finishing that." His voice sounded hoarse.

"Yes. I'll send Green to buy some more."

Icarus swallowed the valerian. He'd become used to the bitter taste, welcomed it almost.

Miss Trentham took away the spoon and rearranged his pillows again. Icarus lay back. She returned to the bed, book in hand, but tonight she didn't sit at the very end; she sat beside him, opened the book, and found her place. "The Siphnians at that time were at the height of their greatness . . ."

It felt cozy having her beside him. Icarus listened to her voice and let his thoughts drift. He shouldn't kiss her tonight, he really shouldn't. But he knew he would—if she offered— because when she kissed him he felt warm and safe and happy, and he needed that feeling too much to turn her down.

His eyelids lowered. He drifted on the sound of Miss Trentham's cool, melodic voice, drifted until her fingers lightly touched his cheek and she said, "You're almost asleep, aren't you?"

Icarus opened his eyes. He freed one arm from his sheets and reached for her, needing to kiss her.

Miss Trentham leaned close and laid her lips on his.

Icarus sighed with pleasure.

They kissed leisurely, unhurriedly, their mouths matching as perfectly as their steps had when they'd danced. Icarus stopped thinking. There was no reason to think. No reason at all. He kissed Miss Trentham's mouth, her jaw, kissed down her throat to the neckline of her nightgown. A dim, half-heard note of caution sounded at the back of his brain. It was dangerous to kiss a woman's throat. Kissing a woman's throat led to kissing her in other places.

Icarus found Miss Trentham's mouth again and kissed her slowly and sleepily, drifting in a cozy, shadowy place where everything was sensation and pleasure and instinct.

He drifted in this place for some time, sinking closer and closer to sleep. After a while, he became aware that Miss Trentham had stopped kissing his mouth and was kissing his throat instead.

His eyes slowly opened. "You shouldn't—"

"Shush," she whispered

He should stop her, but it felt too good, marvelously good—soft lips exploring his throat, a warm tongue tasting his skin. It made his blood hum faintly.

In another time and place that hum would have pushed him towards wakefulness and arousal, but here and now it was comforting, deeply and profoundly comforting, because it made him feel alive and it made him feel loved, even though he knew he was neither of those things.

Icarus closed his eyes again and let himself drift, cocooned in warmth and safety and happiness.

The next time he opened his eyes, it was daylight. Someone was moving quietly, making up the fire.

He propped himself on one elbow and watched Green adroitly coax the coals into flame. "What time is it?"

"Ten o'clock, sir." Green stood and began laying out Icarus's shaving tackle. "Mrs. Reid apologizes for waking you, but she says there's quite a distance to cover today."

Icarus scrubbed his hands through his hair and yawned. "She's right." He climbed out of bed.

A quick wash, a quick shave, three eggs and sirloin, and

they were off. "North or south?" Icarus asked Miss Trentham, when they stepped out into the wintry street.

"North?"

"North it is." There was a hackney stand at the end of the street. Icarus raised his hand, hailing a jarvey.

They circled Bristol as a clock hand does, first the northern parishes, then those to the east, and then south. It was late afternoon by the time they reached Bedminster. The jarvey slowed several times to ask directions, and finally drew up in front of a large church of antiquated appearance. Icarus stepped down from the carriage and helped Miss Trentham alight.

The church of St. John was empty except for a woman arranging the folds of the frontal cloth.

"Excuse me, madam," Icarus said. "Can you tell me where I can find the churchwarden?"

The woman straightened. She had graying brown hair beneath a mobcap, and a plump, pleasant face. "Mr. Crowe? He's gone to Portishead for his grandson's christening. Could my husband help you? This is his parish."

"I'm looking for a Chelsea out-pensioner," Icarus said. "A Sergeant Houghton, recently returned from Portugal."

"Houghton? Poor man. He's staying over by the South Liberty coal-pit, with his sister's family."

Icarus's weariness fell from him. "He's here?"

"Yes."

"Can you furnish us with his direction?"

The vicar's wife gave them Houghton's address. "But this time of day, he's usually on the high street."

"The high street?"

The woman came as far as the church steps and pointed. "It's five minutes from here."

Icarus handed Miss Trentham up into the hackney. The carriage lurched into motion again. He sat forward on the seat, peering out. Bedminster looked a dingy, dreary place.

In the high street, they climbed down once again. Beneath the acrid coalsmoke was a nauseating whiff of tannery.

"Please wait for us," Icarus said, reaching into his pocket for some coins. At the next cross street, a man awkwardly swept the crossing. Icarus glanced down at the coins in his hand—and then back at the crossing-sweeper. He was sweeping awkwardly because he only had one arm.

Icarus chose a coin at random and thrust it at the jarvey. He took Miss Trentham by the elbow and towed her across the street. She didn't protest, didn't ask questions, just caught up her skirts and hurried alongside him.

Icarus was almost running by the time he reached the crossing-sweeper. The man wasn't Houghton. He *couldn't* be Houghton.

The crossing-sweeper looked up. He was a big man, but almost cadaverously thin. His shabby coat hung on his frame, the left sleeve pinned up at the elbow. The face beneath the ragged beard was Houghton's, the brown eyes were Houghton's, but not the Houghton he remembered—alert, confident, vigorous. This Houghton looked as grimy and dispirited as his surroundings.

They stared at each other. Icarus saw Houghton give a blink of recognition. His shoulders straightened, as if he was on parade. "Major Reid, sir?"

"Jesus, man," Icarus said, aghast. "What are you doing here?"

Houghton's jaw tightened beneath the beard. His chin lifted fractionally. "What does it look like? I'm sweeping the crossing."

"But *why?*"

"Because I want to eat."

"But you have a pension!"

"Pension's half-yearly, sir."

Icarus opened his mouth, and shut it again.

"Shall we find somewhere to sit and talk?" Miss Trentham suggested. "A pot of tea would be nice, and I'm sure Sergeant

Houghton would like something warm to drink if he's been standing out here all day."

*C*HAPTER 29

*T*hey repaired to the nearest inn, taking seats by the fireplace in the coffee room. Icarus ordered tea for Miss Trentham, coffee for himself and Houghton, bread-and-butter, and whatever cakes were on hand. He opened his mouth to introduce Miss Trentham as his wife, and found himself unable to lie to Houghton. He simply could *not* force the words from his tongue. "This is my friend, Miss Trentham," he said awkwardly, and Miss Trentham lifted her eyebrows slightly and flicked him a thoughtful glance, and smiled at Houghton and said she was pleased to make his acquaintance.

"You're from Bedminster?" Icarus said, to make conversation. Houghton seemed even shabbier and grimier in these surroundings—and the man was aware of it. He looked deeply uncomfortable.

"Yes, sir."

As a sergeant talking to a major, Houghton had never been uncomfortable. He'd been respectful, but confident. Forthright. Assured. A man who'd known his own worth.

And now he was little better than a beggar.

The tea and coffee arrived, with bread-and-butter, ratafia biscuits, and plum cake.

Houghton was hungry—Icarus could see it in his eyes—but the man had too much pride to behave as if he was. He politely waited for Miss Trentham to make her selection, then took one slice of bread-and-butter.

Icarus sipped his coffee, almost choking on his outrage. Houghton, reduced to this?

"What are you doing here, sir?"

"Looking for you."

"Me, sir?"

"Yes. Have some plum cake." Icarus now understood how Miss Trentham felt. He wanted to open Houghton's mouth and shove the plate's worth of cake down the man's throat.

Houghton hesitated, and took a small slice. "Why are you looking for me?"

He could scarcely have been given an easier opening, but Icarus found himself unable to ask the question outright. Houghton would be offended—and rightly so. "A couple of reasons," he said, prevaricating. "I heard you'd lost an arm. I'm sorry."

Houghton met his eyes, and then nodded.

"I only found out a couple of weeks ago," Icarus said. "I had the fever, after Vimeiro. Lost six weeks. Can't remember much at all."

"You do look a bit hagged, sir."

So do you, Icarus wanted to say. He held out the plate of ratafia biscuits. "Try these."

Houghton hesitated, and took one.

Icarus put the plate back on the side table. He leaned his elbows on his knees. "I'm trying to find out what happened at Vimeiro—not the battle itself, but the day before. I was hoping you could help me piece it together."

Houghton's eyebrows rose. "Of course, sir."

"Dunlop told me you were looking for me that day. You had a message for me. Do you remember?"

Houghton blinked. "Message for you?" His eyes narrowed in memory. "That's right, sir. Colonel Armstrong wanted to speak to you when you got back."

"That was the message?"

"Yes, sir."

"Do you remember what Dunlop told you?"

"Told me not to bother him with messages for you, because you wouldn't be back 'til after dark."

"Did he tell you where I'd be, at any time that day?"

Houghton snorted. "Told me where and when you were meeting your scouts, stupid clunch. As if I wanted to know!" His gaze flicked to Miss Trentham, and he colored faintly. "Begging your pardon, ma'am."

"Did you tell anyone what he told you?"

"I told Colonel Armstrong you wouldn't be back until after dark."

"Did you tell Armstrong when and where I was meeting the scouts?"

"No, sir."

"Did you tell anyone else?"

Houghton shook his head. "No, sir. Why?"

Icarus glanced at Miss Trentham. She gave a tiny nod.

He looked back at Houghton. "We were ambushed that day, my scouts and I. Someone told the French where we were meeting, and when." He put out one hand and gripped Houghton's wrist fiercely. "I didn't think it was you. I *never* thought it was you. I'm checking everyone. Even you, even Matlock—and I *know* neither of you would have said anything to anyone!"

He saw Houghton's affront, felt the tension in his wrist.

"I didn't think it was you," Icarus repeated, holding Houghton's gaze. "I would have staked my life on it!"

Perhaps Houghton had some of Miss Trentham's knack of hearing truthfulness, for his rigidity eased fractionally. He gave a short nod.

Icarus released the man's wrist. He had the answer to his question; he could leave now. He stayed seated. "Tell me about your arm. What happened?"

"Not much to tell, sir." Houghton's voice was stiffer than it had been before. "Musket ball through the elbow."

"I'm sorry," Icarus said again.

Houghton shrugged aside his sympathy. "Could have been worse. Could have been my leg."

Icarus thought of the old soldier he'd met begging in Basingstoke. He would *not* let that happen to Houghton. "Does it pain you?"

"Not much," Houghton said, brusquely. He reached for his coffee cup.

Icarus refused to be deterred. "Tell me about your circumstances. You're living with your sister?"

Houghton put down his cup. He was tense again, with pride not affront, if Icarus read him aright. He made as if to stand. Miss Trentham beat him to it, rising to her feet, murmuring, "Pray excuse me. That painting over there, quite intriguing . . ." She crossed to the farthest corner of the coffee room and peered at a painting on the wall.

Icarus was deeply grateful for her tact. "Tell me about your circumstances, Sergeant."

"I'm fine, sir," Houghton said, standing. "Thank you for the coffee—"

"For God's sake, man, *sit*. I'm not going to offer you pity, so put your hackles down!"

Houghton hesitated.

"Sit," Icarus told him. "And stop being so damned stiff-necked!"

After a moment, Houghton sat again, on the very edge of his seat.

"Tell me how it is, Sergeant." Icarus leaned forward again, his elbows on his knees. "And let's have the wood with no bark on it."

Houghton's mouth compressed. He looked down at his cracked brogues.

"You're living with your sister," Icarus prompted.

"Yes, sir."

"And?"

For a moment he thought Houghton would tell him it was

none of his business, and then the man sighed, and all the stiff pride went out of him, and he looked tired and defeated. "She's got eight children, sir, and a ninth on the way. Joe, that's her husband, he works in the coal-pit, and Susan takes in laundry when she can, but they can barely afford to feed themselves, let alone me. They were all living in one room when I got here. I used my back-pay to move 'em somewhere better—two and a half rooms—but I can't take food out of their mouths. Not with eight children, and a ninth on the way!" His voice held a note of despair.

"I understand why you're sweeping the crossing."

"It's all I'm good for," Houghton said bitterly. "Brings in a few pennies."

"Nonsense! I can think of a dozen things you could do. You have a damned good head on your shoulders."

"And only one arm!"

"Admiral Nelson had only one arm—and look what he accomplished."

"I'm not an admiral. I'm not even a sergeant any longer."

Icarus couldn't dispute this truth. He shoved the plate of plum cake at Houghton. "Eat, man."

Houghton's jaw firmed stubbornly. Did he think it was charity?

Wasn't it? Chastened, Icarus took a slice of plum cake and two ratafia biscuits. "Eat," he said again, and began to do so himself, biting into a ratafia biscuit, tasting sugar and almonds.

After a moment, Houghton chose another slice of bread-and-butter.

Icarus chewed slowly, pondering what was he going to do with Houghton. Something that would provide the man with a decent living. Something that *wasn't* charity. He chased the ratafia biscuit down with a mouthful of coffee. "Do you like it here? Bristol. Bedminster."

Houghton shook his head. "I joined the army to get away from the coal-pits, and now I'm back amongst 'em again." He grimaced. "Leastways, I can't work in 'em now." He looked down at his plate. "I wish Joe didn't. M' father died in the pits, and what if Joe does, too? What would Susan do then, with nine children?"

"Is there nothing else Joe can do?"

Houghton shrugged. "There's the brickyards and the rope-walks, but they don't pay half as well. Nothing does."

Which left the problem of feeding nine children.

Icarus ate a piece of plum cake. Could he set Houghton and his brother-in-law up as shopkeepers? The nine children could live over the shop. "What's Joe like?"

Houghton shrugged again. "He's a good enough fellow. Works hard. Doesn't drink overmuch. Doesn't hit m' sister." He picked up a ratafia biscuit and contemplated it, and then burst out: "I just wish he'd stop swiving her! I know it's his right and all, but *nine* children, and him barely earning enough to feed them! He says it's God's will, but to my mind, it's *Joe's* will."

Icarus grunted a laugh.

Houghton glanced up sharply, and for a moment Icarus was afraid he'd offended him—and then Houghton's face relaxed and he smiled faintly, wryly, ruefully, and shrugged and ate the ratafia biscuit.

Icarus offered him the plate of plum cake. "Have another piece."

Houghton did.

Icarus chewed on his second ratafia biscuit, and pondered what to do with Houghton. Not a shop with Joe, not after hearing the pent-up frustration in Houghton's voice. And not something near the coal-pits. And not outright charity.

He examined the man's face. Houghton had been a damned good sergeant. Conscientious, smart, courageous. Tough, but fair. Not a bully. And not lazy. A good judge of character, able to distinguish shirkers at a glance.

The seed of an idea sprouted in Icarus's mind. "You can read and write, Sergeant?"

Houghton nodded.

Icarus pushed the plate of bread-and-butter towards him.

"Have some more." He watched Houghton select another slice of bread-and-butter, and let the idea flower. Yes, it could work—and not only that, it could work *well.*

"I sold out, you know."

Houghton looked up, his disbelief clear to see. "You, sir?"

Icarus nodded.

"Why?"

Why? Because he'd betrayed his own side. "My health," Icarus said. "I haven't long to live."

"Sir . . ." Houghton put down his bread-and-butter. "I'm sorry."

Icarus waved aside the sympathy. "I have a project in mind, Sergeant, and I'm hoping you can help me with it."

"Of course, sir." Houghton glanced at his pinned-up sleeve, and his mouth tightened. "If I can."

"You can," Icarus said. "Better than most men." He ordered his thoughts, and leaned forward. "I have a significant amount of prize money and I had planned to leave it to charity—veterans' charities—but what I'm now thinking is that I'd like to set up businesses where injured soldiers can *earn* their livings."

Houghton stiffened slightly. Bracing himself for unwelcome altruism?

Icarus forged on with his idea. "You'd rather earn your living than be the object of charity—and there are plenty of men like you—and I'd like to make that possible—only I don't know exactly *what* businesses to set up, and I need someone to help me decide, and to help me set them up, and select the men to employ, and make sure the money is used wisely, and oversee everything once I'm gone. So, you see, Sergeant, I'm not offering you charity; I'm offering you a *job.*"

Houghton didn't look stiff anymore; he looked dumbstruck. After a moment, he swallowed, and found his voice. "Why me, sir?"

"Because you were an outstanding sergeant. And because I know I can trust you." He held his hand out. "Will you be my partner in this? I can think of no one I'd rather work with."

Houghton swallowed again. Icarus thought he saw a glimmer of moisture in the man's eyes. The sergeant blinked, and nodded, and gripped Icarus's hand firmly. "Yes, sir. Thank you, sir."

"No, thank *you*. I shall work you hard, you know!"

Houghton smiled. "I hope so, sir."

Icarus looked around for Miss Trentham. She had abandoned her perusal of the painting and taken a seat by the window, giving them privacy. "Miss Trentham and I are leaving for Exeter tomorrow. Come with us. The sooner you and I start planning, the better."

Houghton glanced down at himself. "Sir, I'm not fit to be seen with you."

"A wash and shave, and you will be. We'll get you some clothes in Exeter. Until then you can wear mine; we're close enough in size."

"Wear your clothes, sir? I can't do that!" Houghton looked so appalled that Icarus almost laughed.

"You most certainly can. In fact, I insist on it! And I hope you'll join us at the Swan in Bristol tonight."

"The Swan?" Dismay flickered across Houghton's face. Icarus could almost see the man wondering how much it would cost.

"As my employee," Icarus said firmly. "Unless you wish to sleep another night at your sister's?"

Houghton hesitated. "No, sir. But I must take my leave of her."

"Of course you must." Icarus fished a few coins from his pocket. "This is for a hackney to the Swan. Come just as you are. My man Green will turn you out as spick as a new pin."

Houghton hesitated, and took the coins.

Icarus pulled out his pocketbook. "And this is for your sister and all those children."

Houghton looked down his nose at the banknote Icarus held out, and made no move to take it.

"It's not charity, Sergeant," Icarus told him. "So take that look off your face. You'll be *earning* this."

Houghton eyed him for a long moment, and reluctantly took the banknote.

Icarus tucked his pocketbook away, thankful to have jumped that hurdle, and glanced at Miss Trentham again. "Ah . . . there's something I ought to explain, before you join us at the Swan." He tugged at his neckcloth. "The thing is, everyone, including our servants, believes Miss Trentham is my wife." He felt himself flush under Houghton's incredulous stare, and hurried into an explanation, telling Houghton almost everything that had happened in the past three weeks. He left out Miss Trentham's fortune, and her visits to his bedchamber, and he omitted all reference to the creek at Vimeiro. When he'd finished, Houghton's expression hovered somewhere between bemusement and laughter. "Would you mind, Sergeant—just for the next week or so—falling in with our charade? I hate to ask it of you, but her reputation . . ."

"I shall call her Mrs. Reid, sir."

"Thank you," Icarus said, deeply relieved. "We would be much obliged."

CHAPTER 30

"$\mathcal{J}$ apologize," he said to Miss Trentham, when they were back in the hackney carriage. "I just . . . I *couldn't* lie to him."

"No." She tilted her head to one side and surveyed him gravely. "You hold Sergeant Houghton in high esteem."

Icarus nodded. He looked down at his gloved hands, and then back at her. "I told him about our charade," he confessed. "Because, the thing is . . . he's coming to Exeter with us. I'm going to take him as my partner—because I trust him, and because I can't just *leave* him here!"

She studied him silently, and then gave a nod. "The sergeant won't accept charity, but he'll accept employment."

"Yes," Icarus said, relieved that she understood. And then he wondered at himself for doubting she would. Miss Trentham was astute and perceptive. She'd taken Sergeant Houghton's measure at a glance. "Thank you for giving us privacy. I'm grateful to you." And he was grateful to her for more than that. Far more.

Back at the Swan, he spoke to both Green and Eliza. "For God's sake, don't offer him pity! Treat him as if he has two arms, unless for some reason he *does* need help, in which case be matter-of-fact about offering it. Green, he has the room next to you. I wish you to look after him as you would me, but *don't* fuss over him."

"Yes, sir."

"He should be here shortly. See that his room's made ready, please, and put out a change of my clothes for him. He'll need a bath and a shave. How are you at cutting hair?"

"I've never cut anyone's hair, sir," Green said apologetically.

"Never mind. He can see a barber tomorrow."

Sergeant Houghton arrived at dusk. Icarus showed him to his room, introduced him to Green, and left.

An hour and a half later, the door to the private parlor opened. Icarus glanced up from the *Bristol Mercury*. His mouth dropped open.

The shabby crossing-sweeper had been transformed. Gone were the ragged clothes and the grime, gone the shaggy hair, gone the beard. Instead, Houghton was clean, combed, shaved, and dressed in top boots and breeches, a waistcoat, and a tailcoat with the left arm pinned up. A neckcloth was neatly arranged at his throat.

Icarus closed his mouth. He stood hastily. "Good Lord, man. Have you seen yourself in a mirror?"

"I have, sir." Houghton's expression was hard to read. Icarus guessed that he was self-conscious about his borrowed finery, perhaps even faintly embarrassed.

"I'm glad to see my clothes fit." He crossed to Houghton and shook his hand. "Can you bear to wear them until Exeter?"

"Of course, sir."

Icarus released his hand. "Have a seat. Miss Trentham will be down shortly. Would you like something to drink? Claret? Sherry?"

"No, thank you, sir."

This Houghton was closer to the man he remembered, but

still not quite him. Less confident, slightly stiff. *He's a coalminer's son wearing gentleman's clothes,* Icarus reminded himself. *Of course he feels awkward.*

The parlor door opened again and Miss Trentham entered the room. She halted, and looked them both up and down. "Goodness, how alike the two of you are! No one could mistake you for anything but soldiers." There was nothing aloof in her manner. Her smile was warm and friendly. "I must say, you clean up very well, Sergeant!"

Before dinner was served, Icarus found a moment to run upstairs. "Green, you've performed a miracle! And you even cut his hair!"

"Eliza cut his hair, sir."

"Did she? Well, I must thank her for that, then—but everything else is due to you! *Thank* you."

He pressed a guinea into Green's hand and hurried back downstairs, arriving in the parlor half a minute in advance of the meal. The landlord supervised the placing of the dishes. Eight dishes tonight. The smell made Icarus's mouth water.

Miss Trentham glanced at the meal, and gave the landlord a nod of approval. The man nodded back, looking pleased with himself.

Icarus examined the dinner. It took him a moment to realize what it was that Miss Trentham had seen: there was no dish that would pose a problem for a one-handed man.

He looked at Miss Trentham. Was this her doing?

Houghton had noticed, too. He became fractionally less self-conscious.

Miss Trentham was Tish tonight. Within ten minutes of sitting at the table, she'd managed to put Houghton completely at his ease. Within fifteen minutes, she'd even made him laugh. Not only that, she cheerfully browbeat Houghton into eating two helpings of everything. "You *must* have more of the fricassee, Sergeant. You need to put some meat on your bones!"

Icarus glanced at Houghton, and discovered that the man wasn't offended; on the contrary, he was amused.

Houghton liked Miss Trentham. And Miss Trentham liked Houghton.

Icarus felt a prick of something that might almost be—but most definitely *wasn't*—jealousy. This so disconcerted him that he ate a second portion of fricassee himself. And later, a second portion of syllabub. Finally, full almost to bursting, he pushed his plate away.

After the servants had cleared the covers from the table, they sat talking. Icarus leaned back in his chair. It had been a long time since he'd had an evening like this, mellow and relaxed, with friends.

The clock on the mantelpiece struck ten. He glanced at it, surprised.

Miss Trentham looked surprised, too. "Is that the time? Poor Eliza will be wondering where I am!" She stood, and held out her hand to Houghton. "Eliza tells me she's responsible for your hair, and I must say, she did a good job!"

"She did indeed, ma'am." Houghton took her hand in a friendly clasp.

Miss Trentham smiled at him, exactly as she had smiled at Matlock and Lucas Kemp. "I'm glad you decided to come to Exeter with us, Sergeant."

"So am I." Houghton released her hand and turned to Icarus. "Good night, sir."

"Good night, Sergeant."

Houghton left the parlor. Miss Trentham made to follow him, but Icarus detained her with a light touch on her arm. She glanced at him, her eyebrows lifting.

"The meal. Was that your doing?"

"My doing?"

"It needed no knife."

"Oh, yes. I thought it would be more comfortable for him. He was bound to feel self-conscious."

Icarus took both of her hands in his and looked down at her. "Bless you."

Miss Trentham colored faintly. "Any hostess would have done the same."

Icarus gazed down at her. She was wearing a gown of soft sage green, and her eyes were green, too. He frowned. Hadn't they been gray yesterday? "Your eyes change color."

"No, they don't," Miss Trentham said. She tried to pull her hands from his grip.

Icarus didn't release them. "They were gray yesterday, and blue the day before. And now they're green again."

"My eyes aren't *any* particular color," Miss Trentham said, tugging her hands again.

Icarus tightened his grip. "They're definitely green today."

Miss Trentham stopped trying to free her hands. "They're a little bit green," she said, in an extremely patient voice. "And a little bit blue, and a little bit gray. They're not any one color."

Icarus looked at her eyes more closely. She was correct— and *in*correct. Her eyes weren't green or blue or gray; they were the color of the sea. "I like them."

Miss Trentham flushed faintly. She tried to pull her hands free again.

Icarus retained his clasp on them. "Thank you for tonight. Thank you for seeing to the meal. Thank you for putting Houghton at his ease. Thank you for making him eat so much. I know I don't thank you as often as I ought to, and I want you to know that I'm grateful for everything you do. Deeply grateful." He bent and kissed her lips.

He felt her jolt of surprise, heard her intake of breath— and then her hands clasped his back, and her lips softened beneath his, and they were kissing properly, the way they did at night in his bedchamber—and then the door opened, and they broke apart, Miss Trentham blushing furiously.

A maidservant entered the parlor and began tidying the room.

Miss Trentham muttered a hasty good night, and fled. Icarus felt scarcely less discomposed than she was. Lord, what had made him kiss her here in the parlor, where anyone could walk in on them!

He climbed the stairs to his room in a state of mild perturbation and stood for a moment looking at the tray Green had prepared: the brandy bottle, the new vial of valerian. He could almost taste their flavors in his mouth.

I shouldn't let her come to me. I should latch my door. But even as he peeled out of his tailcoat, he knew he wouldn't. Miss Trentham's nighttime visits had become almost as important to him as the air he breathed.

C HAPTER 31

L etty grasped Reid's shoulder, shook it hard, and stepped back. "Icarus, wake up!" How familiar everything had become, a routine that had grown up between them. She plumped up Reid's pillows, poured brandy—a quarter of a glass only, because that was all he'd drunk last night—uncorked the valerian and measured out a teaspoon, and opened Herodotus to the page she'd marked. She read until his eyelids were heavy and his breathing slow, then she slipped the ribbon between the pages again and put the book aside. She reached out and smoothed Reid's hair back from his brow, as if he was a child. *I love you, Icarus Reid,* she whispered silently.

He didn't love her. She knew that without needing to be told. Reid had kissed her in the parlor in an impulse of gratitude, and he would kiss her again shortly because it had become their habit, but he didn't love her.

Letty studied his face for a moment—the dark eyelashes, the strong cheekbones, the hard angle of his jaw. Reid's voice echoed in her ears, as it had for the past two days. *I'm dead already, don't y' see? Been dead for months.*

He believed it. Truly believed it.

She smoothed his hair again, letting the strands slide through her fingers. He was like a character in a Faerie tale, trapped in a state of not-quite-death, needing someone to bring him to life again.

"How do I save you, Icarus Reid?" Letty said under her breath.

Reid's eyes blinked drowsily open. "Did you say something?"

"No." She bent closer and kissed him.

Reid turned his head towards her, sleepily seeking her mouth.

They kissed for several minutes. Heat flushed over Letty's skin, but beneath the heat was a deep, cold ache of sadness. How could she save him?

Reid's kiss grew sleepier. Letty lifted her lips from his mouth and pressed them instead to his throat. Reid uttered a low sound of pleasure, almost a sigh.

She kissed her way down his throat to the open collar of his nightshirt and then back up again, nibbling lightly with her teeth, licking. Reid filled her senses: the taste of salt on her tongue, the pliant warmth of his skin, the faint prickle of whiskers.

Reid liked being kissed like this. If he was a cat, he'd be purring right now. That low sound he made in his throat almost *was* a purr.

Letty repeated what she'd done, nibbling her way down his throat. This time Reid uttered no sound. His breathing was slow and even.

She lifted her mouth from his skin. "Icarus?" she whispered. "Are you asleep?"

He made no reply. His eyes were closed. He was asleep.

Letty gazed down at his face and loved him and grieved for him and wished with all her heart that she knew how to make him happy.

Abruptly, she had a flash of memory: Tom kneeling in front of Lucas. The expression on Lucas's face had been one of utter bliss: eyes closed, lips parted.

She would like to make Reid look like that.

The thought—once it had formed—refused to be ignored. It sat in her skull, large and loud and blatant, crowding out absolutely everything else. She *could* make Reid look like that, couldn't she? If she kissed him as Tom had kissed Lucas.

Letty heard her heart thump loudly in her chest. She felt nervousness prickle in her blood. *I can't. I daren't. It's not respectable.*

And then she felt ashamed of herself. She'd dared to go to Marshalsea Prison, hadn't she? Even though that had been scandalous and outrageous and not something a lady would do. She'd dared to go to Basingstoke and to come to Bristol. If she'd done those things for Reid, surely she could do this for him, too? Her gift to him: a moment of pure happiness.

But still she hesitated—and that also shamed her, because surely a woman who loved a man wouldn't hesitate, not if she knew she could make him happy, and she *did* know it. No one who'd seen Lucas's face could doubt that this kind of kiss gave a man pleasure.

Go on, Julia whispered at her shoulder.

Julia would have done it without hesitation, just as she'd done everything without hesitation—climbing trees and sliding down banisters and racing the boys on her pony. Julia had lived life boldly, and her joy in living had been contagious, and everyone had loved her for it.

Just do it, Tish! How many times had Julia told her that over the years?

Very well, she'd be Julia: she'd just do it.

Letty resolutely peeled back the bedclothes. Reid's linen nightshirt was rumpled, the hem bunched around his knees. She gently eased it higher, exposing his thighs. In the candle-light, Reid's skin was a pale golden color.

The nervousness spiked, became almost fear—and Letty set her jaw in determination and drew the nightshirt up to his waist. Her gaze skittered away, and then back. Away again. And back. Her nervousness became . . . bemusement.

When she'd been nineteen, Julia had found sketches made by their Uncle George during his Grand Tour—chateaux and churches, lakes and vertiginous mountains—and nude classical statues.

She and Julia had spent some time studying the sketches of the statues, quite baffled.

Later, Julia had shown her next-oldest and recently married sister the sketches, and inquired as to how the finger-shaped appendage dangling from a man's groin could make a woman pregnant.

That explanation had been even more baffling.

Letty bunched the nightshirt at Reid's waist and gazed at him in perplexity. The thick thatch of dark hair was nothing like the sketches, but she should have expected it—indeed, if she'd thought of it at all, she *must* have expected it—and the size and shape of Reid's organ was . . . not what she'd imagined either. From the sketches, one could deduce that a man's organ was no larger than his little finger, but Reid's organ was thicker and longer—she glanced at Reid's hand, lying limp on his chest—*significantly* thicker and longer—and his testicles were as large and plump as goose eggs.

Letty swallowed. Her nervousness returned. Her mouth was dry, her throat dry. She felt cowardly and craven. She wanted to lower the nightshirt and pull up the covers and hurry back to her bedchamber—and then she remembered the expression on Lucas's face. *That* was what she wanted for Reid: pure, unadulterated pleasure.

She gazed at his groin, at the dark hair and thick, limp, rosy organ, and inhaled a shallow, nervous breath and bent low and tentatively kissed him.

The skin of Reid's organ was soft and warm beneath her lips. She inhaled his scent—clean linen and soap and a subtle musky odor that was intensely and unmistakably *male*. The musky odor wasn't unpleasant; on the contrary, it was oddly invigorating. Letty kissed him again, and then parted her lips and cautiously licked, tasting the salt on his skin.

She inhaled Reid's scent, and licked again, trailing her tongue down his limp organ to the very end and back again. He uttered a low sound, almost a grunt. Encouraged, Letty did it again, slowly and thoroughly.

Reid groaned. His organ twitched beneath her lips. His skin seemed warmer than it had been and his organ to have increased in size.

Letty raised her head. Yes, his organ had grown a good inch. In fact, it was no longer entirely limp. And it was rosier than it had been. Improbable as it seemed—impossible even—Julia's sister had been correct: a man's organ *did* grow.

Julia's sister had also said that it would become quite hard, almost as hard as a carrot, and stick straight out. At the time, she and Julia had known they were being roasted. Now, Letty wasn't quite so certain.

She glanced at Reid's face. His eyes were closed, but his lips were slightly parted. Although he was asleep, he appeared to be enjoying what she was doing.

Letty bent over him again, and kissed her way down his organ several more times. It twitched and swelled and stiffened beneath her ministrations. It wasn't limp at all now; it jutted up from the hair at his groin like a tree rising from a thicket of bracken, and its crown reminded her of nothing so much as a plump, ruddy plum.

She ran her tongue over that plum-like crown, caressing, exploring, tracing its contours, savoring its taste. This elicited a groan. Encouraged, Letty repeated what she'd done—Reid seemed to particularly like it when her tongue touched the ridge of skin beneath that ruddy, bulbous crest. He groaned whenever she licked there. She lingered at this spot for a time, and then raised her head and looked at his face. Reid appeared to be in a state of beatific bliss, eyes closed, lips parted, cheeks flushed.

Pleased, Letty bent her attention back to his organ. If she hadn't witnessed its transformation, she wouldn't have believed it possible—the thing had doubled in size and gone from soft

215

to rigid. One could be forgiven for thinking his organ had caught a fever, so hot to the touch it was, so rosily red.

Letty licked that plum-like crown again, licked that ridge of skin again. How intimate it was to kiss a man like this, intimate and quite extraordinarily exhilarating. Emboldened, she drew the head of his organ into her mouth, pillowing it with her tongue.

Reid uttered another groan. Letty deduced that he liked the sensation of being in her mouth. She liked it, too. His organ felt large and hot and smooth and hard, resting on her tongue. Experimentally, she sucked lightly. Reid seemed to catch his breath. He uttered a low moan. His whole body twitched.

Encouraged by this reaction, Letty sucked again. Reid caught his breath again. His body twitched again.

Letty sucked several times, each time a little more strongly. Reid seemed to like it very much. He was no longer relaxed, though. His breath was coming faster, his body shifting restlessly, and his hips had a tendency to lift off the bed each time she sucked, as if his organ was trying to thrust itself further into her mouth. She was compelled to take hold of his shaft with one hand. That was another exhilarating sensation. How *hot* he was, how hard, straining against her fingers, seeming almost to pulse.

Letty sucked again, even more strongly, and this time the shaft definitely *did* pulse in her hand, and his organ pulsed on her tongue, too, and liquid spurted into her mouth.

Startled, Letty recoiled. Reid's organ slipped from her mouth, pulsed again in her hand, and more liquid spurted onto her cheek. An unusual taste blossomed on her tongue, bitter, salty, but not unpleasant—and then—in an instant of shocked comprehension—she realized what the liquid was.

It was Reid's *seed*.

The instant of shock was followed by an instant of utter panic. Could she become pregnant from swallowing Reid's seed? Letty scrambled off the bed, wiping her cheek. His seed was warm and slightly sticky to the touch.

Reid had woken. He pushed up on his elbows, looking quite dazed, his silver eyes dark and dilated, his cheeks flushed. "What the devil?"

She saw him focus on her, standing beside the bed—and then on the sheets pulled back and his nightshirt around his waist and his organ resting back on its nest of hair, not quite completely limp again.

His expression changed—she saw his shock, saw his horror—and he hauled the bedclothes up to cover himself. "What the—"The flush had completely drained from his face. "I didn't—we didn't—"He sat bolt upright and said frantically, "Tell me we didn't!"

"I kissed you the way Tom was kissing Lucas," Letty confessed.

Reid stared at her, his mouth open, his expression utterly appalled. Letty thought that he almost wasn't breathing, he was so shocked.

His reaction told her how grossly she'd strayed past the bounds of propriety. Letty felt herself flush. "I thought you might like it. It was only a kiss, after all."

"A kiss? Jesus Christ! That's not a *kiss*! It's as good as having sex!"

"Can I become pregnant?" Letty asked, uneasily aware of the taste of his seed in her mouth.

"What? No, of course not. But it's not—"The beatific bliss she'd glimpsed on Reid's face a few minutes ago was gone. He looked wholly agitated, clutching the bedclothes to his chest. "You shouldn't have done it!"

"If I can't become pregnant, why is it so terrible?"

"Why?" Reid stared at her, and then he said, "Christ," thickly, and dropped his head back on the pillows and pressed the heels of his hands to his eyes.

Letty bit her lip. She hadn't meant to upset Reid; she'd wanted only to please him, to give him the gift of happiness for a few moments. "Icarus . . ." She sat beside him on the bed. "It's not so dreadful, is it? Only you and I know of it."

"Please go," he said.

"But—"

"Please leave my room."

Tears rushed to her eyes. Letty stood and picked up her chamberstick and quietly left the bedchamber.

*C*HAPTER 32

November 23rd, 1808
Somersetshire

*I*t was raining when they left Bristol. Their party now numbering five, Reid hired two post-chaises to convey them to Exeter. Letty traveled in the foremost carriage with him and Houghton. She had the very strong impression that Reid would have preferred *not* to be in the same carriage as her; he seemed unable to meet her eyes today, and whenever he addressed her, he spoke to her shoulder.

They journeyed south through a gray, wet landscape. Letty spent the first hour studying her gloves, plucking at the fingertips, wishing she'd not given in to the impulse to kiss Reid's organ. And really, in the light of day, it was difficult to understand why she'd done something so bold and scandalous and obviously wrong.

She loved Reid, and she'd wanted to give him bliss, and she'd allowed those things to override good sense and prudence. She'd tried to be Julia, and that had been a mistake, because she wasn't Julia, had never been Julia, and never would be—and now there was this terrible awkwardness between them, and Reid couldn't even look her in the eye.

She thought she could guess why he was so embarrassed: she'd seen a part of his body that no woman other than his wife should ever see. *Or a whore,* she reminded herself, and that was an unsettling thought, and she plucked at the fingertips of her gloves and wished even more fervently that she'd not given into the impulse last night.

This was what came of trying to be Julia. And, now that she thought of it, Julia had almost broken an arm falling out of one of the trees she'd climbed, and she *had* broken her neck jumping a fence that was too high for her horse, and why hadn't she remembered that last night?

Reid's conversation with Houghton tugged at her attention. The two men were discussing what businesses might usefully employ crippled soldiers. Reid appeared to have the intention of setting up several enterprises and funding them with his prize money. Letty found herself listening as they discussed and discarded half a dozen possibilities. "I won't have them picking oakum, like inmates in a workhouse," Reid said. "Or selling doormats and boot blacking door-to-door. A man needs some dignity!"

Houghton favored a bakery. "I'd be no use as a baker," he said, with a shrug of his truncated arm. "But anyone with two hands can knead bread. It wouldn't matter how many legs he had."

Reid expanded on this theme, proposing a confectioner's shop. "Like Gunter's, with ices and wafers and all kinds of sweetmeats."

From here, they moved to discussion of other types of business. Houghton suggested a tavern, or a chandler's shop selling turpentine and pitch and rope and all the supplies a sailing ship would need. The conversation took a turn at this point. Reid, it appeared, was very taken with the idea of a farm. "If a man has spent years campaigning, he'd hardly wish to be confined indoors. I know I wouldn't."

Letty listened with interest—and growing hope. Reid was thinking ahead, looking to the future. Had he changed his mind about dying?

"I'll put everything in your name," Reid said. "Right from the start. That way, there'll be no complications when I die."

Letty's hope was extinguished.

They took refreshments at the posting inn in Shepton Mallet, twenty miles south of Bristol. Reid escorted Letty to the coffee room, saw her seated by the fire, and managed to avoid looking her in the eye or speaking to her directly.

Letty sipped her tea and nibbled her bread-and-butter and worried. She'd rescued Eliza, and Reid had rescued Green and Houghton, but who would rescue Reid?

I'm dead already, he'd said, and his voice had rung with truth.

It seemed to her that the only person who could rescue Reid was Reid himself. He didn't need money, he didn't need a protector; he needed to *want* to live.

She wished she could reach inside his skull and rearrange his thinking, wished she could find the part of his brain that thought he was already dead and amputate it, as the surgeon had amputated Houghton's arm. But she couldn't. The only tools she had at her disposal were words.

Words that she'd spoken before, and that Reid had not listened to.

After everyone had partaken of refreshments, they braved the rain again. Their progress was slow. Great puddles lay across the road and the horses were often brought to a walk. The rain came down more heavily, drumming on the carriage roof.

Letty peered out at the postilions. "The poor postboys are half-drowned!"

"We'll not make Taunton," Houghton said.

"No," Reid said. "We'll have to put up at the next posting inn."

But ten minutes later, the rain stopped drumming on the roof, and ten minutes after that, it stopped entirely. And ten minutes after *that*, so did the carriage.

Houghton glanced out. "Road's flooded." He opened the door and jumped down, his boots splashing in a puddle.

Letty looked out after him. Ahead, the road had transformed itself into a pond.

Reid climbed down from the carriage. Letty followed.

Houghton stood at the water's edge, surveying the flooding. "Less than twenty yards across, and it doesn't look more than two feet deep at the most. What do you think, sir? Shall we try to push on?"

Letty glanced at Reid, and then a second time, more sharply. His face reminded her of the day he'd been tossed by his horse: the rigidity of his muscles, the faint flare of his nostrils.

He was terrified of the water.

"I think we should turn back," Letty said briskly. "For all we know, it gets worse further on." She turned to the postilion astride the outside leader. "Is there an inn nearby?"

With a jingle of harnesses, the second post-chaise-and-four pulled up behind them.

The postilion wiped his dripping nose. "There's one half a mile back, ma'am."

"Turn the carriage, please. We'll stay there for the night."

The inn in question was a humble establishment, a short way off the post road. The single ostler was thrown into a state of agitation by the arrival of eight post-horses and four postilions, and the landlord was so surprised by the appearance of Quality on his doorstep that he was temporarily lost for words. He overcame his stupefaction, bowed low several times, begged them to step inside, and called urgently for his wife.

The Two Geese was a rustic establishment with low ceilings and crooked floors, but it was clean and dry and able to accommodate five unexpected guests. "There's two bedchambers at the front," the apple-cheeked landlady said, bobbing yet another curtsy. "And three at the back. And the postboys may sleep in the stables, ma'am."

"Excellent," Letty said.

She selected the front two bedchambers for herself and Reid, and left Eliza laying out a change of clothes, while she ventured down to the kitchen. There she found the landlady and another female, considerably flustered. "Quite discombobulated, I am!" the landlady declaimed, wringing her hands. "What I'm to feed 'em, I'm sure I don't know! They'll be wantin' half a dozen dishes laid afore 'em, and there's only that goose and the last of the beef, and as for dessert—" She broke off when she saw Letty, and her plump cheeks grew even rosier. "Beggin' your pardon, ma'am. I didn't see you standin' there."

Letty spent the next few minutes assuring the landlady that their needs were simple and that they were happy to sit down to a dinner consisting of only two dishes. "My husband and Mr. Houghton were soldiers, you know. They have no patience with finicky food; they much prefer a plain meal!"

She then broached the subject of Houghton's one-handedness.

The landlady rose to the occasion. "Goose pie would be just the thing, and we can turn the beef into a stew. We'll be sure to cut the meat up small, ma'am, of that you can be certain!"

"Thank you," Letty said. "And I assure you, we need no dessert."

But the light of zeal was in the landlady's eye. "Apple tansey," she declared. "It'll be just the thing!"

The Two Geese possessed no private parlor. Letty dined in the coffee room with Reid and the sergeant, while Eliza and Green took their dinner in the kitchen. Reid managed to pass the entire evening without once meeting her eyes, and every time that he looked past her instead of at her or spoke to her shoulder and not her face it felt as if he'd given her the cut direct in the middle of a ballroom. Was he never going to look at her again? Letty struggled not to show her mortification, her anxiety, struggled to maintain a light, cheerful conversation.

After the meal, she sat by the fire with a book, while Reid and Houghton played two games of backgammon. It was impossible to read. The words looked like scratches made by sparrows. She stared blindly at the pages and thought about Reid not looking at her and wondered how on earth she could make things right between them again.

The rain resumed. Letty listened to drops striking the windowpanes, and while she listened, she came to a decision.

After the second game, Houghton yawned and declared himself ready for bed.

"I'll retire, too," Reid said.

Letty closed her book and took a deep breath. "Icarus, may I please have a word with you before you go? Good night, Sergeant."

She waited until Houghton had shut the door before looking at Reid.

He didn't meet her eyes, choosing instead to gaze at the fire. "You wish to speak with me?"

"Yes," Letty said. "I want to apologize for last night. It was not my intention to offend you."

A grimace flickered across Reid's face. He turned his head further from her. Letty understood from those two reactions that he would have preferred that she hadn't mentioned the incident. She bit her lip, aware that she'd embarrassed him again. Silence grew between them. "I'm sorry," she said hesitantly. "I truly am. I didn't realize it was such a terrible thing to do."

Reid turned his head to look at her. He met her gaze for the first time that day. The impact of his silver eyes made her breath catch in her throat. "You don't understand, do you?"

"I don't know," Letty said, even more hesitantly. "Are you embarrassed that I saw you?"

Color rose in Reid's face. He looked away again.

"Can't we just forget it happened? Please?"

Reid looked back at her. He seemed to be debating what to say. Finally, he said, "What you did last night was a sexual act and you *can't* do things like that to people without their consent! Imagine how you'd feel if you woke up and found that I'd done something like that to you."

Letty considered these words. If she woke to discover her nightgown up around her waist and Reid leaning over her, touching her intimately . . . she wouldn't just feel embarrassed, she'd feel violated.

That's what she'd done to him.

With that realization came a sick, cold feeling in her belly. "It was a violation, wasn't it? I violated your privacy, and your trust in me."

"Yes," Reid said.

Tears filled her eyes. "I'm sorry! I didn't mean to! I thought you'd like it. Lucas liked it. He looked so happy!"

Reid's mouth tightened. "I wish you'd never seen that."

So did Letty. She hunted for her handkerchief. "I'm sorry. I thought it was just another way of kissing someone. I mean, I guessed that it wasn't quite respectable—"

"Not quite respectable?" Reid gave a humorless laugh. "Good God, I can hardly think of anything *less* respectable!

It's an extremely lewd sexual act. A man would *never* ask it of his wife."

"I'm sorry," Letty said again, wiping her eyes.

Reid sighed. "Don't cry, Letty. It's not worth crying over." It was the first time he'd ever called her by her Christian name, and that made the tears come even faster. Letty sniffed, and tried to blink them back, and mopped her cheeks.

Reid crossed to where she sat. "Don't cry," he said again, and he lowered himself to perch awkwardly on the chair alongside her. "Please, Letty. It's not worth it."

Letty clutched the handkerchief tightly. "I give you my word I won't do it again—my word of honor!—if . . . if you can bring yourself to believe me?"

"Of course I believe you," Reid said, and it was true, and that made more tears spill from her eyes.

Letty wiped them away. "I'm sorry about last night," she said, in a small, shaky voice.

"I know," Reid said.

The tears stopped coming so fast, and then they stopped coming at all. Letty was able to dry her cheeks and blow her nose and fold up the handkerchief.

They sat quietly for several minutes, watching the fire, and it felt as if they were friends again. Letty's thoughts became less agitated. She found herself pondering several questions. "Icarus? What I did last night . . . is it something that generally only men do to each other?"

Reid recoiled slightly in his chair. "What? No!"

"But Tom—"

"Forget you ever saw that!"

Forget it? Did he not realize how impossible that was? The scene was imprinted in her memory, as vivid as if she'd witnessed it only yesterday. But Letty obediently turned her mind from it and instead sifted through everything Reid had said tonight. Lewd. The sort of thing a man wouldn't ask of his wife. "Is it something that only fallen women do?"

Reid looked as if he didn't want to answer this question. Finally, he said, "In the main, yes."

"But why?" Letty said, folding her damp handkerchief even smaller. "I don't see what's so dreadful about it. It wasn't unpleasant in the slightest."

Color mounted in Reid's cheeks. He returned his attention to the fire. "It's exceedingly intimate."

That, Letty could concede—the scent of his skin, the taste of his seed—but even so . . . "Wives *never* do it?"

"Most would not."

Letty reflected on this answer for a moment, remembering the pure bliss on Reid's face last night. "Don't their husbands want them to?"

Reid noticed that the fire needed more wood. He pushed to his feet and laid another log on the embers and spent some time arranging it to best advantage.

"Don't their husbands want them to?" Letty repeated.

Reid straightened. "I wouldn't know," he said repressively. "Having never been married myself."

"Do you think that's why so many men are unfaithful to their wives?"

"I can't possibly comment." Reid fished his watch from his pocket. "Goodness, is that the time? I shall bid you good night." He bowed politely, and hastened from the coffee room.

CHAPTER 33

*L*etty jerked awake a short time after one o'clock. She heard rain on the windowpanes, and the sound of a man crying out in distress. She flung back her bedclothes, fumbled for the tinderbox, and threw her shawl around her shoulders.

Reid came out of his nightmare berserker-mad, lunging up from the bedclothes—and struck his head on the low ceiling. He gave a grunt. His legs folded and he sat abruptly on the bed, his expression a mixture of shock, pain, and bewilderment.

"Icarus? Are you all right?"

Reid bowed his head into his hands with a groan.

"Icarus?" Letty went to him, and cautiously touched his shoulder. The berserker fury had drained from his muscles. "Icarus, did you hurt yourself? Is it bleeding?"

He didn't reply, but he did let her gently run her fingers through his hair until she found the swelling. To her relief, there was no blood.

Letty put her arms around him. "Poor darling," she whispered.

Reid didn't hear the endearment. He sat with his forehead resting against her shoulder, his breath wheezing in his throat, his whole body shaking from the nightmare. Letty laid her cheek against his hair and rocked him gently, as if he was a

228

child. "Hush," she whispered, stroking the nape of his neck.

When his breathing had steadied, she released him and straightened his bedclothes and rearranged his pillows. "Sit back."

Clumsily, Reid obeyed.

Letty pulled the covers up, poured a quarter of a glass of brandy, and sat beside him while he sipped. He needed both hands to hold the glass steady. "Does your head hurt terribly?" she asked when he'd finished.

Reid glanced at her. His eyelashes were spiky with tears. "No."

Letty's heart clenched painfully with love for him. She took the glass and climbed off the bed and poured Reid a teaspoon of valerian. "Here."

Reid swallowed the valerian.

"Would you like me to read to you?" Letty asked diffidently.

Reid looked at her and hesitated, and she knew that they were both thinking about last night. The hesitation drew so long that she was certain Reid was going to say *No,* but instead he gave a brief nod.

He trusted her.

Letty had to swallow a sudden lump in her throat. She picked up Herodotus and sat at the end of the bed. "Aristagoras, the author of the Ionian revolt . . ."

She didn't stop reading when Reid's eyelids grew heavy, nor did she lean over and kiss him; she didn't think she could endure it if he rebuffed her tonight. She read eight pages, ten pages, twelve, until Reid was deeply and profoundly asleep, and then she closed the book and sat looking at him in the candlelight: the bony, beautiful face, peaceful now in sleep; the slow rise and fall of his chest.

How could Reid believe he was dead?

She hugged Herodotus and watched him sleep. Rain pattered steadily against the windowpanes. The night chill sank into her skin, making her shiver. Finally, Letty climbed off the bed. She laid her fingertips lightly and fleetingly on Reid's brow, and then tiptoed from the room.

It was still raining in the morning. The landlord informed them that the post road was under water in several places. "Then I think we should stay here," Letty said.

Embroidery was *not* her favorite way of passing time, but there was little else to do. Letty stitched by the fire, while Reid and Houghton sat at the table, deep in discussion. She listened idly while they debated the merits of a confectioner's shop over a bakery over a chandlery and then argued back and forth over whether to purchase a farm or two as well.

In the early afternoon the rain eased to a drizzle, and two hours after that it stopped entirely. Letty put aside her embroidery with relief. "I'm going for a walk. Do either of you wish to come?"

Both men looked up. "A walk?" Houghton said. "Absolutely! You coming, sir?"

They set out fifteen minutes later—with the addition of Eliza and Green—heading east along a narrow lane pocked with overflowing potholes. Letty strode briskly in her sturdiest leather half boots, inhaling air redolent with woodsmoke and decaying leaves. Houghton matched his stride to hers. "Good to be outside," he said.

"Isn't it just!"

They walked for half a mile, coming to a junction with an even narrower lane. "The landlord said we can take this one north for a mile," Houghton said. "There's another lane that'll bring us back to the inn. It's not signposted, but he says it's bounded by a ditch with a good crop of withies, so we can't miss it."

"Withies?"

"Willow shoots. For making baskets."

The landlord was correct; the ditch of withies was unmistakable, although to Letty's eye they looked more like reeds than willow shoots. Green produced a penknife from his pocket and managed, without getting his feet wet, to harvest one withy. Watching him, Letty thought how boyish he looked—and how unlike the dispirited young man shoveling manure in Basingstoke. She glanced from Green's beaming face to Reid's solemn one.

Houghton stood alongside Reid, and for a moment the likeness between the two men made her blink. Houghton had craggy features and his eyes were brown not silver, but even so, he and Reid were extraordinarily similar. Both large men, grown too thin. Both with tanned skin and direct, alert gazes. Both with the same hard, faintly dangerous edge. One could tell at a glance they were soldiers—and that they'd killed in battle.

Houghton spoke with a West Country accent, but in every other respect, he and Reid could be brothers. Was that why Reid was so determined to rescue him?

Letty glanced at Houghton's empty left sleeve. The men's brotherhood went deeper than the eye could see. Both had been crippled at Vimeiro, even if only Houghton's wounds were visible.

She looked at Reid again. He needed rescuing even more than Houghton had.

But she didn't know how to save him.

Reid noticed her glance. "Shall we continue?"

Letty nodded.

They walked without speaking, the mud sucking at their boots. The lane was scarcely wide enough for a cart, more path than road. Letty glanced back. Houghton had lingered at the withies with Green and Eliza. She heard their laughter, faintly.

She studied Reid's face. He was gazing out across the flat, dank, wet landscape, and even though he was within touching distance he seemed as remote and unapproachable as if he were on the other side of the ocean.

How could she save him?

The only tools at her disposal were words.

Letty chewed on her lower lip, and imagined repeating what she'd said at Whiteoaks. Reid would be angry. Furious.

But *someone* had to say something.

Reluctance and urgency wrestled in her breast, and for several minutes the reluctance won out—if she spoke to Reid on this subject again, their newly patched friendship would be sundered. He'd look at her with dislike glittering in his eyes and speak to her with curt hostility in his voice, and she wasn't certain she could bear it.

But if she didn't speak of it, Reid would continue on his path, and that would be a thousand times worse.

Letty's sense of urgency grew. Pressure built inside her until it felt as if she would burst. She *had* to try again.

"Icarus?"

Reid glanced at her. "Mmm?"

Letty took a deep breath. She felt sick with nervousness. "I asked you a question at Whiteoaks, and you never answered it."

"Didn't I? I beg your pardon. You'll have to refresh my memory."

The feeling of nausea increased. Letty took another deep breath and grabbed hold of her courage. "If Pereira had told the French what you told them—and if he'd survived—what fate would you have wanted for him?"

Reid halted. He glanced sharply back at the others, out of earshot at the withy ditch.

"Would you have wished him dead?"

Reid's gaze swung back to her. She saw outrage gather on his face.

"Or would you have thought that he'd already suffered more than any man can endure, and that he deserved forgiveness instead?"

"That is none of your business."

"I've made it my business," Letty told him. "And I intend to keep asking until you give me an answer. Would you have wished—in your heart—for Pereira to hang?"

Reid's face was pale with fury. He turned from her and began striding down the lane, his boots spraying muddy water.

Letty hurried to catch up. "It's a simple question, Icarus. Yes, or no."

Reid didn't reply. He walked faster.

Letty stretched her legs, almost running. "Yes, or no?" she said urgently.

Reid halted, and swung round to face her. "For God's sake, woman!" His voice was almost a shout. "Leave me alone!"

"Would you have wished Pereira to hang?"

Reid was breathing heavily, his eyes bright and angry, his nostrils flared.

"Yes, or no?"

"Yes!" he flung at her. "Yes! Of course I would!" He swung from her again, striding fast, paying no attention to the puddles.

Letty stayed where she was for several seconds, hearing the *clang* in her ears. Did Reid know he was lying to himself? Then she gathered up her skirts and hurried anxiously after him.

The lane narrowed further. Overgrown hedges crowded close on either side. Letty was out of breath by the time she caught up with Reid. The lane made a sharp left turn, ducked through a grove of willows, dipped into a hollow where water flowed sluggishly—

Reid splashed knee-deep into the water before he caught himself. He recoiled so violently that he almost fell over. Letty saw panic flare across his face.

"Icarus!" She caught his arm, steadying him, drawing him several paces back from the water.

Reid shrugged his arm free.

233

"Are you all right?"

He inhaled a wheezing breath and bent over, bracing his hands on his knees. His hat fell off.

Letty picked it up. Cold water sloshed in her half boots. Reid's face was tense, his eyes squeezed shut, muscles knotted in his jaw. She judged him very close to vomiting.

If I ever find the men who did this to him, I will kill them myself.

Letty gripped Reid's hat in her hands and wondered how to rescue him, and then she bent until her mouth was close to his ear. "You lied to me, back there. You wouldn't have wanted Pereira to hang. You would have wanted him to live."

Reid's eyes opened. "No," he said hoarsely.

"You're lying, Icarus. If Pereira had told them, and if he'd survived, you'd have wanted him to live."

Reid shook his head. He straightened to his full height. His mouth was grim.

Letty handed him his hat. "You're lying to yourself, and you need to acknowledge that." She turned and headed back in the direction of the withy ditch. She made herself stand tall, made herself walk briskly, but inside she was trembling.

*C*HAPTER 34

*I*carus tried to conceal his ill temper, but he knew Green and Houghton had noticed. He smiled tightly, and offered the excuse of a headache. To Miss Trentham, he offered no excuse. She knew exactly why he was angry.

He ate his dinner grimly, ignoring Miss Trentham's promptings that he have a second helping of pie and another serving of suet pudding.

Houghton ate seconds.

After the meal, Icarus was strongly tempted to go up to his bedchamber and have a slug of brandy. He didn't. He played two games of backgammon with Houghton and then excused himself—saying a coldly courteous good night to Miss Trentham—and climbed the stairs to his bedchamber. That infernal woman. Talking about things she had no knowledge of. How *dared* she talk of poor, damned Pereira?

Icarus paused at the top of the stairs and squeezed his eyes shut and tried not to remember. But he couldn't hold the memories back: Pereira begging them to stop. Pereira sobbing and gasping and choking and vomiting. Pereira telling them in desperate, thickly accented French, *Oui, oui, c'est vrai. C'est vrai!*

And the bastards had still killed him.

Icarus blinked several times and inhaled deeply through his nose and opened the door to his bedchamber. He pasted a stiff smile on his face and let Green help him out of his boots and his tailcoat and then sent the boy away.

When he went to lock the door, he discovered this was impossible: there was no keyhole. Worse, there wasn't even a latch. His stool was too short to jam beneath the door handle, and the washstand too tall.

"Fuck," he said, under his breath.

The brandy bottle sat on the bedside table, beckoning him.

Icarus poured himself a glass, drained it in one swallow, coughed, caught his breath, and put the glass back on the tray. He saw Pereira in his mind's eye: lanky in his uniform, with a boyish face and dark, eager eyes.

Miss Trentham had been correct: he wouldn't have wanted Pereira to hang.

Icarus sat on the edge of the bed and bowed his head into his hands. He wished this was over. He wished he was in his grave.

The floorboards outside his door creaked.

Icarus stood swiftly—ducking his head—and flung the door open. Miss Trentham stood in the corridor, her hand on her own door handle, her face dimly visible. He saw her eyebrows lift. "Icarus?"

"I don't want you in my room tonight," he told her coldly.

Miss Trentham's expression became perfectly blank.

"Do you hear me? I won't have you in my room tonight!"

Miss Trentham lifted her chin and met his gaze straightly. "I have no intention of lying awake half the night listening to you scream. If your nightmares wake *me*, you may be certain that I shall wake *you*."

Icarus hissed a sharp, angry breath at her. "You are the most dreadful woman it has ever been my misfortune to meet!"

Her face tightened as if he'd struck her; she'd heard *that* truth.

Icarus turned on his stockinged heel and stalked into his bedchamber, closing the door with a muted slam. Once in his room, his rage drained away. He sat on the edge of his bed and bowed his head into his hands again. *I wish I was in my grave.*

He lay on stony ground, bound hand and foot, retching helplessly, more dead than alive, water streaming from his mouth, from his nose, from his hair, from his clothes—and already they were heaving him up again, carrying him back to the creek. Icarus wheezed desperately for breath. The rage that had sustained him was gone; he'd vomited it up long ago. *Please, God, please.*

But God didn't hear him, and here was the creek again, black water glinting in the moonlight.

Icarus thrashed weakly, frantically. "No! No! Please!"

He was dumped facedown alongside Pereira's sodden corpse. Someone crouched and gripped his hair, forcing his head up. "The northeast ridge, it is not defended, yes? C'est vrai?"

Icarus struggled to breathe, water rattling in his throat.

His hair was released. A curt order was barked. Rough hands gripped him, lifted him. Icarus saw the gleam of moon-lit water. Panic took over. "It's true!" he screamed hoarsely. "It's true!"

His captors dumped him on the ground again. The fingers dug into his hair, lifting his head. "Dis-moi. Tell me."

Hot, despairing tears leaked from his eyes. "C'est vrai," he choked out.

His hair was released. His head fell forward.

He heard the hasty crunch of footsteps, heard hurried voices. The footsteps and voices receded. Silence came. Echoing, empty silence.

Icarus pressed his face into the stony soil, and wept.

"Icarus!" Someone shook his shoulder. "Icarus, wake up!"

Icarus wrestled his way to wakefulness. His eyes slitted open. He saw shadowy bedhangings and a pale, anxious face. "Icarus?"

With consciousness came no ease. He'd told them. Oh, God, he'd *told* them.

Icarus turned his face into the pillow and cried as despairingly as he had at Vimeiro.

"Icarus?" Someone stroked his hair. "Icarus?"

He couldn't stop crying, couldn't stop the huge, wrenching sobs, couldn't catch his breath.

"Icarus . . ." The person gathered him in her arms, rocked him gently. "Hush, hush . . ."

He wept endless tears, while someone held him, and rocked him, and stroked his hair. An eternity passed. He finally ran out of tears, but not of despair. He was submerged in despair, drowning in despair.

Gentle fingers wiped his face. "Go to sleep, Icarus."

He recognized the voice: Letty Trentham.

It was her arms around him, her warmth in his bed. Dimly, at the back of his brain, beneath the fog of despair, beneath the exhaustion, he knew he should turn her out of his bedchamber, but he didn't want her to stop holding him, didn't want her to leave.

"Go to sleep," she whispered again, and Icarus obeyed.

She was gone when he woke, but he could tell she'd spent the night with him; it wasn't just the dent in the pillow and the rumpled hollow under the bedcovers, it was the empty feeling in his bed, as if someone had been holding him until only a few minutes ago.

Icarus touched where she'd lain. The sheets were still faintly warm.

Green tiptoed in half an hour later, and drew open the curtains when he found Icarus awake. "Sergeant Houghton walked down to the post road, sir, and he says it's no longer flooded."

Icarus sat up slowly. His head felt thick and his limbs lethargic. He wanted to curl up in a dark, quiet place and close his eyes and never open them again.

"We should be able to reach Taunton today," Green said cheerfully, laying out the razor and strop.

Icarus washed and shaved and dressed and ate and climbed into the post-chaise, and climbed out of it again in Taunton, but none of it seemed real. He spent the day in a fog of despair that he couldn't fight his way out of. He was aware of Houghton and Miss Trentham and Green watching him anxiously, but the fog was so dense, and wrapped so thickly around him, that he couldn't free himself. He lay awake that night, staring blindly up at the ceiling. Tonight was going to be one of those nights that was as long as a year, where every second was endless—

"Icarus!"

Icarus fell off his horse and scrambled to his feet, flailing with his fists. They wouldn't take him this time. He'd fight to the death rather than be captured.

His fist connected with something. He heard someone fall.

"Icarus, *stop!*"

He halted, panting, blinking.

His surroundings came into focus: four-poster bed, washstand, fireplace, candle burning in a chamberstick. And on the floor at his feet, Miss Trentham.

Icarus stared down at her stupidly.

"Icarus?"

Awareness washed over him. Icarus staggered under the weight of it and heard himself groan. He dragged air into his lungs, but couldn't find speech.

"Icarus?" Miss Trentham said again, cautiously.

With the awareness came belated horror. He'd struck her again. He held out his hand to her and helped her to her feet. His arm was trembling. His whole body was trembling. "You all right?"

"Yes. Are you?"

He nodded dumbly, and lurched down to sit on the edge of the bed. "Sorry. Didn't mean to."

"Of course you didn't." Miss Trentham briskly rearranged his pillows and straightened the bedclothes. "In you get."

Icarus climbed into bed.

"Here."

He swallowed a quarter of a glass of brandy. And then a teaspoon of valerian. Miss Trentham sat beside him and opened Herodotus. "On the side of the barbarians, the number of vessels was six hundred . . ."

After she'd turned the first page, Icarus reached out and took her hand. "Did I hurt you?"

"No."

"I'm sorry I hit you."

She glanced at him and smiled. "I know."

Some of his guilt subsided. He lay listening to her cool, quiet voice and holding on to her warm hand. His eyelids grew heavy. He could no longer keep them open. Miss Trentham's voice slowed, then stopped.

Icarus blinked open his eyes with effort. He didn't want her to go. He wanted her to stay here all night.

He turned his face towards her, and Miss Trentham hesitated and then bent to lightly kiss him.

Icarus sighed with pleasure.

They kissed, and kissed some more, and his arms were around her, and he heard himself say sleepily against her mouth, "Don' go."

Miss Trentham stopped kissing him. She grew very still. "I'm the most dreadful woman you've ever met."

Icarus tried to open his eyes, but his eyelids were too heavy. "'S true," he said. "But you're also the best. The worst, an' the best."

Miss Trentham huffed a faint laugh. She seemed to relax. She kissed him again, lingering on his lower lip, and then pressed her mouth to his throat.

A low, purring hum kindled in his blood. Icarus uttered a wordless sound of pleasure.

Miss Trentham kissed his throat again and his blood hummed and it was a marvelous feeling, absolutely the most marvelous feeling in the world. This must be how embers in a banked fire felt—warm and safe and alive and snug and slumberous.

Icarus gave himself up to it, let himself float on it, let himself drift to sleep, warm and safe and happy.

He half-woke at dawn. Someone bent over him, pressed a light kiss to his cheek, whispered in his ear. Icarus sank back to sleep before catching the words. He didn't wake again until several hours later, and even then not fully. He lay for some time, warm and drowsy. Reality began to intrude. He heard voices in the street outside, heard the distant rattle of carriage wheels, heard the muffled thump of footsteps descending the staircase.

Icarus yawned, and stretched, and rolled over—and was confronted by a pillow that someone else had clearly slept on. He blinked. Memory washed over him. Letty Trentham. He'd asked her to sleep in his bed. It had been Letty Trentham who'd bent over him at dawn, Letty Trentham who'd whispered in his ear.

You're not dead, Icarus Reid, she'd said. *Do you hear me? You're not dead.*

His warm, drowsy contentment congealed.

Icarus sat up and flung back the bedclothes.

He'd *asked* Letty Trentham to spend the night in his bed? What in God's name had induced him to do that? It was unforgivable! Inexcusable!

Icarus climbed out of bed, mortification cold in his belly. *No brandy tonight,* he told himself, jerking open the curtains. Not one mouthful. Not even one drop.

CHAPTER 35

$\mathscr{T}$hey reached Exeter after darkness had fallen. Icarus directed the postilions to a hotel on Cathedral Close that had been recommended to him as a quiet and superior establishment. It was certainly superior, but it was also much larger than he'd anticipated. "Perhaps we should find somewhere more discreet."

"I'm wearing a veil," Miss Trentham said. "No one will recognize me."

Icarus wasn't so certain. He thought that anyone who knew Miss Trentham well would recognize her, veil or not. The austere elegance of her clothes was unmistakable, as was her cool poise.

They didn't dine until nearly eight o'clock. Icarus saw at a glance that Miss Trentham had spoken to the kitchen staff. Of the ten superb dishes arranged on the table, only the roasted chicken would present Houghton with difficulty. Icarus carved for them all, slicing the breast meat wafer thin. *You should be able to cut that with a fork*, he wanted to say, but set his tongue between his teeth. Houghton wouldn't want to be fussed over.

They lingered over the meal. Miss Trentham was Tish again. She'd been Tish every evening since Houghton had joined them. It was irrational to feel jealous, but he did. Icarus frowned down at his plate and stabbed a piece of baked salmon with his fork. He should be glad if she and Houghton made a match of it.

Miss Trentham was wearing a gown of soft lavender and a pretty shawl the color of dusty grapes. In the nearly four weeks he'd known her, she had yet to wear strong, bright colors. She seemed to prefer muted shades—sage green, dove gray, soft blue, lavender. They suited her pale skin and blonde-brown hair and sea-colored eyes.

Icarus blinked, and looked more closely at Miss Trentham's eyes. Tonight they were lavender-gray.

She caught his glance and smiled a Tish-smile that made her look quite extraordinarily attractive—the curve of her cheeks, the curve of her lips, the smoky lavender of her eyes. "What do you plan for tomorrow?"

"Uh . . ." Icarus blinked again, feeling momentarily off balance. He gathered his wits. "The receiving office, for Cuthbertson's address, and then the sergeant and I are going shopping for clothes."

Miss Trentham grinned at Houghton, looking even more like Tish than before. "You have my sympathy, Sergeant."

Houghton pulled a humorous face, but his glance at Icarus was faintly discomfited. Why was that? But even as Icarus asked himself the question, he knew the answer: Because Houghton had no money.

"I'll advance you some of your salary," Icarus told the sergeant, helping himself to another portion of veal pie. "More pie? Or would you like some more chicken?"

He chewed his food stolidly, trying not to notice how attractive Miss Trentham was—such an intelligent, interesting face. *No brandy tonight,* he told himself. *Not one single drop.*

Icarus repeated the words as he climbed into bed—*No brandy, no brandy*—but when he heaved out of his nightmare several hours later, it took all his effort just to breathe, all his willpower not to vomit. He accepted the quarter-glass Miss Trentham handed him without a second thought. By the time he'd drunk the brandy, the urge to vomit had gone. He swallowed the valerian and lay back on his pillows. Lazy warmth permeated his limbs. He watched Miss Trentham pick up Herodotus. She came to the bed and smiled down at him and stroked his hair back from his brow.

Icarus smiled sleepily at her.

Miss Trentham settled herself cross-legged on the bed beside him. She opened the book.

Icarus held her hand and listened to the quiet rise and fall of her voice. His eyelids drooped lower and lower.

After an eon, he realized that Miss Trentham had stopped reading. He turned his head, searching for her, not wanting her to go.

She didn't leave. Instead, she leaned down and kissed him.

Icarus sighed with pleasure and kissed her back. Another eon drifted past, an eon of warm, languid kisses.

"Would you like me to stay?" Miss Trentham whispered against his mouth.

Icarus knew this was a question that should alarm him. Why? Cogs turned slowly in his brain. Memory grudgingly unfurled. He'd made a decision that morning: No brandy. No asking Miss Trentham to stay the night with him.

It was too late to hold by his first decision; he wasn't top-heavy, but he was definitely mellow, his wits slow, his inhibitions floating somewhere out of reach—and since when had a quarter of a glass of brandy been enough to do that to him? *Since you were six weeks in bed with the fever,* a little voice said in his head.

"Would you like me to stay?"

Icarus wrestled with his conscience, but his conscience was weak tonight, and all he could think of was how much he *wanted* her to stay.

"Icarus? Yes, or no?"

There were two answers he could truthfully give her. No, he didn't want her to stay, because it was wrong and reprehensible and dangerous to her reputation. Yes, he wanted her to stay, because when she held him he felt safe and happy.

Icarus settled on the truth that gave him what he craved, even though he knew he didn't deserve it and even though he knew he'd regret it in the morning. "Yes."

CHAPTER 36

November 27th, 1808
Exeter, Devonshire

$\mathcal{I}$carus slept the night in Miss Trentham's arms, feeling warm and safe and happy. He roused briefly at dawn to hear her voice in his ear—*You're not dead, Icarus Reid*—and then fell back into deep, dreamless sleep. He didn't wake until Green opened the curtains. Icarus drowsily watched him lay out the shaving tackle and today's clothes. A good lad, Green. Cheerful, hard-working, diligent in his duties. He made a mental note: *Ask Houghton to hire Green when I'm gone.* Houghton would treat the lad well.

"What's the time?"

"Ten o'clock, sir."

Icarus pushed back the bedcovers and sat up, reluctant to leave the bed's warmth and the sense of safety and happiness that lingered there. He rubbed his face and raked his hands through his hair. *You're not dead,* Letty Trentham had said when she left him, and it was true that he felt like a man again, not a staggering corpse—but it was also true that he *was* dead. He'd been dead ever since he'd uttered those terrible, unpardonable words: *It's true. C'est vrai.*

Icarus lowered his hands, and clenched them together. He didn't deserve Letty Trentham's kindness or her kisses, and he certainly didn't deserve to have her hold him while he slept.

And she didn't deserve to be used by him.

She deserved a good man, someone decent and honorable who treated her with respect, who valued her not for her ability to hear lies but for herself, because she was strong and generous and compassionate, and altogether a remarkable woman.

Icarus sat on the edge of the bed and felt ashamed of himself.

"Are you all right, sir?"

Icarus looked at Green. "No brandy tonight," he said. "Only the valerian."

"Very good, sir."

He and Houghton visited the postal receiving office, where they learned that Colonel Cuthbertson's mail went to Okehampton, on the edge of Dartmoor some twenty miles from Exeter. Then, armed with a list provided by the hotel proprietor, Icarus took Houghton to a tailor, a boot maker, a hatter, and a haberdasher's, outfitting him from head to toe—stockings and drawers, breeches and pantaloons, shirts, nightshirts, waistcoats, tailcoats and a greatcoat, boots, shoes, hats and gloves, neckcloths. "What have we forgotten, Houghton?" he said, glancing around the haberdasher's. A cornucopia of items met his gaze: bolts of fabric, ribbons and laces, muffs and fans and reticules, clocked stockings and plain stockings, handkerchiefs and gloves, parasols and umbrellas. "Handkerchiefs. And would you like an umbrella?"

"No, sir."

Icarus glanced around again. His gaze alighted on a display of knitted coin purses. "Choose a coin purse, as well."

Outside on the street, Icarus examined the list. Only the leather goods shop remained. He pulled out his pocket watch, and glanced at the time. "We must get you a watch."

"Sir," Houghton said desperately. "I don't need all this!"

Icarus slid the watch back into his waistcoat pocket. "You're to be my representative, Houghton. You must dress the part."

"But I'm not a gentleman! I don't speak right! All this—" Houghton's gesture included more than just the haberdasher's shop, "—is as much use as dressing a monkey in a man's costume!"

Icarus eyed him. Houghton's face was flushed.

This was important. Too important to brush off. Icarus felt carefully for his words. "Tell me, Sergeant . . . did you judge the men in your charge by who their parents were, or by their character?"

Houghton's gaze fell. "By their character," he muttered.

"And what made you respect an officer most? His birth, or his character?"

Houghton pressed his lips together. "His character," he admitted again.

Icarus stepped closer, ignoring the passersby jostling them. He pitched his voice low: "It doesn't matter who your parents were, or how you talk, Sergeant. What matters is who *you* are—and you're a better man than most I've known. You're not a monkey dressed in a costume, you're not *playing* the part of a gentleman; in your character, you *are* a gentleman."

Houghton's cheeks reddened. He glanced up, meeting Icarus's eyes.

Icarus clapped him on the shoulder. "Come on, man, let's find that leather goods shop. You need luggage—and a pocketbook!"

The purchases made, they walked back to the hotel. Icarus ordered two post-chaises for twelve thirty the next day. An edgy sense of anticipation built in him. He knew he'd find Cuthbertson tomorrow.

He could think of no reason for Cuthbertson to pass information to the French, but he had a feeling—a feeling close to certainty—that Cuthbertson had.

Why? Why would he do such a thing?

He found himself fidgeting during dinner. Miss Trentham had to suggest, twice, quite firmly, that he eat. After the meal, he played backgammon with Houghton. His mind was on Cuthbertson. He lost both games.

Up in his bedchamber, he noted that Green had remembered to remove the brandy. Not that it mattered tonight; he doubted he'd sleep. His head was full of Cuthbertson. Was he the traitor?

Icarus blew out his candle and lay staring up at the dark ceiling. *Cuthbertson.*

But he did fall asleep, and it wasn't Cuthbertson he dreamed of, but a creek in Portugal, and when Letty Trentham woke him, he almost fell out of bed trying to hit her.

Icarus struggled back to full consciousness. Deep shudders wracked him. His breath wheezed in his throat.

"Where's the brandy?"

"Told Green I didn' want it," he said hoarsely.

Miss Trentham put her hands on her hips. "Well, that was foolish, wasn't it?"

Yes. Very foolish. There was nothing he wanted more right now than some brandy.

Icarus sat hunched on the edge of the bed, struggling to control his breathing, shaking like a leaf in a windstorm, dimly aware of Miss Trentham opening cupboards, opening drawers. She finally found the brandy bottle in his portmanteau, underneath the high bed. Her search had produced no glass. Miss Trentham plucked the small, decorative vase from the mantelpiece, wiped out the dust with a corner of her shawl, and poured brandy into it.

"Not too much," Icarus said. "A few mouthfuls only."

Miss Trentham glanced at him, and stopped pouring, and when she gave him the vase he was relieved to see that there was barely a finger's width of brandy in it.

Icarus sipped while she straightened his bedding. He drank slowly, savoring each small mouthful. The brandy's warmth crept through his body. Muscle by muscle, he felt himself relax. His breathing steadied, his shuddering stopped.

"Would you like more?" Miss Trentham asked, when he'd finished.

Icarus did want more, but he shook his head.

Miss Trentham took the empty vase and placed it back on the mantelpiece. She measured out a teaspoon of valerian.

Icarus swallowed it.

Miss Trentham climbed up on the bed and sat cross-legged beside him. She opened Herodotus, flicking through the pages, looking for the marker.

"Letty," Icarus said firmly. "Tonight you're not going to sleep here."

Miss Trentham looked up from Herodotus.

"It's *wrong*," Icarus said. "You must know that it's wrong!"

Her expression didn't change in any way that he could put his finger on, except that it *did* change, infinitesimally, almost imperceptibly—and he wasn't sure how to interpret that alteration. Contempt? Miss Trentham knew as well as he that everything they did at night was wrong. It was wrong that she entered his bedchamber. Wrong that she sat on his bed and read to him. Wrong that they kissed.

And he'd allowed those things to happen because they comforted him. Icarus's shame increased. "Perhaps you should leave now."

Miss Trentham looked down at the open book on her lap. She hadn't seemed aloof before, but she suddenly seemed so now, as if she'd drawn into herself. "Is that what you want?"

Icarus was unable to reply truthfully *and* honorably at the same time. He chose an indirect answer instead: "You shouldn't be in here."

"Shouldn't?" Miss Trentham's mouth twisted wryly. "A friend of mine used to say that *shouldn't* was a word that took the joy out of life." Her lips lost their wry twist; her expression became sad. "She's dead now, because she *shouldn't* have put her horse at a fence it couldn't jump."

Icarus thought he knew which friend she meant: Lucas Kemp's twin sister. Someone for whom Miss Trentham had worn blacks for a full year. "I'm sorry."

Miss Trentham closed Herodotus and put the book to one side. "I wanted to ask you something tonight."

"What?"

"You won't like it. You'll think it a question I *shouldn't* ask."

"What?" Icarus said again, warily.

Miss Trentham hesitated and bit her lip, and then she took a deep breath and lifted her chin and met his eyes squarely, and she so visibly gathered her courage and her resolution that Icarus knew he *definitely* didn't want to hear what she was going to say.

"Please will you let me kiss you the way Tom kissed Lucas?"

Icarus recoiled against the pillows. "No!"

"Why not?"

Why not? There were so many reasons why not. A thousand reasons why not. "Because . . . because it would be contemptible of me to allow you to do that!"

Her gaze was steady on his face. "Why would it be contemptible?"

Icarus thought of Matlock kneeling at Lucas Kemp's feet, and then he imagined Miss Trentham kneeling at his own feet, and his cock pulsed and his breath choked in his throat and for a moment he couldn't speak, couldn't do anything more than shake his head vehemently.

"Why would it be contemptible?"

"Because it *would*! Because . . . because my behavior

towards you has been—from the very outset!—unforgivable, and if I allowed you to do that, it would be more unforgivable than everything else put together!"

Miss Trentham surveyed him, her gaze serious, and it felt as if she could see inside him, could see his heart beating fast and agitatedly, could see the shameful images in his head.

"From my point of view it wouldn't be contemptible or unforgivable. I would consider it a . . . a gift. But if you feel yourself unequal to it, then of course you may refuse."

A gift? Icarus stared at her in utter disbelief. He was either drunk or dreaming. "You actually *want* to do it?"

Her gaze lowered. She blushed. "I wouldn't be asking if I didn't want to."

Icarus was rendered speechless with astonishment.

Miss Trentham took one end of her shawl and began to pleat the border, directing her words to her fingers, not to him. "Tomorrow we'll reach Okehampton and find Colonel Cuthbertson, and it will likely be he who betrayed you, and . . . and then I'll go back to London and we'll never see each other again."

Never see Letty Trentham again? It gave Icarus a funny feeling in his chest.

"And I thought . . . while we still have the opportunity . . . perhaps we could do this?" Her blush deepened, and her fingers busily, nervously, pleated the shawl. "If you can bring yourself to allow it."

Icarus's cock pulsed again. He clutched the bedclothes to his chest like a barrier. "Allow it? Of course I can't allow it! It would be inexcusably selfish of me!"

"Selfish?" Miss Trentham stopped pleating the shawl and glanced at him, a puzzled frown on her brow. "How would it be selfish of you?"

Icarus looked away. Because if he allowed her to do that to him, he'd be using her as he'd use a whore, and of all the ways he'd used her, that would be the worst.

Miss Trentham waited several seconds, and asked her question again. "How would it be selfish of you?"

He looked back at her, Letitia Trentham, England's greatest heiress, sitting on his bed in a nightgown and shawl, discussing oral congress with him, and for a moment his incredulity was so great that he almost laughed from it.

"Icarus? I see how it is selfish of *me*, but I don't see how it is selfish of *you*."

His laughter quenched. It *was* happening—and if there was one thing he knew about Miss Trentham's character, it was that she was persistent. She wasn't going to stop asking her question until he'd answered it.

"Icarus?"

He looked away again, and tried to frame his reply. "It would be selfish because . . . because I would be taking pleasure from you and not giving any back, and that's *wrong*—I couldn't possibly allow it! Not unless—" Abruptly, he halted. A whole realm of possibilities suddenly opened out in front of him.

"Unless what?"

Icarus glanced at her. Letty Trentham. Her long braid was slightly disheveled and her nightgown wrinkled, and she looked tempting and approachable and quite extraordinarily attractive.

His cock gave a strong pulse.

But using his mouth on Miss Trentham would be almost as reprehensible as allowing her to use her mouth on him. The two acts wouldn't cancel each other out; they'd *compound* the dishonor to her.

"Unless what, Icarus?"

He hesitated, and knew that she would keep asking until he answered. "Unless you allow me to reciprocate."

Miss Trentham's expression grew wary. "You'll have to explain what you mean by that."

"I mean that I could only allow you to kiss me *that* way if you allowed me to return the favor."

She recoiled slightly. He saw her shock, saw her instinctive grimace of distaste. "You mean . . . kiss me down there?"

"Yes."

Silence stretched for several seconds.

"Would you want to?" Miss Trentham asked, in an extremely dubious tone.

Icarus imagined tasting her intimately, and felt his cock stir. "Yes."

Miss Trentham wasn't going to let him. He could see it clearly on her face: the embarrassment, the reluctance. She was going to refuse and he should be relieved—he *was* relieved—because oral congress between them would be utterly inexcusable.

"All right," Miss Trentham said, and while Icarus was still gaping at her, she picked up Herodotus and found her marker. "When the Persian commanders and crews—"

"You agree?"

She glanced up, and nodded.

Heat suddenly flared between them. Icarus stared into her sea-colored eyes and heard his heartbeat hammering in his ears. He knew he should turn her out of his room . . . but he also knew that he wasn't going to.

He reached out and took the book from her and closed it. "Forget Herodotus."

CHAPTER 37

A vivid blush mounted in Miss Trentham's cheeks. She looked shy and self-conscious and awkward and apprehensive and embarrassed, all at the same time.

Icarus was abruptly ashamed of himself. He looked away from her. "Letty, we can't do this. You should go."

"But you agreed!"

He glanced back at her.

"Don't change your mind," Miss Trentham said urgently, laying her hand on his. "*Please,* Icarus."

Icarus hesitated. Was it wrong to give her what she wanted? Or wrong not to? Or was this one of those times when *every* choice was wrong?

I would consider it a gift, Miss Trentham had said.

It wasn't a gift an honorable man would give her. But they both knew he wasn't honorable.

"Please, Icarus."

He looked at her, and heard the plea in her voice—and knew that he was lost. He was going to do it. Because Letty Trentham wanted it, and because he wanted it, and because this could be the last night they ever spent together.

"You need some brandy. Where's that bottle?" Icarus climbed out of bed and splashed brandy into the bottom of the vase. He didn't want Miss Trentham self-conscious and awkward; he wanted her relaxed. He wanted her to enjoy what he was about to do to her. He gave her the vase. "It's not enough to make you drunk, I promise."

The first sip made Miss Trentham cough and choke. Her eyes watered. "You like this?"

"It has its time and place."

Miss Trentham drank the brandy stoically. Icarus sat on the bed alongside her, and listened to the hard, fast beating of his heart, and felt heat gather in his groin, and knew that he had no honor. No honor at all.

"Do you feel a little more relaxed?" he asked, when she'd finished.

Miss Trentham bit her lip, and glanced at him shyly, and nodded.

He put an arm around her shoulders and drew her close. *I'm going to miss you,* he thought, and then he kissed her gently. After a faint hesitation, she kissed him back.

Icarus kissed Miss Trentham until all trace of her shyness had gone and she was warm and breathless in his arms, then he stretched out and patted the bed alongside him. "Lie here."

She blushed, and did as he bid.

Icarus kissed her again, lingering on her lower lip, licking, nibbling, sucking lightly, making her gasp and tremble, and then he reached down and tugged her nightgown up to her knees.

Miss Trentham tensed slightly. "Relax," Icarus whispered against her mouth. He kissed her again, and eased her nightgown up another inch.

He kissed her a dozen times, and each time he drew the nightgown higher, until her thighs were almost fully bared. One more tug, and her groin would be exposed to his gaze.

Hot blood hummed eagerly in his cock, but Miss Trentham was tense again. Icarus kissed her. "Don't be afraid. I won't hurt you."

"I'm not afraid. I'm embarrassed."

"Don't be. You have a beautiful body." And she did. Her bare legs were long and slender. He could easily imagine them wrapped around his hips, a fantasy that made his cock twitch strongly.

Icarus laid a hand lightly on her knee. "Relax." Miss Trentham resisted for a fraction of a second, and then allowed him to part her legs and slowly stroke up her inner thigh. Her skin was impossibly smooth. Smoother than silk.

His cock stirred again.

Icarus let his hand slide all the way to the top of her leg. Was that the tickle of hair against his fingertips, or was he imagining that, too?

He looked at his hand, brown against the creamy paleness of her skin, and at the bunched-up nightgown hiding her groin, and then he tore his gaze from Letty Trentham's legs, and looked at her face. Her lips were rosy from his kisses. "You can return to your bedchamber if you wish. At any moment, if you want to stop, just say so."

"If I stop, you won't let me reciprocate. Will you?"

"No."

"Then I shan't ask you to stop." And then she bit her lip and said anxiously, "You don't have to do this, you know. Honestly! I won't think you're selfish if you don't—"

"I want to," Icarus said.

His need must have been audible in his voice, because her gaze dropped and she blushed.

"I want to," Icarus said again, more softly, almost a whisper, and he pushed her nightgown up to her waist. His cock gave an eager twitch at the sight of that little thatch of hair. He almost groaned. God, how he *wanted* this.

Icarus bent his head and inhaled her scent. It went straight to his loins. His cock didn't just twitch this time, it surged. If it had a voice, it would have barked an order: *Hurry up! Do it!*

Icarus settled himself between Letty Trentham's long, slender legs, and bent to the business of reciprocation. He laid a trail of tickling kisses up her inner thighs, then let his fingers wander through that thatch of hair—surprisingly silky, silkier than any woman he'd lain with—and parted her inner lips, stroking and teasing with his fingertips, finding her hot and damp and responsive—and dipped his head to let his warm breath tickle over her sensitive flesh—Lord, but she smelled amazing—and then tasted her.

Letty Trentham tasted just as good as she smelled. Icarus closed his eyes for a moment, a silent hum resonating in his throat, savoring her scent, savoring her taste. His cock was rock-hard, furnace-hot. He might climax just from this. Then he opened his eyes and set to work, teasing her with his fingers, with his mouth, with his teeth and tongue. He didn't need to look at her face to know that she liked it; her body told him—the tiny moans, the helpless shifting of her hips. She was hot and juicy and throbbing and absolutely ready to be bedded. Icarus felt a little spasm of pleasure ripple through her. He slid a finger inside her, licked—

Her body convulsed.

Icarus kept licking, kept stroking his finger inside her, until the convulsions died to mere tremors, then he sat up and drew her nightgown down and looked at her face. She wasn't Miss Trentham, cool and aloof. She wasn't Tish, lively and attractive. She was Letty, flushed and dark-eyed and indescribably tempting.

Icarus stared at her. His cock pulsed, pushing against his nightshirt, hot and aching. He wanted to mount her, wanted to sink himself to the hilt in her heat and ride her until they both cried out with pleasure.

Letty blinked, and moistened her lips. "Is that what it feels like for you?"

Icarus nodded.

"I understand why so many men have mistresses." She sat up. "My turn."

They both looked at his lap, where his cock tented his nightshirt. It looked as if he had a dueling pistol growing there. Icarus felt his face become scarlet with embarrassment.

"Lie down," she said.

He obeyed, clumsy with anticipation and arousal and need and shame, resting awkwardly back on the pillows. Letty drew his nightshirt up—and there was his cock, thick and ruddy, straining to attention like a soldier on parade.

Icarus couldn't think. Couldn't speak. Couldn't move.

"Do you consent to this, Icarus?"

He dragged his gaze from his cock, and stared at her. His breath was coming short and fast, and his heartbeat thundered in his ears.

Letty Trentham took his silence for assent. She bent her head and licked that smooth, crimson head.

Icarus's breath strangled in his throat. *Oh, God.*

She licked a second time. Every bone in his body turned to liquid. Icarus squeezed his eyes shut. This wasn't happening. It couldn't be happening.

But it *was* happening. Most definitely. He felt her soft lips, felt her warm, tickling breath, felt her tongue, supple and hot and velvety. Oh, God, her *tongue.*

Letty Trentham seemed to know exactly where to lick. Icarus heard himself panting, heard himself groaning. There was no space in his head for embarrassment or self-conscious-ness or shame. Every part of him was drowning in pleasure. *Oh, God.* She drew him into her soft, hot mouth. His hips flexed helplessly. His toes curled in ecstasy. He heard himself whimper.

Icarus managed one coherent thought—*I must stop her before I climax*—but then Letty Trentham sucked his cock lightly, and again more strongly, and he stopped being able to think at all. Time distorted, twisting in on itself, each second excruciatingly long, and then his climax burst through him like a thunderstorm, lightning bolts of pleasure burning through every vein in his body, illuminating him until he must glow like a bonfire.

Icarus didn't notice Letty Trentham pulling down his nightshirt, nor did he notice her rearranging the bedclothes, tucking the blankets up to his chin. He felt as if he was floating several feet above the mattress.

"You are not dead, Icarus Reid," she whispered in his ear as he plummeted towards sleep. "Do you hear me? You're *not* dead."

CHAPTER 38

November 28th, 1808
Devonshire

Letty watched Reid and Houghton plow their way through breakfast. Reid was embarrassed by memory of last night—she'd seen it in the way his cheeks had colored faintly when he'd first entered the room—but at least he was able to meet her eyes this morning. His manner became easier as the minutes passed. By the time breakfast was over, it was as if the intimacies in his bedchamber had never happened.

But they *had* happened. She could remember what he'd done to her, what she'd done to him. Those latter memories were the ones she dwelled on, the ones she returned to time and time again: Reid's taste and his scent, the shape of him in her mouth, the heat and the smooth hardness, the helpless noises he'd uttered. And most precious of all—the memory she hugged to herself—was the expression of dazed bliss on his face afterwards.

Reid pushed away his plate. "The carriages are ordered for twelve thirty. Sergeant Houghton and I have a little business to attend to. We'll be back by twelve fifteen at the latest. Will you be all right here?"

Letty nodded, and sipped her tea.

Houghton pushed his chair back. "I'll just fetch my hat, sir."

Reid stayed seated. When the door had closed, he said, "I want to buy him a pocket watch. I think he'll refuse it. He's touchy about charity."

Letty folded her napkin. "If you make it a gift?"

"That's what I was intending, but I don't think he'll be comfortable with it." He sighed, and ran a hand through his hair.

"Buy him a watch from a pawn shop. Something cheap, but functional."

"A pawn shop?" Reid frowned thoughtfully. "Yes, that's an idea." The frown cleared. "An excellent idea! And then I'll leave him *my* watch in my will. He can't object to that!"

Letty almost choked on her tea.

Reid didn't notice. He was pushing back his chair. "Is there anything I can get for you in town?"

Letty managed a stiff smile. "No, thank you." She stood and walked to the window and looked blindly out. Reid still intended to die?

Hot tears rushed to her eyes. What should she do? Yell at him? Grab his coat lapels and shake him? Slap him? Or sit on the floor at his feet and cry?

Outside, a coach-and-four pulled up with a faint clatter of wheels and jingle of harnesses. A liveried footman jumped down from the rumble seat and hurried to let down the steps.

If she told him it would break her heart if he died, would Reid change his mind?

Perhaps. But what a terrible burden to place on him; Reid had burdens enough. And what did her heart mean to him anyway? He didn't want her love. All he wanted from her was her ability to hear lies.

The coach had a team of matched blacks and a nobleman's crest on the door. A lady stepped down from the carriage.

Letty blinked back her tears. The lady was elegant, notably pregnant, and wore spectacles. A second lady descended the steps, also pregnant, but of diminutive stature and pretty rather than elegant—and then two men. Letty stiffened, and stared.

"What?" Reid said, coming to stand beside her.

"Lord Cosgrove and Sir Barnaby Ware."

"Suitors of yours?"

"No." Letty peered down at the two men. They stood talking to one another. As she watched, Cosgrove said something, grinning, that made Sir Barnaby throw back his head and laugh. "They're friends again."

"Friends?"

"They always were friends—best of friends!—and then Cosgrove's first wife died and there was a *dreadful* scandal, and they fell out, and I was so sorry, because I liked them both very much." She examined the two ladies. "Those must be their wives." Who was married to whom? Sir Barnaby answered her question, giving his arm to the petite blonde, smiling down at her, laying his hand on top of hers.

Letty turned away from the window. "I must fetch my veil. If they're staying here . . ."

She hurried from the private parlor.

Her desire to indulge in a bout of tears was thwarted by Eliza's presence in her bedchamber. "I've laid out your traveling cloak, ma'am, and your hat," she said cheerfully. "And the packing's almost done."

"Thank you." Letty placed the hat on her head, arranged the veil over it, and retreated back to the private parlor. It was empty, but even so, she dared not cry. A servant might walk in at any moment.

She sat by the window, rigidly tense, rigidly miserable. *Damn you, Icarus Reid.* How could he not see that he had every reason to live?

He couldn't see it, because he was a soldier. Breath, blood, and bones, a soldier.

It didn't matter that Reid had endured more than any man could be expected to endure. It didn't matter that his confession hadn't cost General Wellesley the battle, that no Englishmen had died because of it. What mattered was his betrayal.

Reid was a soldier, and he'd betrayed his own side, and his life had stopped at that point.

Letty sat with clasped hands and bowed head. *What can I say to him? How do I make him see that he deserves to live?*

Everything that she could think of saying, she'd already said.

A distant clock struck twelve sonorous notes. Letty sighed, and stood, and crossed to the door. The corridor was empty, but a voice floated to her ears. An agitated voice. "But I didn't, ma'am! I'm no thief!"

"You may tell that to the constable," a woman grimly replied.

Letty headed in the direction of the voices, and found herself looking up a staircase. The landlord's wife and a chambermaid were descending. The chambermaid's face was flushed and swollen from crying.

"Excuse me, madam," Letty said, raising her veil. "May I ask what's the matter?"

The landlady halted, and looked her up and down. With obvious effort, her mouth found a smile. "Mrs. Reid. Nothing's the matter. Just a little misunderstanding with one of the maids. I apologize if we disturbed you."

"You didn't disturb me. But I shall be *very* disturbed if you take this young woman to the constable."

The landlady lost her smile.

"I have an ear for the truth and I can tell you that your servant is speaking truthfully. Whatever has been lost, she didn't take."

The landlady eyed Letty. "Lady Shipley said she did."

"Then Lady Shipley is mistaken. May I ask what's missing?"

The landlady hesitated, and then said, "A pair of earrings. Diamond earrings."

Letty looked at the weeping chambermaid. "Did you take them?"

The girl shook her head frantically. "No, ma'am!"

"Do you know who took them?"

"No!"

Letty transferred her gaze to the landlady. "Your maid is telling the truth. The earrings must have been misplaced."

"Lady Shipley's room has been searched twice, top to toe," the landlady said heavily, and Letty saw that the grimness was a mask. Beneath it, the woman was almost as upset as the chambermaid. "And her luggage has been searched, too. I saw to it myself."

"Then perhaps Lady Shipley is mistaken. Perhaps she never brought the earrings with her at all."

"She wore them yesterday," the landlady said, even more heavily. "And Martha here is the only one who's been in that room."

No wonder the poor girl was distraught. A maidservant's word against a noblewoman's. The girl could find herself transported.

"Lady Shipley doesn't have a maid?"

"Not with her. She was taken ill."

"Hmm," Letty said, and wondered whether the maid was ill—or fictitious. She began to feel a strong interest in meeting Lady Shipley. "I'm not familiar with Lady Shipley. Where does she come from?"

"Yorkshire."

Yorkshire was conveniently far away. So far away that no one in Exeter could be expected to know anything about Lady Shipley.

"Where is she now? I'd like to speak with her."

The landlady glanced up the staircase. Letty's ears caught the sound of slow, measured footsteps descending. The landlady heard them, too. She looked at Letty.

"I promise I shan't make matters worse," Letty said. "And I will very likely make them much better."

The landlady hesitated a moment, then towed the maid down the last two steps to the landing and thrust the girl behind her, so she was half-hidden. Then she composed her face and folded her hands at her waist.

The footsteps grew more audible. *Creak, creak,* went the stair treads. The stiff black bombazine hem of a gown appeared, and then the gown itself, and then its wearer's face.

Lady Shipley was a stout woman, with graying hair and a square fleshy face. She had a small, displeased mouth and an imperious nose. A high-crowned black bonnet sat on her head, and in one black-gloved hand she carried a black reticule. She halted on the final step and looked down her beaked nose at them.

"Lady Shipley?" Letty asked.

Lady Shipley stared coldly at her for several seconds, and then inclined her head. "I am Lady Shipley."

Letty listened to the *clang* in her ears, and felt her heartbeat speed up. "My name is Reid. I understand that you've lost some earrings. Perhaps I can help find them?"

"They are not lost; they've been stolen." The words were spoken in an icy, affronted voice—and were wholly false. Lady Shipley transferred her arctic glare from Letty to the landlady. "And if you expect me to pay my bill, when one of your thieving servants has stolen earrings worth three thousand pounds, you are quite mistaken!"

The landlady opened her mouth, but Letty lifted two fingers in a tiny gesture, silencing her.

"I understand that your room has been searched twice, but are you *quite* certain that the earrings are missing?"

"Of course I'm certain!"

Clang.

"Perhaps they're in your reticule? Or in a pocket?"

Lady Shipley drew herself up majestically. "They most certainly are not!"

Clang.

Letty tried to smile diffidently. "Are you certain they're not in a pocket? I myself have misplaced items in pockets."

"They are not in a pocket!" A bell-tone of truth underlay the irate voice.

Letty's eyes caught movement: coming up the stairs were the landlord and a wide-eyed, anxious young waiter. The landlord looked as grim as his wife.

"Then your reticule, perhaps?"

Lady Shipley swelled with indignation. "Of course they're not in my reticule! Do you think I've not looked there a dozen times already?"

Clang.

The landlord hurried forward, his hands clasped in petition. "Lady Shipley—"

Lady Shipley swung to face him. "I demand to leave this thieves' den of a hotel!" she said, in a carrying voice. "I have never been more shocked in my life. You may be certain I shall tell *all* my acquaintances in London!" She caught sight of the maidservant, cringing behind the landlady, and swelled with wrath. "There she is! That nasty little thief! Why is she not clapped in irons? Where is the constable?"

The landlord gestured to the white-faced waiter. The lad turned and hurried down the stairs.

"I wouldn't if I were you," Letty said. "Lady Shipley's earrings have not been stolen."

Everyone swung to face her. The waiter halted on the stairs, and looked back up at her.

"Lady Shipley's earrings are in her reticule."

Lady Shipley inhaled an outraged breath, her chest swelling majestically. "They most certainly are not!"

Clang.

Letty smiled politely. "They're in your reticule, Lady Shipley. I suggest you take another look."

Lady Shipley clutched the reticule to her bosom. "I have never been so insulted in my life!"

"On second thoughts," Letty said. "Perhaps we *should* call for a constable, and he can look in your reticule?"

Lady Shipley lifted her jowled chin even higher. Was that

panic in the dark eyes? "I refuse to listen to any more of this nonsense."

Letty glanced down the staircase and met the waiter's eyes. "Fetch the constable. And hurry!"

A spasm of panic crossed Lady Shipley's face. "No! Wait!"

The waiter halted in mid-step.

There was a long moment of silence, when no one moved. Letty saw Lady Shipley swallow convulsively, saw her eyes dart from side to side as if looking for an escape.

"Would you like to check it now, while we're all here? That way no mistakes can be made." Letty caught the landlord's eye and tried to convey a message.

The man must have understood it. He stepped forward. "A good idea. Best to check, before the constable comes." His voice was not quite neutral, and held a hint of steel.

An occasional table stood in the corridor. The landlord took the vase from it and gave it to his wife, then opened his hand in a gesture. "You may empty your reticule here, Lady Shipley."

Lady Shipley clutched the reticule more tightly to her massive bosom. "I had rather do it in my room."

"I had rather you did it here." The steel was unmistakable this time.

Lady Shipley hesitated.

The landlord glanced down the staircase. "Walter, the constable."

The waiter didn't move; Lady Shipley did. She stalked forward and opened her reticule and began laying items on the little table: a handkerchief, a bottle of scent, a second handkerchief, hartshorn and *sal volatile,* a coin purse. "There! You see? No earrings."

"Tip it up," Letty suggested. "They may have fallen to the bottom."

Lady Shipley glared at her.

"Yes, tip it up," the landlord said. "Or the constable can."

Lady Shipley pressed her lips together, and tipped the

reticule upside down. A tiny object wrapped in black ribbon and fastened with a pin fell out.

They all looked at it. Lady Shipley was breathing heavily through her nose.

"Would you like to open it, Lady Shipley?" the landlord said, his tone barely cordial. "Or shall I?"

Lady Shipley fumbled with the pin and unwrapped the black ribbon. Inside lay two diamond earrings.

The waiter came up the stairs. He peered over his employer's shoulder.

"Fetch the constable, Walter," the landlord said.

"No!" cried Lady Shipley. "It was a mistake! I forgot!"

Clang. Clang.

The landlord glanced at his wife, who stood with tightly folded lips holding the vase.

"I would suggest that you *do* send for the constable," Letty said quietly. "This woman isn't who she claims to be. Her name is not Lady Shipley."

Lady Shipley drew a deep breath. "How dare you!" she said in a throbbing voice.

The woman certainly looked the part of a dowager noblewoman—the black bombazine, the imperious nose, the haughty manner—but Letty rather thought she was an adventuress. "Have you done this before? To avoid paying your bill?"

"How *dare* you insinuate such a thing!"

"Have you?"

Lady Shipley drew herself up even higher. "Of course not!"

Clang.

Letty met the landlord's eyes. "Send for the constable. Tell him that this woman's name isn't Lady Shipley and that she's played this trick before." Her gaze shifted to the tear-stained chambermaid, half-hidden behind the landlady. "Some other poor girl may have been accused of theft."

The landlord nodded. "Walter," he said, not looking at the waiter. "Fetch the constable." He smiled tightly at the false

270

Lady Shipley. "Madam, I suggest you wait here, in this parlor." He took two steps sideways and opened a door. "My wife and I will wait with you."

Lady Shipley fumbled her belongings back into the reticule. Her face was blotched with color, her hands trembling. Letty felt no pity for her.

The landlady placed the vase back on the little table. "Martha, go wash your face, dear," she said in a low voice, and then she met Letty's eyes and gave a nod. "Thank you very much, Mrs. Reid."

"You're welcome."

The echo of the waiter's rapid footsteps died away. Lady Shipley reluctantly entered the parlor. The landlady followed, looking martial. The chambermaid departed down the stairs, wiping her face.

The landlord paused in the parlor doorway, looking at Letty. "Madam? Will you wait for the constable with us?"

Letty suddenly remembered that her own identity in Exeter was as false as Lady Shipley's. She shook her head and tried to sound regretful: "We're leaving shortly. I'm certain you won't need my testimony; you and your wife witnessed everything I did."

The landlord nodded. "We're very much obliged to you." He stepped into the parlor and closed the door.

Letty stood for a moment in the empty corridor. She blew out a breath.

"That was masterful!"

Letty jumped, and jerked round.

Sir Barnaby's wife stood in the half-open doorway of another private parlor, petite and pregnant, her bright blue eyes fixed intently on Letty's face. "One might almost have thought it was magic, the way you could tell she was lying."

"Oh, no! Not magic!" Letty said, hearing the *clang* in her own words. "Just a knack."

Lady Ware shook her head. "*I* have a knack for seeing when people lie, but I couldn't have done what you just did. To me, it looked like magic."

271

"It wasn't," Letty said, and felt herself color. If Lady Ware truly *did* have a knack, she'd know that for a lie.

Lady Ware's lips twitched in a smile. Her head cocked to one side. "I could almost believe you had a Faerie godmother," she said, musingly. "You don't, do you, by any chance?"

CHAPTER 39

Letty's heart seemed to halt for an instant. *What* had Lady Ware just said?

"I have a Faerie godmother," Lady Ware said. "A terrifying creature! She has the blackest eyes and teeth like a fox. Her name's Baletongue."

Letty stared at her, struck speechless.

Lady Ware grinned. Dimples sprang to life in her cheeks. "You *do* have a Faerie godmother. I can tell from your face."

Letty swallowed, and found her voice. "Baletongue?"

"That's what my mother called her. No one knows her true name."

Letty swallowed again. She heard her heartbeat in her ears. "My mother called her Baletongue, too."

Lady Ware opened the door to the parlor wide. "Well, come in, then! Don't stand out there in the corridor!"

Letty obeyed, feeling dazed.

Lady Ware gestured to a chair. "We must be cousins. How long are you here? Charlotte will want to meet you!"

"Charlotte?"

"Countess Cosgrove. She's one of us, too." Lady Ware sat and leaned forward, her gaze avid. "To think that we're cousins!"

273

Letty stared back. "You're Sir Barnaby Ware's wife?"

Lady Ware promptly held out her hand. "Anne Ware, but you must call me Merry. Everyone does!"

Letty shook hands with her. Lady Ware's handclasp was firm. "My name's Letitia. Letty."

"I know who you are. You were pointed out to me in London. But I didn't know we were cousins." Lady Ware's gaze sharpened with interest. "Or that you'd married. I must have missed that announcement in the newspapers! Who is Mr. Reid?"

Letty felt her face grow warm. She looked away from that bright, eager stare. "I'm not married. My relationship with Mr. Reid is purely business." *Clang*. She hurried on: "He needed my knack, and it was easier to travel together if we pretended to be married, but we're not." She glanced back at Lady Ware. "No one knows I've come here, you see."

"You're traveling incognito?" Lady Ware's eyebrows lifted. She didn't look outraged; she looked fascinated.

Letty bit her lip, and nodded.

"How thrilling!" From her expression, Lady Ware was bursting with questions.

Letty hurried into speech: "You saw me in London? I'm afraid I don't recall meeting you."

"Oh, we never met," Lady Ware said, cheerfully. "I moved in different circles to you. But you were pointed out to me on several occasions."

Letty pulled a face. "The great heiress?"

"The great heiress who wouldn't marry." Lady Ware's eyes sparkled with curiosity. "Did you refuse them all because they were lying?"

Letty nodded.

"Then you've had your gift for a while?"

Letty nodded again. "Since I was twenty-one."

"It was twenty-five with Charlotte and me." Lady Ware jumped to her feet and crossed to the window and peered out. "Oh, how I wish Charlotte were here! She will *so* want

274

to meet you!" She turned to face Letty. "Neither of us knows anyone else who has Baletongue for a godmother."

"I don't know anyone else either," Letty admitted. "I thought it was just me."

Lady Ware grinned. "No. There's now three of us!" She came swiftly back to her chair and sat, graceful despite her rounded belly. "Did she terrify you, Baletongue?"

Letty shivered in memory. "Yes." Distantly, she heard a clock toll the quarter hour. She should go upstairs and check that the luggage had been carried down, but she couldn't make herself move. She gazed at Lady Ware. This woman was *family*. Real, flesh-and-blood family. "Did she terrify you?"

"I was in a panic at the time, otherwise I'm sure she would have scared me witless. And as for poor Charlotte, she didn't know about Baletongue *at all*. It was a complete surprise to her!"

Letty heard footsteps in the corridor outside, and the timbre of male voices. The waiter returning with a constable? Sir Barnaby and Cosgrove? "Does Sir Barnaby know?"

"Yes. And Marcus knows, too. Cosgrove, I mean."

Letty nodded. More footsteps strode past. This time she recognized the voices: Reid and Houghton. She glanced at the door. Was Reid looking for her? "I must go. Mr. Reid is leaving in a few minutes."

"But we've only just met!"

"I know. But Mr. Reid's business is critical." Letty stood. She felt almost agitated.

"Of course it is!" Lady Ware rose and clasped Letty's hands. "Else you wouldn't be here, would you?"

Letty shook her head. Foolishly, she felt close to tears.

"When will the business be concluded? When can we meet again? Here, take my card." Lady Ware released Letty's hands and rummaged hastily in her reticule. "You *must* come and stay just as soon as you can! We can all become acquainted. Charlotte and I live within sight of each other, you know."

Letty took the proffered card and clutched it tightly.

"May I tell Charlotte about you? Please? She won't breathe a word, I promise! Neither of us will. We know how to keep a secret."

Letty hesitated, and then nodded.

"Oh! To meet you like this, and then have you vanish!" Lady Ware's posture was eloquent with frustration—her face, her hands. Then she laughed ruefully. "But at least I *did* meet you. To think, we might never have known about each other!" She stood on tiptoe and kissed Letty's cheek. "I'm *so* glad to have found you."

Letty's tears were even closer to the surface. She blinked them back. "And I, you."

Lady Ware crossed to the door and opened it. "I hope your business with Mr. Reid is concluded swiftly," she said, and then her expression became dismayed. "What have I said to make you look like that?"

Letty tried to find a smile. "It is . . . unhappy business."

Lady Ware closed the door again. "Do you need help?"

The concern on Lady Ware's face, the seriousness in her voice, brought the tears closer to the surface. Letty gathered her composure. "No, thank you. Mr. Reid's business is . . . is of a very private nature. It is best kept secret."

"Is this Mr. Reid bothering you?" Lady Ware asked bluntly. "Has he forced you to come here?"

"Oh, no! He would never—! I *chose* to accompany him!"

Lady Ware studied her for a moment, and gave a decisive nod. "Very well. But if you *do* need help, you must promise to ask for it. And if it's not something *I* can help with, then Barnaby will. We live half a day's ride from here."

"Thank you. You're very kind."

"Promise me!"

Letty gave a shaky laugh. "I promise."

Lady Ware opened the door again. "I wish you . . ." She paused, frowning, choosing her words. "I wish you the best possible outcome to your business with Mr. Reid."

"Thank you."

"And I wish to see you again soon."

"You will." Letty hugged Lady Ware. "Thank you."

Lady Ware hugged her back, and then pushed her gently but firmly out into the corridor. "Go help your Mr. Reid."

Letty hesitated, and turned back to her. "What gift did you choose?"

"Not the one I'd planned on choosing." Lady Ware smiled wryly. "Go! Your Mr. Reid will be waiting. I'll tell you it all when I see you next."

CHAPTER 40

Reid was indeed waiting for her upstairs. "There you are!" he said, with a look of relief. "Are you ready to leave?"

"Yes." Letty donned the traveling cloak that Eliza held out. Her fingers fumbled with the clasp. She had cousins. *Real* cousins.

Reid said in a low voice: "It worked. The pawn shop. Thank you for suggesting it."

"Good." Letty looked at the card Lady Ware had given her. *Two* cousins.

Houghton came striding along the corridor. "Everything's loaded, sir."

"Excellent," Reid said. "Let's be off."

Letty glanced up distractedly. "Gratuities?"

"Done," Reid said.

The dazed distraction gave way to jittering exhilaration as Letty went down the stairs. She had two cousins. Flesh-and-blood cousins. Cousins who shared the same secret heritage. Cousins who'd met Baletongue and chosen Faerie gifts.

Excitement fizzed in her veins, bright and effervescent, mounting with each step that she took. This must be how a champagne bottle felt when it was shaken—pressure building, bubbles hissing and humming and popping and sparkling.

By the time they descended the final flight of stairs, Letty felt as if she might burst.

Two cousins!

They stepped outside into cool, gray daylight. Two post-chaises-and-four were drawn up, ready to depart. Letty opened her hand again and looked at the card tucked into her gloved palm. *Lady Anne Ware. Woodhuish House.*

What gift had Lady Ware chosen? What gift had Countess Cosgrove chosen?

Belatedly, she realized Reid was talking to her. "I beg your pardon?"

Reid narrowed his eyes. "Are you all right?"

"I'm . . ." Letty looked down at the card again. *Cousins.* Excitement jittered and sparked in her blood. She felt it burning in her fingertips, felt it tingling on her scalp. It fermented in her chest in great iridescent bubbles.

She would *burst* if she didn't tell someone.

But there was no one she could tell.

She glanced at Reid—the strong cheekbones, the silver eyes, the stern jaw. Reid was a man who could keep secrets.

Letty turned impulsively to Houghton. "Sergeant, there's something I need to tell Mr. Reid. Something of a . . . a confidential nature. Would you mind traveling with Eliza and Green for the first stage?"

Houghton's eyebrows lifted. "Not at all."

Reid's eyebrows lifted, too, but he said nothing until they'd climbed into the post-chaise. "What's this about?" he said, settling on the seat opposite her.

It was almost impossible to sit still. Euphoria bubbled in Letty's veins. She opened her hand again and stared at Lady Ware's card. *Should* she tell Reid?

"Letty? Is something wrong?"

The words brought her head up. Reid had used her first name, something he rarely did.

Letty took a deep breath, trying to quell the jittering, bubbling excitement. "If I tell you something, will you *promise* to never tell another soul?"

Reid's eyebrows twitched upwards. "I promise."

Letty had the sensation that she was poised on the edge of a precipice, arms outstretched. She inhaled another breath, felt a moment of trepidation—and took the leap. "You know my knack for hearing lies? Well, it's not really a knack, it's a gift from my godmother. My Faerie godmother."

Reid's expression didn't alter dramatically, he made no exclamations of shock or disbelief, but Letty saw his blink of surprise, saw his shoulders stiffen, saw the muscles in his face tighten fractionally.

She plunged into explanation. "You see, a long time ago—*centuries* ago—one of my ancestors earned a Faerie gift, and it was passed down to her daughters, and to their daughters, and all the way down to my mother, and then to me, and on my twenty-first birthday, I was allowed to choose a gift, and I chose hearing truth from lies. I couldn't hear lies before then. You could have told me as many lies as you wished and I wouldn't have known!"

Reid was staring at her as if she'd transformed into one of the ostriches in the Royal Menagerie.

Letty hurried on. "It's the same gift my mother had—she advised me to choose it because of the fortune—and I didn't make my début until I was twenty-one because before then I'd have probably married the first fortune hunter I met because I couldn't hear his lies.

"And today, at the hotel—not fifteen minutes ago!—I met someone else who has the same Faerie godmother, and . . . and I've never met anyone else, other than my mother, and it's the most exciting thing that's ever happened to me!"

She tried to read Reid's expression. Skepticism? Wariness? Worry?

"I know it sounds preposterous and impossible, but *think,* Icarus! I can hear *every single lie.* That's not natural! It's not humanly possible! It *has* to be magic. There's nothing else it could be!"

She thought Reid was leaning fractionally away from her,

as if he'd found himself trapped in the post-chaise with a lunatic.

"*Ask* me about it, Icarus!" Letty said urgently. "What do you want to know?"

Reid stayed silent, eyeing her.

"*Ask* me!"

For a long, terrible moment she thought he'd ignore her request, and then he moistened his lips and said, "Why twenty-one?" She could tell from his voice—cool, carefully neutral—that he didn't believe her.

Letty clutched Lady Ware's card more tightly, aware of a sinking feeling in her stomach. This hadn't been a good idea. Better to have stayed silent and burst than to have Reid look at her like this.

"There are three different lines of descent," she told him. "One from each of my ancestor's three daughters. The women in my line receive their gifts on their twenty-first birthdays. Lady W— The person I met today received hers on her twenty-fifth birthday, which means she's descended from a different daughter." The blood connection she and Lady Ware shared was extremely tenuous—but they *were* still cousins.

Reid's expression was singularly dubious.

"What else would you like to know?" Letty asked desperately. "Ask me!"

"When did this ancestress of yours live?"

"About five hundred years ago."

"Letty . . ." Reid took a deep breath. "If this woman lived so long ago, and if all her descendants have a Faerie godmother and can do magic, then hundreds of people across England would have magic. Thousands of people. There'd be magic everywhere." His tone was very reasonable, patient, almost gentle. "Your mother was mistaken." He didn't say 'You are mistaken' but it was clearly implied.

"It's direct descent through daughters only," Letty said, her desperation congealing into a sick sense of dismay. He wasn't going to believe her. "My mother was the only daughter of an only daughter of an only daughter. That's why I never knew of anyone else like me."

Reid sighed. "Letty . . ."

"It's *true*, Icarus! I'd show you Baletongue if I could, but she only comes once, and only then if we're alone."

Reid's expression became even more skeptical.

Letty hurried on: "No one knows her real name, but we call her Baletongue because she's so *baleful*. She's got the blackest eyes and sharp teeth like an animal, and she's quite dangerous! She tricked my great-great-grandmother into choosing a gift that sent her mad."

Reid's lips compressed. Clearly, he thought she was mad, too.

"What would make you believe?" Letty said urgently. "There must be something! Tell me a hundred things, and I'll tell you whether they're true or not—and I'll get them all right! Please, Icarus!"

A thought flickered across his face. She could almost read his mind: *I'll prove to her she's wrong*. He sat up slightly on the seat. "My grandfather was a twin."

"True."

"My father was a twin."

"True."

"Two of my brothers are twins."

"False."

"Ah . . . my oldest brother's name is Zeus."

"True."

"His daughters are twins."

"True."

"Their names are Andromeda and Pandora."

"Andromeda is true, Pandora is not."

"Their names are Andromeda and Persephone."

"True."

The post-chaise rattled out of Exeter. For the next two miles Reid told truths and lies until Letty's ears were ringing. Finally, he ran down to a halt.

They sat in silence, eyeing each other. Reid's expression was deeply dubious.

Letty leaned forward. "It's not *natural,* Icarus. Is it?"

Reid glanced away from her.

"It's not natural!" Letty persisted. "Is it?"

He looked out of the window for a long moment, and then back at her. "No," he admitted.

"But you don't believe it's magic, do you?"

Reid blew out a breath. "I don't know."

It was the truth, and better than an outright *No.*

"You don't *want* to believe."

Reid looked at her for several seconds. "No. I don't."

"Why not?"

He looked away, grimaced. "I don't know. It's . . ."

Letty waited silently.

"It's challenging," Reid said finally. "It turns everything I believe in upside down. I'm not comfortable with it." He met her eyes.

Letty bit her lip, and looked down at the card she still held in her hand. It was limp and creased. "I'm sorry. I shouldn't have told you. I was too excited." Some secrets were meant to stay secrets. She had allowed euphoria to overwhelm good judgment.

"If . . ." Reid paused, and then continued slowly: "If what you have told me is true, and if you have just met another person like you . . . then I understand your excitement."

Letty lifted her gaze. Contrition washed through her. He'd been happier not knowing. "I'm sorry," she said again, and she changed her seat, sitting on the squab beside him and slipping her hand into his. "Forget I told you."

Reid uttered a dry laugh. "Forget? Jesus, Letty, it's not the sort of thing you forget!"

"I'm sorry," she said again, even more contritely.

Reid sighed, and he pulled his hand free and put his arm around her shoulders, drawing her close. "It's all right."

Letty leaned her head against his shoulder, and listened to the very faint bell-note in his voice. It was all right, just.

CHAPTER 41

Okehampton was a small market town on the edge of Dartmoor. The posting inn was unable to accommodate them, but the innkeeper directed them to another establishment, with dormer windows beneath a peaked roof, and ivy growing up its walls.

Reid pulled out his pocket watch, and gave a grimace.

"Go to the receiving office," Letty told him. "I'll see us settled in here."

Reid glanced at her, but didn't argue.

Letty watched him stride away, and then turned back to the landlord. "May I look over the rooms, please?"

The Sleeping Mallard was smaller and quieter than the posting inn, and enchantingly quaint. The largest bedchamber at the back had a pretty view over an orchard, some pastures, and a river. Adjoining it was a chamber clearly intended for a servant, small and plain and with a bare minimum of furniture.

Letty eyed the door that connected the two rooms. "My husband shall have the large bedchamber. I'll take this one."

"This one?" The landlord, a Mr. Thackeray, blinked his surprise. "But surely—"

"I like the view," Letty said. She liked the door even more.

She wouldn't have to worry about not hearing Reid cry out.

The rooms allocated, Letty went down to the kitchen to discuss a dinner that wouldn't require the use of a knife. Mrs. Thackeray was as amiable as her husband, and more than willing to modify her menu.

Reid returned twenty minutes later, with the news that Colonel Cuthbertson had a house on the moor. "A good five miles from here," he said, shoving a hand through his hair. "We wouldn't get there before dark."

Letty heard this news with relief. "We'll go first thing tomorrow morning. Is he at home?"

"Yes. His groom rides in to pick up the London papers each day."

They ate a quiet dinner. No one spoke much. Letty had little appetite. The elation of meeting Lady Ware had totally evaporated; in its place was an anxious dread.

"Do you think it's him?" she asked. "Cuthbertson?"

"Yes," Reid said. "I don't know why he'd do such a thing—but I think he did it."

"Perhaps he told several people, like Dunlop." Perhaps this wasn't the end of Reid's quest, but merely a way station.

"Cuthbertson? No." Reid shook his head. So did Houghton. "He gossiped about women, not military matters."

Letty looked down at her dessert. *Then we are very close to the end,* she thought.

She couldn't have Reid; she knew that. She'd always known that. She was reconciled to it. But she *wasn't* reconciled to Reid's death.

How could she make him want to live?

She glanced at Reid, at Houghton. The two men seemed more alike than ever this evening, both monosyllabic, both grim.

Houghton understood the importance of tomorrow's confrontation in a way that Letty couldn't. He'd been at Vimeiro. He knew Cuthbertson. Perhaps he'd even known the murdered Portuguese scouts.

But there were things *she* understood that Houghton didn't.

Letty listlessly stirred her curd pudding with her spoon. How could she make Reid *want* to live?

~~~~

That night, Reid slept for less than two hours before falling into his nightmare. He woke fighting, not crying, to Letty's great relief. The blind berserker madness, she could cope with; the terrible, anguished tears were almost unbearable.

She plumped up his pillows, straightened his bedclothes, gave him a quarter of a glass of brandy and a teaspoon of valerian, and settled herself cross-legged alongside him on the bed. Reid didn't suggest that she leave. "When the Persian commanders and crews saw the Greeks thus boldly sailing . . ."

At the end of the first paragraph, she took his hand. Such a large, warm hand—such strong, lean fingers.

She found herself glancing frequently at him while she read. The single candle painted huge hollows beneath his cheekbones. Reid might be listening to her voice, but she doubted he was listening to the words. His gaze was distant, as if he looked at something beyond the bedchamber, and there was a small frown on his brow. She thought he must be thinking of Cuthbertson, but when she paused to turn the page, Reid said, "Have you told anyone else what you told me today?"

Letty glanced at him, surprised. "About my Faerie godmother?"

Reid gave a tiny grimace, as if the words *Faerie godmother* pained him. "Yes."

"No. Only you. Although . . ." She looked down at the page, not seeing the words. "I did tell Julia and Lucas about my gift. Sort of. I did what I did with you today—which was foolish, but it was the day after my birthday, and I was so excited . . ." Excited that she could finally make her début, excited about the prospect of love and courtship and marriage. More fool her. "But I didn't tell them it was magic; I said it was a trick I'd learned. I didn't quite dare to tell them about Baletongue. I thought they'd think I was mad." She glanced at Reid. "Like you did."

Reid said nothing, but the faint twitch of his lips was wry.

Letty waited a moment, in case he had more questions, then looked back at the book.

"What magic can she do? This woman you met."

Letty glanced at him again. "I don't know. We spoke for less than five minutes."

Reid frowned. "You'll meet with her again?"

"Yes. As soon as I can." Once she and Reid had parted ways and she'd gone back to being Letitia Trentham.

"Is it safe?"

"Of course it is!" Letty managed a smile. "She's not a monster, Icarus. She's a perfectly respectable woman."

Reid's frown didn't ease—but he didn't ask her to reveal Lady Ware's name.

Letty looked back at Herodotus, blinked several times, inhaled a steadying breath, and read another two pages. Reid's eyelids drooped lower and lower. His hand grew limp in her clasp. If she read much more, he'd be asleep. Letty released his hand, closed the book, and placed it on the bedside table. "Icarus?"

Reid's eyelids lifted. His eyes focused slowly on her face.

Letty gazed at him. She had the sense—even more strongly and urgently than she'd had last night—that time was running out. Tomorrow Reid's quest ended. Tomorrow everything changed. Tomorrow she could find herself in a post-chaise heading back to London—without Icarus Reid. She had to grab what she could *while* she could, even if it meant being brazen and bold. Even if it meant saying and doing things she ought to be ashamed of. She felt Julia at her shoulder, heard her whisper in her ear: *Do it, Tish.*

"Icarus, please let me kiss you the way Tom was kissing Lucas."

Reid winced, closing his eyes. "Letty . . ."

"Please, Icarus." She leaned over and kissed his cheek lightly, kissed his jaw, kissed the corner of his mouth, and with each kiss she thought, *I love you, Icarus Reid.*

Reid sighed. He turned his head on the pillow, his mouth seeking hers. His hand found the back of her head, cupping it gently.

Their lips clung together for a long moment. *I love you,* she thought.

"Please," Letty whispered against his mouth. "You don't have to reciprocate. Honestly."

"Yes, I do," Reid said, and then he kissed her some more, and said, "All right."

And so they did.

CHAPTER 42

November 29th, 1808
Okehampton, Devonshire

$\mathcal{D}$artmoor had a rugged, desolate beauty, but Icarus was in no mood to appreciate it. He was as edgy as he'd been before a battle, tense and alert and restless. He clenched his hands together and managed to sit still, managed not to fidget. Letty Trentham, seated across from him in the carriage, made no attempt at conversation. She wasn't Tish this morning; she looked pale and tired and sad.

Icarus turned his head and gazed out the window, seeing rough, rolling heath and upthrusting outcrops of gray rock. They were coming to the end of this search. A sense of urgency had been building in him all morning, and underneath the urgency was a strong pang of regret. He would miss Letty Trentham. She could try the patience of a saint, but she was also . . .

His thoughts ground to a halt, trying to find an adjective that fitted her. The closest he could come was that Letty Trentham would make an excellent officer. She had the strength of character necessary, the intelligence, the courage. She didn't pull her punches and she didn't turn from daunting tasks. If she thought something needed to be said, she said it. If she thought something needed to be done, she did it.

If Letty Trentham were a soldier, he would be glad to serve with her.

The carriage slowed and made a right turn, lurching over a rough, narrow track. Leafless trees came into view, a drystone wall, a dour house built of gray stone.

The carriage slowed again, made another turn, and came to a halt in front of the house. Icarus stared out the window. Colonel Cuthbertson lived *here*?

He climbed slowly down from the carriage, examining the house in disbelief. Cuthbertson was flamboyant and swaggering and libidinous, happiest when in a brothel working his way through the women on offer. This place looked the exact opposite of a brothel; it looked like a damned prison.

He turned and handed Miss Trentham down from the carriage. "Walk the horses," he told the coachman. "We shouldn't be above fifteen minutes."

His boots crunched over the gravel and echoed flatly on the gray stone slab of the doorstep. He hammered the door-knocker loudly.

Icarus counted the seconds in his head, aware of Miss Trentham's hand resting lightly on his arm, aware of the ever-tightening coil of anticipation in his belly. His muscles were taut, his heartbeat slightly elevated.

After fourteen seconds, a housemaid opened the door. Icarus looked her over. Her shape was lush and her bodice slightly too low. He wondered how many times a day the colonel flipped up her skirts and swived her.

"Is Colonel Cuthbertson in?" he asked.

The maid bobbed a curtsy. "Yes, sir."

"Tell him Major Reid is here to see him."

They waited in the unlit entrance hall while the maid hurried off. Heavy oil paintings frowned down at them. The house didn't feel like a home; it felt like an abandoned museum, chilly, musty, long neglected.

The maid returned, and led them to a small north-facing dining room. Cuthbertson sat at the table, the remains of a substantial breakfast spread before him. The colonel was only in his early forties, but he'd gone to seed since Icarus had last seen him. His hair needed a trim, and so did his sideburns. Always heavyset, he was now edging towards stoutness.

"Reid. This is a surprise." Cuthbertson climbed to his feet. He gave Miss Trentham a swift survey and almost visibly dismissed her as unattractive, made a perfunctory bow in her direction, and offered her a seat.

Miss Trentham declined.

Cuthbertson shrugged, and sat again. "What brings you to Dartmoor?"

"You."

"Me?"

"Yes." Icarus crossed to the window and turned, so he could see both Cuthbertson and Miss Trentham. "I was surprised to hear you'd sold out."

"Oh . . ." Cuthbertson shrugged. "I'd had my fill of soldiering. Twenty-five years was enough."

Off to one side, Miss Trentham silently shook her head. Cuthbertson was already lying.

Icarus glanced out the window. The outlook was bleak: skeletal trees, scrubby moor, gray stone. It was the last place he'd expect a man like Cuthbertson to end up. "Why here? Why Dartmoor?"

"M' aunt left me it. Can't stand the place, but I'm rather short of funds at the moment. You know how it is, Major."

"But you just sold out." Surely the man hadn't run through his commission already? A colonelcy was worth several thousand pounds.

Cuthbertson opened one hand in a throwaway gesture.

Lord, the man was even more of a wastrel than Icarus had thought. Which could explain his act of treason—*if* it had been Cuthbertson.

Icarus leaned his hip against the windowsill, trying to look casual. "I wanted to ask you about Vimeiro."

"Vimeiro?" A fleeting grimace crossed Cuthbertson's face. He fussed with the teapot. "Would you like a cup?" he asked Miss Trentham. "Would you, Reid?"

Icarus shook his head.

Cuthbertson refilled his teacup. "What about Vimeiro?" he said, not looking at Icarus's face.

"Grantham says he told you where I was meeting my scouts," Icarus said. "I wondered whether you'd told anyone?"

"Me? Good Lord, no!" Cuthbertson uttered an overly hearty laugh, and swallowed some tea.

Icarus didn't need Miss Trentham's headshake to know that the man was lying. His heart gave a great kick in his chest.

This was his traitor.

He stayed where he was, leaning against the windowsill, every muscle taut. "Who did you tell?"

Cuthbertson arranged his features into an expression of offended dignity. "I just told you, Major: No one!"

Icarus shook his head. "You and I both know you're lying, Colonel. You told someone. Who was it?"

Cuthbertson put down his teacup with a clatter. "I don't have to listen to this." He stood, and made for the door.

Icarus reached it before Cuthbertson had fully opened it. He pushed the door forcefully shut, making it shudder in the doorframe, and turned the key and pocketed it. "Who did you tell?"

Cuthbertson drew himself up. "I order you to unlock that door, Major!"

Icarus gave him a thin smile. "Neither of us is in the army now." He took several steps back, until he could see Miss Trentham again. "Did you tell the French?"

"No!"

Miss Trentham nodded. The colonel was telling the truth.

"Another Englishman?"

"No. Give me that key!"

Miss Trentham nodded again.

"A villager?"

"The key, Reid."

"A villager?"

"No!" Behind Cuthbertson, Miss Trentham shook her head.

The colonel took two stiff-legged strides towards him and reached for the pocket that held the key. Icarus caught the man's wrist and twisted it sideways.

Cuthbertson staggered, and caught his balance. He tried to wrench his wrist free. "How dare you lay a hand on me in my own house!"

"You told one of the villagers. Who?"

The colonel was breathing heavily, his face ruddy with outrage. "I don't have to put up with this!"

Icarus released the man's wrist and took a step back. "No. You don't. I'm happy to take this to a court-martial. Are you?"

Cuthbertson rubbed his wrist. "Court-martial?" He laughed, a flat, angry sound. "Don't be absurd."

"Who did you tell?"

They matched stares. Cuthbertson looked away first. "A woman. I don't remember her name. Maria something."

Miss Trentham gave a small nod.

"A woman?" Icarus said, in disbelief. "You told a woman? Why in God's name would you do that?"

Cuthbertson shrugged, and walked back to the table and picked up his teacup again.

"She was a whore, wasn't she?" Cuthbertson had told a damned *whore*.

"The best fuck I had the whole time I was in Portugal." Cuthbertson sipped his tea. "Get out of my house."

Icarus clenched his hands, and mastered the urge to smash the man's teacup into his face. "What did you tell her?"

Cuthbertson shrugged again. "This and that."

"Where I was meeting my scouts?"

Cuthbertson shrugged a third time. "I can't remember."

Miss Trentham shook her head.

"You damned well *do* remember." Icarus took a pace towards him. He was trembling with fury. "You told her, didn't you?"

Cuthbertson eyed him. "I might have."

"*Why?*" The word exploded out of him.

Cuthbertson put down the teacup. "She was afraid. Needed to feel safe before she could get in the mood. You know how it is, Major. Nervous creatures, females."

"Jesus Christ! You told a fucking *whore* because she was scared? You—" He caught sight of Miss Trentham standing tense and white-faced on the other side of the table. She shook her head. Because Cuthbertson had lied? Or because his own language had descended into the gutter?

Icarus shut his mouth. He inhaled a hissing breath through his nose, and struggled to rein in his rage. *Control yourself, man. Letty's here.* But fury roared in his chest like flames in a furnace. "Your whore told the French. You realize that, don't you? They were waiting for us. *Waiting* for us!"

Cuthbertson looked away.

"Men *died* because of you."

Cuthbertson shrugged. "A couple of Portuguese."

The next few seconds were hazy. Rage possessed him. He knew he hit Cuthbertson, but he had no idea how many times—all he knew was that he was going to *kill* the fucking son of a—

"Icarus, *stop!*" That sharp, commanding voice jerked him to a halt.

Icarus lowered his fists. He shook his head, trying to clear it. He was panting, his chest heaving. What had just happened?

At his feet, Cuthbertson wheezed, spitting blood on the carpet.

Icarus stepped back, and shook his head again. "Sorry," he told Miss Trentham. "I didn't . . . I didn't mean to do that." His voice seemed to come from very far away.

"Let me talk to him, Icarus." It wasn't a suggestion; it was a command.

Icarus took another step back. He let his hands fall to his sides.

CHAPTER 43

$\mathcal{I}$carus watched Miss Trentham crouch alongside Cuthbertson. "I can hear when people tell lies," she said, in a conversational tone. "And you have told a number of lies this morning, Colonel Cuthbertson."

Cuthbertson lifted his head and glared at her.

"You didn't tell Maria about the rendezvous because she was afraid, did you?"

Cuthbertson wheezed, and said nothing.

"Tell me, Colonel. Or I shall let Icarus hit you again."

"Bitch," Cuthbertson muttered.

Icarus took a jerky step forward, hands clenched.

"It would be best if you answered my question, Colonel. As you can see, Icarus has a short temper. Maria wasn't afraid, was she?"

Cuthbertson pressed his bloody lips together.

"*Was* she?"

Icarus took another step forward.

Cuthbertson didn't cringe from him, but he did speak: "She was afraid at first, but I told her we outnumbered the French, they didn't stand a chance. That settled her down. She spread her legs willingly enough."

"In that case, why did you tell her about Reid and his scouts?"

"She wanted to know how I knew we outnumbered them. I said we had scouts out."

"Why did you tell her the time and place of Reid's rendezvous?"

Cuthbertson didn't reply. He wiped his bloody mouth with one hand.

"Answer her," Icarus said, in a gravelly voice.

Cuthbertson glanced at him, and away. He said nothing.

Enlightenment came suddenly. "You were showing off, weren't you? Puffing yourself up. Trying to impress her."

Cuthbertson wiped his mouth again, ignoring the question.

Icarus took a step forward and took the colonel by the nape of his neck and shook him hard.

"I would answer him, if I were you," Miss Trentham said.

Cuthbertson wrenched free. He glared up at Icarus. "So? What if I was? She was a tasty bit of luncheon; thought I might have her for supper, too, if she was willing."

Icarus squeezed his eyes shut. He held on to his temper with effort. Men were dead—good men—because Cuthbertson had bragged to a whore?

"What else did you tell Maria?"

Icarus opened his eyes and stared down at Cuthbertson. He wanted to rip off the man's head. Rage was a wolf in his chest, pacing, gnashing its teeth.

"Nothing."

"Colonel, may I remind you that I can hear when you lie? And that Icarus has a very short temper."

Cuthbertson set his lips together and rubbed the back of his neck and glowered up at Icarus.

"What else did you tell her?" Miss Trentham's voice was relentless.

"I told her how many men we had," Cuthbertson said sullenly. "And where they were to be placed."

Icarus squeezed his eyes shut again. He was going to *kill* Cuthbertson.

"One of the ridges had no men stationed on it. Did you tell her that?"

Icarus opened his eyes.

"Yes," Cuthbertson said, even more sullenly. "Not that it mattered! The French never got near it. Wellesley blocked them in time."

Icarus turned away. It was either that, or pound Cuthbertson into the carpet.

"And why did you leave the army?" Miss Trentham asked. "It wasn't because you wanted to."

Icarus turned back.

Cuthbertson took a handkerchief from his pocket and pressed it to his bleeding mouth.

"Why?" Miss Trentham asked again, a steely edge to her voice.

"Wellesley made me," Cuthbertson said, the words muffled by his handkerchief. "Said he had a good mind to press for a dishonorable discharge. Said it was my fault Reid and his men were caught."

"He *what*?" Icarus said.

Cuthbertson scowled at him from behind the bloody handkerchief.

"He knew about Maria?" Miss Trentham asked.

"He knew she was missing, gone to the French. The whole damned village was in a clamor about it. And he knew I'd been with her. Didn't believe me when I said I hadn't told her anything."

Wellesley had always been damned astute.

"Why was the village in a clamor?" Miss Trentham asked.

Cuthbertson lowered the handkerchief. "Because she was some alderman's widow, or whatever they call it over there— and she ran off to be with a French officer."

Icarus had a flash of memory, so intense it almost made him grunt: the town square in Vimeiro in the baking heat of August. For a brief instant, he actually *smelled* Vimeiro, actually tasted it on his tongue. The memory unfolded in his mind: he saw three women come out of the church, stepping from shadow into sunlight, widows dressed in black. The youngest of them had drawn his eye, dark-eyed and voluptuous, with milky skin and a ripe, wine-red mouth and lustrous black hair beneath her mantilla. Hell, she'd drawn *every* man's eye.

"What happened to Maria?" Miss Trentham asked.

"Dead, I hope. Bitch cost me my colonelcy."

Icarus shook his head. Cuthbertson had lost his colonelcy himself.

"The general forced you to resign your commission?" Miss Trentham asked.

Cuthbertson glowered at her, and dabbed his mouth with the handkerchief. "Said he was cleaning out his house. Got rid of me and Dunlop and Grantham. Twenty-five years of service, and he threatened me with a dishonorable discharge!" His tone was aggrieved.

"He should have done more than threaten," Icarus said flatly. "He should have had you court-martialed. I'll repair that omission."

"Court-martial?" Cuthbertson snorted, and lurched to his feet. "I'd like to see you try."

"You will. Why else do you think I'm here? You'll get to dance on the end of a rope. And I shall have the pleasure of watching."

Cuthbertson wasn't intimidated. He curled his split lip in a sneer. "Wellesley's fucking golden boy. I'm sorry the French didn't kill you, too."

They did kill me, Icarus thought.

Cuthbertson turned to the table, picked up his napkin, pressed it to his bloody mouth. "All this fuss over a couple of worthless Portuguese—"

"I wouldn't say that, if I were you," Miss Trentham said coldly.

Cuthbertson ignored her. "Worthless Portuguese! What's another damned peasant dead?"

"Three scouts," Icarus said, between his teeth. "And a cavalry officer."

Cuthbertson snorted. "That boy with his ridiculous mustachios? Lord, if I didn't laugh every time I saw him—"

Icarus hit him, right in the middle of his sneering, smirking face.

Cuthbertson tumbled backwards over the table, tried to catch his balance, and hit the floor with a yelp. Icarus followed him to the floor, driving his fist into the man's face again and again—

"Icarus!"

Icarus halted with his fist pulled back.

"Don't kill him."

Icarus hissed out a breath. Rage bellowed in his chest. He flipped Cuthbertson over on his stomach and sank his fingers in the man's overlong hair, grinding Cuthbertson's face into the carpet, pressing hard. "Pereira is *dead* because of you—and he didn't die easily. They completely *broke* him. Because of *you*." He was sobbing with rage, or maybe with grief. How *dared* Cuthbertson dismiss Pereira as a joke? "He was a courageous soldier, and he deserved a better death!"

Cuthbertson struggled weakly, gurgling in his throat.

Icarus leaned down and snarled in the man's ear: "You were never a soldier. You're nothing more than a mutton-monger, following your cock, betraying men who trusted you for the sake of a quick *fuck*." He ground Cuthbertson's face into the carpet with that last word, pressing with all his weight.

"Icarus!" There was a stern note of warning in Miss Trentham's voice.

Icarus released Cuthbertson and pushed to his feet, swinging away from her, striding to the window. He was shaking—shaking as violently as he did after his nightmares—and hot tears were running down his face. He scrubbed them away roughly and tried to catch his breath, tried to capture his composure.

He turned around and watched Cuthbertson roll painfully over and push up to sit. The colonel fingered his gory nose, and spat blood. "You son of a bitch. Don't think I won't lay charges—"

"Do," Icarus said, his voice harsh. "Because I intend to lay charges against you. You're going to face a court-martial. For Pereira and my three scouts, you're going to *hang*." He crossed to Cuthbertson. "On your feet."

"Must we take him with us?" Miss Trentham asked. Her voice was neutral, but his ears caught the undertone of distaste.

Icarus hesitated, and glanced at her, and then down at the colonel. Revulsion rose in his throat like bile. Letty Trentham deserved many things, but an hour spent in Cuthbertson's company in the close confines of a carriage definitely wasn't one of them.

He crouched, so he was eye to eye with Cuthbertson. "I'll be back for you this afternoon. You'd better be here. Understood?"

Cuthbertson inhaled a wheezing breath and spat at him. The bloody spittle landed on the man's own waistcoat.

"I'll take that as a yes." Icarus showed his teeth in a smile. "It would be useless to run; you've got no money."

He stood and crossed to the door, pulling the key from his pocket. His fingers were shaking so badly he couldn't insert it in the lock.

Miss Trentham wordlessly took the key and unlocked the door.

CHAPTER 44

$\mathcal{I}$carus had blood on his gloves. Cuthbertson's blood. He stripped them off and balled them up and climbed into the carriage. He didn't speak. Neither did Miss Trentham. He sat, his elbows on his knees, his head in his hands, his eyes squeezed shut. Thoughts lurched in his head, disjointed and fragmented. He felt almost drunk, felt almost like vomiting. Cuthbertson had betrayed them for the sake of a five-minute fuck?

The trembling stopped after the first mile. His thoughts became less fragmented. Icarus lifted his head and looked at Letty Trentham, seated in the opposite corner.

"I apologize. My behavior was unpardonable. My language—"

"Under the circumstances, I think that your behavior and language were perfectly pardonable." She looked at him for a long moment, her face pale and grave. "Icarus, what did you mean about Lieutenant Pereira? What did you mean when you said he'd broken?"

The question stung like a slap. He felt the muscles in his face tighten, felt himself flinch.

He looked away from her and clenched his hands together. Outside, Dartmoor stretched, bare and bleak.

Letty Trentham didn't repeat her question, but it hung in the air between them. Finally, Icarus forced himself to answer. "I meant that he was so desperate for them to stop that he would have told them anything. He would have given up his own mother."

"Did he tell them that ridge was undefended?"

Icarus looked down at his clenched hands. He didn't hear the clatter of the carriage jolting over the rough lane; he heard Pereira struggling to breathe, water rattling in his throat. "Yes."

"Before or after you told them?"

"Before."

"I don't understand. If Maria had told them, and Lieutenant Pereira had told them, why did they make *you* tell them, too?"

"I was a British major. My word held more weight."

He saw Lieutenant Pereira in his mind's eye, little more than a boy despite the flourishing mustachios, eager and idealistic, willing to give his life for his country.

Well, he had. But not heroically in battle. His life had been choked out of him over agonizing hours.

Pereira hadn't deserved to be broken, and having been broken, he certainly hadn't deserved to die.

And Cuthbertson had dared to *mock* him?

Black rage swept through him again, and—as at Cuthbertson's—grief was inescapably mixed with it. His throat tightened. His nose stung. His eyes burned. God, he was going to cry.

Icarus leaned his elbows on his knees, lowered his head into his hands, and squeezed his eyes shut.

Letty Trentham moved, coming to sit beside him. She didn't hug him, didn't kiss his cheek or murmur soothing words; she just rested one hand on his back.

Her silent comfort, her hand on his back, made his throat choke even tighter, made his eyes burn even more fiercely. It took every scrap of willpower Icarus possessed to force back the tears. "I want to kill him." His voice was low, thick, hoarse.

"I know."

They traveled the rest of the way to Okehampton in silence, side by side, her hand resting on his back. Icarus's thoughts were fixed on Vimeiro. He saw each scout die again, heard Pereira begging, saw his sodden corpse.

It had been no grand plot, no treason for the sake of idealism or money, for love or fear. The scouts and Pereira had died because of Cuthbertson's insatiable itch for sex.

For weeks he'd been focused on this moment—on finding the traitor, on forcing a confession—and now that he had, there was no sense of triumph. He felt weary and deflated. And sick. Sick with the sordid, venal stupidity of it all.

The road became smoother. The carriage picked up its pace. Five minutes later, they trotted into Okehampton. Icarus lifted his head and watched the Sleeping Mallard come into view. The sign above the entrance swayed in the breeze liked a hanged man on the gallows. His eyes focused on the movement.

For Pereira's sake, and for the three scouts, Cuthbertson would hang.

Reid paid off the coachman and requested his services again later that day. Everything about him was grim—his manner, his expression, his voice. Sergeant Houghton looked at his face and forbore to ask questions, but he touched Letty's elbow and drew her aside. "It was Cuthbertson?"

Letty nodded.

Houghton shook his head in bafflement. "Why?"

"To impress a woman."

"Huh. That sounds like the colonel." Houghton's gaze slid to Reid, still talking to the coachman. "He doesn't look pleased about it."

"He's not. Cuthbertson was . . ." She searched for the correct word. "Offensive. Extremely offensive. Icarus lost his temper."

Houghton glanced at her. "The major never loses his temper."

"He did today. He hit Cuthbertson a number of times."

Houghton's eyebrows rose. "Reid did?"

Letty nodded.

"In front of you?"

Letty nodded again. And what was worse, Reid had cried. She didn't tell Houghton that, though. "Will you please go with him when he collects the colonel? I dislike the thought of them being alone together. Icarus could be provoked into something he might regret."

"Of course I'll go with him."

"Thank you."

They ate a silent luncheon in the private parlor. Reid didn't put any food on his plate; he looked at the goose and turkey pie as if he didn't recognize it for what it was. Letty opened her mouth to urge him to eat, and then closed it again. Reid had retreated somewhere beyond reach.

Houghton must have come to the same conclusion. He kept glancing at Reid, glancing at the empty plate, but he said nothing. When he'd finished eating, he looked at Letty, his thoughts clear to read on his face: *What do we do?*

Letty shook her head. She had no idea what to do.

The clock on the mantelpiece chimed one o'clock. Reid came out of his bleak reverie. He pushed back his chair and stood. "Excuse me. I must find the constable."

Houghton pushed back his chair, too, and stood. "*I'll* find the constable. You need to eat."

Reid blinked, and looked blankly down at his plate. "I'm not hungry."

"I'll find the constable," Houghton said again, even more firmly. "An army marches on its stomach. You know that, sir."

Reid's gaze jerked to the sergeant. He clearly recognized

the aphorism. For a moment, it looked as if he'd choose to ignore Houghton's words, and then he gave a nod, and resumed his seat. "Tell him I'll be bringing a guest for his lock-up this afternoon. Four-ish."

"Yes, sir."

Letty met Houghton's eyes and gave a nod, thanking him silently.

Houghton nodded back, and left.

Letty returned her attention to Reid. He was regarding the pie with marked lack of interest.

"Would you prefer something plainer? I'll ask for bread-and-butter, shall I?"

Reid had eaten one slice of bread-and-butter when Houghton returned. The sergeant was almost running. He shut the door with something close to a slam, caught his breath, and blurted: "Cuthbertson's dead!

CHAPTER 45

The words seemed to strike Reid with the force of a battle-ax. He rocked back in his chair. His lips parted, but no words came out.

"Dead?" Letty said sharply. "How?"

"Shot himself in the head." Houghton put two fingers to his temple. "The constable was called away not half an hour ago. Him and the doctor both."

"Are you *certain* it was Colonel Cuthbertson?"

"Yes."

"And he's definitely dead?"

"Yes."

Letty looked at Reid. The blood had drained from his face. He seemed stunned speechless.

"Sir?" Houghton said. "Are you all right?"

Reid shoved his chair back and stood. "Cuthbertson's dead?"

"Yes, sir."

Reid's eyes seemed to burn in his pale face. Letty pushed back her own chair and stood. "Icarus?"

If he heard her, he gave no sign of it. He looked through her as if she didn't exist and turned towards the door, moving like a man who was half-blind.

Houghton stepped aside.

Reid fumbled with the handle, pulled the door open, and stepped out into the corridor.

Letty and Houghton looked at each other.

"I'll go after him," Houghton said.

"No, I will. See if you can find that coachman—tell him not to put the horses to. I think the carriage came from the posting inn."

"Yes, ma'am," Houghton said automatically, and then, "But the major—"

"I'll see he doesn't come to any harm."

Letty gathered her skirts in one hand and ran up to Reid's room. He wasn't there. She hurried down the dim staircase and burst out into the inn's forecourt. Not come to any harm? She couldn't keep Reid from harming himself if he chose to. No one could.

She spun on her heel. The quiet backstreet stretched empty in both directions. A silent scream built in her throat: *Reid!*

She ran to the far end of the yard. A lane led towards the river. Reid was halfway down it, walking with that same half-blind gait.

Letty hurried after him.

The lane ran past the orchard and turned left when it met the river. Reid turned left, too.

Letty followed, fifty yards back.

Reid walked for nearly a mile, not caring where he stepped, paying no attention to the mud and the puddles. The lane passed through a dark grove of willow trees. When it emerged into open daylight, Reid was nowhere to be seen.

Panic kicked in Letty's chest. She turned and plunged back into the gloom of the trees.

She nearly ran right past Reid. He was almost invisible: a man in a dark tailcoat with dark hair standing ankle-deep in dark water behind a dark curtain of willows.

Letty's heart seemed to stop beating. Was he going to drown himself?

She stood frozen with horror while Reid took a step. The water rose over the top of his boots.

Reid! But her voice was locked in her throat. She hurried down to the river, heedless of brambles and mud, her heart pounding almost hard enough to burst from her chest.

Reid lowered himself to sit in the water, moving with slow stiffness, as if his joints were made of rusted iron.

Letty halted on the riverbank and stared at him. Reid's eyes were squeezed shut, his teeth gritted, his face gray beneath its tan. He was visibly shaking.

What was he doing?

Understanding dawned. Reid wasn't trying to kill himself. He was trying to break free of Vimeiro.

She remembered his frantic panic when he'd fallen in the stream, remembered how he'd vomited, how he'd struggled to breathe. What Herculean effort was it taking him to sit in this river, with water wetting the lowest fold of his neckcloth?

Letty gathered up her skirts and stepped into the river. Water filled her half boots and climbed up her legs, so cold it stung. She walked with clumsy care to where Reid sat and lowered herself alongside him. Water rose to her collarbone.

Reid's eyes opened. His head jerked round. She saw how close to the surface his panic was.

"It's all right," Letty said, and moved closer, so her shoulder touched his. She groped through the water and found his hand.

Reid didn't speak. His fingers gripped hers tightly.

They sat silently, while the river flowed around them. Letty's skin burned with cold. Reid's eyes were tightly shut again. He was shaking as violently as he did after a nightmare, wheezing, his breath hissing fast and shallow between clenched teeth.

Letty held his hand, and leaned her shoulder against his, and grew steadily colder. Her skin no longer burned; it ached. The chill sank through her clothes, sank through her flesh, sank deep into her bones—but Reid's breathing was growing slower, deeper, easier. He no longer wheezed so hoarsely, no longer hissed through his teeth with each inhalation.

Finally, his breath stopped wheezing at all. He was still shaking, but so was she, deep shudders that rocked her to her core. *We'll freeze to death,* Letty thought. But she didn't stand and clamber ashore. She would stay with Reid as long as it took.

Reid made no move to stand. Nor did he release her hand.

Letty clamped her jaw tight to stop her teeth chattering. Her skin was ice, her flesh was ice, her blood was ice.

Finally Reid spoke: "I don't know what to do." His voice was low, almost inaudible.

I don't know what to do. It was a statement, and it was also a plea.

Letty had the feeling that her next words might be the most important ones she ever spoke in her life. She hesitated, selecting them with great care. "You have a choice, Icarus. You can choose to die, or you can choose to live." She paused. "It's not a choice that your scouts or Lieutenant Pereira were given."

There was a lot more she wanted to say. *Choose to live, Icarus! Choose it in their honor. Choose it for yourself.* But she bit the words back. Reid needed to come to those conclusions himself. If he could.

Reid didn't say anything. Nor did he look at her. Nor did he pull his hand from her grip.

Letty let another frozen minute slide past, then released his hand and climbed stiffly to her feet. Water streamed from her gown. Her body ached. Her teeth chattered. "Come back to the inn. You're too cold to think."

Reid turned his head and looked up at her. He was pale-faced, but not gray, and his eyes were neither burning nor blind.

Letty held her hand out to him.

Reid took it and let her pull him to his feet.

Back at the inn, Letty gave Reid into Green's care. "What happened?" the valet said, aghast.

"We fell in the river," Letty said, hearing the *clang* of her lie. She turned to Houghton, standing anxiously at her shoulder. "Sergeant, go down to the kitchen and tell them Mr. Reid needs a hot bath *now*."

"Yes, ma'am." The sergeant clattered down the stairs, and reappeared two minutes later, when Letty was helping Green peel Reid out of his sodden, clinging tailcoat. "Is he all right?"

Letty didn't know, but she said, "Yes," and then: "Sergeant, I'd like hot bricks in his bed—as many as you can find!—and see what food they have in the kitchen. He needs something hot to eat. A good, hearty soup, if you can find it. Put him to bed, make him eat as much as you possibly can—force it down his throat, if you have to!—and give him quarter of a glass of brandy and a teaspoon of valerian—Green will know where it is."

"Yes, ma'am." Houghton hesitated. "Did he hit his head when he fell? He looks . . . odd."

Numb, was how Reid looked. Numb with more than cold. He was somewhere deep inside his own head, not responding to remarks, moving like a sleepwalker.

Too much had happened to him today.

"It's the cold," Letty said.

Houghton accepted this with a dubious nod, and hurried downstairs to the kitchen again.

Houghton had ordered a bath for her, too. By the time Letty had bathed and dressed in dry clothes, she'd finally stopped shivering. Eliza insisted on wrapping two shawls around her shoulders. Letty hastened next door. Reid's bedchamber was cozy, the fire blazing high, and Reid himself was in bed. She could tell at a glance that he'd drunk both the brandy and the valerian; his eyes were drowsy and heavy-lidded.

Letty crossed to where Sergeant Houghton stood at the bedside. "He had more than a pint of soup, ma'am. Mutton and barley, it was. Good and rich."

"Thank you, Sergeant." She reached out and touched Reid's brow lightly, and then his cheek. He wasn't shivering, and his skin felt comfortably warm.

"I don't think he'll take a chill," Green said, hovering anxiously on the other side of the bed. "The bathwater was hot, and there's six bricks in his bed."

"Excellent," Letty said. She looked around for Herodotus. "I'll read until he falls asleep."

Reid was asleep before the end of the third page. Letty closed the book and looked at his face for a long moment, then put the book aside and stood. "I would like one or the other of you to stay with him while he sleeps," she told Houghton and Green in a low voice. "If he should have a nightmare, wake him immediately. But be careful—he can strike out."

Both men nodded.

Letty hesitated. How to describe Reid's mental state after one of his nightmares? She decided not to. "Fetch me when he wakes—especially if he has a nightmare."

Reid didn't wake before dark. Houghton dined with her in the parlor. The covers hadn't long been removed when the landlord, Mr. Thackeray, tapped on the door and entered, a portentous look on his face. "The parish constable to see Mr. Reid, ma'am."

Letty exchanged a glance with Sergeant Houghton.

"Show him in here, please."

The parish constable entered the parlor half a minute later. Letty looked the man over. Middle-aged and thickset, with a no-nonsense expression on his face. She rose and shook his hand politely, trying to gauge his temperament. "Good evening, Constable. I'm Mrs. Reid, and this is my husband's friend, Sergeant Houghton."

"Ma'am," the constable said stiffly. "Sergeant."

"I understand you wish to speak with my husband? He fell in the river and I've put him to bed." Letty smiled apologetically. "He's sedated, I'm afraid—fast asleep."

The constable looked put out. He opened his mouth.

"Please be seated, Constable," Letty said, resuming her seat. "I gather you're here about that business with Colonel Cuthbertson?"

The constable hesitated, and sat. "Major Reid visited him this morning."

"Yes, we both did. And before you ask, yes, there was an altercation, and yes, my husband did hit Colonel Cuthbertson." She paused, trying to read the constable's face. Should she be open, or evasive? "Colonel Cuthbertson was responsible for the deaths of four of my husband's men in Portugal, and Icarus—my husband—wished to bring him before a military court-martial."

The constable's face folded into a frown. "Court-martial?"

"Yes. My husband was to have fetched Colonel Cuthbertson away this afternoon."

The constable eyed her. "Where was Major Reid at midday today?"

"Here, with the sergeant and me. We were just sitting down to luncheon. Weren't we, Sergeant?"

"Yes," Houghton said. "The coachman can confirm that Major Reid returned here shortly before twelve, and the waiter will tell you that we all sat down to lunch shortly afterwards." His voice held a note Letty hadn't heard before. This was Houghton being a sergeant. "Not only that, the major sent me to the lock-up to tell you he'd be bringing in Cuthbertson this afternoon. When I got there, you'd just left."

The parish constable digested these facts, turning his hat over in his hands.

"Do you think Colonel Cuthbertson has been murdered?" Letty asked, her tone a careful combination of diffidence and concern. "Did he not leave a note?"

The constable pursed his lips, clearly debating the wisdom of answering this question. "He didn't leave a note."

"Does it look like murder?"

The constable hesitated. "Not rightly, no. But the maid said there'd been a Major Reid to visit earlier, and there'd been violence."

"There was," Letty said. "But my husband didn't shoot the colonel. He wanted to see him hang. Which fate, one must guess, the colonel wished to avoid." She let this comment hang in the air for a moment. "If you would like to speak with my husband, I suggest you return tomorrow, but as Sergeant Houghton has said, both the coachman and the waiter will confirm that he was here at midday."

The constable cogitated on this for several seconds, and nodded.

Letty stood, and held out her hand to him again. "It is good of you to be so thorough, Constable."

The constable shook her hand. "It's what the parish pays me for," he said gruffly.

When the man had gone, Letty turned to Houghton. "What do you think?"

"Officious, but not a fool. He won't be back."

CHAPTER 46

Reid was still sleeping when Letty retired at ten o'clock. She sent Green to bed, and left the door open between her bedchamber and Reid's, but Reid didn't rouse in the night. He was still asleep when she rose the next morning.

"Is he all right?" Green whispered anxiously.

Reid wasn't flushed, he wasn't shivering, his breathing slow and steady and quiet. "I don't think he has a fever," Letty whispered back. "He's just tired. Will you sit with him, please? And let me know when he wakes?"

It was past eleven when Reid finally woke. Houghton brought the news. "No, don't go to him, ma'am—Green's got everything in hand."

"How is he?"

"Well enough," Houghton said. "But he says he'll take his breakfast in bed."

Letty pondered these ominous words. Breakfast in bed? Reid? But when she entered the bedchamber half an hour later, Reid didn't look ill. He was sitting up in bed, his face shaved, his hair combed, and from the evidence of the depleted tray Green was removing, he'd eaten a good breakfast.

She studied his face. "How do you feel?"

"Fine," Reid said, and yawned. "Tired."

"You slept twenty hours."

"So Green tells me. I feel like I could sleep twenty more."

"Then do! Lie down. I'll read for a bit."

Letty rearranged his pillows, and pulled up a stool, and opened Herodotus. Even without brandy and valerian, Reid was asleep after six pages. He woke again in the middle of the afternoon, ate soup and bread-and-butter, played one game of backgammon with Houghton, and fell asleep again. "Is he all right?" Houghton asked worriedly, over dinner.

"I think so," Letty said. She *hoped* so. "He's been under immense strain the past few months. I think his body needs to rest."

"He told me he was dying. You don't think . . . He's not . . ." Houghton took a deep breath. "This isn't the end, is it?"

Letty shook his head. "I think he's finally healing."

"I hope you're right, ma'am."

So did Letty.

Reid woke at nine that evening, ate, played another game of backgammon, listened to four more pages of Herodotus, and slept the night through, thus setting the pattern for the next three days. Green, whose attachment to Reid bordered on worship, sat with him whenever he slept during the day; when Reid was awake, Houghton played backgammon with him and Letty read Herodotus. The days slipped by lazily. Each night, Green left out brandy and valerian and Letty opened the adjoining door, but Reid had no nightmares.

On the third day, Letty wrote a letter to her putative chaperone, Mrs. Sitwell, telling her that she'd decided to stay longer in Andover, and to not to look for her for another two weeks. Yet another lie to add to her tally—and she felt a pang of guilt—but how could she leave Reid now, when he was deciding whether he wanted to live or to die?

She posted the letter, and hoped Mrs. Sitwell wouldn't examine the postmark.

During the daytime, while Reid slept, Letty walked out with Eliza or Houghton, rambling alongside the river, exploring the ruins of Okehampton castle, climbing up onto the moor. The more time she spent with Eliza, the more she liked the girl. Eliza was barely seventeen, but she was cheerful and stoic and possessed an unexpectedly shrewd intelligence—and now that she'd lost her overawed shyness, she showed glimpses of an impish sense of humor.

I shall be sorry to send her to the lying-in hospital, Letty thought, as she strolled on the moor one day with Eliza. She'd have to ensure the girl found a good position afterwards, somewhere safe. She fell to wondering whether she could employ Eliza in her own household . . . but that would mean confessing that she wasn't Mrs. Reid, and would the girl wish to have a liar for a mistress?

Letty sighed, and gazed unseeingly across Dartmoor, and saw the balance scales in her mind's eye. The weight of her lies was substantial, but the weight of the deaths was far greater. Not merely three deaths, as she'd once thought, but many, many deaths. All of Lieutenant Pereira's deaths, all of Reid's deaths.

She regretted the lies she had told, wished they hadn't been necessary—and knew that she'd do the same again if she had to.

"I think that's Dinger Tor, ma'am."

Letty blinked, and discovered that she was staring at a distant outcrop of rock.

"Jeremy says one of the villagers told him a giant used to live there."

"Jeremy?"

Eliza flushed a pretty pink. "Sergeant Houghton, I should say, ma'am. He's teaching me to play backgammon." And then she said, anxiously: "You don't mind, do you?"

"Of course not." It wasn't Houghton's one arm that made him safe company for Eliza; it was his integrity.

The very next day, Sergeant Houghton himself brought up the subject of Eliza's future. "I know it's not my place, ma'am, but what exactly do you plan for Miss Marshall?"

Letty abandoned her perusal of the ruins of the Okehampton castle bailey, and examined Houghton's face instead. "What has she told you?"

"Everything." He paused. "At least, I think she's told me everything."

Letty surveyed him. "And what's that?"

"That she was raped," Houghton said bluntly "And turned off, and her aunt wouldn't take her in—and you rescued her."

Letty nodded. Eliza *had* told him everything. "My plan is to send her to a lying-in hospital in Holborn, a clean, well-run place. She doesn't wish to keep the child, so it shall go to a good foundling home. And then I'll see to it that Eliza finds a respectable position. I should like it to be in my own household, but . . . that would mean telling her I'm Miss Trentham, not Mrs. Reid, and if she knew *that* I doubt she'd wish to be employed by me."

"You think not?"

"I have deceived her, Sergeant."

"And saved her. Your kindness to Miss Marshall must make her forgiveness certain."

Perhaps. Or perhaps not. Letty eyed the sergeant, remembering Eliza's pink blush yesterday. "Do you like Eliza, Sergeant?"

Houghton went faintly pink himself. He looked away. "I'm not courting her, if that's what you mean, ma'am."

"You may, with my good wishes."

Houghton studied the remains of the bailey for several seconds, and then met her eyes. "I'm twelve years older than her, and I have only one arm."

"So?"

"So, I'm not a good husband for her."

"Nonsense! It's a man's character that determines whether he'll be a good husband, not the number of arms he has. And as for your age, if Eliza doesn't care, then I don't see why you should."

Houghton's lips compressed. He looked down at the grass growing where flagstones had been hundreds of years ago.

"Eliza needs a good friend," Letty said gently. "And perhaps, in time, that good friend can become her husband."

Houghton's lips compressed further. He dug the heel of his boot into the turf, gouging out a clod. "I'd like to see him flogged, the man who raped her. If I had both arms, I'd do it myself."

"Then it's just as well you *don't* have both arms!" Letty told him. "For he's a squire's son and you'd end up in gaol, and how would *that* help Eliza?"

Houghton glanced at her sharply—and then acknowledged the truth of her words with a wry grimace.

"Come." Letty held out her hand. "Let's climb the motte."

Houghton dutifully offered her his right arm. They strolled up the incline of the old motte to where the ruined keep stood, its crumbling turret sticking up like a warped gray finger.

Letty gazed out towards the village, her hand tucked into the crook of Houghton's arm. A very strong arm, thick with muscle, warm and alive. "Does your left arm pain you, Sergeant?"

Houghton didn't answer.

Letty glanced at him. Had she offended him? No; Houghton looked pensive, not angry.

"Not so much now. The worst part is, I keep forgetting it's gone. I go to use it, and . . . it's not there." He smiled crookedly at her. "I'll get used to it. It's already a lot better than it was. In time I'll forget I ever had two arms."

No, Sergeant, she thought. *You won't forget.*

Letty released his arm, and impulsively hugged him. "I do like you, Sergeant. Very much! And I hope you *will* marry Eliza!"

CHAPTER 47

$\mathcal{I}$carus knew it was winter, knew that the days were growing shorter and darker and colder, but he couldn't shake the feeling that it was spring and that outside everything was being reborn—buds bursting forth on bare branches, lambs prancing in the pastures. Nor could he shake the feeling of lazy convalescence. He knew he should abandon his bed and hire post-chaises and haul everyone back to London, but he simply couldn't muster any enthusiasm, and so, every day, he let it slide. When Letty Trentham told him she'd put off her return for another two weeks, Icarus nodded his relief and stopped thinking about departure at all.

He didn't think about Vimeiro, either. He knew it had happened, could remember every detail if he wanted to, but it seemed very distant, something that had happened to him in another life.

On the fifth day after Cuthbertson's death, Icarus left his bed—but he only went as far as the parlor, where a merry fire burned, and where there were scones warm from the griddle, and clotted cream and sticky strawberry jam, and a pot of tea. Icarus stayed there all afternoon, talking with Houghton, talking with Letty Trentham, while rain pattered against the windowpanes.

The conversation wandered in many directions, and finally drifted to his planned charity for invalided soldiers. "I've been making notes," Houghton said. "I'll fetch them. Won't be a moment, sir!"

Icarus looked at the tea tray, where the last scone lay amid a litter of crumbs, and contemplated eating it.

"Icarus?"

He glanced at Letty Trentham. She was wearing the lavender gown today, and her eyes were lavender, too.

"If you don't mind my asking . . . how do you feel?"

Icarus gave up contemplation of the scone and considered this question. He felt well. But that didn't quite capture it. He thought for a minute, and finally understood what it was that he felt. "I feel alive."

Letty hadn't looked anxious, but he realized now that she had been. He saw her shoulders relax slightly. She smiled, and her changeable eyes seemed to sparkle, as if they filled with tears, and then she blinked and the illusion was gone; no tears, just a smile. She didn't say anything, just nodded, and when Houghton returned a moment later with a sheaf of notes in his hand, she picked up her book and read, while he and the sergeant fell into discussion of the intricacies of setting up a bakery.

That evening, rather than backgammon, Letty Trentham proposed a game of Commerce. "They have the cards and counters here, you know. Sergeant, would you like to play?"

Houghton hesitated. "I shouldn't be fast enough. I can't hold cards *and* play them."

"I may have a solution to that," Letty said, and she produced a small wooden bookstand, with a sloping back and a lip that Houghton could set his cards on. "Shall we try?"

They played Commerce. The first hand was sedate, but by the third hand they were all three of them as rowdy as children. When Houghton narrowly beat Letty Trentham in the final round, Icarus looked at them both—Houghton chuckling and

Letty shaking her head ruefully—and he laughed with the sheer pleasure of the moment.

It felt good to laugh. Good to have friends. Good to be alive again.

That evening, after Green had gone and Icarus was climbing into bed, someone knocked softly on the door between his bedchamber and the next. He hesitated, and then said, "Yes?"

The door opened. Letty Trentham stood there in her nightgown.

They stared at each other for a long moment. Letty Trentham had been Tish while they played Commerce, relaxed and laughing. She wasn't Tish now; she looked shy and almost diffident, as if expecting a rebuff. "May I read to you tonight?"

She was asking more than that, and they both knew it.

Icarus hesitated. He shouldn't invite her into his room. He *knew* he shouldn't. But longing overcame good sense. "Yes."

CHAPTER 48

*L*etty Trentham did read to him, sitting cross-legged on the bed, but only four pages. She closed the book and glanced at him, with the same shy diffidence she'd shown in the doorway.

They held each other's gaze for a long moment, and then Icarus reached out and drew her close enough to kiss. Her lips were warm and soft and perfect.

Icarus gave a deep sigh of pleasure, and drew her even closer. He'd missed this: kissing Letty Trentham.

Later, he kissed his way up her inner thighs and brought her to a shuddering climax, and after that, Letty returned the favor. It seemed hypocritical to refuse consent when she'd done it before.

They fell asleep in the warm, cozy, rumpled bed, holding each other. For the sixth night in a row, Icarus had no nightmares, and for the sixth morning in a row, he woke feeling alive.

That afternoon, when he and Houghton were debating the merits of London over Exeter as the site of the inaugural bakery, Letty Trentham and Green and Eliza returned from a walk on the moor.

"Look what we found, sir," Green said, depositing a bundle wrapped in one of Miss Trentham's shawls on the hearthrug.

The bundle moved.

Green peeled open the shawl. Inside was a puppy. It had huge dark eyes and a muddy black-and-tan coat. Icarus could see every one of its ribs.

"I thought you might like him," Letty Trentham said hesitantly. "He has three black paws, like the dog you had when you were a boy."

Ulysses had been black and white, and had looked nothing like this pup, but Icarus was aware of three pairs of eyes beseeching him. He got up from his chair, and crouched beside the puppy, holding out his hand for it to sniff.

"He's going to be big," Houghton said, crouching alongside him. "Look at the size of his paws."

The puppy did indeed have huge paws. It timidly wagged its tail and licked Icarus's hand.

"Of course I'll keep him," Icarus heard himself say.

Green beamed at him. "I'll wash him," he said, bundling the pup up again.

"And I'll find some food," Eliza said. "The poor wee thing's starving!"

"Not so wee," Houghton said, once Green and Eliza had gone.

"No," Icarus said ruefully. He glanced at Letty Trentham. Her gown and her eyes were green today.

"You don't mind?" she said, faintly anxious.

"I don't mind." He smiled, and held out his hand to her.

She slipped her hand into his, and squeezed his fingers lightly. "I'm glad. Because I couldn't leave him to starve up on the moor, and I *know* I couldn't order him drowned!"

Icarus grimaced. "No."

"What will you call him, sir?"

324

Icarus thought for a moment. "Ajax Telamon. The giant, Ajax."

Ajax spent the evening snoring on the hearthrug, his belly rounded with food. "As soon as he wakes, we must take him outside," Icarus said. It had been a long time since he'd had charge of a puppy, but he remembered that much: when puppies woke, they peed.

Ajax woke—and peed outside—and then Green bore him off to his bedchamber, where he'd set up a basket and an old horse blanket. And later that evening, after they'd all retired, Letty Trentham read to Icarus again, and after that she spent the night in his bed.

The days drifted past, slipping into a gentle routine: a morning stroll with Ajax gamboling at his feet, lunchtime discussions with Houghton, afternoon rambles with Letty Trentham, card games in the evening. And food. And laughter. Ajax's ribs became less prominent. He learned to sit on command. He made everyone laugh. He made everyone love him. Icarus, sitting by the fire one damp afternoon, with Ajax sprawled across his lap, warm and bony and deeply asleep, thought that he'd never felt so content in his life. He pulled one of the pup's velvety ears slowly through his fingers—Ajax's favorite caress. How easy it was to make a dog happy. And how happy they made people in turn. He'd forgotten that in the years since he'd buried Ulysses, forgotten how infectious a dog's joy in life was.

He glanced at Letty Trentham, mending a torn hem,

and at Houghton writing notes at the table, and his sense of contentment swelled until it felt as if he overflowed with it.

And if the days slipped into a routine, so, too, did the nights. Every night, after everyone had retired, Letty knocked on his door, and every night Icarus asked her to come in. And every night, he had no nightmares.

He had the feeling—a feeling so strong it was a conviction—that he wasn't the only one sleeping better now. He *knew* that Pereira and the scouts rested more peacefully in their graves. And he knew that Pereira's soul was no longer anguished.

On the tenth evening after Cuthbertson's death, after a close-run game of Commerce, Letty Trentham packed up the cards and counters. She'd been laughing while they played, but now her expression was sober. "I must return to London soon."

Icarus's contentment drained away. "How soon?"

"Oh . . ." She squared the cards. "I need to leave here the day after tomorrow."

Icarus glanced at Houghton. He looked as somber as Letty. None of them wished this to end.

But it had to come to an end. He'd always known that.

That evening, Letty Trentham read from Herodotus for twenty minutes. "How many pages are left?" Icarus asked, when she put the book aside.

"Three. Would you like me to finish?"

"No."

He didn't want Letty to ever stop reading to him. He didn't

want any of this to end. But it had to. If one chose to live, life went on. One couldn't sit forever in an inn on the edge of Dartmoor, however much one wanted to. Letty Trentham had to return to the world of the *ton,* and he had to forge ahead with his new life.

Icarus gathered Letty close and kissed her. Her mouth was as perfect as it had been last night, as perfect as it had been every night. Icarus kissed her slowly and thoroughly, regretfully. He was going to miss Letty's mouth. And her voice. And her changeable eyes. And her company.

He should ask her to marry him—it was the honorable thing to do after the intimacies they'd indulged in—but Letty could hear lies. She'd ask whether he truly wanted to marry her, and he'd have to say *No.* He didn't want to marry anyone. Not yet. Maybe not ever. He liked Letty, liked her a lot—more than any woman he'd ever known—but marriage? Marriage was being a good husband and a good father, and he wasn't certain he could do either of those things. He wasn't yet certain that he could succeed at being *alive.*

Yesterday he'd been alive, and today he was alive, but what if he woke up tomorrow and he was dead again?

He kissed Letty's mouth, and then her throat. Warm anticipation built in his body. He wanted to kneel between her legs, wanted to run his hands up her inner thighs, wanted to inhale her secret, intimate scent and lick inside her.

"Icarus?"

"Mmm?"

"Can we do it properly tonight?"

It took a few seconds for the words to sink in. Icarus stopped kissing her throat. He raised his head and blinked, focusing on her candlelit face. "What?"

"Can we please do it properly tonight?"

"Of course not!" Icarus pushed away from her, sitting up in the bed. "You'd no longer be a virgin. When you marry, your husband would know!"

"I shan't marry."

"Of course you'll marry!"

Letty sat up, too. "Icarus, I've been on the Marriage Mart for six years. I've been proposed to by nearly two hundred men, and not one of them—not one!—wanted to marry me for myself. It's not going to happen."

Icarus shook his head. "You'll meet someone."

"I'm taking myself off the Marriage Mart," Letty said. "I've had enough."

"But . . ." he said stupidly. "But . . . what will you do?"

She looked past his shoulder. A fleeting expression of sadness crossed her face, and then her lips compressed slightly and she met his eyes again and lifted her chin. "I shall establish a lying-in hospital and foundling homes and a school, like my mother."

"Foundling homes?"

"I always intended to, after I married. But I shall do it now."

Icarus stared at her, dismayed. "But Letty—"

"My mind is made up," she said firmly. "But I do want to know what it's like to lie with a man, so would you please do it?"

Icarus shook his head. "Letty, you *know* I can't! You'd no longer be a virg—"

"Have you not listened to a word I've said? I shall *never* marry."

He couldn't hear lies the way she could, but he heard the vehemence in her voice. Letty meant it: she would never marry.

"Please, Icarus." Her tone was beseeching. "This will be my only chance. I know I'll never meet a man I like more than you! Please will you do it?"

Was she saying she loved him?

Icarus recoiled inwardly. He wasn't worthy of anyone's love, and Letty Trentham understood that better than any person on this earth. She'd seen him at his worst. She *knew* how far he'd fallen.

No, she couldn't love him. No woman could.

But she was attracted to him, and there was no denying that he was attracted to her. No denying that he wanted to bed her.

Icarus made one last attempt to dissuade her. "You might fall pregnant."

Letty gave a lopsided smile. "A child would be nice."

Icarus looked away. His throat was inexplicably tight. He swallowed. "Letty . . ."

She touched his arm lightly. "Please, Icarus."

Icarus knew he was lost. How could he reject that plea? How could he ignore that light touch on his arm?

He turned his head and looked at her. Letty Trentham. Not pretty, but poised and interesting and eye-catching. The woman he wanted more than any other in the world. "If it's what you wish."

CHAPTER 49

$\mathcal{I}$carus had never bedded a virgin before, but he knew that it was meant to be a painful experience for women. This knowledge was surprisingly unnerving. The last thing he wanted was to hurt Letty Trentham. *Take it slowly,* he told himself. *And bring her to a climax beforehand.*

So he took it slowly—undoing the mother-of-pearl buttons that fastened the nightgown high at her throat, peeling the garment off her, shucking his own nightshirt, stretching his body alongside hers in the warm bed.

Clothed, Letty looked boyishly thin. Unclothed, there was nothing boyish about her. Everything was feminine: the gentle curve of her hips, the slender waist, the small, pert breasts.

Icarus set himself to the agreeable task of learning the slopes and contours of her body. He trailed his mouth over every inch of her skin, explored her long, long legs, discovered that her breasts perfectly filled his mouth, learned that she shivered when he kissed the tender hollow of her elbow. Letty was shy, and also eager, and as curious to acquaint herself with his body as he was to acquaint himself with hers. She tasted his skin, licking, taking small nibbling bites that made his cock twitch and his body tremble helplessly. Time slipped past. The candle burned lower in its chamberstick. Icarus found his way back to Letty's mouth and kissed her hungrily. Their legs were entwined, their bodies pressed close, bare skin to bare skin, hot, eager, breathless.

Icarus dragged his lips from hers, and inhaled a shuddering breath. "You certain about this?"

"Yes."

He knelt between Letty's legs and tongued her to a climax, as he had for the past five nights, but this time he didn't stop there. This time, he settled himself over her and let his throbbing cock rest at her entrance. "It will likely hurt a bit," he told her, his voice slightly ragged. "It may even make you bleed."

"I know."

"Tell me if it hurts too much, and I'll stop." His voice almost strangled on that last word, but he *would* stop. He'd stop if it hurt her, and he'd stop before he spilled his seed.

Icarus let himself sink slowly into her, half-inch by half-inch. It was the most exquisite sensation. She was tight and hot and slick—

Letty stiffened.

"It hurts?" His voice was barely intelligible.

"Yes."

"Let's . . . wait . . . a bit."

Icarus counted to one hundred in his head, trying not to shake, his cock several inches inside her. He pressed his lips to Letty's temple—light, soothing kisses—and paid attention to the tension in her body. Slowly, she relaxed.

"All right?" he said, when he'd counted to one hundred twice.

"Yes."

Icarus let himself sink deeper into her. Slowly. Slowly. When he was almost fully sheathed, Letty clutched his arm, her fingers digging deep. He didn't need to ask if it hurt; he knew it did. Her body was rigid, her breath hissing between her teeth.

Icarus held himself still and counted to one hundred again. His body shook. His hips wanted to flex, his cock wanted to plunge fully into her. *Eighty-eight, eighty-nine, ninety.* By two hundred, Letty's grip on his arm had eased. By three hundred, the tension had ebbed from her body. Icarus let himself slide the last inch into her. His eyes closed with the sheer pleasure of it. A silent groan reverberated in his chest. It took him several seconds to find his voice. "How's that?"

"It's not comfortable," Letty said breathlessly.

Her honesty made him laugh—and having laughed, he almost lost control. Icarus squeezed his eyes shut. *Don't move,* he told himself. *Don't move.* He counted to twenty, inhaled a shallow breath, opened his eyes, and lowered his head and found Letty's mouth. He kissed her leisurely, lingeringly, giving her body time to adjust to having him inside her. "Still uncomfortable?" he murmured against her lips.

"Not so much."

Icarus withdrew halfway, and carefully thrust into her again. It was even harder this time to hold himself in check.

Letty didn't tense.

"Did that hurt?" His voice was hoarse.

"No."

He did it again, slowly, and a third time. It was becoming almost impossible to rein himself back. "All right?"

"Yes." Letty's hips rose slightly. He recognized that movement as a silent request for more, and gave it to her—another careful withdrawal and thrust. Her hips lifted again and she clutched him, uttering a sound between a gasp and a moan.

Icarus gratefully released his control. His movements became faster, firmer. He and Letty fell into an instinctive rhythm, not languid, not energetic, but somewhere perfectly in between. Icarus stopped paying attention to anything but the glide of his body over hers, the glide of his cock inside her. The feeling of connection between them was intense, more intense than he'd ever experienced in his life. He felt it in his blood, in his bones. This wasn't just sex; this was something much more profound.

Letty climaxed, clutching his arm, crying out, but Icarus

didn't withdraw. He didn't want to lose the connection, the feeling of completion on a deep, visceral level. He and Letty Trentham were meant for each other. He knew it with utter certainty.

And so, when his balls tightened and the spasms started, he didn't pull away, but let his seed spill into her. The climax jolted through him, from his toes all the way to his scalp, shuddering and powerful.

The shudders died to mere tremors, and then to nothing, and still Icarus didn't withdraw. He wanted to stay inside Letty forever. He gathered her in his arms, and rolled so that she lay on top of him, and then he acknowledged the truth to himself—he loved Letty Trentham.

Icarus drank in the moment: Letty warm and relaxed in his embrace, her cheek pillowed on his shoulder, his cock nestled inside her. He felt a fierce tenderness, a fierce possessiveness. He tightened his arms around her, not wanting her to ever leave him.

Letty didn't seem to want to. She made no move to climb off him.

The candle flickered and guttered, and then died, leaving them in darkness, and still Icarus held her, and still Letty made no attempt to free herself from his embrace.

"How was it?" Icarus asked finally.

Letty was silent for a long moment. "Much better than I thought it would be." She sounded sad.

Icarus wished he could see her face. "Are you all right?"

"Yes," Letty said, sounding even sadder, and now she did move, pushing away.

Icarus opened his arms and let her climb off him. Panic stirred in his chest. "Do you regret it?" Had Letty not felt that same sense of connection, of utter and absolute *rightness*?

"Regret it?" Letty reached out and found his face and traced his lips with her fingertips. "No, I'm glad we did it." She leaned over and kissed him. "You are the only man I'd ever want to do that with, Icarus Reid."

His panic subsided. That had been almost a declaration of love, hadn't it?

Letty didn't pull on her nightgown and tiptoe back to her own bedchamber; she curled up alongside him in the bed, naked and warm. Icarus rolled on his side and gathered her close, tucking her into the curve of his body.

He fell asleep holding her, planning their future.

CHAPTER 50

December 9th, 1808
Okehampton, Devonshire

Reid waylaid Letty in the corridor outside the parlor the next morning. "How are you? How do you feel?"

"Very well. And you?"

"No, I mean . . ." He lowered his voice. "Are you sore?"

She was heart-sore, but that wasn't what he meant. "No."

He nodded his relief, and shuffled his feet in an un-Icarus-like manner. "Letty . . . do you *have* to leave for London tomorrow?"

"Yes."

"But if you're taking yourself off the Marriage Mart, then there's no reason—"

"I still have to return before I'm missed. I owe it to my family not to distress them. And if Mrs. Sitwell thinks she's lost me she'll be beside herself."

Reid accepted this with another nod, and shuffled his feet and seemed about to say something more—and then he turned and opened the door to the parlor. The waiter was laying out breakfast.

Houghton arrived, bringing Ajax, and they sat down to eat. Letty had little appetite. Melancholy had taken up residence in her chest and she felt a disconcerting inclination to cry. Determinedly, she buttered a piece of toast and made conversation with Sergeant Houghton. The sergeant was unrecognizable as the bearded, gaunt, filthy crossing-sweeper of two and a half weeks ago. She thought even his own sister wouldn't recognize him. This was who Houghton was meant to be. Confident, alert, good-humored.

Reid had altered almost past recognition, too. He was no longer the man she'd met at the Hammonds' ball. The strain and the haggard exhaustion were gone, the tension and the grimness. He looked ten years younger.

Ten years younger, yes, but Reid was in an odd mood this morning, his mind not on his food or the conversation. He was distracted, fidgeting with his cutlery, poking his breakfast around the plate, shifting in his seat as if barely restraining himself from rushing off somewhere. "Do you have a middle name?" he asked abruptly, when Letty was buttering her second piece of toast.

She glanced up. "Who? Me, or Sergeant Houghton?"

Reid flushed beneath his tan. "Um, both of you."

Letty and Houghton exchanged a glance. The sergeant shrugged. "John."

"Louisa."

They both looked at Reid. "Mine's John, too," he said, and then he bent his attention to his food, pushing it around the plate again.

Houghton and Letty exchanged another glance. Houghton shrugged, and embarked on his third egg.

Letty finished her toast slowly, trying to ignore the deep, dark ache of her love for Reid. She stole a look at his face, noting the hard planes, the stark angles, the strong bones. An intensely masculine face—and yet also beautiful. And even more beautiful than his face were his hands.

She gazed at Reid's hands—lean and strong and

tanned—and the deep, dark, hopeless love grew until it was almost impossible to breathe.

Reid pushed back his chair. "I need to go to Exeter today. Urgent business. I don't know when I'll be back. Tonight, I hope—but I may be delayed until tomorrow."

The words jerked Letty from her melancholy. She stared at him, her lips parting in silent protest.

Houghton half-rose. "Shall I come, sir?" Ajax half-rose, too, on the rug by the fire, ears pricked, hope blatant on his black-and-tan face.

Reid shook his head. "It's nothing to do with our business. I'd be much obliged if you'd stay here and look out for Miss Trentham."

"Of course, sir."

Reid came around the table and took Letty's hands, clasping them in his. "I'm coming back," he said, and she heard the note of truth in his voice. "If not tonight, then definitely tomorrow. *Promise* me you won't leave for London before I return."

Letty managed not to clutch at his hands, managed to smile at him and say in a perfectly normal voice, "Of course I promise."

"Thank you." Reid released her hands and strode to the door. Ajax got there at the same time he did, almost falling over himself in his eagerness. "No, scamp, you stay here." Reid patted the pup, tugged his ears gently, and strode from the room. The door shut firmly behind him.

Ajax sat down and whimpered.

Letty looked at Houghton. "What's put him in such a pother?"

Houghton shrugged, and shook his head.

Reid didn't return that evening, or the next morning. Letty grew as jittery as Reid had been. She couldn't sit still, couldn't embroider, couldn't read. She fidgeted with her shawl, with her cuffs, with the cord of the blind in the parlor. Ajax caught her mood, and took to following her anxiously and whining whenever he caught her eye. "This is ridiculous!" she told him. "Let's go for a walk."

But when they returned, Reid still wasn't back. The waiter set the table for luncheon. Letty and Houghton were taking their seats when rapid footsteps sounded in the corridor. Ajax sat up, his ears pricked. Letty's heart gave a little kick in her chest. The door opened and Reid strode in.

Ajax uttered a yelp, and bounded to greet him.

"Hello, scamp. Yes, I'm delighted to see you, too. No, don't scratch my boots, please." Reid gave the pup a hearty rub.

"Excellent timing, sir," Houghton said, a grin splitting his face. "We had them lay a place for you."

Letty stared down at her plate. It was that, or devour Reid with her eyes.

"Good. I'm starved!" Reid pulled out his chair and sat.

Letty lifted her gaze to him. Dark hair, tanned skin, high cheekbones. God, he was beautiful.

"Did your business go well?" she asked, as Reid peeled off his gloves.

Reid glanced at her, and the impact of his silver eyes almost took her breath away. "It took a little longer than I'd thought, but yes, it went well. Very well."

Reid's trip to Exeter might have gone well, but he was no less restless than he'd been yesterday morning. He reminded Letty of a child waiting for Christmas. He ate fast, as if impatient to get to whatever came next.

Houghton picked up on Reid's edginess. He caught Letty's eye and gave her a *What's going on?* look.

Letty shook her head. She pushed her food around her plate. Her appetite had deserted her. What she most wanted to do was cry. Instead, painstakingly, she forced herself to eat a portion of cold chicken.

When she'd finished, Letty folded her napkin and laid it beside her plate. She stared at the tablecloth, rather than Reid's face. "Icarus, I must leave today."

"I know," he said. "We can make it as far as Exeter tonight. I just . . . I need to speak with you privately first."

Letty glanced at him. "With me?"

"Yes."

"I'll take Ajax outside." Houghton pushed back his chair and stood.

Ajax, who'd been dozing by the fire, woke with a jerk and scrambled to his feet. "Come along, m'boy," the sergeant said. "Let's get you some fresh air."

The door closed behind Houghton and the pup.

Reid stood and crossed to the fireplace. From outside came the faint rattle of carriage wheels.

"What is it, Icarus?"

Reid didn't answer. He shoved a hand through his hair, tugged twice at his neckcloth, and paced to the window and then back to the fireplace. He was so jittery he seemed ready to burst out of his skin.

Letty stared at him in worry. "Icarus, what's wrong?"

"Nothing's wrong." He took a step towards her. "Letty—"

The door swung open. Bernard Trentham strode into the room. His outraged glare went from her to Reid and back to her again. "Letitia!"

CHAPTER 51

*L*etty's mouth fell open. She stood hastily. "Bernard?"

Bernard closed the door with a suspicion of a slam. "How *dare* you disgrace us like this? You have brought shame upon our family! Your behavior—"

"Good afternoon, Trentham," Reid said politely.

Bernard rounded on him. "You!" he spat. "You corrupt, amoral—"

"How did you find us?" Reid asked.

"You may well ask!" Bernard cried wrathfully. He bristled like an enraged tomcat—his tufty eyebrows bristled, his wispy hair bristled, his shirt-points and neckcloth and coat-tails bristled. Even the tassels of his Hessians seemed to bristle. He snatched a crumpled letter from his pocket. "Letitia, in her depravity—"

Reid plucked the letter from Bernard's fingers. He glanced at its direction. "Mrs. Sitwell?"

"My chaperone in London. I sent her a letter." Letty clutched the back of her chair. She felt disoriented, almost dizzy. Bernard, here? "I didn't think she'd notice the postmark."

"She didn't!" Bernard said. "But you may be certain that I did! How you came to be so lost to propriety, so lost to what you *owe* us—"

"That's all very well," Reid said. "But have you told anyone about this?"

Bernard drew himself up. "Of course not!"

"Then I fail to see what all this fuss is about," Reid said, handing the letter back to Bernard.

"You seduced Letitia! You—"

"He did not!" Letty cried, at the same time Reid said, "No one seduced anyone."

Bernard ignored them both. "You have ruined Letitia—"

"No, he hasn't!"

"You *are* ruined, Letitia." Bernard dug in his pocket again and thrust a folded piece of paper at Reid. "I *insist* that you marry!"

"Don't be ridiculous!" Letty felt herself bristle—not with wrath, but with protectiveness. Invisible hackles rose down her spine. She took a step forward. She would *not* let Bernard force Reid into a marriage he didn't want. "There's no call for us to marry."

Reid made no move to take the paper Bernard held out. "What is it?"

"A marriage license, you . . . you *cur*."

"Thank you, but I have one of my own."

"You?" Bernard's upper lip curled in theatrical contempt. "I doubt it."

Reid slid a hand into his breast pocket and drew out a folded piece of paper that looked identical to Bernard's.

Bernard snatched it from him and perused it swiftly. "The Bishop of Exeter?"

The Bishop of Exeter?

Emotions superseded one another swiftly in Letty's breast: disbelief, then painful hope—and then dismay. Reid didn't want a wife; he'd told her that quite truthfully only last month.

Then why had he procured a marriage license?

The answer to that was obvious: like Bernard, Reid believed he'd ruined her.

341

The invisible hackles wilted. A cold, sick sensation grew in Letty's stomach.

Reid reclaimed the marriage license and returned it to his pocket. "Thank you for coming all this way, Trentham, but I prefer to use my own license." He crossed to the door and opened it. "Have a good journey."

Bernard didn't move. "If you think for *one* moment that I'm going to leave before I've seen you married to Letitia—"

"I do think it," Reid said. He took Bernard by the elbow and steered him politely but firmly to the open door. "I'll send an announcement to the newspapers. Good day."

Bernard tore his elbow free. He raised a fist.

Letty stepped hastily forward. "Bernard!"

"I wouldn't, if I were you," Reid said civilly. "After all, we'll be seeing each other at Christmas for the rest of our lives."

He propelled Bernard gently into the corridor, closed the door and locked it, and turned to face Letty.

Letty stared at him, and felt her heart break in her chest. Icarus Reid, whom she loved more than she'd ever loved anyone—and whom she was going to have to set free.

Reid met her gaze squarely, but his face was tense. Was he afraid of her reaction?

Letty swallowed, and tried to make a joke. "I never visit Bernard at Christmas."

"Thank heavens for that!" Reid pushed away from the door. "Letty, we need to talk."

"Yes, we do." Letty turned away from him and crossed to the trio of armchairs beside the fireplace, sitting sedately, drawing her composure about her as she'd draw a cloak. "You don't have to marry me, you know. I am *not* ruined, regardless of what you and Bernard may believe."

"I don't think you're ruined," Reid said, coming to stand in front of her.

"Then why did you get a marriage license?"

"Because I want to marry you."

Letty frowned at the bell-note of truth in his voice. Her

gift had never been wrong before. "But you don't want to marry *any* woman. You told me so in London, and it was true!"

"I've changed my mind." Again, his voice rang with truthfulness. Reid drew a second armchair closer and sat on the very edge of the seat, leaning forward, his hands clenched together, knuckles sharp. For an instant, he reminded her of the man she'd met at the Hammonds' ball. "Letty, I know I've given you no reason to think I'd be a good husband, but if you'll give me a chance . . ." His silver eyes beseeched her. "I think I *could* be a good husband. I'll try my damnedest to be one!"

"I have no doubt you'd be an excellent husband, Icarus." What she *did* doubt was his reason for offering for her. "Why do you wish to marry me?"

"Because I love you," Reid said, and then blushed beneath his tan.

Letty stared at him, hearing the truth in his voice. After a moment, she found her voice. "Me?"

"Yes."

"But . . . but I'm plain, and I'm bossy, and . . . and I'm the most dreadful woman you've ever met!"

"For heaven's sake, Letty, you know I was angry when I said that! You are *not* dreadful. And you're not plain! I *like* how you look."

Letty lost the ability to breathe. He meant it. Reid actually liked how she looked.

"You are a bit bossy," Reid admitted. "But there's nothing wrong with that. I'd far rather have a strong-minded wife than a meek one." He paused, and then said, "Although I imagine we'll butt heads from time to time."

Letty would rather butt heads with Reid than with anyone else, but she had no air in her lungs to say the words aloud.

"I want to marry you because I think we fit together. And because you make me happy."

Tears rushed to Letty's eyes. "You make me happy, too," she managed to say, and then she burst into tears.

343

"Letty!" Reid rose from his chair, his expression aghast.

"I'm sorry," Letty sobbed, hunting for her handkerchief. "I don't know why I'm crying. I *want* to marry you. I want it more than anything in this world!"

"You do?"

Letty nodded, and by huge effort of willpower managed to stop the tears. She took a deep, shuddering breath, and blotted her eyes. When she'd finished doing that, she discovered that Reid was kneeling in front of her. "Will you please marry me, Letty Trentham?"

"Yes," Letty said, and she slid from the chair and put her arms around him and hugged him tightly. The tears came again, spilling from her eyes.

Reid hugged her back, just as tightly, and then he stood and swung her up, and sat in the armchair she'd just vacated, settling her on his lap, holding her close. Letty burrowed into his embrace, trying to press herself even closer. "I love you," she said, into his shoulder.

"I love you, too," he said, and it was *true*.

They sat like that for long minutes, Reid's arms warm and strong around her. Letty knew she'd never been so happy in her life. She was bursting with emotions—joy, wonder, love— and mixed in with the joy and the wonder and the love was an eager excitement for the future. She couldn't wait to be Reid's wife, to stand at his side while their lives unfolded.

She wiped her eyes, and spoke to his shoulder again: "Do you wish to rejoin the army? I'm sure Wellesley would be delighted to have you back."

Reid didn't tense, but she felt the change in him, a stillness.

Letty raised her head. "Icarus?"

"I can't be a soldier again."

"If it's what you want to do, I don't mind. I'd be happy to follow the drum." She'd follow him anywhere.

Reid shook his head. "I can't. Not after what I did."

Letty opened her mouth to protest.

"If I wore that uniform, I couldn't live with myself."

Letty closed her mouth, and bit her lip. Tears gathered in her eyes. She ducked her head and rested her cheek against his shoulder again, so he couldn't see them.

Reid might no longer have nightmares, he might feel alive again, he might *want* to live, but demons still rode on his shoulders. They probably always would.

"You were right about Pereira," Reid said quietly. He stroked the nape of her neck, a light caress. "If he'd survived, I would have wanted him to live. I'd have wanted him to be happy—if he could, carrying such a burden."

"Do you think it's possible?" Letty whispered. "To be happy, with such a burden?"

Reid didn't answer immediately. His fingers rested warmly on the nape of her neck. "Last month, I'd have said no. Now . . . I know it's possible."

Letty closed her eyes. She would do whatever was in her power to make him happy. Anything and everything.

They sat silently for several minutes, and then Reid took an audible breath. He didn't shift in the armchair, but she felt the change in his mood. "Before we marry, I think you should know that I have my eye on your fortune."

Letty blinked at the truth in his voice, and lifted her head—and then understood what he meant. "Your charity for invalided veterans?"

"Yes."

She rested her cheek on Reid's shoulder again. "I have more than enough money for your charity and my charity *and* for our children."

"I won't spend too much, I promise."

"You may spend a lot, if you wish." Letty smoothed his coat lapel with one hand. "I've always thought that if I have children, I shouldn't like them to have large fortunes. A moderate fortune is all very well, but an extravagant one is . . . an encumbrance."

"That quite puts my mind at rest," Reid said dryly.

Letty lifted her head and met his eyes. "Trust me, we'll be doing our children a favor if we spend a great deal of my money."

Reid looked amused. "Yes, ma'am."

Letty's heart seemed to stop in her chest. That faint smile, those silver eyes.

She loved this man.

She leaned forward and kissed him. Reid's arms tightened around her. He returned the kiss with enthusiasm.

When they were both breathless, Letty rested her head on his shoulder again. "When can we get married?"

"As soon as you like."

"Tomorrow?"

"Tomorrow." Reid stroked the curve of her hip. "I'll ride over to the next parish and talk with the vicar. I think it's best if we don't marry in Okehampton—we'd shock the Thackerays—and I should like to stay here for a couple more days."

"I'd like that, too." The Sleeping Mallard felt like home in a way the house in London never had.

Reid was silent a moment, stroking her hip. "Matlock will be pleased to hear we're marrying. He puffed you up to me."

"Tom?" Letty sat up on his lap. "He didn't!" But she could hear it was true.

"He told me no one has a style quite like you. And he was right."

Letty blushed.

"You are the most elegant woman I've ever met, Letty Trentham. And the most interesting."

Letty's cheeks became even hotter. She hid her face against Reid's shoulder again. "I'll write to Lucas and Tom today." A wisp of memory floated through her mind: Bernard waving her letter in Reid's face. "Thank you for not hitting Bernard."

"Hit him? I should think not!" Reid's hand halted in its stroking. His body seemed to tense fractionally. "I know you've seen me use violence, but you needn't worry about me hitting anyone ever again, because I won't. I *swear* it." He hesitated. "You're not afraid of me, are you?"

Letty sat up on his lap again. Reid looked exactly as his voice had sounded: anxious.

"Of course I'm not afraid of you!"

Reid gave a crooked smile. "I wouldn't be surprised if you were. You've seen me at my worst."

"Then I look forward to seeing you at your best." Letty leaned forward and pressed her lips to his. "Go and find us a vicar, Icarus."

$\mathscr{A}$FTERWARDS

The next twelve months were busy ones.

The Reids bought a rambling, red brick manor in Devonshire called Lincombe Park. It has ivy growing up its walls and odd turrets and strange staircases and a view of the sea. The Reids love living there. So does Ajax.

Sergeant Houghton bought a house within half a mile of Lincombe Park. It also has a view of the sea, and roses climbing over the door. When the village tavern came up for sale, Sergeant Houghton bought that, too. His sister and her nine children and her husband live there now. Joe's a good publican and the business is thriving.

Reid and Houghton opened a bakery in Exeter. It did so well, they opened four more. They also bought a small, run-down farm. With the help of Sir Barnaby Ware—who knows a lot about farming—they're converting it into a property that invalided soldiers can run. If it's successful, they plan to buy more farms.

Mrs. Reid established a lying-in hospital for poor women in Exeter. Eliza Marshall gave birth there—and decided to keep her baby. She named the child Mary Letitia.

Three months after Mary Letitia's birth, Sergeant Houghton married Eliza and adopted her daughter. The Houghtons are very happy in their home with the roses over the door, far happier than they ever dreamed was possible.

Reid offered Green a position as his secretary. Green turned it down; he's content being Reid's valet. Reid's new secretary is an ex-rifleman with only one leg.

Mrs. Reid is pregnant. It might be twins.

$\mathscr{A}$UTHOR'S $\mathscr{N}$OTE

The quote "An army marches on its stomach" is attributed to both Frederick the Great (1712-1786) and to Napoleon (1769-1821). I choose to believe that Frederick the Great uttered it first, and that my ex-soldiers in 1808 are familiar with it.

On the subject of attributions, I confess that the quotations from *The Histories of Herodotus* are taken from the translation by George Rawlinson, published a few decades after the events of this novel. Earlier translations do exist, but I was unable to locate any copies. I don't think Letty or Icarus noticed the difference, and I hope you didn't either.

You may recognize General Wellesley as the man who led Britain's army to victory in the Peninsular campaign and who vanquished Napoleon at the Battle of Waterloo. He is most familiar to us as the Duke of Wellington, a title he acquired several years after the events depicted in this novel.

The Battle of Vimeiro took place on August 21st, 1808. The northeastern ridge wasn't occupied by British troops and the French did attempt to take it, but were repulsed.

General Wellesley had a number of aides-de-camp and one of them really was dismissed for insubordination at the exact same time that my fictitious Dunlop was discharged from his service.

Wellesley also had exploring officers on his staff. The most famous of these men was Colquhoun Grant, who scouted behind enemy lines in British uniform. Grant was captured by the French in 1812, but later escaped.

Do you like listening to books?
The Baleful Godmother series is available in audio!

Praise for the narrators:

**"An intelligent, well-paced performance
that shows once again why Ms. Landor is such a
beloved narrator of historical romance."**
~ AudioGals, on *Ruining Miss Wrotham*

**"Landor really gets under the skins of the leads, unerringly
pinpointing the emotional heart of their relationship."**
~ Caz's Reading Room, on *Trusting Miss Trentham*

**"Landor delivers another flawless performance.
Accomplished, nuanced, emotionally resonant."**
~ AudioGals, on *Unmasking Miss Appleby*

**"As usual Hamish Long is amazing! All the characters
come alive. A pure delight to listen to."**
~ Audible reviewer, on *Claiming Mister Kemp*

Available wherever audiobooks are sold.

Listen to samples at
www.emilylarkin.com/audio-books

$\mathcal{T}$HANK $\mathcal{Y}$OU

Thanks for reading *Trusting Miss Trentham*. I hope you enjoyed it!

If you'd like to be notified whenever I release a new book, please join my readers' group, which you can find at www.emilylarkin.com/newsletter.

If you enjoyed this book, please consider leaving a review on Goodreads or elsewhere. Reviews and word of mouth help other readers to find books and are the best gift you can give an author.

Trusting Miss Trentham is part of the Baleful Godmother series. I'm currently giving free digital copies of the series prequel, *The Fey Quartet*, and the first novel in the series, *Unmasking Miss Appleby*, to anyone who joins my readers' group. You'll also receive exclusive bonus scenes and other goodies. Here's the link: www.emilylarkin.com/starter-library.

The next book in the Baleful Godmother series is *Claiming Mister Kemp*, a short romance novel featuring Tom Matlock and Lucas Kemp. *Claiming Mister Kemp* stands as a companion novel to *Trusting Miss Trentham* and a number of its events occur at the same time as those in *Trusting Miss Trentham*.

For the first chapter of *Claiming Mister Kemp*, please keep reading.

If male-male romances aren't your cup of tea, then I invite you to read the first two chapters of *Ruining Miss Wrotham,* a triple award-winning Baleful Godmother novel about a young lady who's searching for her missing sister and the rake who steps forward to help her.

The first two chapters of *Ruining Miss Wrotham* can be found after the *Claiming Mister Kemp* excerpt.

CLAIMING
Mister Kemp

October 6th, 1808
London

*L*ieutenant Thomas Matlock trod briskly up the steps of Albany Chambers and rapped on the door to Lucas Kemp's rooms. The moon shone cold and bright overhead and an icy breeze fingered its way between the folds of his military greatcoat.

His knock sounded loudly—and was followed by silence.

Tom knocked a second time, less hopefully, and then dug in his pocket for the key. He unlocked the door and let himself in to the entrance hall. "Lucas?"

The set of rooms was dark and silent.

He called out again, this time for Lucas's manservant, "Smollet?" and was met with more silence.

Tom sighed, and hefted the bottle in his hand, and debated what to do. Did he want to traipse all over London looking for Lucas? He wasn't dressed for the clubs; he still wore the clothes he'd traveled in all day. *You should have stopped to shave and change, idiot.*

Tom sighed again. He placed the bottle on the little table in the entrance hall, where Lucas could hardly fail to see it when he came in—then picked it up again and ventured into the sitting room, carefully picking his way past dimly seen furniture to the cold fireplace. There, he placed the bottle in the center of the mantelpiece, label facing outwards. "Happy birthday, Lu," he said quietly.

Someone muttered behind him.

Tom jerked around.

The sitting room was dark, and beyond it was the entrance hall, and beyond that, the open door and the courtyard. The distant lamplight made the rooms as black as the inside of a tomb.

As black—but not as silent. His ears caught the sound of someone breathing.

The hair on Tom's scalp pricked upright. "Hello?" he said cautiously, and then—because this *was* Lucas's sitting room and who else but Lucas would be here?—"Lucas? Is that you?"

The muttering came again, like a man talking in his sleep.

Tom strode out to the entrance hall, found the chamber-stick and tinderbox where Smollet always left them, lit the candle and returned to the sitting room. The shadows retreated to the corners, showing him the familiar furniture: tables and chairs, desk and bookcases. Lots of bookcases, because Lucas liked reading even more than he liked boxing and riding.

Two winged armchairs had long ago staked out territory on either side of the fireplace, hulking leather beasts with brass studs burnished from years of use. In the nearest one, a man slouched, eyes shut, chin sunk on his chest.

"Lucas? What the devil are you doing here in the dark?" But he could answer that question himself: Lucas was drunk. A *lot* drunk.

"Where's that man of yours?" Tom demanded. "Smollet?"

Lucas's eyelids rose heavily. He stared at Tom without recognition, blinked twice, and closed his eyes.

"Hello, Tom," Tom said, under his breath. "Welcome back to England, Tom. Nice to see you again, Tom." He bent and spoke close to Lucas's ear: "Where's Smollet, Lu?"

Lucas was usually punctilious about his appearance. No one would ever call him a peacock—he liked sober colors and plain tailoring—but he was always immaculate, almost fastidiously so. Not tonight. His guinea-gold hair stuck up in tufts, his collar-points had wilted, and he wore no neckcloth at all. Fumes wafted from him. Cognac, judging from the smell. Tom peered at Lucas more closely in the candlelight. Moisture glinted on his cheeks, glinted in his eyelashes. Lucas wasn't just drunk; he'd been crying.

Tom had seen soldiers cry after battle. Hell, he'd cried himself, a couple of times. But a man's tears had never had quite this effect on him before. His throat tightened and his heart seemed to clench inside his ribcage.

He cleared his throat and shook Lucas's shoulder roughly. "Where's that damned man of yours?"

Lucas's eyelids flickered again.

"Smollet, Lu. Where is he?" *And what the devil does he mean by leaving you here in the cold and the dark?*

"Gave 'im the night off," Lucas muttered.

Tom straightened, and sighed. "Then I guess it's up to me to put you to bed."

Tom closed the door to the courtyard, lit two more candles, and went into Lucas's bedchamber, where he kindled the fire, turned back the covers, and set one candle on the bedside table. Then he returned to the sitting room and stared down at Lucas, sprawled in the armchair, disheveled and drunk. It didn't take any feat of insight to guess why Lucas had chosen to spend his twenty-seventh birthday like this. The solitude, the alcohol, the tears were because of his dead twin sister, Julia.

Tom shook Lucas's shoulder gently. "Come on, Lu. Time for bed."

Lucas hunched away from his hand. "Go 'way," he mumbled, not opening his eyes.

Tom uttered a faint laugh. This wasn't the welcome he'd imagined. "No. I'm staying until you get into bed."

"Want t' be alone."

"Tough. I'm not Smollet. You can't tell me what to do." He took Lucas's arm and tried to haul him from the armchair.

Lucas pulled free. His eyes slitted open. He clumsily swung a blow.

"Easy, man," Tom said, catching the fist.

Lucas's eyes came fully open, his fist clenched in Tom's hand—and then Lucas blinked, and bafflement crossed his face. His fist sagged. He peered at Tom owlishly. "Tom? That you, Tom?"

"Yes. Come on, on your feet."

Lucas's brow creased with confusion. "You're in Portugal."

"No, you cod's head, I'm right here. On your feet." He hauled on Lucas's arm again, and this time Lucas didn't try to strike him.

Lucas was six foot two and built like a prizefighter, but Tom was two inches taller, and if he was leaner than Lucas, he was almost as strong. A grunt and a mighty heave and he had Lucas on his feet.

"You're in Portugal," Lucas said again, swaying.

"I'm back for the inquiry into the Convention of Cintra."

"Huh?"

"I'll explain it later. *When you're not drunker than a sailor.* He slung Lucas's slack arm over his shoulder. "Come on. Bed."

Lucas couldn't walk a straight line. Not only that, his legs kept buckling. Tom was out of breath by the time they reached the bedroom door. "Jesus, Lu, how much cognac did you have?"

"Dunno," Lucas said, and uttered a discreet burp.

"You'd better not shoot the cat," Tom said, warningly.

"Not tha' drunk," Lucas said, leaning bonelessly against him.

"Yes, you are—and I swear to God, Lu, if you vomit on me I'm going to shove you headfirst into the nearest privy."

Lucas huffed a faint, cognac-scented laugh, and then sighed heavily. "I missed you."

Tom tightened his grip on him. *I missed you, too.* He

permitted himself to rest his cheek against Lucas's hair for a brief second, and then thought, *Fuck it,* and pressed his face into Lucas's hair and inhaled deeply.

Lucas didn't notice; he was too drunk.

Tom closed his eyes and inhaled two more breaths. Nineteen years of friendship, and this was the closest they'd ever physically been. Almost hugging.

Tom thought about the battlefield, and he thought about musket balls and death, and he thought about all the years he'd loved Lucas and been too afraid to do anything about it. He thought about opportunities missed and opportunities lost, and then he thought, *This time I'm not going to be a coward.* Because this time could be the last time. In fact, this time shouldn't be happening at all. He should be buried in Portugal—but by the damnedest miracle he was still alive, and he was *not* going to waste this chance.

Like to read the rest?
Claiming Mister Kemp is available now.

RUINING
Miss Wrotham

CHAPTER 1

July 15th, 1812
London

$\mathcal{N}$ell Wrotham had two godmothers. One had given her a bible when she was christened and a copy of Fordyce's *Sermons for Young Women* when she turned twelve. Her father had insisted that Nell read the sermons and she had dutifully obeyed.

Nell's second godmother hadn't given her a gift yet and Nell's father hadn't known about her, because *that* godmother was a Faerie and her existence was a deep, dark secret. Her name was Baletongue and she would only come once, on Nell's twenty-third birthday, and when she came she would grant Nell one wish.

Nell was wishing as the stagecoach she sat in rattled towards London. She was wishing that her twenty-third birthday had been yesterday, or perhaps today, or at the very latest, tomorrow. But it wasn't. She still had a week to wait.

She sat on the lumpy seat, pressed close by a stout widow on one side and an even stouter attorney's clerk on the other. Nell's fingers were neatly folded over her reticule, her expression calm, her agitation hidden. *A well-bred lady never shows her emotions*—one of the many maxims drilled into her by her father. Her father, whose rigid, unforgiving righteousness was at the root of this disaster.

Nell clutched her reticule more tightly and wished for the thousandth time that her birthday was sooner—and prayed that when her Faerie godmother finally came it wouldn't be too late.

CHAPTER 2

$\mathcal{M}$ordecai Black reached London as the clocks were striking noon. The streets were dusty and the traffic sluggish. The air trapped between the buildings had a fetid undertone. He drew the curricle to a halt outside the Golden Cross Inn, thrust the reins at his groom, and jumped down.

The inn's yard thronged with porters and passengers, all of them hot and sweaty and irritable, but Mordecai had no difficulty traversing the crowd. People looked at him and prudently stepped aside.

The taproom was busy, the coffee room slightly less so. "Your master?" he asked a serving-man.

Mordecai followed the man's directions and found the innkeeper in a stuffy back office, bent over a ledger, tallying rows of numbers.

"The stagecoach from Bath that arrived this morning . . . are any of the passengers putting up here?"

The innkeeper looked up with a scowl on his brow, clearly annoyed by the interruption. He opened his mouth, took in Mordecai's size—and thought better of what he'd been about to say.

"A woman arrived this morning from Bath," Mordecai said. "Traveling alone. Is she staying here?"

"There was a woman." The innkeeper put aside his quill

and reached for a smaller ledger. Not accounts, but room allocations. He ran his finger down the entries and halted at one.

Mordecai's heart began to beat faster, a drumbeat of hope and nervousness. He was acutely aware of the document tucked into his breast pocket.

"Mrs. Webster," the innkeeper said. "Yes, she's putting up here."

"Mrs. Webster?"

"Yes."

"It's Miss Wrotham I'm looking for."

The innkeeper closed the ledger. "Then she is staying elsewhere."

W, Mordecai thought. *Wrotham. Webster.* "What does she look like? Young, slim, dark brown hair?"

"I wouldn't call her young," the innkeeper said. "Or slim."

Mordecai's hopeful nervousness evaporated. In its place was a feeling that was part unease, part worry. He went outside to speak with the porters. Half a crown each and a glance at his face bought him their full attention.

Some days it annoyed him that his appearance intimidated people; today it was useful, but only one porter had noticed Miss Wrotham. None of them had seen her leave the inn's yard.

Mordecai drove to Grosvenor Square, avoiding the other carriages by habit, scarcely noticing the landmarks. How the devil was he to find Miss Wrotham in a city the size of London?

The curricle rattled into the great square and there, on the far side, was his townhouse, a towering edifice with columns and a Palladian pediment and four rows of windows rising one above the other. Lord Dereham's house until eight months ago, and now Dereham's bastard's house. He'd heard the linkboys call it that—Dereham's bastard's house—not as a slur on his character, but merely acknowledging the truth of his birth: Dereham's natural son. Dereham's bastard.

Mordecai drew the curricle to a halt and clambered stiffly down. The hours he'd spent on the road were catching up with him: the journey to Bath, the journey back again, no rest in between.

"Take it round to the stables," he told the groom. "Have the rest of the day off."

The curricle clattered away over the cobblestones, but Mordecai didn't climb the steps to his front door.

Miss Wrotham was somewhere in London. Alone.

Mordecai stripped off his gloves and rubbed his face, felt grit and sweat and stubble. He needed food, a shave, a cold bath, fresh clothes. And maybe a nap.

He turned on his heel and stared across the square, seeing tall buildings, hazy rooftops, chimneys. The city seemed suddenly full of dangers. He felt a twinge of fear—an emotion he was unused to. He stood six foot five and weighed two hundred pounds and he knew how to fight, he was *good* at fighting, but Miss Wrotham was none of those things. And she was female, and alone in London without friends or protectors, and she had no experience of abbesses and cutpurses and bullyboys.

The sense of fear became stronger, laced with anxiety. *Where the blazes is she?*

Behind him, he heard his front door open. Mordecai looked around. His butler peered down the steps at him. "Sir?"

"I'm going for a walk."

He went to Halfmoon Street, five minutes' fast walk from Grosvenor Square. The Dalrymples' house was closed and shuttered, the knocker removed from the door—they were away, but Miss Wrotham *must* have known that; the Dalrymples were her cousins and she knew as well as anyone that they spent every summer in the country. So why had she come to London, and how the devil was he to find her?

Mordecai hesitated on the doorstep of the shuttered house, sweating, tired, worried. God, it was warm in London, the air close and still and sticky, no breeze to ease the heat.

He loosened his neckcloth and rubbed his face again, stubble rasping under his hand. There was one other person Miss Wrotham knew in London.

Mordecai strode around to Berkeley Square telling himself that he was a fool, that the last person Miss Wrotham would visit was Roger—the man had jilted her, for God's sake!

Halfmoon Street to Berkeley Square took all of two minutes. Mordecai's pace slowed when he neared Roger's house. It was a handsome building, but not as handsome as his own townhouse, nor as large.

He wondered what the linkboys called it.

Mordecai halted at the foot of the steps. *A fool's errand, this. Roger won't know, and if he did, he'd delight in not telling me.* And then he felt the prickling anxiety again. He touched his fingertips to the marriage license in his breast pocket, took a deep breath, and climbed the steps of the new Lord Dereham's house.

The butler opened the door.

"Afternoon, Bolger. My cousin in?"

The butler's lips tightened at the word *cousin,* a tiny spasm of distaste. He looked as if he wished he had permission to close the door in Mordecai's face. "Lord Dereham is at home, sir," he said woodenly.

"I'll see him."

The entrance hall was similar to Mordecai's own: the high ceiling molded and painted by Robert Adam, the long stretch of marble floor, the doors to dining room, drawing room, and library on either side, the staircase at the end. There the resemblance ended; Mordecai didn't decorate his entrance hall with footmen. Vases were decoration, a Robert Adam ceiling was decoration, but his footmen were not. Roger's footmen were, poor sods. Four of them stood in their curling wigs and gold-braided livery, two on either side of the hall, backs to the wall, chins up, eyes staring blankly ahead. Human statues. Mordecai almost snorted. *Why in God's name must he have one standing here all day, let alone four?*

But he knew the answer: the footmen were because Roger liked to flaunt his wealth, and there were four because Roger liked symmetry. Two footmen would have been too few, and three or five unacceptable.

"Lord Dereham is momentarily occupied," the butler said, his expression dyspeptic, as if Mordecai's kinship to his master pained him as much as it pained Roger. "If you will step into the library, I shall inform him of your arrival." He gave a stiff-necked nod, and one of the footmen sprang to open the library door.

Mordecai had taken half a dozen steps towards the library, wondering how long the butler and Roger would choose to keep him waiting, when the drawing room door opened abruptly and a young lady strode out. "—hiding behind excuses. A *hen* has more courage than you!"

Mordecai halted.

He'd been truly and deeply surprised twice in his life. Once, when his father had come to claim him, and the second time when Henry Wright had stood up for him at Eton. This moment qualified as the third. He was so astonished that he gaped. Eleanor Wrotham was here? In Roger's house?

"If you won't help me, I'll find someone who has the gumption to do so!" Miss Wrotham was magnificent in her scorn, eyes flashing, voice ringing, cheeks flushed.

And then he saw the tears trembling on her eyelashes. She wasn't merely angry; she was upset.

Miss Wrotham didn't see him. She crossed the entrance hall briskly, flung open the door before Bolger could reach it, and marched outside.

Roger emerged from the drawing room—red-faced and righteous, his blond hair sleek with pomade. Mordecai ignored his cousin. He strode after Miss Wrotham and shut the door firmly in Bolger's face. "Miss Wrotham!" He took the steps two at a time.

Miss Wrotham halted on the flagway and glanced back. He saw surprise cross her face—a brief, wide-eyed flare of astonishment—and then the surprise snuffed out and she was once again her father's daughter, haughty and aloof.

Mordecai stared down at her and knew in his bones that she was the one woman in all the world whom he was meant to marry. Not because of her appearance and her breeding—those had been Roger's reason for offering for her—but because of what lay beneath those things: the clear-eyed intelligence, the suppressed passion, the spirit bursting to be free.

He trod down the last three steps. "I'll help you," he said. "Whatever it is, I'll help."

Miss Wrotham's eyebrows lifted slightly. She looked him up and down.

Mordecai was suddenly acutely aware of what he must look like: sweaty, hulking, unshaven, dressed in clothes that had been elegant yesterday, but today were wrinkled and travel-stained.

He resisted the urge to tighten his neckcloth and brush the dust from his coat, but it was impossible not to feel embarrassed. Of all the ways he'd imagined meeting Miss Wrotham again, this wasn't one of them. He felt a faint blush creep into his cheeks—and when was the last time he'd blushed? Years ago.

Mordecai endured her scrutiny, and wished he knew what Miss Wrotham thought of him. Not what she thought of his appearance—it was obvious what anyone would think of his appearance right now—but what she thought of *him*. Mordecai Black. Earl's son. Bastard.

Society accepted him—his father's sponsorship had seen to that—but not everyone liked him. Roger certainly didn't. Miss Wrotham's father—a high stickler—hadn't either. He'd thought Mordecai unworthy of his daughter's hand, but the man was dead now and the only opinion that mattered was Miss Wrotham's. What did *she* think? Did those astute eyes see past his reputation as a rake? Did she see who he truly was?

Perhaps she did, because instead of turning away from him as a prudent and respectable young woman should, Miss Wrotham said, "I need to go to Seven Dials, but none of the jarveys will take me—they say it's no place for a lady."

Seven Dials? Mordecai stared at her in astonishment. "They're correct."

"Will you take me there, Mr. Black?"

"No." He shook his head emphatically. "Absolutely not. If you have business there, allow me to go in your stead."

"I have to go myself."

"Seven Dials is little more than taverns and brothels," Mordecai told her bluntly. "It's not a place you should visit."

"My sister's there." Miss Wrotham's aloofness slipped. Desperation and urgency were clear to read on her face. "She's in terrible trouble. She needs my help."

Mordecai's eyebrows lifted. The sister who'd plunged the Wrotham family into disgrace? Who'd ruined Miss Wrotham's marriage prospects and caused Roger to jilt her? "Is this the sister who, er . . ." *Ran off with a soldier.*

"I have only one sister."

And whatever that sister had done, Miss Wrotham obviously still cared about her.

Mordecai hesitated. If Miss Wrotham's sister was in Seven Dials, then her fortunes had sunk very low. "I'll bring her to you. It's best that you don't—"

"I'm going with you."

"Miss Wrotham—"

"Mr. Black, you would terrify her!"

371

Mordecai felt himself flush. "I assure you that I'll treat your sister with respect," he said stiffly.

"It's not that," Miss Wrotham said, with an impatient wave of her hand. "Oh, don't you see? You look *dangerous,* and she's scared enough as it is . . . and I *have* to go with you. She's my sister!"

Mordecai looked down at her and saw fierce determination on her face and stubbornness in the set of her chin—the spirit he'd admired last year, no longer suppressed but burning brightly. And then he thought of trying to persuade a frightened young woman who didn't know him from Adam to trust him enough to get in a carriage with him. He grimaced inwardly.

"Please," Miss Wrotham said, and she reached out and touched his arm, a gesture that was somehow both reckless and cautious at the same time, as if she thought that merely laying her hand on his sleeve might ruin her.

Mordecai's awareness of her flared. The last of his resolve crumbled. He gave a reluctant nod. "We'll go together."

Relief and hope illuminated Miss Wrotham's face—and then the urgency returned. She gripped his arm, her fingers digging deeply into his sleeve. "Can we go now? Where's your carriage?"

"In the stables. A hackney will be quicker."

"They'll refuse—"

"They'll not refuse me."

Like to read the rest?
Ruining Miss Wrotham is available now.

$\mathscr{A}$CKNOWLEDGMENTS

A number of people helped to make this book what it is. Foremost among them is my sterling developmental editor, Laura Cifelli Stibich, who made this story immeasurably better. (Seriously, she did.)

I also owe many thanks to my hardworking copyeditor, Maria Fairchild, and eagle-eyed proofreader, Martin O'Hearn.

The series logo was designed by Kim Killion, of the Killion Group, and the cover and the print formatting are the work of Jane D. Smith. Thank you, Jane!

And last—but definitely not least—my thanks go to my parents, without whose support this book would not have been published.

Emily Larkin grew up in a house full of books. Her mother was a librarian and her father a novelist, so perhaps it's not surprising that she became a writer.

Emily has studied a number of subjects, including geology and geophysics, canine behavior, and ancient Greek. Her varied career includes stints as a field assistant in Antarctica and a waitress on the Isle of Skye, as well as five vintages in New Zealand's wine industry.

She loves to travel and has lived in Sweden, backpacked in Europe and North America, and traveled overland in the Middle East, China, and North Africa.

She enjoys climbing hills, reading, and watching reruns of *Buffy the Vampire Slayer* and *Firefly*.

Emily writes historical romances as Emily Larkin and fantasy novels as Emily Gee. Her websites are www.emilylarkin.com and www.emilygee.com.

Never miss a new Emily Larkin book. Join her readers' group at www.emilylarkin.com/newsletter and receive free digital copies of *The Fey Quartet* and *Unmasking Miss Appleby*, as well as exclusive bonus scenes and other goodies.

$\mathcal{O}$THER $\mathcal{W}$ORKS

THE BALEFUL GODMOTHER SERIES

Prequel
The Fey Quartet novella collection:
Maythorn's Wish
Hazel's Promise
Ivy's Choice
Larkspur's Quest

Original Series
Unmasking Miss Appleby
Resisting Miss Merryweather
Trusting Miss Trentham
Claiming Mister Kemp
Ruining Miss Wrotham
Discovering Miss Dalrymple

Garland Cousins
Primrose and the Dreadful Duke
Violet and the Bow Street Runner

Pryor Cousins
Octavius and the Perfect Governess
Decimus and the Wary Widow

OTHER HISTORICAL ROMANCES

The Earl's Dilemma
My Lady Thief
Lady Isabella's Ogre
Lieutenant Mayhew's Catastrophes

The Midnight Quill Trio
The Countess's Groom
The Spinster's Secret
The Baronet's Bride

FANTASY NOVELS
(Written as Emily Gee)

Thief With No Shadow
The Laurentine Spy

The Cursed Kingdoms Trilogy
The Sentinel Mage
The Fire Prince
The Blood Curse

38455092R00224